DAVID EBSWORTH is the pen name of writer Dave McCall, a former negotiator for Britain's Transport & General Workers' Union. He was born in Liverpool but has lived in Wrexham, North Wales, with his wife Ann since 1981.

Following his retirement, Dave began to write historical fiction in 2009 and has subsequently published five novels: political thrillers dealing with the 1745 Jacobite rebellion, the 1879 Anglo-Zulu War, the Battle of Waterloo, warlord rivalry in sixth century Britain, and the Spanish Civil War. This sixth book, *Until the Curtain Falls* returns to that same Spanish conflict, following the story of journalist Jack Telford who, as it happens, is also the main protagonist in a separate novella, *The Lisbon Labyrinth*.

Each of Dave's novels has been critically acclaimed by the Historical Novel Society and been awarded the coveted BRAG. Medallion for independent authors. His work in progress is a series of a further nine novellas, covering the years from 1911 until 1919 and the lives of a Liverpudlian-Welsh family embroiled in the Suffragette movement.

Until the Curtain Falls is also the first of Dave's books to be translated into another language, through the work of Kelly Thornhill (Adventures in Spanish) – a specialist provider of tutoring and translation services based in Cheshire, UK – and an editorial team in Alicante. This Spanish version is also published by SilverWood Books.

For more information on the author and his work, visit his website at www.davidebsworth.com.

D1333810

Also by David Ebsworth

The Jacobites' Apprentice
A story of the 1745 Rebellion. Finalist in the
Historical Novel Society's 2014 Indie Award

The Assassin's Mark
A political thriller set towards the end of the Spanish Civil War. The first
of the Jack Telford stories and the sequel to which is *Until the Curtain Falls*.
"This is not a novel you will be able to put down."
– Rachel Malone, Historical Novel Society

The Kraals of Ulundi: A Novel of the Zulu War
Picks up the story of the Zulu War where Michael Caine left off.
"An accomplished, rich, beautifully produced and very rewarding read
that brings a lesser-known era of history to life."
– Cristoph Fischer, Historical Novel Society

The Last Campaign of Marianne Tambour: A Novel of Waterloo
Action and intrigue based on the real-life exploits of two women who
fought, in their own right, within Napoleon's army.
"Superb! David Ebsworth has really brought these dramatic events to life.
His description of the fighting is particularly vivid and compelling."
– Andrew W. Field, author of *Waterloo: The French Perspective* and the
companion volume, *Prelude to Waterloo, Quatre Bras*

The Song-Sayer's Lament
"A rich, glorious, intricate tapestry of the time we know of as the Dark Ages,
With echoes of Rosemary Sutcliff's magnificent *Sword at Sunset* and Mary
Stewart's, Crystal Cave series, this is at once a fast, fierce tale of the old gods
versus the new, of old politics and honour replaced by venal expediency –
and of humanity in the face of implacable disease as the first great plague
swept through. It's steeped in authenticity and heart. I loved it!"
– Manda Scott, author of the bestselling Boudica series and *Into the Fire*

Until
the
Curtain
Falls

DAVID EBSWORTH

SilverWood

Published in 2017 by the author
using SilverWood Books Empowered Publishing®

SilverWood Books Ltd
14 Small Street, Bristol, BS1 1DE, United Kingdom
www.silverwoodbooks.co.uk

ISBN 978-1-78132-643-5 (paperback)
ISBN 978-1-78132-644-2 (ebook)

British Library Cataloguing in Publication Data
A CIP catalogue record for this book is available from the British Library

Page design and typesetting by SilverWood Books
Printed on responsibly sourced paper

Dedicated to the memory of my dear friend, Chamorro

Dedicated also to the work of Spain's Asociación para la Recuperación de la Memoria Histórica, the International Brigades Memorial Trust, and the Abraham Lincoln Brigade Archives

And dedicated to Joe C Dwek CBE and his Family Trust for their considerable support in the publishing process for this novel

Chapter One

Friday 30th September 1938

The image of the woman Telford had just killed would not leave him. He was almost sure she deserved to die. And, if he hadn't drowned her first, he was fairly certain that he himself would now be dead.

So far as I can be certain of any damned thing, any more. Jack shivered, naked except for his bathing costume, as he crouched among the tombstones and granite memorials, the rhododendrons, and the strewn pine needles under his bare and filthy feet. He was suffering from shock, he supposed. And cold. *God, how I hate being cold.* Still dripping from the Bay of San Sebastián's September waters. The salt stinging his hungry belly too. Deep scratches raked by Carter's nails before she had finally succumbed and been swept away from him.

What time? he wondered. Morning still, of course. But no later than ten. It couldn't be. She'd been positive they could get a swim and be back at the hotel again in time for their train to Irún and the French border at eleven-fifteen. But the boy who'd carried their towels would be waiting for them at the beach hut. And how long before he raised the alarm? Jack had no idea, but this was a mess.

Carter-Holt was a celebrity, after all. Holder of Franco's coveted Red Cross of Military Merit. One of the most famous right-wing international correspondents of her day. *Christ*, he thought, *if only they knew!* A brilliant cover for one of Stalin's agents. Her crazy scheme for assassinating *El Caudillo* when they had all been presented to him in Santiago de Compostela – those of the tour group still left, at least, after Covadonga. Telford a willing accomplice in Carter's plan. Yet the whole thing had gone to cock, ended in a farce.

If only I'd left well alone. But he had not. And on the journey back to San Sebastián he had pushed the thing just too far, discovered that her plan included setting up Jack as her mark, her dupe, to take the blame for Franco's death if the attempt had worked. But worse, she'd also finally admitted her part in the death of poor Julia Britten, back when the tour had begun, less than two weeks earlier. Julia had smoked her, it seemed, and paid the price. In their own ways, Julia and then Jack had chosen curiosity over acquiescence and each had suffered the aftermath.

They'd all been on the trip together, fourteen of them, enticed for mixed reasons to take part in one of the Battlefield Tours that Franco's rebel government had recently established. A propaganda exercise. A good one. For the outcome of Spain's civil war was still very much in the balance, more than two years after Franco's military coup had failed to immediately oust the elected Popular Front Republicans. And these tours were running every week now, bringing folk – mostly those already fans of Hitler, or Mussolini, naturally – from all over Europe to hear the myths being spun about Franco, crusader against the Red Menace.

All on the trip together! Including the Holdens. Nazi supporters. Leading members of the Anglo-German Fellowship. Still at the Hotel María Cristina and waiting for the same train home. Even if the bellboy didn't raise the alarm, busybody Dorothea Holden would certainly do so.

Less than an hour, Jack told himself. *Either back to the hotel and make up some story about an accident, or...* But there were the scratches on Jack's belly. *And if they search Carter's room,* he thought, *what then? Or the body washes up on the shore.* And, anyway, there was something else in his dulled brain. An instinct that he should remain lost. For it was not pure serendipity that had caused Telford to clamber out of the waves onto the esplanade, the Paseo Nuevo, then run for the path, which cut up through woodland on this northern slope of Mount Urgull to the English Cemetery here.

Close to him stood the reddish stone monument, military figures and the dedication. *In memory of those courageous British soldiers who gave their life for the flag of their country and for the independence and the freedom of Spain.* But Jack crouched in the shadow of a particular tombstone. Smaller. A more intimate inscription. *Colonel F C Telford. Died on the fourth of July, 1837.*

In truth, he had no real idea who this person might be. Only that he was one of the ten thousand men from the British Legion of Volunteers

2

who came here to fight and die for Spain in that earlier civil war – a hundred years earlier – like so many men from the International Brigades had done more recently. At least, until the Republican Government, now based in Barcelona, had decided they should all be repatriated. But Telford imagined he saw the Colonel again now, as he had done on the beach only an hour earlier, in company with the ghost of Jack's suicidally dead father. The pale spectre of a young man, scarlet tunic, who whispered in Jack's ear. *Will you fight now? Or still the pacifist coward?* The same taunt as before.

'I killed her, didn't I?' said Jack. 'Isn't that what you wanted? Tried to help kill Franco too, for Christ's sake.'

Yet he knew there was unfinished business for him, here in Spain. Knew there was a ticking clock eating the minutes available to him. A quick glance to check that he was unobserved, then crawling up through the bushes, sprinting across the track, which climbed up to Mount Urgull's summit. Jack spurned that easier route in favour of the thick shrubs, with their pungent resins, their armies of ants, their birdsong, their incessant crickets, until he finally came cautiously to the ruins of the La Mota Castle. He wasn't cold any more, at least. In fact he'd worked up a fair sweat. Their guide, the fascist Irishman, Brendan Murphy, had brought them here at the start of the tour, and Jack hoped to hell there would be no other intrepid travellers on the ramparts today. He was in luck. Nobody. So he scrambled over the tumbled stones, now in the full glare of the sun, and edged down to the old chapel, that memorable view through the trees to the town and the bay below.

The bay. Valerie Carter-Holt's body was down there somewhere. Perhaps already tumbling back and forth with the tide. *No,* he thought, *the tide's only just on the turn.* And he saw again how, after the confession, the angry words, she had waited for him in the water, eased down the straps of her bathing suit. Those exquisite tiny breasts.

'Shall I let my hair down for you, Jack?' she had said, then begun to fiddle with the ornamental pin that held her bun in place. *The pin, Jack. Why did she have the pin?* He had convinced himself it was poisoned. Another assassin's tool. She had struggled, of course. Fought like a demon. And he glanced down at the gashes she had clawed in his gut.

A while then, he thought. But only until the alarm was raised. Less than an hour. And if Carter-Holt was found dead, he convinced himself, his only hope of escape was if Jack Telford was deemed to have drowned at her side too. So, no going back to the hotel.

Escape how, exactly? If I go back down there, into the old town, I'll stick out like a sore thumb. Stupid, pink English face. Big ears. Red nose. Swimming costume. I need money. Something to wear.

Most of all, at that moment, he needed a smoke. And his smokes were back at the Hotel María Cristina. Along with his clothes. The expensive Greaves of London brown leather weekend bag stamped with his initials – a rare luxury for a modestly paid journalist like Jack. The newspaper clippings he had collected, and the note-pads filled with all the observations he had made, the pieces he had written, during the past two weeks, his fact-finding mission on behalf of *Reynold's News*. The bag contained his Hugo's Spanish Grammar too. And that prized copy of Richard Geoghegan's *Doctor Esperanto's International Language*. There was Julia Britten's scrapbook also. Not in the bag itself but left upon his bedside table. It had given him the clue to her death – and Carter-Holt's possible part in it. *Will it find its way back to England?* he wondered. And how long before word reached London that he'd drowned? How would his friends and family take the news? How long before he could get word to them that he was, after all, still alive? But remaining free long enough to send them that happy news still required him to be dressed, and have some cash in his pockets.

So steal what you need, Jack, my lad.

Great idea. And then, when they find Carter's body, rocking and rolling in the waves, the Englishman, Telford, missing too, you think they won't ask questions? You think those poor sods down here are so flush with money and clothes that they won't report the theft?

He was looking at the tempting sight of fishermen's wives and mothers, hanging their wash. A different sort of flapping, glistening catch, dripping from poles and lines stretched across the broken ground at the edge of their *barrio*, below him. Just to the right, two modest steamers in one harbour basin, the smaller boats bobbing in the second, now safely moored within the harbour wall, yet the oily stink of their morning's work still wafting up to make him gag. Larger fishing boats hauled up on the quayside, and a couple of small trucks, some business being transacted.

But what if we stole a little here, a little there? he thought. *And maybe one day, I'll come back. Apologise. Make amends.*

Oh yes, Jack. How pathetically English.

He glanced again around the corner of the old chapel. Still nobody. He tried the ancient, studded door. Open. Not much inside. A crucifix on the far wall. A couple of broken pews. No altar. But a tiered tray, just inside the gloom. Small votive candles. Stubs mainly. *Lit for whom?* he pondered. Not the fisherman, that was sure. They had their own church, down in the *barrio*. But he knew that, in truth, the candles were burned by other visitors to this place. A prayer for the soul of a cancer-stricken relative, a lost child, a dying husband. And Jack was not a religious man, though neither was he entirely free of the inherent human superstitions from which, he believed, all religions stemmed – so that he ran his fingers reluctantly over the dark and crumbling pine box screwed to the dusty stone beside the candle tray, and let them rest a moment upon the coin slot in the nailed lid. He tested the firmness of its fixing, found it to be feeble. Two guilt-trembling hands now, trying to shake it free. He looked around for a tool, a lever. Then stopped. Startled. Thought he heard a sound. Somebody edging stealthily outside. It sounded like the soft scratch of a shoe's sole. Just a single step on dusty gravel. A pause, followed seconds later by another cautious movement. Telford's heart raced. He pressed himself against the wall, started with fright and cursed himself for a fool when a lizard, six inches long, scampered through the doorway and stopped just inside. He aimed a kick in its general direction, then gave up all pretense at caution, lifted his joined fists and brought them down upon the money-box so hard that its sides splintered, coins tinkling to the floor, left it hanging from the half-dislodged, rust-riddled screws.

Jack poked his fingers inside, drew out just a few grubby bank notes, all of one *peseta* denomination and, surprisingly, not all printed as the Burgos currency of Franco's alternative government, the only ones constituting legal tender here in the Nationalist Zone. Two of them were Republican *pesetas*. Worthless. And he doubted they had been here since before San Sebastián fell to Franco's forces. So some mean-minded soul had decided to put them in the poor box, presumably assuming that God wouldn't mind, or couldn't tell the difference. It made him feel better about taking the contents. The coins were a mixed bag too though, in total, the 'heist' – as the Americans might call it these days – had made him richer by no more than twelve *pesetas*. *Better than nothing, all the same,* he thought, making an involuntary and curt obeisance to the crucifix.

Another check around the doorway, then back out into the blazing sun, gripping his newfound fortune tightly in a crime-soaked fist. He followed the ramparts to the left, to one of those typically Spanish round sentry boxes – a *garita*, he recalled, from a childhood pirate story – from which, through the trees, he could just discern temptation. The hotel, pocked by the bullets from those days when supporters of Franco's rebellion had held out there against the local Basque militia. But San Sebastián had surrendered to the Nationalists just two years ago and was now firmly in fascist hands. Return to the hotel was out of the question.

A train whistle in the distance, just beyond the old town and close to the cathedral. Tiny smoke signal smudges bursting above the rooftop terrain of tiles. Not the train to Irún and the border though. Too early still for that. Just. But another temptation. How quickly he could get away, if only it were possible to reach that station. Yet the problem remained. No clothes. And twelve *pesetas*.

Jack made his decision. Back along the ramparts, he scrambled over the loosely tumbling rocks of an old wall, slithered down the coarse scree towards a path, scratched his legs bloody on some local variety of thistle, then followed the winding route down in a crouching run, now trying to keep the boats and fishermen's barrio always in sight.

He froze.

At the next bend in the track was a guard post. The swaggering peril of a Guardia Civil trooper in his polished three-cornered hat. Jack had no fond memories of the Guardia. His reception at the frontier had been less than friendly. And after Julia Britten's terrible death – murder, as he now knew – there had been the interrogations. That pig of a man, *Teniente* Enrique Álvaro Turbides of the Guardia's Public Order and Prevention Service. Telford inwardly murmured a quick and hypocritical blessing that the sentry was focused on the town, not the castle, then began to creep back the way he'd come. Step by cautious step. Holding his breath. His heart beating so fast he was sure the trooper must hear it. His bare feet suddenly absurdly loud on the painful gravel. He trod on a stone, almost cried out. Cringed as the Guardia began to turn towards him, fingering the rifle sling at his shoulder. But the fellow was looking down at his own tunic breast pocket and Jack slipped behind the bole of a pine, heady with its resin sweetness. He tried to still the racing in his chest, the trembling of his hands, until a more compelling smell overwhelmed the tree's own essence, and he swore silently. The Guardia had lit a cigarette, and the heavenly drifting smoke almost made Telford cry.

Women's voices wafted up to him from the houses, harsher than the wood smoke on which they were carried. Loud voices. That way the Spanish had of always sounding like they were on the verge of coming to blows when, in truth, they were probably just discussing the price of lentils at the local market. The word *fishwives* came to mind but, then, that was precisely what these women of the *barrio* would be. He was still above them, crouched – almost frantic now – behind the battlements of the castle's lowest defensive wall, against which the old two-storey houses had been built, a couple of rows dropping down to the quayside, narrow alleys separating one row from the next.

Through the languid lines of sun-stroked washing beyond, an early group of schoolchildren was being led, two-by-two, to the Aquarium. This had been a stupid idea. The only one that had come to him. But stupid. Too many people around. And himself in a bathing costume. He'd be lucky to last five minutes without being picked up. And the washing lines, which had seemed so tempting ten minutes ago, now looked entirely unattainable. But he edged along the rampart in any case, towards the steps he could see away to the left, near the taller blocks, closer to the Casino and the modern white brilliance of the Royal Yachting Club with its jetty.

His first piece of luck. Like all the other houses along the quay, the last one he passed before reaching the stairway boasted a wooden balcony, and the good *señora* who lived there had chosen to use its south-facing upper rail in preference to the communal drying grounds. Even better, there was no noise from the house. But the only garment that seemed even vaguely useful was a pair of canvas breeches, of the sort he'd frequently seen fishermen wear during his travels along the coast. He set down his money, snatched the breeches, knew at once they were too big for him. Still damp as well. And not quite rid of their fishy odour. Yet he pulled them over his bare legs with gratitude, pulled the waist cord tight above his hips, stuffed the *pesetas* into a deep pocket. They reached only to his shins, though he could not have felt better-dressed had he been outfitted on Savile Row.

For dramatic effect, he rubbed some muck into his face and mouse-brown hair, then looked down at the pallid flesh of his torso, knew he still looked absurdly out-of-place. Yet it would have to suffice, and Telford began to step out with increased confidence, no longer trying to hide, but limping a little as his pampered feet faultlessly found every sharp edge of the stony path between the houses. But he found his next gift from the gods at the first corner. Washing lines he'd not noticed before, strung between the walls along an alley that cascaded down onto the waterfront. A few pairs of men's drawers, which he chose to ignore even though the breeches were already chafing him, and a workman's coarse shirt. Somewhere within the house a woman was scolding her children and Jack deftly slid the garment from the thick string – then almost jumped out of his skin as a dog growled, low and menacing, right behind him.

Telford spun around, his nerves in tatters now. He was no more fond of dogs than he was of the Guardia Civil. Yet, here, the threat was more immediate. He'd not noticed the beast – a wire-haired mongrel with bared fangs – for it had been taking the shade in the lee of the house opposite while, just around the corner itself, an old man was sitting quietly in a wicker chair. Jack stood rooted to the spot, the dog shifting to a pouncing crouch, and its hackles raised, the growl now a deep and continuous rumble.

'¿*Quién es?*' said the old man. *Who is it?* And Jack saw that he was blind, an evil burn scar across his forehead and the place where his eyes should have been. And the effect of this injury caught Jack by surprise. A recollection of some lines from *Samson Agonistes*. He was still in shock, of course, from the morning's traumas. He knew that. But the old man brought back memories of Julia Britten too – the blind concert pianist from the tour group, murdered here, at the Hotel María Cristina. He had liked her. A lot. And Jack found that he was shaking violently, choking back a sob. At the same time, images ran fast through his brain, like clips from the Pathé News played too fast on a projector. Images, which took less than an instant, inspired Jack to one of his better judgements. He knew few words of Basque. But those he possessed, he now deployed, trembling as he spoke.

'*Burkide,*' he said. Comrade. Then, '*Kamarada. Lagun.*' Friend.

The old man turned sightless eyes towards him, sniffed once, then reached out his fingers, found the dog's neck, ruffled the fur to quieten the creature. He mumbled something too, though Jack had no idea whether it was meant for him, or for the hound. But he chose to take it as a blessing, a dismissal, and spoke his own farewell, though now in Castilian Spanish.

'*Gracias, amigo*,' he said, then took the shirt, pulled it over his head, thankful that it was almost dry, and took his first cautious step onto the quayside, though frequently looking back to where the man still sat. But his attention soon turned to one of the trucks he had seen earlier. Still there. A van, really. A coat of arms emblazoned on its cab door. And a legend stenciled in white upon its dark blue fitted canvas body. Gran Hotel La Perla, it read. And the address, Plaza del Castillo, 1. Pamplona. Jack consulted his mental gazeteer of Spain. The associations with Hemingway and *The Sun Also Rises*. Somewhere to the south and east, he thought. Not too far, but out of San Sebastián, at least. Navarra, wasn't it? A recollection that Pamplona was one of the first cities to have gone over to the rebels. That General Mola, another of the rebellion's leaders, had been based there when the conflict began – before his death.

The driver had been arguing furiously with three other men outside some sort of warehouse. A cold store perhaps. Impossible to understand the conversation, for they were all yelling at each other. But the driver evidently won the debate, since the better-dressed of the three finally shrugged, waving his arms wildly and, still shouting, disappeared inside to emerge again, seconds later, carrying a wooden box, packed with ice from which fish heads protruded.

The driver, also still unwilling to concede, snatched the small crate and slid it into the back of the van, slammed and bolted the tail-gate, then loosely tied the canvas flaps together.

'*¡Cabrones!*' he shouted, a last defiance, as he climbed into the driver's seat and started his engine. Telford knew that particular expletive. But, as the three men turned their backs, and before he had time to think too much, he was running as fast as his bare feet would allow him, reaching out for a hand-hold and, he hoped, a free ride to Pamplona.

Chapter Two

Saturday 1st October 1938

Jack's stomach still rebelled after its own particular trials of the previous day.

The long and winding road to Pamplona had not provided the most comfortable of journeys. The fish may have been packed in ice but that didn't make them any less malodorous, and their stink, combined with the van's exhaust fumes, the oil its engine was burning like a flare stack, and the jolting, swaying nausea of the switchbacks, had given him nearly three hours of vomiting *mal de mer*. Far worse than anything ever experienced on the Dover ferry.

And though his head had been almost continuously poked through the vehicle's tail sheets, he could remember little else about the journey. Irún he had recognised, of course, but that was really before the nightmare had begun, before the driver swung south onto the road signposted for Bera and begun to climb into the mountains.

There had been the roadblock too, of course. That heart-stopping moment when the van slowed almost to a stop, and Jack had thought they might have reached their destination, almost jumped out, then realised he was too late as the unmistakable voice of military authority demanded papers. And that bloody fool of a driver chose to argue about it. Jack heard the word *pescado*, fish, and knew the game would be up if the soldier, or Guardia, decided to rummage in the back. But he had not done so and, after some more interminable shouting, they were on their way once more, Jack peeking through a gap between the flaps to see that it was, indeed, a Guardia Civil wagon that had stopped them, parked sideways across the road. Looking for him? No, he thought. Too routine. And thank heavens he had been able to hold back his next bout of sickness until the buggers were out of sight around a concealing bend.

Yet, after they crossed the Arga River, the eastern outskirts of

Pamplona had finally begun to bustle about them, obvious from the volume of traffic and the continuous sprawl of suburbs washing one upon the other. So that, when they turned north again, up the Calle de la Estafeta, passed the bullring, Jack knew they must be near the centre and, at the next opportunity, he jumped out onto the busy street. But he followed the van a little way, until he saw it stop outside the narrow side elevation of the Gran Hotel La Perla itself. There'd been a vague recollection that Hemingway had stayed here, watched the bulls run down Estafeta during the Festival of San Fermín. But Jack, too tired to worry about it greatly, retraced his steps back to the corner of Estafeta and the Calle Javier. To his right, steps led up into a large square, the Plaza del Castillo. Busy with boisterous people. Elegant cafés into which this beggar-like version of Jack Telford would never be permitted. But Calle Javier itself seemed more promising. A narrow street, sloping downwards, full of shadows at this hour, and he followed it, ignoring the strange glances cast in his direction. Past a bookshop, a bar and an *estanco* – a tobacco shop. He stopped, desperate for enough nerve to enter, but then moved on until, at the next corner, he came to a church, San Agustín. The word "sanctuary" came to mind, and he walked further along Calle Javier looking for somewhere he might find that precious commodity. Nothing. So he walked back, turned along the modern church façade and came to a small postern gate, open, that gave onto cloisters, which ended abruptly at their southern end, as though once belonging to a larger complex. And there, in a darkened corner, he settled down with his painfully scratched belly, his aching and punctured feet, his still queasy guts, to take stock of his situation and to doze in a succession of fitful nightmares.

His craving for a smoke had been dampened by the sickness in his stomach but, by late afternoon, his nausea had turned to famished hunger and he would almost have killed for a cigarette. Then that unfortunate turn of phrase had fetched back his contrition. Self-loathing. Fear of retribution. His family was not Catholic, but he had grown up among Catholic families, and had somehow assimilated their crushing sense of guilt. Another calculation to be made. And he had ventured from his lair, shambled along the pavement until he came to the *estanco* he had seen earlier. There, after some mumbling and pointing, he succeeded in buying a paper-wrapped pack of twenty *Superiores* and a box of matches.

He cast an anxious though foolish glance at the newspaper headlines. The *ABC de Sevilla*. Copies of *El Heraldo de Aragón* and *La Gaceta del Norte. El Pueblo Vasco* too. And *El Correo Español*, the official organ of the Falange. Then he kicked himself for a fool, had hardly been able to credit that it was still the same day. There would be no word from San Sebastián yet, one way or the other. But the coarse tobacco smoke had soothed his frayed senses, at least, when he got outside. And an equally successful expedition to the bar had equipped him with a bread stick – no longer particularly fresh at this time of the day – and a portion of cheese far bigger than he really wanted.

He had carried them back to the church, two *pesetas* poorer, taken advantage of the fresh water springing from the fountain at the centre of the cloistered garden, then counted the hours slowly, hidden in a corner, chewing on the cheese and his own sacramental bread, all through the church bell summons to evening mass, all through the service itself, not daring to smoke again until the noisy parishioners had left and the place fell silent once more. And there he had spent the night.

By morning it was raining. And there was that rebellious stomach to consider, making him think of practicalities. Toilets, among other things. So, with the bell ringing again in the elegant tower above him, he slipped out through the gate, falling almost naturally into that shambling shuffle he had adopted yesterday evening. Mumbling to himself. The epitome of Pamplona's village fool. For he had noticed on his expedition for the cigarettes that, in this guise, people rarely looked at his face.

At the *estanco*, the morning's papers had not yet arrived, but the bar opposite was open. Old men sitting on stools at the counter. Shouting at each other, as normal. Rasping voices, impossibly deep. But otherwise everything seemed normal. If he had expected a hue and cry, he was disappointed. Guilt still eating at him. Yet the call of nature was even stronger, and he watched the bar's routines until he felt confident enough to step into its gloomy, cigar smoke-filled interior.

'*¡Fuera!*' shouted the stubble-faced man behind the counter. Get out!

Jack almost smiled. His performance as mendicant beggar must have been more convincing than he'd realised. But he opened his fist, showed the barman his meager supply of *pesetas*, and the fellow grunted, jerked his head towards the table by way of permission to enter.

'Cognac?' said Jack. '*Por favor.*'

He would have preferred a coffee, but it did not look as though the brass and copper monster at the far end had seen any of the genuine article for some time, so he opted for the same beverage he'd seen the customers ordering, then sat in a darkened corner, watching once more until, thankfully, one of the men sauntered off through a rear door and came back minutes later, fastening his flies. Jack set down his glass and went through the same door, out into a small yard. Crates, barrels and, tucked away behind, a badly constructed hut with no door, plenty of cockroaches, and a simple hole-in-the-floor squat toilet, stinking to high heaven, but at least squares of newspaper threaded on a string and a metal bucket in which to deposit the used pieces – and Jack was considerate enough to use his matches, setting fire to the contents when he'd finished.

Back inside the bar, he paid his bill, counting out his *céntimos* with miserly care, then shuffled out into the street again. The *estanco* owner was sorting the recently arrived newspapers and Jack picked up a copy of the *Diario de Navarra*, realised from the joyous headlines, articles filling the whole front page, the triumphant photographs that this was Franco's birthday. And more good news for Europe's fascists on the middle pages. The whole continent, it seemed, glorying in the Munich Conference, Prime Minister Chamberlain's decision to appease Hitler still further, to give him a free hand in the Sudetenland. Jack could have wept. Could nobody truly see what was happening to the world? What had the leader of the Republican *guerrilleros* at Covadonga said? Fight the fascists here in Spain – or end up fighting them everywhere else. *Christ almighty*, he thought. And then wondered how his own paper would report this. Tomorrow's edition. What would be the headline in *Reynold's News*? None of this claptrap for Sydney Elliott, that was certain. If Jack knew anything about his editor, he'd likely be the only one in Britain to damn Chamberlain for the buffoon he certainly was. Yet Jack suddenly felt very lost and alone, found himself sobbing quietly, and the shopkeeper beside him, angry, demanding payment for the paper. Another twenty *céntimos* gone. He wanted to peruse more of the local rags, but the proprietor was now looking at him suspiciously, and Jack stumbled back to the cloistered garden, rummaging through the pages for anything about San Sebastián. Nothing. And if Carter-Holt's body had been found, it would have merited a mention. Surely. But not a word even about her disappearance. Or his own.

Tomorrow, then. Maybe tomorrow. But as he settled down in his seclusion, chewing on the last of his bread, another lump of cheese, something did draw his attention. One of many pieces about Pamplona itself. He did his best to translate, cursed again the loss of his Hugo's Spanish Grammar. Yet the gist of the article told him simply that the city was preparing to receive an influx of pilgrims on the Camino de Santiago once more. Among so many other things for which Spain should be thankful to *El Caudillo*, it seemed, was his encouragement of Europe's Catholic Youth to come and see how the country's re-conquest from the Reds had made the famous pilgrimage route safe once more.

Has it ever been anything but safe? Jack wondered. *Except when Franco was charging his bloody armies all over it.*

He'd been in Paris for the 1937 International Exhibition, and the Spanish Pavilion there had not only housed Picasso's now famous painting, but also a towering sculpture by Alberto Sánchez Pérez called *El Pueblo Español Tiene un Camino que Conduce a una Estrella*. The Spanish People Have a Path, which Leads to a Star. It was an obelisk, with a winding spiral path leading to a star at the top. A reference to the religious pilgrim route, of course. But also a symbol of hope for the secular republic. The vision that, despite the civil war, there was a goal. A dream. A hope.

And where does the Camino lead, Jack? He asked himself. Ultimately to Santiago de Compostela, of course. But before that, there was Burgos. And in Burgos there was Franco.

Telford had been astonished at the lack of security around the *Generalísimo* when they had been presented to him. So near. And yet so far. But in Burgos, now the capital of Nationalist Spain? How would it be there? How close could he get to Franco for a second time?

Unfinished business, he thought. *Fight the fascists here – or end up fighting them everywhere else.*

All he needed was a plan to get himself from Pamplona to Burgos.

The mid-morning Mass attracted quite a crowd. Almost a repeat of the service the tour group had attended – most of them, at least – in Irún, two weeks before. That had been a Sunday, of course. But, here in Pamplona, large numbers of the devout seemed keen to receive the

Eucharist on any day of the week. The respectful gathering outside the main door of the church. No women, waiting out here in the drizzle. All men. And either very young or very old. Those of fighting age away at the Front, perhaps. Dark suits. Hats and berets – many of them the large red berets of the Carlists. Then the arrival of some dignitaries. Nazi salutes. Cries of *¡Arriba, España!*

Everybody filed inside, joined the women already seated in the pews, and Jack slipped in behind them, though trying to keep his distance. But that was no problem, for there seemed to be nobody over-keen to share proximity with a shoeless and alien beggar stinking of foul fish. All to the good, and he was soon working over the details of his strategy, through the reverences to the altar, the incense, the Act of Penitence, the *Agnus Dei* and the Communion. He even went forward himself, to accept the flesh and blood of Christ, tried to make sure that the priest noticed him.

What are you, priest? he wondered. *An honourable example of your vocation? Or one of those who, when the rebellion began, pointed his finger. How many political opponents of the coup d'état have been butchered here?* he asked himself. *And not just here. A thousand other places.* Shot just because they'd voted a certain way in the '36 Elections. And yes, he knew all the stories about so-called Red atrocities too. Priests killed. Supporters of the Right. In that initial random madness and terror after the insurrection began. But this was different. Telford knew it was different. Systematic. Planned. By Franco himself. To cleanse Spain of its democracy.

And when the service ended, most of the congregation eventually departed, Jack remained in his seat, waiting to see how things worked in this Church of San Agustín. Thankfully, he did not wait alone. Yet few of those remaining stayed in their original seats. Instead, the two dozen still left began an unseemly race for the pews nearest the dark confessional box, an old lady on two sticks using them to her advantage, and hacking her way to the front. He was not Catholic himself, so had never done this before, had no idea whether, in this particular church, confessions were heard so close after the Mass itself. But he assumed from the agitation and jostling for position that it must be imminent. Even so, some considerable time elapsed before the priest appeared once again, and in that intervening period, more people had arrived. Another older woman; a younger lady with two rebellious and corpulent children;

a middle-aged man missing one leg and using a crutch. Each of them approached the waiting huddle, asked the same question.

'*¿Quién es el último?*' Who's last in line?

The black-robed priest strode briskly towards the group, fiddling with his green stole and exasperation etched into his pinched features. He bellowed at them, and they all edged away along the pews, further from the temptation to sin by eavesdropping. All except the *señora* with the sticks, who waddled to the side of the confessional and was helped by the priest to kneel. It took a while. Longer, more painful, it seemed to Jack, than her short confession was worth. And then the others followed suit, in their allotted order, Telford straining to hear the process, getting the words right in preparation for his own turn. For he had moved up now, taken a new seat closer to the box. Boredom set in, his eyes becoming heavy as he tried to make out the sins for which these people were seeking absolution. But then they were all gone, the last of them, the one-legged man, struggling from the awkward place where he had propped himself against the wall. Jack went to help him, then knelt on the cushion, spoke into the grille those lines he had learned by rote, listening to the loudest of those who had gone before him.

'*En nombre del Padre y del Hijo y del Espíritu Santo. Amen.*'

And the priest replied, in his bored voice.

'*Ave Maria Purísimo.*'

'*Sin pecado concebida,*' said Jack.

'*¿Cuándo fue su última confesión?*' asked the priest. When was your last confession?

Jack hesitated.

'*¿Habla Inglés, Padre?*' he said. Do you speak English, Father?

Silence. And Jack realised that his entire plan fell upon the hope that the priest did, indeed, speak some of his language. Perhaps just a little, he prayed.

'English?' said the priest.

'I'm Irish, Father,' Jack lied. '*Irlandés.*'

'How long sin' you las' confess?'

'A year, Father. And I killed somebody. I came to Spain to fight the Reds. But I ended up killing one of our own. My parish priest said all good Catholics should stand up for General Franco. So I joined O'Duffy.'

'O'Duffy, who is he?'

'A fighter for our Faith, Father. Politician. But our General too. He brought us here from Dublin. Volunteers. Good Catholic boys. Well, I was at Jarama. A place called Ciempozuelos. Lots of us died there. Killed by our own side. A mistake, they said. A company from the Canary Islands. Just arrived at the Front.'

'In war,' said the priest, 'thing 'appens. An' must go fast, my son. Others wait.'

'I'm the last one, Father,' Jack told him, heard the priest sigh.

'You kill there?' he said. 'It is duty of soldier. Kill in war is different. Kill for God here.'

'No,' said Jack. 'I went to hospital. Sick. Vasculitis. And in the next bed was the officer. From that Canary Islands company. I killed him, Father. Then ran away. Tried to get to my regiment. But by then they'd sailed back to Dublin. Now I want to repent. Walk the Camino de Santiago. Beg for God's forgiveness. And after that I'll surrender. To the army. Take my punishment.'

Silence again.

'You kill 'im in purpose?' said the priest.

'On purpose. Yes, Father.'

'Then I cannot give you *absolución*, my son. *Hasta que se rinda.*' Until you surrender. 'You understand?'

Jack knew about the Seal of the Confessional. The theory, at least. But how far could he play this priest?

'I understand, Padre. You will inform the Guardia Civil?'

'You know I cannot,' said the priest. 'You mus' do. Now. Or after you walk Camino. You will walk? Make *penitencia?*'

'I will,' said Jack. 'If I can find shoes.' Then he murmured the only Act of Contrition that he knew. From long, long ago. And only in English. 'My God, I am sorry for my sins with all my heart. I have sinned against You, whom I should love above all things.'

He waited for a response, but the priest simply muttered a prayer and, when the prayer was done, Jack saw the shadowed face come closer to the far side of the grille.

'On the Camino,' said the priest, 'you mus' say El Rosario. Every day. *¿Comprende?*'

'I understand, Father. *Lo comprendo.*'

'Then go in peace, my son.'

'Thanks be to God,' said Jack. He rose from the cushion, began to walk down the aisle, back towards the entrance. It had not gone entirely as he had hoped. Too much reliance on his literary education at Worcester's Royal Grammar School. Victor Hugo. *Les Misérables* firmly on the curriculum. But this priest was no Bishop Myriel. And Jack was no Jean Valjean. No golden candlesticks here. Yet he heard the confessional door open and close behind him.

'*¡Espera!*' shouted the priest. Wait! And Jack almost soiled himself, fearing that the old fool may have decided to ignore the Seal after all. He turned, slowly, saw the priest wringing his hands. 'There are things you need, my son. For the Camino. Shoes. Other things. But will you say me your name, my son?'

Jack smiled.

'Yes, Father,' he smiled, in his best Irish brogue. 'My name is Murphy. Brendan Murphy.'

Chapter Three

Sunday 2nd October 1938

No candlesticks. Yet the gifts from Father Ignacio were worth their own weight in gold. A pair of rope-soled shoes, *alpargatas*. Cast-off workman's trousers, heavy and serviceable. A threadbare, brown woollen cloak, which might at least also serve as a blanket. Canvas satchel. Enamel cup and plate. Straight razor and shaving brush. A stout staff, blessed, to help him on his road. A small, iron replica of a scallop shell, from the priest's personal possessions and, he had said, tying the thing to the top of the staff, a symbol of Saint James himself. A loan – Jack persuasively insisted it should be so – ten more *pesetas*. And, most precious of all, a letter signed by the priest himself. A letter confirming that the bearer, Brendan Murphy, was making pilgrimage to the holy shrine of Saint James the Apostle and should be given every possible assistance. On the back of the letter, some basic instructions for the first leg of his journey.

Naturally, the questions, and Jack's dissembling answers, had swarmed thicker than flies around hams in a *bodega*. What had happened to his uniform? Father Ignacio had pressed him. Cast aside, Jack insisted, when he was on the run. Even the boots? Stolen, when he slept at the roadside, along with his razor and other personal belongings. And where had this hospital been – where he killed the officer? In Valladolid. When he ran, he decided to head for the French border. Then God had spoken to him. Not far from Pamplona. About the Camino. How long had he been on the run then? Many months, he had said. But how had he fed himself? By begging. Stealing too. Yes, another sin. A few Hail Marys added to his daily recital of the Rosary.

Which had reminded Father Ignacio. A final gift if *Señor* Murphy was truly going to complete his penance, he had better carry a rosary with him, had he not? And he had taken from the pocket of his cassock a set of the holy beads and crucifix. They looked like ivory, though Jack thought it more likely to be celluloid, French ivory. Beautifully made, all the same, with the bead pins, connector loops and links all seeming to be silver. For the first time, Jack had begun to feel true guilt, tried to refuse the offering, then decided that the best way to both deflect further questions and, at the same time, diffuse his unwanted self-reproach was to field some interrogation of his own. And he had been on safe ground when asking about Father Ignacio's background. Reminiscences about the village of his birth. His reasons for pursuing this vocation. His first parish. His move to Pamplona. It had all taken time. The tortuous mix of execrable English, sparse Spanish. But when Jack had begun to probe events in the city following the insurrection – the Movement, *el Movimiento*, he carefully chose to call it, using the genteel name by which Franco's supporters referred to their sedition – communication between them started to shrivel. And, by the time he'd gone to bed, in the priest's house this time, he was convinced that Father Ignacio had been up to his neck in atrocity himself.

All of which had helped Telford sleep better.

He was on the road early. Washed and shaved. His goal for the day was Puente La Reina. Twenty-four kilometres – *más o menos*, more or less – according to Father Ignacio, who had given him an additional parting gift – a package of bread, cheese and smoked sausage for his satchel. A last farewell, while the priest was distracted with preparation for early Mass, and Jack was crossing the Plaza del Castillo, with all the Sunday bells of Pamplona's many other churches ringing in his ears. Out along the tree-lined Paseo del Sarasate, with its monuments and statues, keeping his head down as he passed the red berets of Carlist sentries at the Navarra Region's military headquarters. He skirted the Ciudadela fortress, and turned down the Calle Fuente del Hierro, followed the old street until it finally took him into open country, through endless fields of wheat stubble, splashed with the green shoots of a winter crop.

Freedom. Yesterday's showers all gone. Bright sunshine and one of Spain's endless horizons ahead, the road ambling gently up towards a haze-shrouded village that he took to be Cizur Menor. A church. No, two churches, to be precise. A few stunted pines. Kites circling and screeching. The whiff of cowshit from somewhere, mingled with the ever-present smell of burned olive oil. The prickle of sweat on his neck and down his back.

Well, here you are, Jack, he said to himself. *On the Camino de Santiago.* One of them, anyway. The French Camino, they called this one. A different route from that on which the tour group had stood – the coastal route – when they had visited Santillana del Mar. He had no idea how many there were in total. Yet they all led to Santiago. To the place where the remains of Saint James had been found. By a bishop led there with a celestial guide. *Compostela.* The Field of the Star.

Yet, of all the routes, this was the most famous. The most important. Because it passed through Burgos. Burgos, for now the capital of Nationalist Spain. *And in Burgos,* he thought, *is Franco the Monster, in his lair.*

'You'll never do it,' he heard his father's voice beside him – the voice he imagined as his father's, at least. Soft Worcester accent. 'Not near enough guts.'

'And who the hell are you to talk about guts?' Jack sneered at the spectre, his father wearing the old uniform of the British Expeditionary Force. The only way Jack remembered him, from the sepia photograph on his mother's front parlour wall.

'You think it's easy,' said his father. 'But you've no idea.'

Jack had tried to imagine. How terrifying existence in the trenches must have been to persuade a man to suicide, forsake his family, life itself, rather than return there.

'No,' Jack murmured. 'No idea at all. But I'll kill bloody Franco, all the same.'

His feet were already burning by the time he'd passed through Cizur Menor's churchgoers. Three kilometres down. More than twenty still to go. *But what does it matter?* he thought to himself. *I can do it in easier stages, maybe. No point killing myself.* He cursed himself for the phrase, thought of his father again, remembered that there was, indeed, a point. A ticking clock. One with minutes and hours of fluid length. Like actual time, now fleeting, now stretched to endless tedium. Yet always limited. And, here, governed by some certainty that, sooner or later, Carter-Holt's bloated corpse would wash up on a Biscayan beach.

It urged him onwards. Another village off to his right, and then nothing but the narrow road again, climbing more steeply now through the interminable straw-coloured landscape. After an hour, he stopped to soak his feet in a stream shaded by an oasis of flaking eucalyptus trees, exchanging curt greetings with a grizzled goat-herd on the opposite bank while the bells of the old man's plentiful flock clanked and jangled, black flies buzzing around their eyes. A break just long enough to smoke one of the precious *Superiores*, followed by the further monotony of walking alone, the beginning of doubts about his wisdom in choosing such a path, both literally and as a political objective. The sun was strong too, and he had no hat. Never wore hats, as it happened. A minor rebellion against the fashion of the times. And it would never have occurred to him to steal one. But he pulled the cloak up over his head to provide some shade and plodded for a further hour until the track turned to the left and he saw to his horror that it began to climb the flank of a considerable peak. Father Ignacio had said nothing of climbing. But Jack should have known. He had been in Spain only two weeks, but still wondered why he'd never realised how the country bristled with mountains more than anywhere he'd ever been. More than anywhere else in Europe, he imagined, outside Switzerland.

Jack pushed himself along, stopping frequently, chest heaving with exertion as the incline increased, until he came to the biscuit-brown church and sprawl of rural houses and wood smoke which, by the priest's note, must be Zariquiegui – though it was anybody's bet how the damned thing should be pronounced. There was a service just finishing and, Father Ignacio's note in hand, he was trying to roll the syllables around his tongue, calculating the number of points he might score in a game of Crossword Lexicon. And his concentration was little disturbed by those leaving the church, or the few living souls not actually at their worship. Yet he heard the man who sneered at him from a lean-to timber pile, correcting Jack's pronunciation.

'Zariquiegui,' said the man. Tha-ree-kee-*eh*-ghee. '*Aquí estamos.*' Here we are, though there was no welcome in it.

The fellow was perhaps in his mid-forties, wild-eyed, dust-worn suit and collarless shirt, his face rough as coarse sandpaper, nose bent badly out of shape.

'*Gracias,*' Jack replied, at the same time as he heard the first distant drone. It took him a moment to spot the source but, at last, he saw them. Bombers, in formation. Low. Heading towards the village from the west.

Germans then. Or Italians. Or both. Hitler and Mussolini had sent their planes here within days of the rebellion's start. And Jack's first instinct was to run. For he had seen the nightmare chaos and mayhem they'd heaped upon towns like Durango and Guernica. But where were these headed? To Barcelona, perhaps, now the base of Negrín's Republican government, though cut off from the rest of their territory further south. Or to the Ebro, where the Republic's forces were still holding out – so far as Jack knew – despite that months-long battle being all but lost. They were closer now, easily distinguishable, the engines a deep roar.

Telford swore, spat upon the road, then spun around, startled by his own involuntary reaction. But nobody seemed to have noticed. Not then. The man was watching the planes too, a maniac's grin to match the madness in his eyes. He was stamping out some joyful jig, singing to the same tempo.

> *¡Arriba, escuadras, a vencer,*
> *Que en España empieza a amanecer!*

Bloody fascists, thought Jack, and he edged away, towards the farther end of the village, found his way impeded by a different sort of procession. Behind him, the parishioners were also shading their eyes to better view the bombers, or clapping their hands in adulatory delight at seeing them, or picking up the same song.

> *¡España una, España grande!*
> *¡España libre!*
> *¡Arriba, España!*

And, ahead, this second group of locals had stopped too, shouting.

> *¡Arriba, España!*

In their midst was a woman, half-dragged, half-pushed, up the lane and now forced to her stocking-holed knees, the back of her hair yanked back, forcing her to look up at the planes as well, while some age-mottled and toothless *pistolero* spat words into her face.

'*¡Mira!*' he screamed, waving the barrel of his revolver before her eyes. Look! '*Muerte a los Rojos.*' Death to the Reds. Yet the woman showed no fear. She was painfully thin though. Eyes sunk deep into the shadowed eye sockets, and the skin stretched tight over cheek and jawbones.

Jack stepped out faster, feeling the place closing about him, the planes now directly overhead. But he could not look. Without them, he knew, Franco could never have got this far, come so close to victory. And his own country had done nothing to prevent it. Worse, Britain had presided over the Non-Intervention Committee, which prevented most of the free world from helping Spain's beleaguered democracy while, at the same time, turning a blind eye to the belligerent participation of Germany and Italy. *Enemy territory*, he thought, then heard somebody running behind him. He turned, almost knowing what would happen next. The madman from the timber pile. Yelling at him. Unintelligible. Jack shrugged.

'What?' he said. '*¿Qué?*'

The man shouted louder, pointed at the planes, began to berate the neighbours, while Jack struggled to pick up even a word or two. But his gestures were plain enough. He pointed to the bombers, clapped his hands, bade Jack do the same.

'*Peregrino,*' said Jack, shaking his head and trying to keep a friendly smile pasted in place. A pilgrim. And he waved Father Ignacio's letter in the man's face. It was knocked aside. Knocked from his hand. Jack made a grab for it, felt the man catch hold of his coat.

'*¡Rojo!*' the man cried again. '*Traidor rojo.*' Red traitor.

'No,' said Jack. '*Irlandés.*' Irish. '*Soldado del Caudillo.*' One of Franco's soldiers. '*Ahora, peregrino.*' Now a pilgrim. But he managed to find sufficient words to ask what the woman had done. She was on her feet again now, being jostled towards the church.

'*Hija de puta,*' the man replied, though Jack knew this was purely figurative. Unlikely that she was literally a whore's daughter. And the rest he pieced together. Wife of a man fighting for the Republic. A Red traitor, like all his family. The village had sent her away. Didn't want her sort here. But today she had come back. Been caught.

'Very good,' Jack nodded, for want of anything better to say, and bending down to retrieve his letter. But the man stood on it. Deliberately.

'*Venga, Irlandés,*' he said. Come on, Irish. Come and see how we deal with Red whores. Telford had no desire to do so, yet he found himself hauled in the procession's wake. The crowd had stopped now, a single gathering formed in a half-circle just this side of the church. People were spitting at the woman, yelling at her, different insults all shouted at the same time, like a vicious version of an opera's *imbroglio*.

Only one woman stood apart from them. Fastidiously dressed, prim, in the very doorway of the church, a small girl in a white frock clutched at her side. The matron's features were harsh, lips pursed in a cruel smile while, from one of the neighbouring houses, another man came running, brandishing a pair of hair clippers. Their captive's composure broke as soon as she saw the things and, for the first time, she no longer looked straight ahead but, rather, turned from one to another of her tormentors, shouting defiance at each of them. But, in this way, her gaze fell upon the vignette at the church portico and her defiant protests turned to a choked sob.

'Mi María,' Jack heard her cry but, by then, the villager had set to work with his clippers, shorn two twists of raven-black hair that floated down to rest on the stones at her knees. And she struggled then, while men and women of all ages defiled her, held her legs, pinioned her arms, clamped fingers around her face to keep the head locked in place.

Somewhere inside Jack's own head, his brain fought to find the words. Spanish words. But they would not come. He realised, too, that the fellow from the timber pile still held his arm, and Jack wrenched it free, fury filling him.

'No,' he screamed. 'Stop this.' But nobody paid him any heed, and the shears continued to snip, snip, snip. The hair fell thicker and faster. Jack tried to grab at one of the thugs gripping the woman's face, but the madman dragged him back, pulled him to the ground.

'¿Qué hace?' the man shouted down at him. What are you doing? Jack tussled with him, at the same time trying to both haul himself up and also slap away the fellow's restraining hand.

'Take your filthy hands off me,' he screamed. 'And let that woman go.' Yet they did not. There was blood now, running in rivulets from cuts inflicted by careless application of the clippers, and the woman seemed to have fallen into a state of resigned inertia, head bowed to the inevitable while, at the church, the old woman and the white-dressed

25

child still looked on. '*La chica*,' Jack shouted, pointing towards the church. The girl. '*¿Quién es?*' Who is she?

'*Hija de la puta madre*,' the man snarled. Daughter of this whore-mother.

That can't be right, Jack told himself. *This woman's daughter?* If so, what sort of barbarism was this? Why did the old matron not take the girl away? Where was the child's emotion?

'You must stop this,' Jack shouted again, pulled free this time and launched himself at the man wielding the shearing clippers. Pointless, of course, for the humiliation was almost complete, the woman's head now stripped of all but a few tufts, reduced otherwise to a ragged stubble.

Like the wheat fields, he thought, as somebody struck him.

'*Mi María*,' the woman sobbed once more, and Jack saw that, finally, the girl in the white dress was being led away. Not even a backward glance. Nothing. He had the man with the clippers in some sort of wrestler's embrace now, trying to pull him away from his victim. Too little, too late. He realised he was weeping, shouting through his tears and rage that they were fascist bastards. He was hit again. And again. Pushed to the ground, kicked, sat upon, while the old *pistolero* yelled at him, poked the revolver's muzzle into his belly, over and over.

The villagers had laughed at him. Scorned his weakness. Summoned their children to come and look at the spectacle. Then they had dragged him off to this storage hut and slammed shut a rusted bolt so loose that Jack could have kicked the thing open in an instant. But he seemed paralysed, incapable of action. Perhaps the unaccustomed fatigue of his morning's exertion. Maybe the accumulated effects of the past two weeks, and especially the last two days. In part, at least, he was stilled by the relief that he'd not been summarily shot and left by the roadside. Yet he still did not fully understand the villagers' volatility, could not be certain whether his execution had only been postponed, rather than commuted. Or that they would not simply send for the Guardia.

In the depths of his diminished manhood, he wondered who would miss him. The mother and sister that he normally saw each second Thursday of the month? Sydney Elliott, who had given him the post with *Reynold's News*, taken a chance with him, on Sheila Grant Duff's recommendation? Sheila herself, perhaps? Sheila, with whom he had worked on the Saar Plebiscite, back in '35. A friend, certainly. Too professional to allow herself ever to be anything more. He had called her from Santiago, dictated his dispatch. Only three days before. It had cost him a fortune. One hundred and forty-seven *pesetas*. Two pounds. Christ, how he wished he'd had that sort of money back in Pamplona.

Yet it was not the *Civiles* who came to visit his makeshift prison, but the parish priest. He strutted through the door like a nervous pigeon, tiny head pecking back and forth as he stammered some panic-woven words. The sleeves of his cassock flapped as he tried to return the walking stick and shoeprint-dirtied letter, but not a word of English and, from the cacophony of his Spanish, Jack could only distinguish repeated references to Padre Ignacio and Pamplona.

For his part, Jack tried to ask about the woman, about her daughter. Simple questions, which the priest chose not to understand. But there was a blessing, Jack thought, as the plump little fellow ushered him out into the daylight again, clawing at the cloak to remove some of the dust it had gathered in the struggle. No sign now of the woman who'd suffered the attack. Nor her daughter – if, indeed, Jack had understood the thing correctly. The priest's parishioners were lined up outside though, contrite, but no more friendly. Yet bearing gifts. Bread. A skin of wine. And, hungry as he might be, Jack's shame caused him to ignore the offerings. The priest used sign language to indicate that he might stay the night, but Jack declined that too, naturally.

Relief at his escape drove him on up the road, to the highest point on the mountain's shoulder, where he followed the curve to the right, along the ridge, from which he could see his route dropping down before him. Easier walking from there, though his conscience no clearer for his failure to help the woman. A few motor vehicles passed him, and even a battered, smoke-gushing autobus, though nobody thought to stop for him. And, by late afternoon, he had passed through enough of northern Spain's bread basket to last him a lifetime, convinced himself he had passed the same cluster of farm buildings at least two dozen times, and experienced serious attacks of *déja vu* on reaching the outskirts of Uterga and Muruzabal. The same two and three storey houses, heavy stone ground floor walls and, above, flake-painted render, clay-tiled roofs. Similar churches too, it seemed, always appearing at an identical point when he turned a bend.

Yet at least nobody else bothered him and, as he came into Obanos, he referred again to Father Ignacio's note, realised he was only about three more kilometres from his goal for the day. But Jack thought they might just be three too many. It was something of a hike up into the centre of town, a pleasant enough place, through an archway that must once have been part of the town's wall. Beyond, a carefully painted board told him he was standing outside the Church of San Juan Bautista. It was slightly more grand than those he'd passed earlier and, inevitably, there was another Mass in progress. So he would have to wait a while before he could approach the local priest, try to beg a bed for the night.

While he was waiting, he looked around the square, saw that he must be back in civilisation. An attractive café. A green-painted garage too, with a bright CAMPSA petrol pump. At the pump stood Jack's favourite motorcar. A 1931 six-cylinder Talbot M75. Golden yellow. Black trim and bumpers. Beside the car, one foot on the running board and elbow resting nonchalantly on the driver's door, was an Englishman. Without question an Englishman. Sandy hair. Whites and a cricket sweater. Probably Jack's age, around thirty. And, looking furious in the passenger seat, one of the most attractive women Telford had ever seen.

Chapter Four

Monday 3rd October 1938

'How was the room, old fellow?' the Englishman asked. He had taken Telford under his wing the previous evening, almost as soon as Jack broke the ice, imitation Irish charm, by asking whether there was anything he could do to help. But no, Frederick Barnard had thanked him. His exquisitely beautiful passenger was simply angry at the price they'd paid for the petrol. 85 *céntimos* per litre. Daylight robbery, she insisted. But what else could you expect, she had said, with *banditos fascistas* now in control? And she had been even more annoyed when her companion had insisted on driving Jack to Puente La Reina. Now, Barnard eased the Talbot into second gear through a tight Romanesque archway and onto the Pilgrims' Bridge for which the town was named.

'It was kind of you to arrange it,' Jack replied, having put his Irish accent carefully in place and settled himself in the dickey seat. 'Good to have a real bed for a change.'

'But was there no bath in the room?' The woman wrinkled that pretty nose again, as she'd done regularly on the drive from Obanos.

'The clothes, I'm afraid,' said Jack, unable to think of a single plausible reason for the fish market stink that still clung to him. 'I must look like a tramp.'

'Yes, rather,' said Barnard, though he was more interested in the architecture, slowed almost to a halt when they reached the middle of the bridge, its highest point. 'There used to be a shrine here. A chapel, really. The statue of Nuestra Señora del Puy. Very famous. You could have come with us last night. To see the church. Remarkable place.'

'It would have been a real treat, I'm sure,' Jack lied, as he glanced back at the town. It was a fabulous sight, to be fair, the early morning sunlight bathing the place in a warm ochre glow.

'Do the rules of pilgrimage allow you such luxury, Mister Murphy?' said Barnard's companion, the elegant Josefina Ruiz Delgado. 'Although I suppose that if you cannot even bother to walk the Camino, accepting such comforts is neither here nor there.'

The Talbot growled into life again and ran down the far side of the bridge, out into open country, and Jack decided not to take her comments personally.

'You should at least have joined us for dinner,' said Barnard, and gunned the throttle.

'It was a long, hot day,' Jack told him. 'A strange day. And I'd have been happy to walk, *señorita*,' he told Josefina, 'except Mister Barnard can be very persuasive when he sets his mind to something, so.'

She was from Mexico City, and Barnard had met her at the University there, when he had been extending his study of Spanish architecture.

'Why else should we be here?' she said. 'In this wilderness full of freedom's enemies?'

She turned and glowered at him, and Jack imagined the stream of invective she must have directed at Frederick for his temerity in picking him up. But he conjured, too, the speech that the real Brendan Murphy would have delivered to her by way of riposte. How so many of those fighting for Franco were simply believers wanting to protect their Catholic faith. How they were fighting for a new world order. How Franco had done so much to restore the traditional values of Spain. Jack had been subjected to the lecture himself at Galdakao. But he could not bring himself to repeat it. Just the one part.

'This is my home now, *señorita*,' he said. 'And I'd hardly call it a wilderness.'

'And you're on leave, Mister Murphy,' said Frederick Barnard swiftly. 'Isn't that what you said? Walking the Camino for health reasons?'

'Something like that,' Jack told him. 'I have some form of vasculitis.' He had decided to leave out any mention of Brendan Murphy's role as a guide, for Barnard had given him full details of their own journey so far. The sleeper from Paris to Bayonne, then collected the car, driving on to San Sebastián and, of course, a stay at the Hotel María Cristina. That would have been a couple of days before Jack returned there, thankfully, and they'd been in Pamplona since then, so little chance they would have gathered any news about two missing English folk. But best to play on the safe side. 'And you two,' Jack changed the subject. 'Came all the way here to check details for a book, right? A novel, is it?'

'Heavens, no,' Frederick laughed. '*A History of Spanish Architecture*. The blasted thing's taken me ten years. And then, just when it's about to finally be published, some professor in Harvard releases a paper claiming that elements of my research about the Codex are wrong. Can you believe it? I've been visiting these sites since I was just a nipper. And now we've had to come all the blinking way back across the Atlantic just to prove the damned fellow wrong.'

'The Codex?' said Jack. 'I'm sorry, but…'

'The Calixtinus, old man. Twelfth Century. Book Five would be right up your street. Literally. Basically a guidebook for those walking the original Camino to Santiago. Lists all the places of religious interest along the way. Astonishing piece of work. And, in my own book, I've produced the first-ever modern map showing the precise locations of all those sites. Quite a task, I can tell you. But hugely exciting. And then along comes this American chap, never even been to the Peninsula, so far as I can tell.'

'How frustrating for you,' said Jack. 'And look, the *señorita's* right. You can drop me anywhere. I should really be walking.'

'But you've such a long way to go,' said Frederick. 'And I don't believe that Saint James the Apostle would begrudge a man with vasculitis just a modicum of assistance. At least let us take you as far as Logroño.' Jack saw Josefina flinch, shake her head and mutter some Mexican curse. 'Or Burgos. Anyway,' Barnard went on, 'you've still not told us what it was that made yesterday so strange. Nor how you came by all those scratches. It's intriguing.'

'These?' said Jack, and touched the abrasions at the side of his eye. 'Just a stupid scuffle with some villagers back a-ways. They were shaving the head of this poor woman. Husband off fighting. For the Reds though. Fair enough, I suppose. But that's no way to treat a woman, don't you think?'

Josefina snorted with derision.

'*Ay, señor*. Shaved head?' she sneered. 'You must have seen and done far worse yourself, Mister Murphy. No? We read the reports. About the way Franco's animals behave whenever they capture towns from the Popular Front.'

'My darling…' Frederick began.

'No,' said Jack. 'It's fine, sure. Just – Well, all sorts of things happen in war, *señorita*. But yesterday, it wasn't the woman herself so much. It was something to do with it happening there, if you take my drift. On the Camino itself. And there was this child. A little girl. They said she was the woman's daughter. I think that's what they were telling me. Only…'

'Only you did not know,' said Josefina, 'that very often, in such towns, they take away the small children from families that you call the Reds. Take them away and give them to those who will bring them up as good Catholics. As loyal followers of Franco.'

As it happened, Jack did not know that, couldn't remember seeing any reference to such a thing in the British press. And he was also unable to decide whether he felt more ashamed by his ignorance as a journalist, or as his new *alter ego*, Brendan Murphy, the Francoist soldier. But, alongside the shame, there was a deeper anger. That Franco and his thugs could wage war against children in that way, with such impunity. It fired his hatred of the monster.

'I suppose you would have strong views on all this,' said Jack. 'Given the support that Mexico's sent to the Republic, an' all.'

'Not everybody in my country supports the Republic,' she snapped. And she turned again, flashed those flame-filled dark eyes at him. 'There are many supporters of Franco. *Fascistas.*' *Like you*, the eyes seemed to scream.

All the same, thought Jack, *Mexico's the only other country in the world, except Russia, that's provided them with direct help*. Two million dollars-worth of aid, Sydney Elliott had written in one of his editorials. *And plenty of Mexicans over here fighting with the International Brigade volunteers*. Sons of Pancho Villa's own revolutionaries, he supposed. But the International Brigades were being withdrawn now. Some sort of gesture on the part of Prime Minister Negrín. Hoping for a truce maybe. Either that, or the first signs of acceptance that the Republic was beaten. *Christ!* he thought. *But without Franco to lead the Nationalists? Couldn't we still turn all this around? One step at a time though, eh Jack? First, we've got to reach Burgos.*

'And you, Mister Barnard,' said Jack. 'Where would a professional historian of architecture stand on all this?'

'Me?' said Frederick. 'Oh, I'm no more than a gifted amateur in that arena. No, Mister Murphy. You have me pegged wrongly, I'm afraid. You see, by profession, I'm a British diplomat. So you cannot possibly expect me to comment.'

The Talbot raised dust through a string of small villages, up hills and down again, with Frederick Barnard making stops at a bewildering number of Gothic medieval churches, monasteries, castles, bridges and abandoned pilgrim hostels, through Estella, with tales of King Sancho Ramirez, and then on past stories of Moorish warlords, vineyards and Charlemagne. And in the rare moments when he was not engrossed in all this, Barnard had a tendency to sing. Loudly. Snatches of Italian opera. An abysmal noise, like the baying of a bereaved hound, though it gave Jack a chance to think. His life had already been touched closely by one British diplomat in the past two weeks, and it seemed astonishing that he should now be here, in company with another. But he began to feel a further plan forming. Jack had no belief in divine providence. Yet here, surely...

'You like music, Mister Barnard?' Jack shouted to him.

'He likes only to murder music,' said Josefina – the first time, Jack thought, that her mood had lightened somewhat.

'Oh, I am so sorry,' Barnard grimaced. 'We heard *Il Trovatore* on the liner coming across. And now I can't get the blasted thing out of my head. And then we were in San Sebastián. Did I mention? At the hotel. There'd been a terrible tragedy. Awful accident.' Jack willed him to say no more, looked out over the rolling landscape. 'Concert pianist. I doubt you'd have heard of the lady.' Telford experienced some surrogate indignation on Brendan Murphy's behalf. 'But I've seen her play several times,' Barnard went on. *Yes*, thought Jack. *Me too. Poor Julia.* 'Only now,' said Frederick, 'some of the sonatas I heard her play are all jumbled up with the Verdi. It's the very devil.' Jack almost sobbed as, at the morning's end, the car came to a halt in the shadow of another bell tower at the heart of Los Arcos.

'That looks like a decent place to eat,' said Josefina, and pointed to a *bodega* on the far side of the square, at the corner of a narrow alley. It was open-fronted, hams hanging over the bar, and a deeply shadowed interior.

'Fine by me,' said Barnard, and set off across the cobbled road, weaving his way between a string of cows being goaded through the town. 'Will you take some lunch, Mister Murphy? My treat.'

Jack was famished, decided to ignore Josefina's sour-faced pouting.

'That's very kind, sure,' he said, and tagged along behind, shrugging off his cloak and slinging the thing over his shoulder. But as they came to the *bodega*'s entrance, and he could see inside a little better, he realised that a couple of Guardia Civil troopers were leaning against the far end of the counter, rifles propped next to them. 'Though maybe I'll have a smoke outside first,' said Jack. 'Maybe eat later. If I'm hungry.'

'As you wish,' Frederick Barnard told him, while Josefina simply flicked a dismissive hand in the air and didn't even look around. Though, by then, Jack had put some distance between himself and the *bodega*. He lit a cigarette and settled himself near the trunk of an old olive tree, in the shade of a drinking fountain with troughs at each side.

You're a bloody fool, Jack, he told himself. *The Civiles have no reason to be suspicious. And how the hell will you ever get close to Franco if you jump every time there's a policeman around?* But that, he convinced himself, was why he needed a new plan. And he mulled it over in his mind. *Tonight*, he decided. *No, not tonight. Tomorrow morning.*

He was still playing out the steps he needed to take, over and over, too engrossed to hear Josefina's approach.

'You have any more cigarettes left, *Señor* Murphy?' she said, and startled him. He stood, fumbled in his satchel, hoped that she wasn't going to make a habit of this. Then he lit one for each of them.

'Eaten already?' he said.

'Just some cheese and chorizo,' she replied. 'It was good. Reminded me of home.'

'And Mister Barnard?'

'Oh, chatting with your friends, the Civiles.' She saw him wince. 'But you, Mister Murphy. On leave, did you say?' He turned to answer her but, by then, she had leaned closer. 'Or is it on the run?' she whispered, blew smoke in his face. 'A deserter, perhaps.'

'Jesus, Mary and Joseph,' said Jack. 'You've some imagination, *señorita*. No, I'm sorry to disappoint you but I really do have vasculitis. So sick leave. Then back to my regiment.'

'Just in time to drive a final bayonet into Spain's democracy, I suppose,' she sneered.

'Maybe still time for a peace settlement,' said Jack, though he didn't believe such a thing was possible. But Brendan Murphy might have done.

'You are either the world's greatest optimist, or its biggest fool. The fighting on the Ebro is all but over. The Popular Front defeated again. How pleased you must feel with yourself. And next? Your Franco only needs to mop up Barcelona. Then a final attack on Madrid, a push through to Valencia. And ¡ya!' She wiped her hands together. All over.

'Life's full of surprises,' said Jack. 'You never know. Look what happened to Franco's generals. Balmes. Sanjurjo. Mola. The same sort of thing could happen to the Caudillo.'

'Ah, that's my answer then,' she stubbed out the cigarette. 'The world's biggest fool. Balmes was assassinated by Franco because he was only lukewarm about the rebellion. Sanjurjo and Mola both died in plane crashes. Coincidence? I suppose so. But you seriously think that, with Franco dead, there wouldn't be somebody to fill his shoes? That whore's bitch wife of his. Or Carrero Blanco. Some puppet of Hitler or Mussolini. You think they've both invested so much in all this that they'd simply watch it slip through their fingers?'

No, thought Jack, *I don't think that.* And he remembered the words. *If you don't fight the fascists here, you'll have to fight them somewhere else.* But he suddenly doubted his own plan of action. Yet it was all he possessed now. And he could see Frederick Barnard coming out of the *bodega,* waving at them.

'I suppose you're right,' said Jack. 'But how long will you stay in Spain, *señorita?*'

She looked surprised. Disappointed perhaps. A woman who relished a lively argument and was now deprived of that very thing.

'Oh,' she said. 'One more week in Spain, then back to France. We sail for New York from Southampton on the Twentieth of this month.'

So probably ten days, thought Jack, *before Frederick needs his passport at the French border. Maybe ten days, if I'm lucky, before he notices it's missing.*

Chapter Five

Tuesday 4th October 1938

'Another night of luxury, *Señor* Murphy,' said Josefina, when Jack finally went down to breakfast the following morning.

'You've quite spoiled me, *señorita*,' he smiled, refusing to rise to her bait. 'But no more. Today it must be shanks's pony for poor Brendan, I'm afraid.'

'A horse?' she asked, and Frederick spluttered coffee into his napkin.

'Turn of phrase, my dear,' he said. 'Mister Murphy means that he'll be on foot.'

'And are you both packed, ready for the road too?' said Jack. In truth, he had been up early, watching their room, hoping they would follow the same routine as in Puente La Reina. Cases packed, down for breakfast, and then a tip to the porter for fetching the luggage. He just prayed that his guess about the passports was correct also.

'Raring to go,' said Frederick, 'though I wish you'd accept my offer. At least to Burgos.' He winced. And Jack sensed that Josefina had kicked Barnard under the table, for she lowered her head still further towards a plate of eggs. 'Well, breakfast then,' Frederick Barnard suggested, before Jack even had a chance to decline the lift again. 'These eggs are wonderful.'

He looked towards the serving range where several covered platters were arrayed.

'Thanks,' said Jack. 'Now that's an offer I'm glad to accept. He took a napkin-wrapped bundle of cutlery from the table and set a place for himself next to Frederick. Or, rather, next to Frederick's room key. Then he put down his own almost identical key and fob alongside, casually throwing the napkin on top. He took a step towards the breakfast dishes, then stopped, slapping the palm of his hand against his forehead. 'Oh no, wait,' he said. 'I wanted to show you something. Before you go. You'll like it, I think.' And he lifted the napkin, removed the couple's key, left his own in its place.

'A surprise,' said Barnard. 'How delightful.'

'I'll just be a minute,' Jack told him, walked purposefully from the dining room but, once outside, in the Gran Hotel's reception area, he bounded for the stairs, took them two by two, up both flights. He had left a spare blanket just inside his own unlocked door, grabbed it. Then across the corridor. Fumbled with Barnard's lock. Opened it and stepped quickly inside. The cases were on the bed. Two large trunks. No obvious locks but solid straps and buckles. He chose the one with Frederick's initials. Clumsy fingers on leather and brass. Ears straining to hear the slightest noise outside. A clamour like sea-surf pounding in his ears.

Inside the trunk, all was neat. Orderly. The cricket sweater. Toiletries case. Trousers. A shoe bag. Jack carefully removed them, item by item, remembering the exact order and position. And there, beneath the shoes, a leather documents wallet. He was shaking badly, sweating, as he fingered beneath its flap, found Barnard's papers there. The magic words, white on dark blue. *Diplomatic Passport.* Jack removed it and, a little further down, discovered a linen suit. He took that too. And a shirt. Replaced them with the blanket moulded to roughly the right shape. Then he re-packed the upper layer. Only half-satisfied with the result. But it would have to do. He closed the trunk again. How long had he been? Minutes, he supposed, though it felt like hours. Surely they'd be wondering by now. He peered out into the hallway. Locked their door behind him. Threw the clothes and passport into his own room. Back down the stairs. *Steady, Jack, steady.* His heart pounding. His heart in his mouth. And, as he turned into the dining room, he was horrified to see Frederick and Josefina rising from their places, Barnard reaching for the napkin.

'Ah, you're still here,' Jack shouted. 'Good. No, just have a look at this before you go. Please.' He sat down, invited them to take their own seats again. 'Please.'

Jack took from his pocket the rosary, given to him by Father Ignacio, handed the beads across the table and, as the couple took a first cursory glance, he lifted the napkin, wiped his brow, then slipped the stolen key back into place before covering it again.

'The rosary has some special significance, Mister Murphy?' said Barnard.

'A gift,' Jack smiled at him. 'But I was told that it's a rare antique. Very old. I thought you might be able to tell me something about it.'

'You're thinking of selling it perhaps?' said Josefina, with a fair amount of cynicism.

'Holy Mother of God, certainly not!' cried Jack. 'Though, heaven only knows, I've been tempted a few times. You'd never get rich on a soldier's pay, *señorita*.'

Frederick Barnard smiled at him.

'Well, I'm sorry, Mister Murphy. But it's not my specialism, I fear.' He handed back the rosary, and Jack shrugged.

'Never mind,' he said. 'Just curious. Now, about those eggs…'

Jack ate his breakfast but kept a close eye on the hotel lobby, where Barnard checked out and tipped the porter so that their cases might be brought down. But Josefina still hovered near the table.

'They say it's not good,' she told him, 'to walk so far on a full stomach. But perhaps you're not intending to do too much after all, *Señor* Murphy?'

Am I so transparent? Jack asked himself. He hoped that she was concerned about him. Hoped that, if he had spent longer in her company, they might perhaps have become friends. More than friends. She was, after all, astonishingly attractive.

'Not too much, no.' He took Father Ignacio's letter from his pocket, turned it over and consulted the notes. 'See,' he said. 'From here. Logroño to – Ah, Nájera. Twenty-nine kilometres. You're right, sure. That's a fair distance. But after all the pampering I've had these past two days, that'll be a breeze. I feel like a new man. But you, *señorita*. You'll take care of yourself, I hope. Safe enough to be so open about Franco with me, maybe. Not in public though. You know what I mean?'

'Is that a threat, Mister Murphy?' she laughed at him. 'You forget that I'm travelling with a British diplomat, perhaps.'

No, thought Jack, as she flounced off towards the ladies' cloakroom, *I'd not forgotten.*

*

'Really,' Frederick told him, as he pressed the ten-*peseta* notes into Jack's hand on the front steps of the Gran Hotel, 'I insist. Simply a small donation to help you on your way.'

Josefina was already tucked into the Talbot, hadn't even said goodbye, but Jack was more concerned with the trunks, now loaded safely on the luggage rack without Bernard having examined them too closely.

'Well, I'd prefer to think of it as a loan,' he said. *Another loan.* 'Nice to have a few bob for emergencies, you know?'

They shook hands and Jack watched them speed through the hotel gates, out onto the Calle General Zurbano, then turn left on the road out of town. Yet, by then, Jack had counted the money, fifty *pesetas*, and was already running back to his room, where he rolled the suit and shirt tightly within his cloak, then looped the cord to secure each end, slinging the whole thing over one shoulder – tied at his waist like a blanket roll – and the canvas satchel over the other. He could not imagine why Frederick and Josefina might return, but there was always that possibility – and he had no intention of staying here longer than necessary.

He checked his key at the desk, then out into the morning's brightness. His initial stop, the local *estanco*. Quick check on the newspapers. *ABC* first. A full-page photograph of Chamberlain on the front. Peace for Europe, it said. Peace for the future. On page four, praise for Hitler and his responsible attitude to the Munich negotiations. *Incredible*, thought Jack. *Responsible? When he's just succeeded in annexing Czechoslovakia.* Page eight, the valour of Mussolini's Italians fighting here for the Reconquest of Spain from the Reds. And page nine onwards, endless further tributes to Neville Chamberlain. Nothing on San Sebastián. Nothing in the *Diario de Navarra* either, but he bought a copy anyhow, and another packet of *Superiores*.

Second stop, a gentlemen's outfitter on Calle General Vara de Rey. Floor-to-ceiling, wall-to-wall, glass-fronted drawers full of linens, woollens. The heady aroma of sizing and starch. Tightly ranked rails of jackets and trousers. Counter displays of detachable collars, shirt studs, ties and pins, braces, gloves and belts. Hat stands. Shoe racks. And, there, he finally persuaded the shopkeeper that he was serious about buying some decent footwear – was forced to show that he possessed the necessary collateral. *Frederick Barnard be praised*, he thought, before finally settling on a style he would have called Oxfords at home. Wonderfully soft calfskin uppers. Almost olive green. Perfect fit. But just short of five *pesetas*. He contemplated buying socks too, but couldn't remember the word, and was pleasantly surprised at being presented with a pair anyhow.

'*Gratis*,' the man kept repeating. '*Gratis.*'

Jack bowed generously.

'*Gracias*,' he said. '*Y, por favor ¿el autobús para Burgos?*' The bus to Burgos? He was steered outside, pointed back the way he had come, given sign language instructions.

A few streets away, on the Calle Sagasta, an entire gaggle of autobuses crowded outside the bustling San Blas Market, a modern building with enormous arched windows, edged and highlighted with red brick. It was chaos. No obvious way to determine their destinations. And each bus belonging to a separate company. *Los Hispanos. Cinco Villas. Automóviles Luarca SA.* Passengers milling around in the dense clouds of exhaust smoke, shouting, knocking into each other with cases, baskets of food, crates of live poultry.

'Burgos?' Jack asked, repeatedly. Until, at last somebody pointed him to an old Saurer vehicle, covered in fine dust through which the hand-painted words *Autobuses Jimémez* were just discernible. To his amazement, there was an old lady at the side of the vehicle offering passengers a cup of thick hot chocolate, for which she seemed to be expecting seven *pesetas*. But after a few moments, Jack understood that the chocolate was another free gift and that the seven *pesetas* actually purchased a ticket all the way to Burgos itself.

A pencil, he thought. *I should have picked up a pencil. Some paper.*

He missed the process of writing. Hadn't done any for many days. But now he tried to write inside his head. To force the words into his memory. About the smells, which crowded around him even more closely than the other passengers. Burned cooking oil on their clothes. Garlic on their breath. Cigar smoke billowing from the mouths of old men. Chicken shit and feathers from the crates on their knees. Cheap perfume on the hair of testy mothers. Old leather bruised by impatient backsides. The inky smell of newsprint on a dozen pair of hands, as folk argued and shouted, back and forth, across the aisle. He was beginning to love it all.

But Jack balanced his shoebox, blanket roll and satchel on his knee, buried himself inside his own copy of the *Diario de Navarra*. More about Munich. The deal allowing Hitler to annexe those parts of Czechoslovakia, the Sudeten lands, with a preponderance of German-speakers but which, in reality, gave him a free hand to add the whole of that country to his fascist Reich. All in the name of peace. How could the world be so stupid? To believe that appeasing Hitler on the Sudeten issue wouldn't simply encourage him to greater ambition? Hard to stop him, of course. Nobody wanted another war. Nobody was truly prepared to fight one. Nobody except Hitler and Mussolini, who'd been able to use their involvement here in Spain as a dress rehearsal. *And we didn't stop them*, thought Jack. *But there could have been sanctions. And we could at least have stopped Franco. Maybe still not too late to do so.*

It occurred to him that an attempt on Franco's life would almost certainly mean the loss of his own. A lone assassin? How could he possibly avoid capture? And Jack was not especially brave. Not physically brave. Yet the idea that this simple act – the killing of Franco, victory for the Republic even at the eleventh hour, the domino effect, curbing the ambitions of Hitler and Mussolini – might turn Europe from the brink of another horrendous war, was just enough to throw some hidden source of sand upon the fires of Jack's fear. In his early days at school, the Great War had been the conflict waged by various European Coalitions against Napoleon, a hundred years earlier. But that had all changed in 1917, with the carnage on the Western Front. And, by then, Jack's father was dead. Disgrace for the family with his suicide. Jack's simple sense of abandonment. His mother's infectious obsession with pacifism. She would certainly be celebrating Chamberlain as a hero today, he knew. Peace at all costs. But life was never that simple. And certainly never for Jack Telford. Yet he was on his way. On his mission.

There was a flaw, however. Naturally. The lack of a weapon. An instrument of justice. For he doubted that anybody had ever been successfully assassinated with a pilgrim's walking stick. There had been Carter-Holt's Astra automatic – but that was back in the Hotel Maria Cristina, along with the camera and its small caliber pistol, its hollow-point bullets. So he ran through the possibilities. Not a knife.

Or his straight razor. He was sure he'd never be able to use one – even on Franco. Acquiring another gun, then. Or fashioning some sort of explosive device. Or that simple use of a fuel-filled jam jar, a rag fuse, that they called a petrol bomb.

The time trudged past like a lame donkey, painfully slow, as the bus coughed and spluttered through every identical town and village, with Jack jerking awake on each of the hundred occasions when they stopped to collect or disgorge customers. Sometimes he would ask somebody to tell him where they'd reached, and he compared the names with Father Ignacio's note. Nájera. Santo Domingo de la Calzada. Belorado. Atapuerca. Until, finally, after seven hours, they arrived in Burgos.

He had an address in Burgos, though it was no use to him. The name of a church, supplied to him by Father Ignacio. A priest who would provide lodging for an honest pilgrim. But Father Ignacio had dated the letter of introduction. Obvious that Jack – or, rather, Brendan Murphy – could not have got here so quickly without cheating.

So, some sort of hotel then.

The bus had dropped him, along with all the other final passengers, at its terminus on Calle Miranda. He followed some of them to a corner, looked to the right and saw the white skyline towers and filigree spires that could only be the Cathedral, framed by birch and willow trees. He headed in that direction. Traffic over a Romanesque bridge across the river, and through an arched gateway, enormous, carved with medieval statues, which led into the old quarter. There was a maze of narrow alleyways, some of the buildings bomb-damaged. And, after a few minutes, a bar, crowded with older men, smacking down dominoes, slapping down playing cards, swigging down shots of brandy, shouting down their neighbours. Joined to the bar, part of the same establishment, an eating place, a canteen, beginning to fill with local workers' families. And, above both, a sign declaring that this was the Hostal Toledo. There seemed to be no separate door, so Jack ventured into the bar, caused a mere moment of frozen silence, spotted a board with prices nailed next to an interior door. Hard to decipher, but he reckoned that it would cost him six *pesetas* for a room. A fair slice of his remaining money. But he was too beggared to be choosy.

Jack turned to the sweat-stained, stocky little man who was polishing drinking glasses with the tail of his grease-streaked shirt.

'*¿Doce pesetas?*' he said. And he gestured upstairs with his thumb.

'*¿Peregrino?*' smiled the man, through his grey stubble. A pilgrim? He nodded towards Jack's staff, the iron scallop shell. Then he made a walking motion with his fingers. '*¿Camino?*'

'Yes,' said Jack. '*Camino.*' He produced Father Ignacio's letter by way of proof, signed a battered register in Brendan Murphy's name. And only then did he notice the plethora of religious decoration behind the counter. A faded poster for a holy festival. A gaudy picture of the Virgin. A cluster of statuettes, Christ on a donkey and Christ on a cross. A crucifix on the wall. So Jack put his hand on his heart too, and nodded. '*Peregrino. Sí.*'

The man made him understand that, for pilgrims, the rate was just four *pesetas* and fifty *céntimos* – and Telford thought that this probably included a meal. He clarified that he wanted to stay two nights, and he was soon settled in a second-storey room, tiny, dark and noisy with street clamour below, but clean enough. There was a rail to hang clothes, and he carefully unwrapped the linen suit, hoping that some of the creases would fall from it overnight.

Downstairs again, he was served a dish of lentil and bacon stew with great cobs of dry bread and rough red wine, before wandering back out into the alley, smoking a cigarette and trying to fathom his next move. First, to find out where Franco's headquarters might be. To discover whether the monster was even in the city. If so, what were his routines? Where might he worship? And was he most vulnerable in church – as he had been when Jack saw him in Santiago de Compostela? It seemed like a reasonable prospect. But only until he turned the next corner, found another *estanco*.

Outside the *estanco*, a billboard. The words *Diario de Burgos* printed upon it. An advertisement for the city's evening daily. And, below, a sheet of paper pasted to the placard, with a daubed headline. *¡Muerte! Una heroína extranjera de la Reconquista.* Dead. A foreign heroine of the Reconquest. Jack went inside, already knowing what he would find. A small stack of the broadsheets. The headline repeated, mid-way down the front page and, alongside, a grainy photograph. Somewhat out of focus. But unmistakable. The face of Valerie Carter-Holt staring back at him.

Chapter Six

Telford had barely slept. He had studied the article until his head was dizzy with the small print and his eyes ached from the spluttering light offered by the bare bulb hanging from his ceiling. Yet he thought that he now had the thing almost word-perfect.

> The body of a young English woman was discovered this morning on the beaches of San Sebastián. She has now been identified as Señorita Valerie Carter-Holt, daughter of Sir Aubrey Carter-Holt, Secretary to the First Lord of the British Admiralty. Señorita Holt was awarded the Red Cross of Military Merit by Generalísimo Franco himself earlier this year for her bravery as a foreign correspondent, reporting for National Spain on the great victory at Teruel, where she was wounded. Señorita Holt is believed to have drowned during a swimming accident. An English man is also missing, and the authorities are investigating.

Jack understood, of course, that the words were one thing, and the spaces between them entirely another. The points left unsaid perhaps more important than those detailed on the page. The Hotel María Cristina would have been alerted, Carter-Holt's room opened. And there? They would have made some interesting discoveries. No mention. Reasonable, perhaps, since it was unthinkable that the press would have been told the whole story. But then there was the line about a nameless Englishman. They must know Jack's identity. Naturally they did. But not to identify him?

He felt sick to his stomach, head filled with renewed images of the intimacies he had shared with Carter-Holt. Yet none of them more intimate than her final moments. But when he felt strong enough, he dressed in Frederick Barnard's fine linen suit, filled his pockets, wriggled his toes within the unfamiliar Oxfords, and clumped down to the bar, yesterday evening's paper under his arm. He attracted some strange glances both from the customers and the proprietor himself.

'*¿Peregrino?*' said the man. A pilgrim? Sure? The proprietor was wearing the same sweat-stained, grease-streaked shirt from the previous night, but his customary stubbled smile had frozen almost to a grimace of incredulity.

'*Sí,*' Jack snapped at him. '*Peregrino.*' And he took himself off to a table where he tried to read the rest of the news. But it was hard to concentrate and, after a piece of toasted bread daubed with oil and salt, a swallow of insipid coffee, he smoked his first cigarette of the day while creeping back to the Cathedral. At least, that's the way it felt. Head down. Hugging shadows. Frequent stops to cautiously check whether he was followed. Or noticed.

The streets were busy. Traders with barrows. Children heading for school. Men making their way to work. Women struggling beneath basket and bundle burdens. Bustling bureaucrats. And the military. Everywhere. Pale khaki of the Guardia Civil officers. The sun-faded olive drab of Franco's general staff. Red berets of the Carlist *Requetés* commanders. Blue blouses of the Falange. The swaggering jodhpurs and forage caps of Germany's Condor Legion. The light green of Italian majors and colonels. A frightening confidence about them as they strolled the streets with no obvious urgency. There was evidence of bomb damage, of course. But nothing recent. Prisoners-of-war in busy gangs, clearing rubble.

Jack had seen it all before, and he wondered now in which direction he should explore. Back towards the bridge? But he settled, in the end, on following a cluster of Italians heading purposefully down the cobbled Calle Santa Águeda, then left along Calle Barrantes, past a church, past a solid stone wall to the right, tile-topped and protected by barbed wire. They turned along the Paseo de la Isla and arrived, after a few minutes, at a heavily guarded gate. The sentries were all turbaned Moors, tightly controlling the line of personnel visiting the red brick and white limestone Gothic palace visible beyond the wall. Credentials were demanded and checked. And limousines were halted as they swung in from the tree-lined avenue, where scarlet Spahis, with billowing white cloaks, were exercising their horses.

But was this Franco's headquarters? It must be, surely. Though Jack only had time to absorb these few details as he strolled past, knowing that he must not stop, nor show too much interest. He crossed to the tree-lined promenade running down the centre of the avenue, joined a small group paying homage at one of the religious reliquaries displayed along the Paseo. Yet, even there, he dared not linger too long. So he turned right at the next corner, a quiet street with nobody else in sight, and he waited there a few minutes, hidden from view, peering around the brickwork, watching, hoping for a glimpse of El Caudillo. Yet Franco did not appear. And there was something else that Jack needed to do.

This time, it was his own article that he read. And read again. An article written in the bar of the Hotel Sabadell, just across the river, on Calle Merced. An article scribbled on the pages of a notebook he had managed to buy at the *estanco*. Scribbled in pencil. Dated. So that Sydney Elliott might know he was still alive on this day, at least. Though he was certain that this would be his final word to the outside world. And what Sydney would make of the thing, he could not imagine. Jack reported missing in San Sebastián, yet writing from Burgos on a later date. Around the time when Franco's assassination would, hopefully, have dominated the world's headlines. He could not bring himself to mention his plan directly, for superstitious fear that this might somehow bedevil his intentions – to jinx them, as the Americans might say. But the allusion in his copy was plain enough. And the article followed on neatly, he thought, from the one he had filed by telephone from Santiago de Compostela.

On the streets of Burgos, he began, *the high command of Hitler's Germany and Mussolini's Italy struts side by side with that of General Franco. These are the forces which, in shared guilt, continue to sink British Merchant Marine shipping in the Mediterranean with impunity, to kill and maim innocent Spanish women and children, while Prime Minister Chamberlain makes pious speeches about Peace for our Time.* Some of it was a repeat of the points he had made in the earlier piece. About how Hitler was being rewarded for his involvement in Spain with all the minerals and raw materials he needed to complete his re-armament programme. About how the British Embassy in Spain knew this. About his belief that Britain stood on the brink of another global conflict – but this time one that Britain would have caused by turning a blind eye to Spain. Yet he still held that all was not lost. That Franco might still fail. *If only…*

He toyed with the idea that he should include a short personal note to Sydney but finally dismissed any thought of doing so. What could he say, after all, without being deceitful? And he could hardly tell the truth. Anything else would be banal, pointless. So he merely finished by signing "Jack" at the end of the article. Then added, "Hostal Toledo, Burgos" for good measure. He succeeded in begging an envelope from the reception desk, and a pen too, for the address. Yet he struggled considerably with his explanation that he wanted to post the thing, thought he'd succeeded when the fellow behind the counter offered to take it – then passed it back quickly to Jack when he saw that the destination was London. But at least he helped by drawing a small map to the Post Office.

'*Correos,*' he kept repeating, showing Jack that he must carry on along the river to the next bridge – the one he had crossed last night, surely – to the Plaza Conde de Castro.

Jack was glad to leave the place, for it seemed to be hosting some convention of Catholic priests. Black cassocks everywhere, clustered in the entrance lobby, in the doorway itself, so that he had to push himself into a small group of them – through their mixed smells of hair oil, tobacco and incense – to reach the pavement. He was still looking back when he stepped into the road, intending to cross, to take a closer look at the River Arlanzón, but totally oblivious to the traffic flow.

The lorry's horn blared like a trumpet on the Day of Reckoning. Jack spun, should have stepped back but froze instead, his bowels almost emptying with fright. The vehicle's brakes screeched. It slewed sideway. Crates flew from its open back. Explosions. Pomegranate shrapnel bursting free, as a hand grabbed at his collar, dragged him to safety while the wagon finally shuddered to a halt.

'This is twice I save you,' he heard a familiar and melodic female voice, heavily-accented, say to him. And his insides churned, the chill of fear washed over by the warm relief of his escape, all wrapped about with the joy and astonishment, the heart-pounding excitement, of acquaintanceship renewed. Telford looked down into the tiny and elegant face, framed in its familiar coif.

'Sister María Pereda,' he laughed. 'What the hell…' Then the cold frisson of fear returned. *Has she read the papers?* The lorry driver, meanwhile, had jumped from his cab, screaming with rage, arms waving towards his load, the blood-red debris of a hundred *granadas*.

'Please, *Señor*,' she scowled at Jack, 'you must not say blasphemy. And I think you have gone back to England?'

What could he tell her? For the moment, nothing, since she had swirled like a dark dust storm out into the road, finger and tongue wagging in unison until she had silenced the driver, sent him on his unhappy way.

'I decided to stay in Spain a while longer,' said Jack, when she eventually returned to the pavement. 'To come and walk some of the Camino de Santiago.'

'Then you must walk with more care, *Señor* Telford,' she smirked. 'You think Our Lady has no better thing to do than send me for watch you? But the Camino. You see? I told you. I knew. You are a good man. That is why I save you. The first time.'

The first time had been in the square at Santiago de Compostela. At the moment Carter-Holt's assassination attempt against Franco should have been triggered. The plan had all gone to cock, yet Sister María Pereda, blissfully unaware, had still sensed that something was amiss, had stood in front of Jack at the crucial moment. Later she had said there had been fear upon his face. She had not known why. Did not need to know. Did not wish to commit the sin of curiosity. But had warned him. About the dangers of straying too far from safe ground, too far into the forest's edge. *If only she knew*, he thought.

'And you, Sister María Pereda. You were going back to Covadonga. To light a candle for Sister Berthe Schultz.'

There had been two nuns among the tour group. From the Order of Our Lady of the Holy Light. Sent from the Swiss Sanatorium Deutsches Haus by the Director, Herr Alexander, a good friend of the German Führer. A delivery of congratulatory flowers for Franco. But Sister Berthe Schultz had been another of the tour's casualties. Their mission had failed as badly as Carter-Holt's.

'I go tomorrow,' said the nun. 'But first I come here. To meet with Father Josemaría.' She spoke the name as though Jack should know the man, then saw the blank ignorance in Telford's eyes. 'Father Josemaría

Escrivá,' she explained. 'A great man, *Señor*. He will be a saint, I think. For his vision. That every person should work to be a saint too. Our Lord spoke to him. Show him this is the Work of God. *Opus Dei*. And now he is here in Burgos, writing his great book. You know what it is called, *Señor* Telford?' Understanding was beginning to dawn upon him, and he looked back to the hotel, the priests still crowding the doorway. He had indeed heard of Opus Dei. They had become one of Sydney Elliott's *bêtes noires* – a new cult, his editor had claimed, within the Catholic Church. Fascist by nature. Pro-Hitler. Was all that true? He had no idea. Yet he suddenly remembered the moment he had said goodbye to the nun just a few days earlier – his surprise at realising how he had become fond of her, despite her own plainly fascist beliefs. But Father Josemaría Escrivá as the founder of Opus Dei? No, he had not known that. And this great book?

'I'm sorry, Sister María Pereda,' he said. 'But I'm afraid...'

She shook her head.

'In English,' she said, 'it is called *The Way*. In my language, *El Camino*. You see? You walk the Camino de Santiago, and here you come to the Hotel Sabadell, where Father Josemaría writes *El Camino*. Is that not truly the Work of God?' She stepped back, took another look at him. 'But you are not dressed for walk, *Señor*.'

No, he admitted, he was not. But if she would care to accompany him? A stroll along the river? To the Post Office. For he badly needed to buy time, in which to invent a plausible story.

For a person who so eschewed the sin of curiosity, the nun had a great many questions. About the train journey to San Sebastián, after she had said goodbye to him at the station in Santiago – only the previous Thursday evening, not even a full week. About *Señorita* Valerie – she had seemed so angry when she boarded the train. And Sister María Pereda hoped that they had become friends again on the journey. They were good friends after all, were they not? Very good friends, yes?

'Colleagues, really,' said Jack. 'Nothing more.' He had no desire to talk about Carter-Holt. Even to think about her. And there were things he needed to know himself. 'But tell me,' he saw the sparkle fade from her eye as he changed the subject, 'you were taking flowers to the *Caudillo*. Will you deliver them here, instead?'

'They tell me it's not possible.' She looked ruefully back across the river. 'He works so hard for the people. Every day. At the Muguiro.'

'Muguiro?'

She stopped, pointed across the fast, clear flow of the Arlanzón, to the bridge that Jack had used to reach the Hotel Sabadell. A heron flew sedately beneath its central span.

'There,' she said. 'In the trees. You can't see it from here. The Palacio de la Isla. But most people call it the Muguiro. For the family who own it. Though now it is the home of the *Generalísimo*. And his family. And our government too. He does not leave often. Unless for big occasion.'

'I think I must have passed it,' said Jack. 'Earlier. Surrounded by Moroccan guards.' Yes, she told him, that was the place. He resisted the temptation to remind her that the legitimate Spanish Government was currently operating from Barcelona. He suppressed, too, any jibe about Franco's Christian Crusade against that Government being so reliant on Muslim troops from Morocco – who, here, even formed his personal bodyguard. 'But does he go to Mass there too?' he asked.

'Of course not,' she laughed. 'There is Mass every morning in the Cathedral. At seven. The *Generalísimo* goes there. Each day. To pray with the people. You are a clever man, *Señor* Jack,' she beamed at him with those beautiful eyes, and took his arm. 'And you are right. I could take flowers there. It is what Sister Berthe Schultz would want.'

He supposed that he should feel guilty. For his plan was taking shape at last. He could picture the scene. Franco mingling with the adoring congregation as he had done at Santiago de Compostela. Vulnerable. Distracted by those, like Sister María Pereda, who would want to touch him. To receive a blessing from their saviour. To present him with gifts. With flowers. And Jack glimpsed the future. A single shot echoing around the Cathedral. The stunned crowd. The guards struggling, too late, through the press to reach their fallen master. The look of incredulity on the nun's face when she realised what Jack had done, how he had betrayed her. The image wrenched at his guts. For he was indeed fond of her. More than fond. Knew that she was fond of him too – the same as he believed of almost any woman who showed more than a passing interest in him. A flaw in his character of which he was acutely aware. Believed that she was attracted to him too. Yet another picture interposed itself in his mind.

'There was a girl,' he murmured. 'A young girl. Back in a village. I can't remember the name of the place. But the girl was called María too. Isn't that strange?'

The picture changed. Not just a single child, but a hundred, a thousand, dragged from their mothers to be re-educated. And above them, devouring them by the fistful, like that familiar figure of Goya's grotesque ogre, strode Franco. It was fanciful. He knew that. But it stoked his cold fury, all the same.

'It is the name of many girl, here in Spain,' she said. Then she must have caught something in the tone of his voice for, all at once, he found her staring hard into his eyes, as she had done once before. 'And there it is again, *Señor*. What is it that you fear? What happen to this girl in the village?'

'Oh, nothing,' said Jack, and offered her his most reassuring grin. 'It was just the coincidence. But come on. We've got this letter to post.'

And somewhere, he thought, *a pistol to find.*

Chapter Seven

Thursday 6th October 1938

The sky was still lightening when he met her next morning on the steps outside the Cathedral's main entrance in the Plaza de Santa María.

'*Señor*,' she smiled, clutching the flowers she had brought. 'Today you are dress for the walking.'

He pulled Father Ignacio's old cloak more tightly around him, against the early chill.

'I shall be on the road just as soon as I see you safely on the bus to Covadonga,' he lied. He had no real intention of walking anywhere today, for his feet still ached from the hours he had spent, on the previous evening, slogging the streets, avenues and alleyways ofBurgos, blistered from the new shoes, vainly seeking a gun shop. He knew he couldn't afford to buy one, though he'd not ruled out the possibility of further theft. Yet, in the event, he had found nothing but an old hardware shop, which displayed a ruined relic of a revolver among the junk in its window. He would go back there later but, for now, he needed to find out whether, even with a weapon at his disposal, he might get close enough to use it. It depended on the crowd, he supposed. And worshippers were already gathering. Old women in dark shawls, shuffling inside to take their habitual place in the pews, even as a single bell chimed somewhere within the extravagant walls before them. Fifteen minutes to seven. The faithful called forth to first Mass.

'Martinillo,' said Sister María Pereda, gazing up at the Cathedral's façade. 'A small wooden man,' she explained, when Jack showed no sign of comprehension. 'At the church clock. Inside, you will see. He hit the bell.' She stood stiffly to attention, mimed the action. 'Four times each hour,' she said. '*Dong*. And then, every hour, another little man –

Papamoscas – open and close his mouth, wave his arms.' She mimed that too, made Jack laugh.

The first time since…

Yet there was no respite for him, as she swirled and swarmed up through the darkened doorway, dropped to a whisper, showed him Papamoscas and the famous clock high above and to one side of the entrance. She led him around the northern side isle, to the iron-gated side chapels, dripping with gold, with silver, with lurid medieval art. Then she pressed a finger to her lips and drew him to the transept, made an 'O' with her mouth as she stretched a finger towards the double-flighted Golden Staircase. A genuflection, when she reached the crossing of nave and transept.

'Seven hundred years,' she hissed at him, and he was left to guess that she meant the Cathedral's age, for her hushed comment still drew vexed glances from the early penitents kneeling at their quiet and questing contemplations. But she pressed on regardless, pointed to the altarpiece, a strange confection of Gothic and Flamenco, and to the wood-carved choir stalls. Yet Sister María Pereda saved her best surprise until last, leading Jack to the centre of the crossing, where a pink marble slab was set into the floor. A Latin inscription, which he struggled to decipher.

'*Rudericus Didaci Campidoctor*,' he read. And shrugged.

'Rodrigo el Campeador,' she whispered, with great reverence.

'El Cid?' Jack murmured. 'Truly?' He knew the story intimately. Or, at least, he knew it as told in the heroic poem. Jack had already seen the tomb of that other medieval hero, Pelayo – Spain's King Arthur. That had been at Covadonga. And, now, here he stood in the presence of Rodrigo Díaz de Vivar. It made him think of Frederick Barnard, to wonder how many pages in his *History of Spanish Architecture* must be devoted to this one edifice, to the tomb of El Cid. But he only gave a fleeting thought to whether Frederick might yet have noticed that his passport was missing. Instead, his mind was filled with the depressive burden of mortality. His own. Tombs and the dead. It seemed to him that there were three new worshippers in the congregation: the spectre of his deceased father; the ghostly scarlet of Colonel F C Telford; and, joining them, the more recently familiar figure of the *guerrillero* leader who had died at Covadonga, along with Sister Berthe Schultz and all those others.

Waiting for me, he thought. *Well, they won't have to wait long.*

'He saved us,' said the nun, 'from our enemies.' It took a moment for Jack to realise that she was still talking about Rodrigo. 'As *El Generalísimo* must save us now. In these days, *El Caudillo* is our *Cid*, our lord.' It could have been a cue, a theatrical prompt. One that made him bite back the riposte he would otherwise have made. For, at that precise moment, the venerable silence was shattered by raised voices back at the entrance, heads turned, a tumble of newcomers pushing into the nave, folk herded from the door by a couple of gabardine-clad thugs. 'Come!' said Sister María Pereda. She took his arm, hauled him along the aisle, towards the nearer door, only just remembered to curtsy and cross herself before she pushed her way out into the morning again, emerging into a press of people now gathered at the top of the steps. It was less riotous than the occasion, last week, when Franco had made his appearance in Santiago, but the sequence was much the same. A pair of motorcycle outriders circling the square's fountain, then a few limousines, headed by the Fiat Twenty-Eight Hundred State Phaeton. And there he was. General Francisco Franco y Bahamonde.

As before, Jack was disappointed that the creature was so short. *El Caudillo's* plain legionary forage cap was worn at a devil-may-care angle on the satanic head. The pencil-line moustache was cruel rather than debonair. The cavalry boots polished to the point of conceit. The jodhpurs were brash. And the military cape lent him the air of a pantomime villain as he swept it aside so that he could help his wife, Carmen Polo, from the car. Familiar white pearl necklace. Black coat. Black *mantilla*. She, in turn, reached back inside the vehicle, this time to help her daughter step out onto the square.

'*Ay, Carmencita*,' said the nun. '*¡Qué guapa!*' How pretty.

Yes, thought Jack, *but I'd not allowed for the child.* The girl wore a white Communion frock, bore a striking resemblance to her mother. How old? Twelve perhaps. Or thirteen. And while Telford now had little compunction about killing Franco in public, in the presence of the monster's wife, he was less certain about doing so with the child as witness.

'Does the girl come here every day?' he asked.

'Of course,' said Sister María Pereda, and she pushed forward through the small crowd, holding the bouquet of flowers aloft to protect them.

She had timed the manoeuvre to perfection, met the General's family as they reached the top of the steps. She made a short speech, though Jack could not hear her words. She would, he assumed, have brought greetings and congratulations from Herr Alexander and the Sanatorium Deutsches Haus, from her own Motherhouse at Axenstein too. In any case, *Señora* Franco took the flowers from the nun, while other hands stretched out to touch her husband's uniform, to receive his blessing, to soak up salvation.

Jack had stayed inconspicuously at the back of the crowd, leaning on his pilgrim's staff, satisfied that Franco did, indeed, deserve to die. But, as *El Caudillo* extricated himself from the press, led his wife and daughter inside the church, there was a brief moment when the monster paused, turned in Jack's direction. Some sixth sense, perhaps, though no doubt about it. That quizzical expression worn only by those who vaguely recognise somebody, but cannot quite place the who, the what, the where, the when – or the why.

Later, Jack paid the greasy proprietor of the Hostal Toledo for one further night's board and lodging. He was certain now that he wouldn't need more. There was still the gun to be procured, but he had determined that, on the following morning, Franco would die. Perhaps he might even use that glimmer of recognition on the General's part to his advantage. To get closer for the kill. He had thought about it all through the Mass, and afterwards, when he had left Sister María Pereda, though with a promise to meet her again, a final farewell at the bus, which would take her on the circuitous journey to Covadonga.

'I bring you this,' she said, and drew from her habit that copy of the *Beano* he had given her the previous week. To amuse her.

'You finished reading it?' said Jack.

'I think there is much I do not understand about the English,' she smiled, apologetically. 'I keep thinking about Sister Berthe Schultz, what she would say, about such people. Such bad things they do.' She flicked through the pages of comic-strip characters. Hairy Dan. Good King Coke. Puffing Billy. Frosty McNab. Pansy Potter. Wily Willie Winkie. And, on the front cover, Eggo the Ostrich.

'They make children laugh,' said Jack. 'Happy.' But he suddenly felt foolish. Dishonest. Wily Willie Winkie. And, unusually for him when he was in the nun's company, somewhat angered. *A lecture about bad behavior,* he raged to himself, *on setting a poor example, from somebody who thinks that Franco's actions are praiseworthy.* 'In an imperfect world,' he added.

'That is why we should follow the example of Father Josemaría. To live our lives so that each of us works to be a saint. To do the Work of God. The *Opus Dei.*'

'And Franco,' said Jack. 'Is that what he's trying to do? To act like a saint?'

'But of course, *Señor.* You should know that, of all people. You walk the Camino de Santiago. Our saints all have their own path, set for them by God. And Saint Iago the greatest path of all. Santiago Matamoros. Heathen-Slayer. God sent him to deliver us from the heathen. As he has sent *El Caudillo.* He will be a saint one day too, *Señor* Jack. You will see.' And she gave him the sweetest smile, as the bus driver shouted a final call for passengers. Sister María Pereda hefted her suitcase, and two elderly men rushed forward to help her get the thing aboard. 'I think we not meet again,' she said. 'That makes me sad. But God protect you on your walking. And you will see.' She wagged a finger at him. 'How soon *El Caudillo* shall become a saint.'

He smiled back at her as she made her way down the aisle of the bus, a parting wave through the window. *No,* he thought, *we won't meet again.* And her leaving filled him with soul-sucking sadness, silver-tinged with relief that she would not be here tomorrow. Neither to mourn nor despise him.

But is that what I'm doing? Jack wondered, as the vehicle rattled off down Calle Miranda in a cloud of exhaust smoke, backfires bouncing between the buildings. *Helping create a martyr?* It was probably inevitable but, if Sister María Pereda hoped to see Franco's beatification, Jack Telford was happy to help the evil little bastard on the next step of the journey.

Jack sat on his bed for a while, turning the pages of the *Beano* once more until he finally threw it in the empty shoe box, picked up Frederick Barnard's passport instead. His original plan was almost risible. To get himself into Franco's headquarters, posing as Barnard the Diplomat. But this new scheme was better. Killing him on the Cathedral steps would be relatively simple, he now told himself, and he must only shut his mind to the likely presence of the General's wife and daughter.

He picked up the *Beano* again, tore out the centre pages, used them as padding inside the heels of the Oxfords, some protection for his burst blisters. And then, in Frederick Barnard's linen suit, as dapper as he could manage, he worked his way back to the hardware store he had discovered. The ancient revolver still sat in the window, among a jumble of galvanised buckets, farming implements, griddles, nail sacks, hand tools, keys, locks, hinges and chains.

Inside, the scar-faced owner viewed him with suspicion. Or so Jack imagined. Not the usual clientele, he supposed. And there was a risk, of course, that the fellow might run straight to the Guardia Civil. But he hoped his Frederick Barnard deception might set them on the wrong scent just long enough to get him past tomorrow morning as Brendan Murphy the Pilgrim.

'Por favor,' he said to the man. '¿La pistola?' He pointed to the window. '¿Cuánto vale?' The pistol, how much is it?

'¿Papeles?' the man demanded, and Jack produced the passport, watched as the shopkeeper scribbled some details on a piece of paper, next to an extravagantly ornate cash register, then reached into the chaos of his window display. 'Es muy vieja,' he said, handing over the weapon.

Very old? thought Jack, as he slipped the passport back into his pocket. *That's a bit of an understatement.* It was rust-rimmed, the barrel loose, and the inscription 'Oviedo, 1866' etched above the front trigger guard. Not a bit of use.

'Are there others?' Jack managed to ask, eliciting a stream of questions that he struggled to either understand or answer. Yet, after a tortuous exchange, he was satisfied he had made himself clear. A diplomat. You see? The passport again. British. A friend of National Spain. He must drive through the mountains. Stories of *guerrilleros*. *Bandidos*. He needed a gun. Though he had little money. The man had asked how much money. Thirty *pesetas*. And the fellow had laughed at him, looked as though he was a lunatic. Thirty *pesetas* would not even buy this old piece of junk. 'But there are others?' Jack insisted.

The man shook his head, pointed to a couple of tempting yet impractical shotguns mounted on the wall. No, said Jack, causing a Pepperbox pistol to appear from under the counter, even older than the revolver. Jack's turn to laugh. And, finally, pay dirt. The pick of the bunch. Dirt-encrusted, true. Though an automatic. B&H monogram on the brown Bakelite grips, slide bearing the name of a French company, the year 1904. Eight millimetre, the man told him, worked the safety catch, and the small lever behind the trigger, which released the magazine. It was loaded. Seven bullets? Eight? Enough, anyway, for Jack's purpose.

But the price! A hundred *pesetas*, said the man.

'*Treinta*,' Jack told him. Thirty. He laid the bank notes on the counter as the fellow spat some oath, put the automatic away.

'*Cien*,' the man snarled. A hundred.

Jack slapped a further ten *peseta* note on the counter.

'*Cuarenta*,' he said. Forty.

The man shook his head, but grudgingly snarled that he would accept ninety. But Jack was down to his final *peseta* and twenty *céntimos*. All in coins. He dug them out of a trouser pocket, spread them on top of the bank notes, made the fellow understand that there was nothing left. Nothing. Only this. And, from the jacket, he set down Father Ignacio's rosary. The man's eyes widened. He picked up the beads, squinted at them, held them to the light, examined the pins, links and loops.

'¿*Plata?*' he said.

Yes, silver, Jack assured him. He wasn't certain, but the shopkeeper seemed convinced. And Jack patiently acted out his final offer. He would take the gun. The shopkeeper would keep the forty-one *pesetas* and twenty *céntimos*. The rosary too. Plus the Diplomatic Passport. Very valuable. Jack would need to return for it, naturally. So, when he did so, he would also bring back the pistol. The man would keep the cash, the rosary, and still be able to sell the automatic afresh. It was enough to convince the fellow. Though he carefully slid the passport back across the counter after writing down its details. His sign language was an impeccable translation of the Spanish he employed to settle the deal. Seven days, he explained. For Jack to return with the gun. Otherwise, the police.

In the evening, there was lentil and bacon stew again, more rough red wine. A lot of red wine. Enough, Jack hoped, to help him find the sleep he needed. But, first, he needed to get the hang of the weapon.

Practice. Safety catch. Releasing the magazine. Removing the bullets, one by one. Pulling back the slide. Checking there were no bullets in the breech. Firing the thing dry. Bullets back in the magazine. Working the slide again. The gun cocked, ready for action. Safety catch again. The sequence repeated a dozen times. A rattling, rhythmic backdrop to the coal smoke clouds of imagery that blazed through Jack's night along the tracks of cold steel beneath his fingers. Until he finally tucked the pistol under his pillow, changed into his walking things, lay upon the bed fully clothed, tried to empty his brain, to settle his terrors.

There were mind-mulled conversations, in which he attempted explaining himself to his mother, to his sister, to Sheila Grant Duff, and to Sydney Elliott. Visitations from his father and from Colonel F C Telford, more haunting than those in *A Christmas Carol*. The ghostly dead of Covandonga too. Julia Britten, of course. Negotiations with the shopkeeper played out a thousand times. Several mad dashes along the dark corridor to the bathroom. Vomit in the toilet bowl. Visions of his own doom leaping into focus in every fashion of cinematic poster – comic, romantic, dramatic, tragic. Interminable hours, in which sleep would not come, refused to allow him release.

And he was still awake when, before dawn, as he tried to steady his hand enough to shave, to make himself ready for the day, there was the roar of a truck driven fast down the street, headlight glare across his shutters, the grind of gears, the screech of vehicle tyres, shouting and commotion, the explosion of boots on paving, the door of the Hostal Toledo smashed open, and the heavy stamp of feet pounding up the stairs.

Chapter Eight

Friday 7th October 1938, Morning

Like a startled rabbit, Telford froze. He simply froze. No time to contemplate fight or flight. No time even to be afraid. No time to think about hiding the gun. No time to remember the drill for using it. No time to say goodbye to the ghosts of his sleepless night.

How many others have been taken like this? he wondered, as his own door was kicked in. Jack dropped the razor and raised his hands, backed towards the window while the room filled with a tumbling turmoil of Guardia Civil uniforms, levelled rifles and raucous Spanish voices, maniacal hands grabbing at him, clawing his arms. They bundled him out onto the landing, prodded and pushed him down to the ground floor. Seemed to not even trouble with searching the room. Merely manhandled him past the startled owner. Dragged him into the back of a waiting truck. Pulled the canvas flaps loosely together. Punched his ribs when he muttered a feeble protest. Laughed as he rolled back and forth on the corrugated metal floor every time the truck took a corner.

They squealed to a halt, and Jack looked up through a gap in the canvas, saw trees lining the avenue on which they waited. He lifted himself on one elbow, recognised that they were in the Paseo de la Isla, and it wasn't long before he realised the reason why they were stopped. One of the Civiles drew back the flap, while others jostled for position, craned their necks to catch that same glimpse, as Jack did now, of the Fiat Twenty-Eight Hundred's headlights leading the stately convoy off to morning Mass. A brief glimpse, before a boot hammered into his shoulder, crashed him back against the mud-caked steel and somebody spat on his face.

Franco at the Cathedral. Me, here at his headquarters. Not how it was all supposed to happen. *The hardware store,* he supposed. *But why not search the room?* He pictured others sent to do that. Detectives. Agents. Members of Franco's intelligence service, perhaps. Telford's stomach was heaving. Nausea rocked him and his shoulder hurt like hell. Every muscle in his body throbbed, but he managed to lift his arm, wipe the spittle from his cheek before the truck lurched off once more, swung around, through a gateway, gears grinding, tyres on gravel, the engine spluttering, finally dying in a rattle of stinking exhaust smoke.

They hauled him out into the courtyard as dawn's fire flames splintered across the sky from the east, threw the district's bomb-damaged walls into sharp relief, cast deep shadows across the features of a turbaned Spahi sentry, and blazed on the brickwork of the Muguiro Mansion. But his captors did not haul Jack towards the stairway entrance to the mansion itself. Rather, to the outbuildings, stables and garages, behind and to the left. A tack room above, where they pushed him into a chair and, most cruel of all, left him there. Alone. Just his fertile imagination for company. And what seemed like eternity.

The envelope lay on the table before him like a mute accusation, Sydney Elliott's name, the address for the *Reynold's News* office, scrawled in Jack's own familiar handwriting. And the man who had thrown it there had still not spoken, merely tapped the package repeatedly with the tip of his absurdly long cigarette holder. Aristocratic bearing. Uniform – though one cut from such luxurious cloth that it could have come straight from Savile Row. Lean face. Tiny head. Sleek, black oiled hair beneath a red Carlist beret, so stiff that it sat like an academic's mortarboard.

'Well,' the man demanded. 'Who are you?' Impeccable English. The clipped precision of a public school education. That absurd plum-in-the-mouth pronunciation.

'You know,' said Jack, 'that England is the only country in the world in which the upper classes have their own identifiable accent?'

'You find that offensive, do you?'

Jack was transported back to his days at Worcester's Royal Grammar School. He would still have been in the Lower Third. Running in the corridor. A crime that warranted his summons before Jasper, the Head Prefect. Six of the best.

'If anything offends me,' quoted Jack, more or less, 'I try to raise my soul so high that the offense cannot reach it.'

'Ah, Descartes. Bravo, sir. Bravo. Then let me help you.' The fellow took a silver case from the side pocket of his uniform tunic, removed a black-papered cigarette and pressed its gold filter into the holder. 'You are registered at the Hostal Toledo under the name Brendan Murphy. The owner says you are a pilgrim. He says that you showed him a letter. Written by a priest in Pamplona. Claiming that you are also a soldier. Is that correct?'

'Sobranie?' Jack smiled, hungry eyes unable to tear themselves from the cigarette. 'Unusual choice.'

'Redstones of London. Fine tobacco, old boy. I would offer you one. Only, you see, if you are indeed a soldier then I must assume you're also a deserter.'

It wasn't the interrogation Jack had expected. There were clearly guards outside the room. But none inside. This pompous ass was alone. And no direction in the questions towards Franco. Nor the pistol. Nor Carter-Holt. So what did this fool want from him? Or was this some elaborate ploy? He stretched out a hand towards the envelope, turned it slowly on the table with his fingers.

'I wanted to walk the Camino. Thought it would be easier if I pretended to have been a soldier. But I'm not, sir. Therefore not a deserter either.'

'Yet this letter is signed "Jack". And addressed to a man called Sydney Elliott. This *Reynold's News*. A newspaper. I remember it. From London. Filthy little socialist rag, I recall.'

'Yes, that's me. Jack Barnard.' Telford had perhaps found a blade of grass to which he might cling. Perhaps this was some routine arrest. Not linked to his plans at all. Routine, yes. A check on foreigners. He had been treated roughly by the Civiles but, since then – 'If I could go back to the Hostal, I could show you my passport. It's in my jacket pocket.'

He hadn't even dreamed he would need the passport again, had almost been disappointed when the shopkeeper had spurned his offer. It had been a good one, he thought. But at least the damned thing was still in Jack's possession.

'Barnard?' said the man. He tapped the mouthpiece of the cigarette holder against his teeth. 'Not Murphy?'

'First name that came to mind, I'm afraid. I just bought a radio. Murphy B31. Fine model. Six pounds and ten shillings. Without the batteries, of course. That's where I heard a programme about the pilgrims' route.'

'Walking the Camino?' The man laughed. 'But taking time from that endeavor to write scurrilous lies about National Spain. Indeed, about your own country. Such a fine nation. Hard to understand how you can betray her so.'

'It's called freedom of speech. Democracy. If you studied Descartes, you should at least recognise the trait.'

'At Stonyhurst, they taught us to treat Descartes with extreme caution.'

The same Stonyhurst? Jack remembered Stonyhurst from his own time at Manchester University. Jesuit College. Famous. Somewhere near Clitheroe. *So who is he?* he wondered. And then he remembered Arthur Koestler's story again. Koestler had been reporting for the *News Chronicle*. An international legend in the world of journalism. Rabidly anti-Franco. Yet captured by Franco's forces. Only his fame had saved him from the firing squad. Then a prisoner exchange. Arranged by Franco's Press Officer. English-educated, Jack recalled. Don Pablo Merry del Val. His father formerly Spanish Ambassador to Britain – the son now one of Franco's key representatives in London. Could this not be Franco's Press Officer?

'Stonyhurst,' Jack repeated. 'This really is about my article, isn't it?' He felt relief begin to seep through his bones.

'Is that not serious enough for you, Mister Barnard? Working in Spain as a correspondent without authority is a serious crime, sir. You are a son of the Catholic Church, I assume.'

'Naturally.'

'Yet you lied to a priest in Pamplona to acquire false documentation.'

'A sin. Yes, I know. I shall confess at the next opportunity.'

'And the holy sister who was with you at the Post Office?'

'Met her by accident. Asked her for directions to wherever I might post the letter. She insisted on delivering me there herself. An act of charity. Was it she who reported me?'

At last, the man took a lighter from his other pocket, put the tip of the Sobranie to the flame and, with hauteur, blew a genteel cloud of smoke towards the ceiling beams.

'No. The Post Office, Mister Barnard. But what am I to do with you? If you truly wished to walk the Camino de Santiago, you could simply have applied to do so. General Franco has, after all, opened the route again. But here you are. And the clothes, sir.' He used the cigarette holder as a pointer, flicked it back and forth in the direction of Jack's cloak to emphasise the point. 'You must be a man of some means. Yet you dress like a mendicant. It all smacks of deception, I'm afraid. Masquerading as a former soldier too. A sense of espionage, sir, don't you agree? A capital crime. As, indeed, might be your unauthorised journalism.'

The short-lived relief that Jack had experienced was now entirely evaporated.

'Look, old man,' he said, 'I just wanted to walk the Camino as a penance. Issues in my private life, you know? Rather not speak of them, if you don't mind. But I *could* show you the passport. And perhaps give you my parole? My word of honour not to send any more dispatches.'

Jack tried hard to quell his panic. Capital crimes? Koestler's notoriety had indeed been his salvation, but that was collateral which Telford did not possess – in any of his current guises. And there was the simple danger that Merry del Val might simply detain him while the room at the Hostal was searched. Then what? *Christ*, he thought, *what a mess.*

'Parole?' said the man. 'The word of an English gentleman. But, sadly, one who has already been involved in so much duplicity.' He paced the room, then stared hard at Jack. 'On the other hand,' he said, at last, 'our relations with the British Government are delicate just now. Delicate and critical. I doubt they would trouble too much if we should rid them of one more socialist agitator but, all the same...'

Back at the Hostal Toledo, under armed guard, Jack tried to explain to the owner that all was well, tried to find the Spanish word for a mistake. Not for the first time, he realised that, in any crisis, it is usually the linguistic department of one's brain, which shuts down first. Yet it didn't matter because the Guardia Civil trooper was in no mood to permit social intercourse on the part of his prisoner, hurried him up to the room, where Jack quickly produced the passport before his escort could become too curious about anything else. Still, Jack found time to snatch the *Superiores* and his matches as well.

'*Vuelvo,*' he shouted to the owner, as they hustled out past the bar again. I come back. '*Una hora.*' One hour.

I bloody hope so! he thought, and offered his silent companion one of the cigarettes, smoked one himself to help him concentrate.

He tried to calculate whether Frederick Barnard might have reached Burgos by now. Or what if Barnard had simply reported the thing as missing? And then there was the small matter of explaining to Merry del Val – if it was actually him – why he had a Diplomatic Passport. Why it gave his Christian name as Frederick, not Jack. Yet he had time. To invent. He was a journalist, after all. So, by the time he'd been marched back to the sentry post at the Muguiro Mansion's gateway, he had rehearsed the thing well. Frederick Barnard's passport photograph could easily enough pass for Jack's own image. And the name? Yes, his real name was Frederick. Jack simply a nickname. From his youth. He would turn the Diplomatic Passport to his advantage too. Particularly if Merry del Val was genuinely concerned about those fragile international relationships he'd mentioned.

What does that mean anyway, Jack? he thought. Then swore to himself. *No time for distractions. Stay focused. Think, man. Junior post, of course. But where? Nowhere on the Spanish or South American circuit, that's for sure. Somewhere off the beaten track. Not too far though. Denmark? Yes, Copenhagen. Why not! And Barnard's own story for cover. A junior diplomat, but one with a passion for medieval architecture. Thinking of writing a book about the treasures of the Camino. But studied journalism. Friends in the industry. Elliott had asked me to scribble a few lines while I was here. Post him an article. Seemed like a good idea at the time. The extra money. Expensive habits, you see. Perhaps went a bit overboard with the content though. Could see that now. It would undoubtedly cost me the job. So wasn't that punishment enough?*

He would offer to surrender the passport, return to the Hostal just long enough to collect his things, then back to the Muguiro Mansion and they could see him on his way to the border. An irresistible offer, surely. He needed just one more night. Not at the Hostal though. He would hide somewhere. Near the Cathedral maybe. Wait there for Franco's final appearance at Mass. Do what he had to do. But, at the gatehouse, Jack began to feel that something was amiss. As they entered, a fellow in civilian clothes was so deliberately inconspicuous, so carefully avoided any eye contact, that he could not possibly be anything other than a policeman. The man sidled behind them and blocked the doorway. And the exchange between Jack's guard and the sergeant at the desk was guttural and slurred, obviously deliberate, making it hard to make out even a single word that passed between them. For the first time, the Guardia unslung his rifle as though he might use it, turned to Jack, narrowed his eyes and nodded towards the door.

'¡*Fuera!*' he growled. Outside.

Jack obeyed, but his legs began to tremble, panic tightened his chest. What was going on? He tried to track back over his conversation with Merry del Val. Something he'd said? Some detail they'd now checked and found lacking? And there was the plainclothes policeman, crunching behind them down the drive. Yet they did not return to the outhouses, instead entering a side door to the main house, along a cream-painted corridor lined with offices from which curious soldiers and civilians stopped their work to peer at him. Then down a tiled staircase into the basement, past kitchens where pots and pans rattled, the scents of fresh bakery gnawed at his hungry belly. More corridors, until they must have travelled almost the length of the mansion. There was a huddle of men there, conversations halting abruptly as Jack and his guards drew near. They stared at him. He felt his nerve fail, his bladder loosen, his legs almost giving way before the guard pushed him into a dimly lit, brick-vaulted cellar. Wine cellar. Another table. Handcuffs and slender rope coiled on the tabletop. Two chairs. The same man as before, though now bareheaded, without the red beret, carefully examining the label on a dusty bottle and smoking another Sobranie. A second man. Wiry little brute. Arabic features. Sleeves rolled up, smiling at Jack in a way that froze his blood, made him want to piss. There was an instruction, and the Guardia Civil pulled the cloak from Jack's shoulders, shoved him down onto the chair, made a grab for the handcuffs.

'Hey!' Telford shouted. 'But I've got it. The passport.' Though, by then, the Guardia had dragged one of Jack's wrists behind his back, snapped a cuff shut and was rattling the other through the spindles of the chair's rear frame. Jack tried to stand, to struggle free, felt his face explode, world turned upside down in a violent gout of pain. And the Arab-featured man was screaming at him through the swimming fog of fear, helping the Guardia to secure the other cuff, binding Jack's wrists together, but also binding them to the chair itself. He struggled too, though feebly, as they used the rope to similarly tie each of his legs behind those of the chair, his knees pulled painfully apart so that his belly and private parts felt horribly exposed. He tried, stupidly, to pull them in, to protect them, but the position in which he was trussed made that impossible. So he tried to clear his brain instead. And, as he did so, as he strove for rationality, a new smell filled his nostrils. Smoke. Not the Sobranie. Not the raw dark tobacco of the local brands either. A cigar. Footsteps. The door closing. The gentle clink of glass on wood as Merry del Val slid the wine bottle back onto its rack.

'*Teniente*,' said Merry del Val, by way of greeting, and with a level of respect that a mere lieutenant's rank could hardly warrant. But then Jack experienced a similar sense of awe. No, it was apprehension, really. The same sensations Jack had felt on the previous occasions he had encountered the newcomer who now sauntered into Jack's field of vision. The man who'd been sent to investigate Julia Britten's death. And then the events at Covadonga. A man who hadn't trusted Jack, even then. Big man. Like a bear. Deeply tanned. Wide, wet lips. Hooked nose. Sweat-slicked black moustache. *Teniente* Enrique Álvaro Turbides of the Guardia Civil Public Order and Prevention Service. He didn't bother looking at Jack but merely consulted that expensive American watch. Impatient. A simple gesture. Just enough to let Jack know, eloquently, that the *Teniente* had determined this would not take long.

Chapter Nine

Friday 7th October 1938, Afternoon

His lip felt as though it had burst, the inner flesh and fluids bubbling through the wound. He had bitten his tongue too, with the blows he had received. For it had all taken longer than his tormentors had anticipated, their only moment of amusement when he had voided his bladder.

Yet Jack still clung to his lifelines, ignoring the damp discomfort. First, that his lip might not be so badly damaged as it felt – injuries to the lip, he knew, usually exaggerated themselves. Second, that his beatings had so far been confined to a few slaps around the head and a couple of well-placed punches. Third, that the numbness occasioned in his limbs by the restraints, which bound them, seemed to have now spread throughout his body, like some accidental anaesthetic – so that each blow inflicted less pain than the last. And, fourth, that this insensibility had cast him adrift in a state where time lost all meaning. These four things provided Jack with a litany, a private rosary to recite as the interrogation crawled through the day.

'Your stomach, at least, seems to be communicative, Mister Telford,' Merry del Val sneered. It was true, and Jack wondered at the fact. That his belly had been rumbling uncontrollably for a long time. Despite the pain and discomfort, some part of his wayward system still craving to be fed. How was that possible? 'I am sure the Lieutenant would agree to provide some food,' the Spaniard continued, 'if only you would be honest with him.'

'You just told me,' Jack mumbled, through those swollen lips, 'you couldn't trust a word I said.'

'As seekers after truth, it is also necessary that we doubt. You see? Descartes again. But in my experience, Telford, few men wish to face the Almighty with a lie upon their lips.'

'Atheists?' said Jack.

'No such thing as an atheist, old boy, when the *garrote's* screw is tightening at your neck. And we already have the crux of the story, do we not?' He pulled aside the ripped remnant of Jack's shirt again, prodding a finger into one of the deeper scratches on Jack's flesh that had still not fully healed. 'You arrive in San Sebastián with Miss Carter-Holt, a heroine of the *Reconquista*. And you, a self-professed Red sympathiser. The poor young woman's body washed up on the shore only hours later. Flesh and blood under her fingernails. Your disappearance. Your lies, deceptions. And here you turn up in Burgos. Those scratch marks on your stomach and chest. You offer no defence. And the Lieutenant's correct, Telford. A military tribunal cannot help but find you guilty of her murder. The punishment a foregone conclusion, even without that other little matter. Your illegal activity as an enemy journalist. The only question is why. Not why you killed her, but why you chose to come here to Burgos.'

Jack might not be thinking clearly, but he was alert enough to understand the flaw. They had already challenged him with the nature of their discoveries. The Holdens – those Nazi supporters of the Anglo-German Fellowship and self-appointed tour group leaders – reporting the disappearance as soon as Jack and Carter-Holt had failed to return in time for their train to the border. The search. Carter-Holt's body found not long afterwards. A hue and cry gone up to find Telford himself. But all the initial assumptions about his whereabouts faulty, as Jack had intended. It gave him a disproportionate sense of self-satisfaction. Yet it did not explain the flaw. If there had been a search, even a cursory one, they must at least have checked Carter-Holt's room, found the camera. And the gun. Why had they not been raised?

'Do they know?' said Jack. 'At home?'

'The Holdens reported your disappearance to the British Embassy at Hendaye,' Merry del Val replied. 'They, in turn, it seems, contacted your newspaper. They will, I am sure, have posted your obituary by now. We delayed our own announcement as long as possible, of course. But it must be clear to you, Mister Telford. That, to the rest of the world, you are already dead.'

'If already dead, no point in telling anything.'

The Guardia Lieutenant Turbides snapped angrily at the Press Officer, a long and vehement diatribe.

'You see?' Merry del Val told Jack when the *Teniente* finally returned to his cigar. 'He understands more English than you might allow. Or perhaps it's simply his experience in these matters. But he says to remind you that there are more lives at stake than your own.'

Jack chewed on this a moment, decided that his brain was too fogged to understand.

'Who?' he said, genuinely puzzled. A bluff, surely. One of those things that detectives were wont to say.

'The Lieutenant says you left a trail that any fool could follow. Clothes stolen in San Sebastián. Some simple enquiries in the main towns of the region once it was clear you'd not headed for the border. So, Pamplona. The owner of an *estanco* there. Then an easy step to the old priest. Father Ignacio. We've had our suspicions about him for some time. Perhaps we owe you something for adding the final piece.'

Jack was jolted from his insensibilities.

'No,' he said, shook his head to clear it. 'I lied to the priest too. Convinced him I was Franco's man. He believed me. Thought he was helping *your* bloody cause – not mine.'

'Really?' Merry del Val laughed, reported his words to Turbides. Jack couldn't follow the lieutenant's reply, but the menace and malice in his tone was plain enough.

'What's happened to Father Ignacio?' said Jack.

'If what you say is true, Mister Telford, then God will now judge him.' Jack's blood ran cold. *What does that mean?* he wondered. *Surely, they couldn't...* But Merry del Val had pressed on. 'You see?' he said. 'The pain and chaos you've caused. And then, there's the girl, of course.'

'Girl?' He thought about the child, back in – Where was that bloody place? Strange name. Zariquiegui. That was it. Then Jack realised he was on the wrong track.

'Oh, come on, Telford. That was quite some network. The priest. Then your little Red friend from Mexico. I suppose you'll tell me you stole this too?' He waved the passport in Jack's face. 'Clever to have the Englishman report it that way. Quite the innocent, the lieutenant tells me.'

'I barely know them,' Jack protested. 'There's no damned network. Just me. Me!'

Josefina.

'We would have picked her up anyway, I suppose,' said Merry del

Val. 'No ability to control her tongue. And so many loyal citizens happy to come forward. Bear witness to the sedition she's been trying to foment. And then your friend Barnard tries to claim diplomatic immunity for them both. Only he has no documentation to prove his status. He's given his Diplomatic Passport to you, Mister Telford, has he not? A serious error on his part. And by the time his friends at the Embassy manage to show us the errors of our ways, it will regrettably be far too late for *Señorita* Josefina Ruiz Delgado.'

'For God's sake, I stole the thing.'

Jack struggled against the restraints again, was rewarded with a blow to the back of his skull from the Moorish thug.

'A soft spot for her, Mister Telford? Well, you're in a much better position to save her, perhaps, than the Embassy in Hendaye.'

'How do I know you're even holding her?' said Jack.

'Oh, I would seriously caution against asking for physical proof, old boy. You should always be careful what you wish for, eh?'

'I don't even know what you want from me.'

'A simple confession that you assassinated Miss Carter-Holt would help. You. Alone. And then, perhaps, an explanation for your presence here in Burgos. The nature of your little espionage ring.'

'There is no bloody espionage ring,' Jack groaned. 'And Valerie's death was an accident. Nothing but an accident. Maybe my fault, I don't know. It just made me panic. I didn't think anybody would believe me. And I decided to walk the Camino as a penance.'

Merry del Val listened patiently, relayed the words to Turbides again. And when he finally turned back to Telford, there was paternal disappointment in his voice.

'That makes life very difficult for us all, I'm afraid,' he said. 'Particularly difficult for the lieutenant. After all, it's his duty to investigate the murder of a true heroine. A heroine of National Spain. But if you refuse to co-operate, Mister Telford, you leave us with no choice but to make life painful and difficult for you also. And to cast our nets still wider. The holy sister, for instance. She was on her way to Covadonga, I understand?'

Jack realised there are worse things than torture. For example, the simple absence of it. While they worked upon him, there was an immediacy to his existence, the mere struggle to survive, to deal with the beatings, to wax and wane through the agonies of his bound limbs, that sensation for which there is no better name than *pins and needles*. But, left alone, those other demons assailed him without mercy.

The scampering silence of severe trepidation: about the agonies still to come – the imagined cruelties perhaps even worse than those already experienced; and about Sister María Pereda – both the possibility that he might have put her in harm's way as well as the certainty that he must lose her good opinion of him. The stark white walls of guilt: about Father Ignacio; about Josefina Ruiz Delgado; and even about Carter-Holt. The rancid sweat-stench of shame: about his failure to so far carry out the plan; about his readiness to now give it up forever if only he could escape this place; and, more, about his certainty that, if he was given the opportunity to sacrifice Josefina, the priest, almost anybody, to save his own skin, he would certainly take it. The foul vomit taste of deepest, blackest humiliation: about how degraded his life had now become at the hands of these men; about how easily he could be so defiled; about the insignificance of his existence; about the lonely bubble, which now defined his existence; and about his utter uselessness. The rope-burn abrasions of his own sedition: about his abandonment of family and friends; about the grief they would have suffered at news of his death; about the falsehood under which they would live out their lives, never knowing his true fate, never able to seek justice for him. So he railed against the image of his dead father, the spectre now standing before him again.

'Why?' he yelled, tears welling from his eyes. 'Why are you here, and not there? Why not go to them instead? Tell them where I am. Tell them what's happened.'

And he was still yelling when his harassers came back into the room, the Moroccan now carrying a flimsy wooden crate, which he set upon the table.

'You're a fortunate fellow, Telford,' said Merry del Val. 'D'you know that? We've been in touch with the Embassy. Hendaye. Miss Carter-Holt was a British citizen, after all. And her father's eminent position at the Admiralty. It goes against our better judgement but, as I've said, there are bridges to be built. So, if they insist, if they believe this is a matter for your British Justice System, it seems we have little choice.'

The words took some time to settle.

'You're letting me go?'

'Regrettably, yes.' Merry del Val reached into the crate, took out a typed sheet of paper with an official stamp at the top. 'Simply this statement to sign.'

'Statement?'

'A disclaimer, rather. To say we're releasing you to the British Authorities, and your signature to confirm that you have been well-treated.'

Jack laughed.

'Just untie me,' he said. 'I'll sign the damned thing if I can hold a pen. And you want me to write a testimonial about National Spain's hospitality too?' *Bloody politics*, he thought. He knew how bad things looked for the Republic. Fighting on the Ebro all but finished, the Republican forces in retreat and, now, with barely enough weapons left to defend Cataluña. After that, just a matter of time. *But you'd think Britain would be a bit less hasty to kiss Franco's arse.* Well, at least Jack would be free to carry on the fight, while there was still one to be fought. If there was still any chance to pick up the plan again, he would do so. If not, he'd find some other way. Either in Spain, or from home. It all depended, he supposed, on that piece of paper. For he knew that some of the captured International Brigade members had been released on condition that they didn't come back to Spain. But some of them, returning despite that, had been caught again, put up against a wall, they said. 'Untie me,' he repeated. 'Let me see it.'

Lieutenant Turbides muttered something dark, then lit another cigar. A fat cigar. A cloud of fresh smoke.

'The lieutenant says all in good time, Mister Telford. Just a couple of quick questions first.' Merry del Val set down the typewritten sheet, reached into the crate again. He pulled out some newspaper clippings. Jack recognised them. From the *Manchester Guardian*. From *The Times*. The same clippings Jack had brought with him on the trip and left at the hotel in San Sebastián. He was about to speak, then clamped his mouth shut. *What if I sign*, he thought, *but they don't release me? Just one more of the disappeared, these bastards left with my signature clearing them of any responsibility.*

Merry del Val handed the clippings to the Moroccan and, at the same time, Turbides passed his lighter to the man – who held the snatches of newsprint between his fingers, set fire to their edges, let them burn all the way to his fingertips. *So they've had the hotel rooms searched too. And now what?* Jack's note-pads were next, those that he had filled with observations over the previous weeks. Then his Hugo's Spanish Grammar, followed by that prized copy of Richard Geoghegan's *Doctor Esperanto's International Language*. Until the room was filled with smoke far more pungent than that of the cigar, and fragments of black ash were floating everywhere.

'You filth,' said Jack, trying to stifle a new and profound sense of loss. 'You've no intention of releasing me, have you?'

'A colleague of mine once made a wise observation,' Merry del Val smiled at him. 'That, once you have taken everything that a man possesses, there is only one way left to hurt him. You give him something back. Only you give it to him broken, damaged beyond repair. His wife. His daughter. In this case, Telford, your freedom.'

And it worked. For Jack's earlier hopes slipped and stumbled over the snow-shelf of euphoria and crashed against the ice-shard rocks far down in the crevasse depths of despair, while Merry del Val took one more item from the crate. The familiar cover of Julia Britten's scrapbook.

'That's not mine!' Jack snapped.

The Moroccan stepped forward to take the scrapbook, but Merry del Val shook his head, opened the thing and turned a few pages.

'But left in your care, I assume? Or stolen. From yet another victim?'

'You're mad.' Jack nodded towards Turbides. 'He knows very well it wasn't me.' He hesitated, unsure about the consequences of continuing. 'Julia Britten was murdered by your precious heroine of National Spain,' he spat, though the Guardia Civil lieutenant was already screaming at him, stabbing the air with those cigar-filled fingers.

'We already know that you killed Miss Carter-Holt,' said Merry del Val. 'The lieutenant knows it. So why not Miss Britten too? But for what reason, Telford? And why did you keep the book? Did she discover something you'd rather have kept secret?'

'You'd like to think so, wouldn't you? Nice and easy. Two embarrassing deaths solved in one day.'

Merry del Val tossed the scrapbook across the room – in Jack's eyes, an act more violent and terrible than anything to which he, himself, had so far been subjected. Tears welled in his eyes, unbidden and impossible to suppress. He had promised to look after it, to make sure it found its way safely back to England. And now…

'I think we are all a little more concerned about what you were planning next, old boy,' said Merry del Val, and took his next exhibit from the crate. The automatic pistol Jack had purchased – hired, really, here in Burgos. Then a second pistol brandished, waved in Jack's face. Carter-Holt's Astra automatic. 'And perhaps you could specifically explain these?' The man carefully lifted out a matching pair of Agfa Box Forty-Four cameras. 'Two of them. But this,' he hefted one of the cameras in his right hand, 'with an extremely interesting interior.'

Jack recalled the clever mechanism. Small caliber barrel connected to the rear of the lens shutter. Deadly hollow-point bullets. Carter-Holt's plan that Jack should innocently take a photo, kill Franco instead. *And the irony,* he thought. *If she'd only told me the truth, I'd probably have been willing to do it anyway.* But she hadn't done that. She'd duped him. Let him believe that, while he was taking the photo, it would actually be Carter-Holt who would carry out the assassination. With the Astra pistol. Yet Jack knew better now. The Astra was for killing Jack. And Carter-Holt would be a heroine once more. The woman who had shot down Franco's assassin. But everybody on the tour had seen her with the camera so many times. So she needed a second one, left back in her hotel room.

'Where did you find them?' said Jack, though he already knew the answer.

'They just arrived from San Sebastián,' Merry del Val smiled at him. 'The lieutenant had ordered a search of your room at the Hotel María Cristina. We found them there, naturally.'

No, thought Jack. *That room would have been searched days ago. Last Friday? As soon as we were reported missing. Or when her body was found. Must have been quite a puzzle for them. Her case. The pistol. A camera-gun.*

'It must have been difficult for you,' Jack laughed, knowing now that he would never get out of this alive. 'What would your heroine of National Spain be doing with all the tools of an assassin's trade, I wonder?'

'They were found in your room, Mister Telford, not in Miss Carter-Holt's.'

'She may have duped me,' said Jack, 'but what a fool she made of Franco. Fancy having pinned the Red Cross of Military Merit on the very woman who was planning to kill him.' He was still laughing but, by then, the Moroccan thug had gripped his head like a vice, held it still while *Teniente* Enrique Álvaro Turbides of the Guardia Civil's Public Order and Prevention Service casually took the fat cigar from his lips, flicked away the ash and blew on the lit end until it glowed and sparked like the pits of hell. Yet he spoke quietly enough as he peered into Jack's convulsed, contorted face.

'The lieutenant wants to know,' said Merry del Val, 'about the camera. He wonders which eye you intended to use. To kill *El Caudillo?*'

Chapter Ten

Saturday 8th October – Saturday 22nd October 1938

Ask for this great Deliverer now, and find him
Eyeless in Gaza, at the Mill with slaves.

The words went round and around in Jack's head, spinning down into the vortex of his own agonies. Samsonite agonies. A great hollow, burning pain that never left him but which flared to intolerable insistence during the brief mad moments of his consciousness. Shuttered vision through the single eye that remained to him, though even that one barely able to focus. The torments he suffered during the interminable night, left alone, sprawled and writhing on that hard floor, incapable of distinguishing whether he still suffered their tortures or whether his brain simply played again those to which he'd already been subjected. The smells embedded in his nostril. The singeing of his lashes, shriveling long before the cigar caressed his lid. The inextricable mingling of the tobacco's smoke and the sickly scent of his own sizzling flesh. The lingering, leathery odour of the lieutenant's sweaty fingers as he pushed and bored, it seemed, into Jack's skull. And then the boiling, liquid oil as his cornea melted. Distant recollection of another truck. An open truck. The sun. A halt before a gateway and, above the gateway, Saint James slaying heathens. Yet this Saint James seemed to live, to battle the Moors in some warped reality until, finally, Jack slipped once more into darkness.

'Can you hear me?'

Jack decided to ignore the man's voice. *All neat and tidy now,* he thought, and he remembered that they'd brought a priest from somewhere. To hear his confession. When they threatened to take the right eye too. He would have confessed anything at all by then. *All neat and tidy*. Confessions witnessed and recorded by the priest. Yes, he'd planned to kill Franco. Yes, he'd killed Julia Britten because she'd discovered his plan. Yes, he'd killed Carter-Holt because she'd confronted him with the murder. Only Turbides and Merry del Val knew the truth. Or suspected it. The myth of Carter-Holt's loyalty to National Spain intact. Franco's reputation too, as a consequence. But this voice didn't belong to Merry del Val. A real British accent? Northerner?

Jack opened the swollen right eye, saw that some tramp was leaning over him. Filthy, torn shirt. Unshaven. Threadbare blanket around his shoulders. Above his head, a window. No glass, but ripped canvas flapping in the cold whistling wind that stung Jack's many wounds. And today's smell? Hard to define, but stomach-wrenching.

'Smell,' said Jack.

'You'll get used to it,' said the tramp. 'But listen, I need to clean this.'

'Oh, Christ.' Jack convulsed as another spasm of fire raked his left eye socket and the surrounding parts of his skull.

'I can give you an aspirin,' the man apologised. 'That's all we've got. But I must clean that wound.' He called over his shoulder in broken Spanish, and a nun came into view behind him, carrying a bowl. Only, like the man, she seemed to be some vagrant version of a nun, her habit almost as ragged as the fellow's shirt. 'No, don't touch,' he told Jack, who was hardly even aware that he'd lifted his hand. 'God Almighty,' the man swore. 'I need to get all these scorched eyelash fragments out of here.'

The water was cold. Ice-cold. Jack flinched at first, tried to stop the man from touching him. But, after a few minutes, the process began to soothe him and he drifted into something resembling a more peaceful, exhausted rest. Yet it didn't last, the pain soon bringing him more fully awake. The derelict room, he saw, seemed filled with other tramps – at least, down in that dim further end, beyond the makeshift blanket partition that separated this section, where a few others groaned, or shouted in delirium, and the nun-nurse bathed their foreheads. She saw that he was awake, called out in Spanish.

'*Doctor. ¡Venga!*'

The tramp returned, lifted Jack's chin to examine the eye.

'Can you sit?' he said. 'It might help. Stop some of this swelling getting any worse.'

'Where?' said Jack, as the tramp helped prop him up against the wall. He could still not quite fathom why he was alive at all, why they hadn't simply killed him in that room. And he was not entirely sure that he was pleased to have survived. There had been a point at which he had lapsed into a place of peace, resigned himself to the conviction that his torments were over. Forever.

'Our little palace? This is San Pedro de Cardeña. Reminds me of home. But what about you? What the hell have you done to deserve all this? And you're not one of us, are you?'

'One of you?'

'Prisoners of war, lad. Internationals. And others.' He nodded towards the nun, who passed by with yet another priest – though her face was set hard and not a word exchanged between them. The priest crouched by a bundle near the opposite wall. Another patient of this strange infirmary. Face deathly white. Barely audible, rasping breath. The priest spoke, but the nun pushed in front of him, reached inside the man's shirt, lifted a crucifix from his chest, spat some invective into the priest's face.

'What did she say?' Jack whispered.

'That's young Jamie. Irish. Peritonitis. She says that he's a *real* Catholic. That the priest has no claim to be one. That Jamie's already made his peace with God in his own way. It's all shite though, eh? She's here because she's a Basque. From Guernica. Won't toe the fascists' line about the town being destroyed by Anarchists. Refuses to keep her mouth shut about the truth.'

'I was there. Guernica.'

'Yeah, sure you were. And Jamie? Jamie came here to fight the fascists. Like the rest of us. But now? It's just about fighting to survive this sodding place.'

Two weeks went by. The pain subsided briefly, began to itch. A good sign, said the medic – who Jack now knew as Bob Keith, a student doctor from Halifax, Communist Party of Great Britain, of course, and the only medic with the International Brigaders stupid enough, he boasted, to have been caught in the front lines. At Calaceite. But the itching became a torture in itself, and Jack had repeatedly made the mistake of scratching at the bandage.

'Bloody hell,' said Bob 'I knew it. You've infected the sodding thing.'

There was no more infirmary, and he now knew he was lucky. Most patients, like Jamie, simply died there. So Jack relished having been moved along the drafty landing, joining the rest of that tatterdemalion company for the regular routine of the concentration camp. Once a monastery, he had learned, but left to fall into disrepair. Some connection with El Cid here too. Or so the other lads said. And he owed those lads a great deal. He'd been dumped here with nothing but his ripped clothes and rope-soled shoes. No razor. No smokes. Nothing. He wasn't alone in this. But nor was he one of them, so their willingness to share their own limited supplies, the occasional cigarette, touched him deeply.

'Got anything for it?' he said. 'For the itching?'

'Don't be bloody stupid. Try to keep it clean. Shouldn't be any worries about the sepsis though. Sorry, the pus. It'll just come out of its own accord. Wash it regularly. Then dress it again with a clean section of the bandage. If you're lucky, there'll be no systemic upset.'

'Wash?'

'Yes, I know,' said Bob Keith. 'But do your best.' Five hundred prisoners. Five cold water taps. And, most days, no more than a few drops.

They were all herded by armed guards out from the long, spartan chamber, down the stairs, two floors and into the cloistered quadrangle. Normal morning routine. Flag pole. Squad of soldiers. The red and yellow standard of National Spain raised to a bugler's discordant notes. And the sergeant, the one they called *El Palo*, the Stick, shouting out a litany.

'*¡España!*' he yelled, raised his arm in the fascist salute.

'*¡Una!*' called back his men, snapping out their own arms with matching enthusiasm, while the prisoners – perhaps four hundred of them assembled around all four sides of the square – joined in, as required, with a more desultory response and, for the most part, the merest parody of the salute.

'*¡España!*' shouted *El Palo*, and received the required response. '*¡Grande!*' Great. Spain is Great. But when the sergeant called out *España* for the third time, the quadrangle erupted, the prisoners now drowning out their captors.

'*¡Libre!*' they screamed. Free! Their battle cry. Taken up, too, by those unseen Basque and Asturian prisoners in the further sections of the prison. And when they were required to shout El Caudillo's name over and over again, they raucously changed '¡Fran-co! ¡Fran-co!' to 'Fuck-You! Fuck-You!'

'You could always try applying a few drops of the soup,' said Bob, as they were paraded past the breakfast pots and collected their ration. 'Just make sure you take out the bread crumbs.'

Jack examined the contents of his bowl, wondered whether the hot water, vinegar, garlic and olive oil had any more use as a salve than it did for nourishment. Most days it just went straight through him, took him fighting for an urgent turn at one of the holes in the floor that served as latrines.

'Does it look as bad as it feels?' he said.

'You'll win no more bloody beauty contests. Worse than that, the eyelids are too badly damaged to ever close again. That means the eyeball itself will suffer from dehydration. Recurrent infections. But when it's healed a bit, I can put a few sutures in, close the eyelid permanently. Won't be pretty. Better though. Oh, and the Secret Six are interested in your story. After dinner, they'll send for you.'

After dinner? The early afternoon slop of lentils or beans. And, before that, the daily course in Christian studies. Suitably egalitarian. All of them treated as though they were equally stupid, equally beyond the pale of civilisation, regardless of whether they were atheist Reds, greedy Jews, heathen Protestants, inscrutable Buddhists, or even wrong-headed Catholics, Eastern Orthodox or otherwise. Yet many of the Bible study group, Jack had discovered, were regular attendees, getting to the end of one course, managing to fail the simple final test, and immediately starting afresh.

'At least the Stick and his lads leave us alone while we're in here,' he'd been told by one of the regulars. But there was no avoiding *El Palo* later when, after a spell back on their own landing, they were all summoned to mandatory prayers before they could eat. And, before the prayers, the regular requirement to satisfy the guards' sadism. Down the stairs again and out into the yard, but now with the pigs lined on both sides, all with staves or pick handles, groups of the prisoners forced to run that gauntlet, beaten across their buttocks, thighs and backs. And many of the lads had been subjected to this, day after day, for months on end. How they had survived so long, Jack had no idea. Riddled with lice.

Living cheek-by-jowl with all the other species of vermin in that ruined pile. More than half-starved. Raked by scurvy. But he had developed his own mechanism. The first time it had been almost an accident, the bandage slipping down to cover both eyes, forcing him to hold back until almost the end of the line. And, by then, the guards seemed to have tired of their sport. Or perhaps it was beyond even their spectacular depths of cruelty to beat a blind man. So Jack now feigned total blindness whenever he was able, created one of those strange paradoxes by which it sometimes seemed that it was they who could not see him. And, as usual, he was left mostly to his own devices, vaguely amused by the parallel game for which he was now personally responsible – the game in which fellow-prisoners, realising Telford's potential value, jostled for the privilege of being his escort – a role which also offered some immunity, despite the risk of even worse beating while in the scrum to win that coveted position at Jack's elbow.

The ploy worked well enough today, carried Jack safely through the prayer session. *Please God, let there be something better than lentils or beans this day.* The prayers unanswered. Just the usual slop. *And, please God, let me not be on the punishment list today.* For such was the next item on the monotonous itinerary. Those who had been observed earlier as especially sluggish in their fascist salute. Those less than enthusiastic in response to *El Palo's* cries of '¡España!' Those who had posed difficult questions for the priest during Christianity Class. Those who still refused to kneel at prayers. A few each day, dragged off from the food queue, down into the cellar, the *Calabozo*, to be thrashed more systematically with wooden clubs or that strange instrument of punishment fashioned from a bull's pizzle.

'Who are they?' Jack was standing in the queue next to Ed Acken, himself a journalist, and serving with the Americans' Abraham Lincoln Battalion.

'That's Bob Steck,' said Acken. He nodded carefully towards one of the men being marched back towards the building. 'Good guy. In my outfit. Produces our own paper. You seen it?' Yes, Jack had seen it. *The Jaily News.* Excellent. Good for morale. 'And that one?' Acken wagged his thumb at the second victim. 'I interviewed him. South African. But born a Latvian Jew. How about that! Jack Fliar. Don't know the third one though.'

'That's Doyle,' said Bob Keith from just behind them. 'Dublin lad.'

And Doyle was refusing to be manhandled, shook off the guards' hands, march himself towards the *Calobozo*, fist raised in his own clenched-fist salute.

'He'll get an extra pasting for that,' said Acken. 'And how about you, Telford? Joining us this afternoon?'

There it was. The way the routine of brutality took you. An instant of relief that it was somebody else, not you, singled out for the treatment. A further moment of regret for the victims. Then on with the business of the afternoon. Hyman Wallach's chess master class. Or the lessons in motor mechanics, languages, art, or working class history, all part of the self-help programme now dubbed by the prisoners as San Pedro's Institute of Higher Learning.

Thank heaven for the Communist Party, thought Jack, without any sense of irony. For the Party was largely responsible, he knew, for the lessons; for the prisoners' own security patrols; for bringing some semblance of law and order among the inmates – replacing the anarchy and chaos, which had plagued the place, to the delight of the fascists, it was said, when the Internationals first arrived; and for establishing the Camp Committee, the Secret Six.

'The chess?' Jack replied. 'I'd love to. But apparently I've got an interview to attend.'

'Ed tells me you're quite a player, Telford,' said the huge American, Lou Ornitz.

The Camp Committee was meeting, as usual, in that section of the first-floor landing where Hy Wallach ran his chess matches. There were a dozen of them taking place, and they provided good cover for the occasional clandestine meeting in full view of the guards. A couple of small boards fashioned from whatever scraps of wood had been scavenged, and not yet used for firewood, but mostly just scratched onto the cold slabs, and the playing pieces all improvised too.

'Chess?' said Jack, as Ornitz moved a tiny papier-mâché Queen's Pawn to D4.

'I think you know what we mean,' snapped Ryan, the Irish major and a spectator at today's game. Jack had no idea whether he was actually one of the Secret Six since there were far more than that number gathered around this particular match – in which Lou's Chinese opponent, Chen, was toying with a Queen's Knight response, to F6.

'He's just being modest, aren't you, cock?' said the thin-lipped engineer from Salford. One of those irrepressible fellows, Joe Norman. 'Writes well, considering.'

Considering what? Jack wondered. *That I'm not a Party member?*

'Not exactly the *Daily Worker*,' Acken drawled. 'But a decent read, this *Reynold's News*, they tell me.'

'Some right grand comrades in the Co-op,' said Joe Norman. 'Your man, Elliott. Bloody good job. Milk for Spain. And the work getting those Basque kids safe to Britain. Bloody brilliant.'

'Nice of you to say so,' said Jack. 'But I'm still not sure what I can do for you, gentlemen.'

He'd met some of these men a couple of weeks back. Around another chess match. Suspicion. Demands to tell his story. Not once, but several times. Telford wasn't the only civilian here, but he was the one with the strangest story. He'd kept as closely to the truth as possible, but omitted any details which, he thought, might make life difficult. In this version, Jack explained the battlefield tour – hard enough for the Secret Six to swallow in itself. He described his role. The main incidents at Covadonga and Santiago de Compostela. Though he carefully avoided any mention of Carter-Holt's own little game there. He was no more than a casual acquaintance of the woman, he insisted. Her death a simple accident. Yet, because he had been with her at the time, he had been stupid. He had run. And been hunted down by the Guardia Civil. Then accused of acting as an illegal correspondent. Almost as a spy. Well, understandable, Ed Acken had said. Remember the Koestler case? But what was it, they had asked, that the pigs had been trying to get out of him? To blind him, for Christ's sakes? Jack had no answer for them. Wasn't that just the way of the fascists? But the point had been left there, hanging in the air.

'You're certain, Herr Telford,' Karlsen whispered to him now, 'that you were not in Fräulein Carter-Holt's confidence?' Karlsen troubled Jack. He was posing in San Pedro as a former Swedish sailor, also captured at Calaceite, but it seemed widely known that, in reality, he was a cadre of the German Communist Party, high on Hitler's most-wanted list. If his true identity was discovered, he'd be off to Sachsenhausen like a shot.

'She never mentioned Willi Müntzenberg, for example?'

Well, of course she had. According to Carter-Holt, it had been through her work with Müntzenberg, on behalf of the Party, that had first brought her to the attention of the Comintern. And also to the boy, Kurt Tiebermann, with whom she had fallen in love and then lost, killed by the Nazis. But Telford couldn't admit any of that.

'Müntzenberg? I've heard of him. Of course I have. But why on earth would Miss Carter-Holt ever have mentioned him to me? She'd not exactly have been a fellow-traveller, would she?'

'Save that for another day, Karlsen,' said Ornitz, then cursed as he lost a knight to Chen's bishop. 'You see, Mister Telford, we've had some news. He held up a copy of the *Diario de Burgos*. They let us see the papers now. A few letters too.'

It was hard to believe, but the others swore it was true. That, bad as things might be at San Pedro de Cardeña, they were actually better than even just a few weeks before. Sadly, all down to the Republic's defeats on the Ebro. Nobody here really believed the war could be won any more. Franco knew it too. So the prison's régime seemed to have relaxed, if only in those very marginal ways. A few letters coming in. The occasional parcel. The divine gift of tobacco. There'd even been a visit from Lady Austen Chamberlain, early in September. The Prime Minister's sister-in-law, though gone to San Pedro with her own pro-Nazi agenda, so that she could report back on how well the prisoners-of-war were treated by her very good friend, General Franco. It had all backfired, of course, and she had cut short the visit, branding them all as Communist scum.

'We get our news from the pages of Franco's newspapers?' Jack laughed.

'And a certain *estanco* owner in Burgos with a clever eye for coding messages,' said Acken. 'But this news affects you directly, Mister Telford. And it's not the only thing we've heard today. The Camp Commandant has informed Major Ryan that a group of the British Battalion members are being transferred. To San Sebastián. In the next day or so. And then exchanged for Italian prisoners taken by our side.'

'And how does that affect me?' said Jack. 'I don't qualify, do I?'

'Not directly,' Ornitz told him. 'But this affects you.' He waved the newspaper again. 'It seems we've had orders. From the top. Madrid.

Somebody must love you very much, Mister Telford. We've been told to get you out.'

'Madrid?' said Jack. 'I don't know anybody in Madrid. Why...?'

Ornitz shrugged, moved his queen to threaten Chen's advancing rook.

'I guess you'll find out. All I ask is, if you get the chance, remember to tell the story. About this place. If we manage to get you out at all, you can bet your life we'll pay for it. Those of us left here. We'll pay big-time.'

And if I escape, thought Jack, *and then get caught again? What then?* But Frank Ryan must have seen the hesitation in Jack's expression.

'You don't get it, Telford, do you?' said the Irishman. 'You think you can just ride out the rest of the war here. But there was one other thing the Commandant told me. They've ordered a military tribunal. Just for you. Spying. So, whatever it is you're hiding from us, they're going to kill you for it. And sooner, rather than later.'

Chapter Eleven

Monday 24th October 1938

He awoke screaming. They were taking his other eye. And the pain, the suffocating pain…

'Easy, Telford. Easy.'

The Irishman, Ryan, with his hand clamped loosely over Jack's mouth.

'Get off me.'

He prised Ryan's fingers free. Strong, stocky fingers. Fingers that had first squeezed a trigger during the Irish Civil War – the Irish Republican side, naturally. Fingers that had penned lyrical Gaelic prose for *An Reult*. Fingers that had helped write the revolutionary constitution for the Irish Republican Congress.

'We need to talk,' whispered Ryan. 'Now.'

He took Jack's elbow, pulled him to his feet, helped him straighten up after the spine-freezing dampness of one more night spent on the cold slabs.

'It's still on?' said Jack, almost praying that the answer would be no, as they crept around the other restless occupants of the landing. They stole across the corridor, into the narrower room with its evil-smelling latrine holes.

'D'you know,' Ryan said, 'I've been here all these months and still don't know where all the shite goes.' Jack wondered whether he was being philosophical. 'And yeah, it's still fecking on. But, if you make it, Telford, what sort of tale will you tell?'

'I suppose that all depends on what happens in Madrid. Why? What did you have in mind, Major?'

'Well, for example, Mister Telford, what will you say about the British Government's little charades in all this?'

'That's partly what got me into this mess in the first place. I tried to post some copy back to my editor. About the blind eye we're turning to British ships being sunk by the Italians.' He touched his own recently blinded eye for emphasis, smiled at the poor joke. Max Weston, his West Country comedian friend, would have been proud of him, and Jack missed the big buffoon. 'About how we're allowing Hitler to be paid off,' he went on, 'for his involvement here with all the raw materials he needs for re-armament. About how the British Embassy in Madrid knew all about the coup beforehand and did nothing about it. And bloody Chamberlain spouting off about Peace for our Time while all that's been going on.'

'Sodding English,' said Ryan. 'I sometimes think the only decent Englishmen are those stuck in here. Or those who've already gone home wounded. And I'm not even sure about all those. But the rest? No offence, mind, but I wouldn't give a guinea for the lot of them. There's a bigger war than this one coming, Mister Telford. And England will be the sodding cause of it. Not Hitler. Not Mussolini. Bloody England.'

'That's a conclusion I'd already come to, Major. But it must make life difficult for you. In a war between British Imperialism and Nazi Germany, which side does an Irish Republican take?'

'Oh, against the fascists first, eh? Always against the fascists. But there are fascists a-plenty in the British Establishment too. You know that. In your fecking Royal Family too. And all those hangers-on. Like Lady Austen bloody Chamberlain. Will you write about them, Telford? Will you have the balls?'

Jack had never been certain whether he liked Ryan or not, but now he softened towards the man.

'The first thing I'll write about is the way you've all been treated here. The conditions. And the tests.' He'd picked up the stories, time and again, about how the Gestapo, Franco's own Secret Police, and a Spanish psychologist called Vallejo, had conducted their experiments on the prisoners – physical measurements and examination of their heads, their bodies, their genitalia; and so-called intelligence tests – to prove that Marxist sympathisers, Communists and Socialists in general, were somehow mentally defective. 'How did you get on with the tests yourself?'

'You want to see the scars, comrade?' Ryan replied. 'I spent almost a month in the hole, on and off. In solitary.'

'You're a brave man, Major.'

'Brave? Bollocks. I'm just another Marxist mental-case. And they tell me that Ireland's very own Minister for Spain is coming to see me. Maybe even going to hire a lawyer to help get me out of here. Though who knows where I'll actually end up! But you, Mister Telford. You have to take the fight against fascism from here now. Take it back onto the streets of bloody London. For all of us.'

I had hoped, thought Jack, *to take the fight to Franco a bit more directly than that.*

'Yes,' he said, 'somebody else had already told me much the same thing.'

'I hadn't planned on doing this quite so soon,' said Bob Keith. Are you sure you want me to go ahead?'

'Just get on with it,' said Jack, so shaken with fear and doubt that he could barely speak, nor stop his limbs from trembling. He was sitting against the wall at a spot where a rare shaft of morning sunshine blazed a theatrical spotlight on the cracked plaster and Telford's face. He saw Keith nod to the men on either side, and they quickly gripped Jack's arms, his shoulders, his head. And Jack closed his good eye involuntarily as soon as he saw the suture needle and thread. In truth, he barely felt the needle pass through the lower lid of the left one but he yelled when it hooked into the upper part, and he felt the cotton tighten and pull as it closed the lips of raw flesh together. He swore and squirmed through another eternity until it was finally done.

'You see?' Bob murmured. 'Plenty of tears from the right eye. Nothing from the left. It would have dehydrated really fast.' He took a last look at his handiwork, then dug a cigarette from his pocket, pressed it between Jack's lips and lit it for him. 'I've seen worse,' he said. 'Try to keep the dressing clean. And get yourself an eye-patch. I'm told the girls love a bloke with an eye-patch.'

He helped Jack down to the food queue and, today, even Jack wasn't allowed to escape the gauntlet unscathed. *El Palo* and his gang set about them all with particular and indiscriminate vigour.

'Pricks!' Jack heard the American, Steck, curse when they eventually all limped to safer ground. 'Pissed off because some of our lads are getting out of this shit-hole, while those bastards are still stuck here.'

It eased the tension, and Steck promised them there'd be a good cartoon in the next edition of *The Jaily News*.

'Well, let's find out whether you're out of here too, Jack,' said Bob Keith. They'd both spotted the Basque priest, the one who somehow seemed at liberty to wander freely between the Spanish section and this block occupied by the internationals. Jack didn't know what the priest was really called. Nobody did. Impossible to pronounce, the lads said. But he'd been incarcerated in San Pedro for sixteen months already. He'd picked up some broken English too. And since he addressed everybody, individually or collectively, in an identical way, he had earned himself the same reciprocal name – Brother Mine.

There followed one of those melting pot dialogues in which Steck's Mexican Spanish was stewed in a broth of *Euskera*, seasoned with a sprinkling of mostly incorrect Anglo-American phrases from Brother Mine, and stirred frequently with inventive sign language, to produce a stew almost as hard to digest as today's beans.

'I hope to hell I've got this right,' said Steck, finally. 'He says he's spoken to the Commandant and asked whether, when the boys go down for their bath this afternoon, you can go with them, Telford. He's made up some story about how badly you stink. Complaints. Laid it on a bit thick. And then asked what harm it can do. A blind man's not going to go far, after all. So you get to take the first step, at least. But we need a volunteer. To go with you. What about you, Doc?' he said to Bob Keith.

In the weeks that Jack had spent at San Pedro, bath days were always those which elicited the most excitement – and the most argument. They occurred at random, and only involved a few dozen men on each occasion. On average, therefore, the long-term prisoners could expect this rare treat perhaps once every two months. But neither the Commandant, nor any of his subordinates, could truly be bothered with any form of organised system. The Commandant, in any case, was far too preoccupied with his daily sojourn to the Burgos Casino, so it often occurred that the lads were chosen more frequently than the bimonthly allowance or, alternatively, were left off the list entirely. Hence, another administrative function for the Secret Six. Bathing Rota. Yet, today, even this carefully managed list was ignored, and the only men permitted to march that mile-and-a-half to the River Arlanzón – apart from Jack and his companion, along with *El Palo* and a dozen guards, of course – were those forty who had been told they would soon make the spine-tingling journey to the international bridge at Irún, the anticipation almost too much to bear, as they waited to discover whether their exchange for those Italian officers would actually take place. But at least having this priority for being made more presentable was a good sign.

'Tell me what Brother Mine said again,' murmured Jack, as they trudged down the woodland path towards the lane. He'd pulled the bandages over both eyes, feigning total blindness once more, though he'd left a small gap so he could just see where he was going. 'About when we get there.'

'He says that, when you've the chance,' said Bob, 'just follow the riverbank along to the right. There's plenty of cover, apparently. And you'll come to a rocky outcrop. Very prominent. They'll be waiting for you there.'

'That simple? I'm not sure about this.'

He hadn't been sure from the moment he'd been told about the escape plan. Too many things that could go wrong. Could the priest be trusted? The Secret Six certainly seemed to think so. But wasn't it at least possible that being shot while trying to escape might be one way for Merry del Val and that creature, Turbides, to avoid any complications from a Military Tribunal and Jack's execution? And even if there was no hidden agenda here, the escape plan legitimate – and successful – what might be the repercussions? For these men marching with him to the Arlanzón. These men whose hopes were all wound tighter than guitar strings. Those he knew now by name – Ward, Malden, Reid, Sterling, Ellis, Pooley, Lomon, McKenna, and that brilliant artist, Branson. All going home to their families. Or so they hoped. But what if his escape caused the whole damned exchange to be cancelled? And for what? So that Jack Telford, important Jack Telford, could be sent to Madrid? Who the hell, in Madrid, had ever heard of him? He had a bad feeling about all this.

'You're a decent bloke, Jack,' Bob smiled. 'Always worrying about others. But no need. The Italians are desperate for this exchange. They won't let a little thing like your escape get in its way, I'm certain. And these lads wouldn't stand in your way either. If you're needed in Madrid, well...' *Yes*, thought Jack, *a bad feeling.* More guilt to pile on top of his existing uncertainties. About the fates of Father Ignacio and Josefina Ruiz Delgado. About the failure and futility of his plan to kill Franco. About the disillusion Sister María Pereda must now be feeling about him. About the stinging criticism he would certainly face from his father next time the spectre appeared to him. 'Anyhow, just think of it this way,' Bob squeezed Jack's elbow, 'you're getting out of jail free. All these poor buggers have just been told that the Foreign Office will send each of them a four quid Repatriation Bill if they make it home. Good old England, eh?'

'And when Brother Mine says they'll be waiting, do we know who "they" might be?'

But Jack already had a good idea about that. The tour group had been held hostage for a while at Covadonga by a group of *guerrilleros* calling themselves the *Machados*, after the poet, Antonio Machado. It was said that there were many such groups, the remnants from the Republican Army of the North, and forged for about this past year into the Guerrilla Army Corps, achieving notoriety when they had attacked the Carchuna Fortress in the south and sprung three hundred Asturian prisoners.

'Yes, of course,' said Bob Keith. 'They'll be partisans. From the mountains. And they should see you safely to Madrid.'

The lads were like children released from school, running through the shrubs along the Arlanzón's stony margin and hurling themselves, yelling with the shock of the water's cold embrace, into the fast-flowing pools, which eddied here around the stone piers of a crumbling medieval bridge. Jack might have said, hurling themselves fully clothed except, of course, they were not. The garments they possessed were mostly rags but at least they would be rid of those soon since, according to Bob, they would be equipped with new tunics and berets. Courtesy of the Italians. To make them presentable for the exchange. Create the illusion that they'd been well treated. As prisoners-of-war. And Telford envied them.

He had held back from the main group, sheltered by a bush and going through the motions of undressing, fiddling with buttons, trying his best to be inconspicuous while gauging the lie of the land through the narrow slit in the bandage. Bob Keith stood a little apart, to his left, closer to the bridge, closer to the guards. The river flowed in that direction, downstream, to Burgos, Jack calculated. But, to the right, the ground was higher, more thickly wooded, the stream emerging from a modest ravine, singing over rocks where a pair of yellow-breasted wagtails danced and darted.

When you've the chance, Jack, he thought. Wasn't that what he'd been told? *And what might that chance be, exactly?* he wondered.

There was a groan, and he saw Bob clutch his stomach, sink to his knees. Jack assumed the guards had struck him, then realised he might be reading it all wrong. A deliberate distraction maybe. Rifles were still slung and *El Palo* seemed wanting in the brutality he normally displayed when inflicting pain.

Chance, thought Jack, seeing the guards' attention all focused either on Bob Keith or the splashing, playful prisoners. He crouched low, pulled the bandage up from his good eye. One backward glance and a short sprint to the next bush. And the next.

The hairs bristled on the back of his neck. His breath came in short, panting gasps, loud enough to waken the dead. The gravel under his feet noisier than a machine gun burst.

Somebody shouted.

'*¡Fuera! ¡Fuera!*' Out! Get out!

Jack dodged left, to the next clump of cover, looked over his shoulder. Several of the guards at the water's edge, rifles now readied, screaming at the bathers to come ashore.

Crack.

The bullet whistled past Jack's ear, whined as it ricocheted from a rock somewhere beyond him.

'*¡Pare!*' Stop! It sounded like *El Palo* but he was damned if he'd wait to find out.

Run, Jack, run.

He'd covered perhaps half the distance to that bend in the river where it emerged from the ravine. Rocky outcrop, he said to himself. It must be there. Somewhere there.

Boots, crunching fast behind him now. More shouting. An iron taste in his mouth. A sour smell in his nostrils. But his own rope-soled alpargatas were light on his feet. A godsend. Until the ties that bound the right shoe to his ankle snapped, and he stumbled.

Crack.

This time too close for comfort. Missed him by no more than a few inches. And he knew it was all over.

'All right!' he shouted, and stopped, raised his hands. 'All right!' But it didn't save him. Not really. He grinned foolishly at the closest of the guards who, only a yard or two behind him, swung his rifle, smashed the side of Jack's face with the flat of the butt. He went down, thought he felt his cheek bone crack, the sutures biting, almost as though the dead eye was bursting from his head. He rolled. Sideways. Fearing that the guard's boot would find him too. Then scrambled to his feet again, careful to keep his hands above his head. 'I said, all right, for Christ's sake.'

Jack was repaid with a vicious poke in the belly from the rifle's muzzle.

'*Venga, bastardo,*' the guard spat at him, poked him again to get him moving back towards the bridge. '*Y mire.*' Look.

Jack did so. To where Bob Keith was kneeling. To where *El Palo*, standing just behind him, had taken his pistol from its holster, the prisoners drawn up in two ranks.

'No!' Jack screamed, as the pistol jerked. Bob's face disappeared in a blast of blood, brains and bone as the gun's report reached Jack's ears.

And, somehow, it echoed. Twice.

There was a grunt, the guard at Jack's side fell like a burst sack. While the second, the fellow who had hit him with the rifle butt, went spinning past him, clutching his guts.

Telford stared for a moment at the place where that young student doctor from Halifax lay in his own gore. Then at the prisoners-of-war. They were singing. The *Internationale*. Fists raised, while the guards, and *El Palo*, were occupied with their own concerns, taking cover, firing. Jack expected to die, but the bullets all seemed to be flying very wide. If he was, indeed, the mark. And they were flying in both directions.

Another guard fell, and Jack turned, his mouth hanging open from his aching face. He thought he was dreaming. *Guerrilleros.* Six of them, spreading across the open ground, firing. And this one, risen somehow from the dead. The leader of the *Machados* from the siege at Covadonga. Eduardo Pinchón. *Guadalito.* But this was not the *Jefe*. Just a likeness. The fellow yelling at him.

'*¡Venga, idiota!*'

Chapter Twelve

Saturday 5th November 1938

Telford killed his first man, in combat – or almost in combat – twelve days later. And it was a very different experience from the death of Valerie Carter-Holt.

He had been half-dragged, half-carried to the cover of rocks, his face aching, a deep, throbbing pain that jarred his skull with every footfall. They stopped only long enough for a temporary repair to the bindings of his shoes, then up through the rough open country to the east. Mostly woodland, stunted pines. An increasingly ominous sky. Hardly a word exchanged. Jack's mind filled with that repeated image of Bob Keith's slaughter.

For the most part, they had avoided contact with any signs of human habitation but, on occasion, they seemed to make a deliberate excursion to an isolated farmhouse or small hamlet, set the dogs barking, then moved on rapidly. An impossible pace, hour after hour, with Jack's frequent complaints unheeded and his legs, his head, screaming at him for rest, until a return to San Pedro de Cardeña and the prospect of execution seemed a welcome alternative.

But, as the sun went down, away to their right, Jack understood that they had swung south. And begun to climb. Steeply. With every mile the gradients seemed to increase, the darkness become more dense. He could scarcely believe that his companions could even discern a path, and he feared, with every stumbling step, each bruised shin, cracked ankle, rock-scraped finger or stubbed toe that he would be plunged over into some terrible abyss.

It was long, long into the night before they took their first rest, Jack falling among pine needles, branches and stars above him, his chest heaving with exhaustion. He was barely able to drink from the wineskin he was offered, and his stomach rebelled at the coarse sausage and sliver of cheese they had told him to eat.

'Come on,' one of them had demanded. 'Eat. Eat.'

But Jack had simply vomited. Nothing but bile, though his insides constantly retching. He knew he was in shock, uncontrollable trembling. And cold.

'Where do we go?' he had mumbled.

'*Arriba*,' the man had snarled. Up. Then he pointed. 'Into the *sierra*.' And, at that moment, the *guerrillero*'s tone had made Jack feel more like a prisoner than at any time during his incarceration in San Pedro.

The following week had passed with the same monotonous routine. Resting by day, usually in caves, now and again in a deserted, ruined hut. One of the *guerrilleros* making an occasional foray for supplies. Sharing their meagre provisions, always hard cheese or dried sausage, sometimes bread, precious cigarettes, the prized wineskin, water from the mountain streams. Communicating little, even among the partisans themselves.

Periodically, they had heard the sounds of an aircraft, the spluttering drone of a scout plane, and the *guerrilleros* had kept carefully to their cover. At other times, one of the men would return from a foraging trip to report the presence of troops travelling a nearby road, or searching a local village.

'Searching for us?' Jack had asked.

'Searching for you, *cabrón*,' they would reply.

They were a taciturn bunch, ripe with the essence of garlic or sharp tobacco, and Jack had endured long periods of silence in which he practiced Spanish questions in his head, choosing his chances to speak carefully, but rarely receiving anything except one-word responses.

'Where is your home?' he would say, though talking was still painful. And they would tell him Gijón, Cartagena, Córdoba, Jaen. Or nothing at all beyond a grunt or a sneer.

Nor had they shared their names, though he had deduced them, believed he could now distinguish between them. Two called Pepe – who each seemed to know precisely when he, rather than his namesake, was being addressed. Three with, Jack assumed, nicknames. Bigote. Cortadito. Moro. And their leader responding only to his rank, it seemed. *Capitán*. They were well armed, rifles mainly, bandoliers of ammunition, two of them with heavy haversacks, two more with coils of climbing rope. And the *Capitán* with a light machine gun strapped to his back, a hefty revolver at his waist.

But with each night that passed, Jack had adjusted to the routine. His face felt considerably better. The bruises from his beatings, from the rifle butt, and his first clumsy attempts at keeping up with the group, had all but disappeared. His periods of rest were less disturbed by nightmares and he felt, in general, fitter than he had ever been in all his thirty years. Even his missing eye troubled him marginally less, though there was often a burning sensation, like a hot ball of lead buried within his cheek and, whenever that eased, he was left with a terrible itching. Yet, at least, the sutures had held – just.

And then, in the early hours of the day he calculated to be the twelfth since his escape, something had changed. The men became more animated, talked at length in rasping whispers that Jack could not follow. Their latest foraging had been especially fruitful, so they lit a fire in their cave, ate and drank more than their normal rations. And the one called Bigote began to sing.

'*Si me quieres escribir, ya sabes mi paradero.*'

It was haunting. And Jack understood those first lines.

'*Si me quieres escribir, ya sabes mi paradero.*'

The repetition helped. If you want to write to me, you know where I am posted.

'*Tercera Brigada Mixta, primera línea de fuego.*'

The Third Mixed Brigade, in the first line of fire.

But, after that, it all became somewhat confused. Odd snatches. Something about bridges. And rivers. Franco. Madrid.

'Where are we?' he asked, not for the first time.

'In the Sierra de la Demanda,' replied the *Capitán*, and caught Jack by surprise with the fullness of his answer. 'Above the road from Burgos to Soria.'

Jack had no idea where Soria might be.

'On the road to Madrid?' he asked.

'First, we have work to do. Here. In the morning.'

But the *Capitán* would not be drawn further and, as the first glimmer of daylight appeared, they left the cave and scrambled, in single file, down a precipitous goat path, through thick scrub, until they came to a wide ledge of rock. Below them, nestled into woodland of pine and eucalyptus, was a squat building surrounded by low walls which, on the farther side, edged a road running east to west. In front of the building, another track joined the road from the south, having crossed a wooden bridge over a sluggish stream and, alongside the track, beyond the bridge, a low, circular concrete structure – a defensive position, Jack thought, for a machine gun perhaps.

They crept down through the trees until they could see the rear of the main blockhouse more clearly, and the pair of Guardia Civil sentries patrolling the grounds, one along the front, one along the back, their respective paths crossing every couple of minutes at the sides. This particular side, a shadowed doorway, down a few overgrown steps, and itself protected by a solid, L-shaped blast wall and roof.

The rear of the building had no windows but, rather, narrow slits high up towards the tiled roof, where thick round beams protruded from the stonework. And Jack hardly dared breathe as the *Capitán* began to silently deploy his men. One of the Pepes slipping through the trees to the opposite side with his rifle. Bigote here, quietly slipping a round into the breech of his own gun. Cortadito creeping down almost to the road. Moro slipping the haversack from his back and filling his jacket pockets with grenades. Then handing a second batch to Pepe Two, who also unslung his climbing rope and quickly fashioned a slipknot noose at one end.

'And you,' the *Capitán* poked Jack hard in the chest, merely mouthing the words, punctuating them by pointing at the ground. 'Stay here. Here!'

Jack offered him a sarcastic salute. They'd never given him a weapon, and they were unlikely ever to do so. Little choice, therefore, except obey. Obey and watch. As the *Capitán* put the tips of two fingers to his teeth and whistled a blackbird's trill, quickly answered by Pepe One and Cortadito, both now out of sight. There were seconds of silence apart from a few notes of true birdsong, the crunch of the sentries' boots on sand and gravel, and the discordant rumble as the Guardia Civil trooper now making his way towards them hummed some melancholy tune – a death chant, Jack thought, as the first shot spun the fellow around, slammed him into the corner of the blockhouse.

The second sentry's eyes widened, impossibly, briefly, as the *Capitán* cut him down at the very instant he also came into view.

'¡Vaya! ¡Vaya!' he yelled, and Pepe Two went as he was bidden, vaulting the low wall and sprinting into the building's shadows, just as rifles jutted from the high slit-windows, and shots began to whine into the trees around Jack's head.

A suicide mission? he wondered, for the blockhouse must be well defended and the garrison surely equipped with wireless communication to summon help. But, by now, Pepe Two had widened the noose in his rope, begun to swing it like a cowboy's lasso – Jack suffered a pang of childhood nostalgia for the many times he'd seen Tom Mix or Will Roger perform this selfsame feat on the cinema screen – and stepped back from the wall in time to launch the lariat upwards, catch the noose on one of those protruding beams and, monkey-like, scale the stonework until he could swing himself up, to sit astride the timber, above and to one side of the nearest loophole. From that position, he took a grenade from a bulging pocket, slipped out the pin, counted carefully and flicked the thing backwards through the slit. By the time it exploded, the *guerrillero* had clambered upright onto the beam and jumped to the next, teetered precariously, then repeated his trick with the hand grenades until smoke billowed from three loopholes and the whole early morning stunk of burning wood and cordite.

It was then that two Civiles came stumbling up the steps from the side door, shrouded in more smoke, unarmed, hands raised.

'¡Vengan, bastardos!' shouted the *Capitán*, gestured with the machine gun for them to cross the open ground, climb the walls and come into the trees, where Bigote covered them with his rifle. But there was still firing from the blockhouse, and the swarthy one called Moro ran over to the blast wall, tossed three grenades of his own through the open doorway. One dull retort after another, echoed inside. As though inside a metal drum. Screams. But no more shots. And two more defenders finally emerged, one of them bleeding heavily from a wicked face wound and virtually carried by his companion. As they came out, Moro edged his way within, disappeared into the darkness. There was a shot. Then two more, before he emerged again, grinning.

The partisans, meanwhile, wasted no time in gathering around their leader, received further quick-fire orders, so that Pepe One and Pepe Two – the latter back on solid ground once more – and Cortadito emptied the contents of another two haversacks to remove explosives, fuses and a detonator box. Jack still had occasional nightmares about a similar detonator, and his experiences with those other *guerrilleros* at Covadonga. He shuddered at the memory, while the three partisans dodged through the trees, off towards the bridge and its pillbox.

'What do you think, English? The *Capitán* shouted, jerked a thumb towards the four prisoners. 'We kill them now?'

Jack glanced at the fellow with the blast damage to his face, writhing in agony against a eucalyptus trunk, and groaning loudly as his head twisted from side to side. He wanted desperately to remind the *Capitán* that these men had surrendered. But it was another Spanish verb he didn't know. Not then. So he raised his hands, as the Civiles had done.

'Prisoners,' he said. 'Prisoners of the war.'

The partisans laughed. One of them cursed and spat. And Telford felt like a fool, thought he saw his father standing among them, also laughing at him. An idiot again, especially when he saw the captured Civiles smiling too. Fatalistic smiles, Jack thought.

'The English!' sneered the *Capitán*, and shook his head. One of the Civiles did likewise.

There was gunfire, over towards the bridge. Two muffled explosions. *Crump. Crump.* More shooting. Birds startled out of the branches.

The *Capitán* persuaded Moro to share his precious cigarettes, offered smokes to the captives, then to Jack as an afterthought. They all accepted. All except the face-wounded man who had now lapsed into unconsciousness.

'Where are you from, bastards?' the *Capitán* asked them.

'Here,' they shrugged. Yes, here. And one of them from Soria.

'Good to die at home,' said the *Capitán*, and the Civiles agreed with him.

A louder explosion. The pillbox, Jack assumed, and saw a plume of smoke spiral above the treetops.

'*Capitán*,' he said. 'Why kill?'

'Idiot!' he was told again. And then the *Capitán* drew the revolver from his belt. 'Come,' he said to the prisoners. 'It's time.'

The three men stood. The three able to do so. They took a last, painful draw on their cigarettes, while the *Capitán* shot the wounded fellow at close range, through the already damaged head. The rest of the partisans moved away, deeper into the trees, though Jack couldn't bring himself to join them.

'*Capitán!*' he pleaded again, while one of the Civiles began to chant.

'*¡España!*' he shouted.

'*¡Arriba!*' cried the other two, as the *Capitán* put a bullet through the first of their brains.

Jack flinched, remembered the way Bob Keith had been butchered in a similar way.

'*¡España!*' the man's voice choked, and he bit his lip so hard that it bled, dribbled through the bristle of his chin.

Why don't they run? thought Jack. He looked around, frantically, hoping for something to happen. *Instead of just…*

No chanted reply this time. Simply a second, reverberating shot. Blood and sludge splattering Jack's own face. The second prisoner slumping in slow motion at his feet. Then the *Capitán* swearing, fiddling with the revolver, trying to squeeze the trigger. Nothing.

The surviving prisoner saw his chance. Took it. Looked quickly around, then pushed his would-be executioner hard, sent the *Capitán* sprawling, the machine gun slipping from his shoulder, skittering across the pine needles. The Guardia ran. Leapt the wall in a single bound, legs pumping him towards the far side of the compound.

Jack turned to the *Capitán*, saw him sitting quietly on his haunches, smiling, the revolver hanging between his knees. Something about his nonchalance turned Jack's stomach. It boiled inside him.

'What is this?' he yelled in English, knowing that his words weren't understood. 'Some bloody game? He's getting away, you bastard. And you want him dead, don't you? Don't you?' There was no brake for his fury. His runaway senses driven by two wrestling titans: the just and compassionate Telford, desperately hoping the man would escape; and the vengeful, haunted Telford who saw no more than poor Bob Keith, his own frustrations, the loss of his eye – the torment of that itching that almost drove him crazy in itself.

He ran for the machine gun, gave no thought to its operation or whether it was still ready to fire.

Yes, his father yelled in his ear. *An eye for an eye, Jack.*

'No, English!' he could hear the *Capitán* yelling at him. But, by then, Jack was at the wall, the escaped trooper almost past the far end of the building. Jack pointed the barrel, squeezed the trigger, felt the bloody gun jerk almost from his grip. The noise was deafening. The stench acrid. Every muscle of his face, and chest, and arms, and shoulders shaken as though by an earthquake. Until the magazine was empty. The world suddenly still. A gesture. A statement. Nothing more.

'There,' he sobbed. 'You wanted him dead. Now he's bloody dead.'

Away across the open ground, sprawled against the blockhouse wall, lay the Guardia Civil.

'¡Cabrón!' said the Capitán, and snatched the machine gun from Jack's trembling hands. 'That one we wanted to go free!'

Chapter Thirteen

Friday 18th November – Saturday 3rd December 1938

It took some time to explain. And, by then, the rest of the partisans were long gone, headed east, leaving Jack alone with the *Capitán* travelling south though a line of lower hills, ground more open than any since they'd left the Arlanzón, all those weeks past.

'The Civiles,' the *Capitán* had told him, in painfully patient Spanish, 'they see you. I call you English. So they will remember. I kill them. All except one. He runs. Tells his friends you are here. Then Bigote and the others go east. They make problems. For the *fascistas*. In villages. The Civiles follow. The army too. They think they follow you. East. But you and me, we go south. It was a good plan. Until you kill that bastard. Idiot! Now – Who knows?'

Even so, they had travelled several days before Jack properly understood that the *Capitán*'s fumbling with the revolver had been nothing but pantomime. It was obvious – now. If he'd wanted him dead, the *Capitán* would have used the machine gun himself. The *guerrilleros*' disappearance into the trees, and leaving the *Capitán* alone with his prisoners, part of the same game. Indeed, even the attack, he now realised, on the Guardia Civil barracks itself, nothing but a ploy to attract attention. No real strategic point at all. A few Civiles killed, and easily replaced. The machine gun emplacement hardly damaged, Jack had seen, when they crossed the bridge. And the bridge itself entirely untouched.

'Why is it important?' he had asked, during a halt in which the *Capitán* had insisted on cutting and lacing an eye patch from a piece of haversack flap. 'Me,' Jack had pressed him. 'In Madrid.'

'Orders,' the *Capitán* had replied. Nothing more, except to hold up the patch. 'There,' he said. 'Now I won't have to look at that mess any more.' Yet he had insisted on examining the sutures closely. 'They have to come out, English.'

A rare moment of intimacy, almost tenderness, despite the pulling pain of their removal, during which Jack had sworn that the wound must surely have opened again. There'd been no time to feel sorry for himself, though, their march soon resumed. Jack possessed proper boots now, at least. Bigote had chosen them for him from the dead Civiles, packed them with straw in the toes to make them fit. And he had taken the rope-soled *alpargatas* with him, perhaps to help with the false trail. But the Guardia blockhouse had yielded more treasures for Jack's benefit. A heavy overcoat, though it did not seem like standard issue for the Civiles. Cigarettes too, enough for Jack and each of the *guerrilleros* to receive a paper-wrapped packet.

Yet every gift granted by life, Jack knew, had a price and, in this case, the currency of his payment was remorse. Jack's remorse. Soul-shattering. He had killed twice in little more than a month. The first time partly through fear. A sense of self-defence. The second time through his confused state of mind. The dizzy chaos of battle. Sucked into barbarism. But, on each occasion, in uncontrollable anger. He no longer recognised himself. Began to wonder whether his experiences had somehow driven him over into insanity.

There was another side to this remorse, too. Remorse that stemmed from those times he had written about this conflict, made judgements about the cheapness of life here. Judgements about the propensity of the Spanish people to wage such a war, one upon the other. And now here he was, civilised Jack Telford, British Jack Telford, hoisted on a petard of his own contrition.

Though if he felt such remorse still, surely this was his salvation. Not Catholic, but experiencing Catholic guilt. *Hold that guilt, Jack*, he thought. *Nurture it. And it will keep you safe. Guilt is the salvation that turns our primal impulses into the maturity of conscience. Guilt is always to be followed. Welcome guilt with open arms, for it will stand between you and iniquity.*

All the same, there was one aspect from which no amount of guilt could protect him. The worst thing about both killings. The true cause of his remorse. That they had been so very, very easy.

*

For most of the moonlit night, they followed a shallow valley and its sparse river – identified by the *Capitán* as the Escalote – until, just before daybreak, they saw the lights of a village ahead, swung up onto a tree-lined ridge that skirted the place and found a sheltered dingle where they might rest for the day. It overlooked the village cemetery, cypress trees along two sides, a wall of ochre stone around the whole. Inside, crosses and tombs, the houses of the dead, cast long shadows.

'Where are we?' said Jack. And the *Capitán* impatiently consulted the tattered map from inside his jacket. As usual, after a few moments, he shrugged and folded the map away again.

'Barcones,' he said. 'Perhaps Barcones. Who knows?' He settled down to sleep, pulled the cap over his eyes. 'But tonight, we cross into Castilla La Mancha.'

The significance was lost on Jack, though the name made him think of Cervantes. And windmills again. For they had passed close to thousands of the damned things. Or so it seemed.

He tried to sleep too. Calculated afresh the number of days since his escape, set them against his mental calendar. Then returned to his regular current pastime – playing afresh the conundrum of Madrid, the reason he was being taken there.

'I had a plan,' he said, suddenly, in his best Spanish. 'In Burgos. A plan to kill Franco.'

'English,' the *Capitán* groaned, 'I want to sleep.'

'It is the truth. My plan to kill Franco.'

'Then perhaps that is the reason they want you in Madrid. To find out whether your plan was good. To find out if you killed the bastard. But I think we would know by now. *¿Vale?*'

No need for sarcasm, thought Jack.

'I am in the prison. Before I can kill Franco. Of course. But who? In Madrid. Who wants me?'

'*El León*. He wants you.'

'The Lion?'

'The Lion. Yes. A general. *My* general.'

The sound of a truck cut through the questions forming in Jack's brain, dividing and multiplying like single-cell organisms. The *Capitán* rolled onto his belly, pressed himself into the dirt, then edged up the bank so he could peer over the hollow's lip. Jack did the same, scratched his hands on some thorny rock plant. Below him, a cloud of dust rose around the engine's protests, the jerking grind of gears. And it settled upon the cemetery gates with the cries of armed men, the more distant tolling of a bell from the village church.

Men like these he had seen before. Everywhere from Irún to Santiago de Compostela. Every time the tour group had been treated to a propaganda-soaked civic reception. Both the well-healed officials who had sat down to eat with them, but also the blue-shirted, heavily armed thugs with their Nazi salutes, crowding around each town hall and church.

'*¿Falangistas?*' Jack whispered.

The *Capitán* nodded, as the men pushed and prodded four bound prisoners into that part of the cemetery not yet sown with the village's dead. There was a wide but shallow trench, already dug in one corner, and it required no real prescience to know what would happen next.

Jack turned onto his back, tapped the machine gun now lying at the *Capitán*'s side, but the *guerrillero* snatched the weapon away, out of Telford's reach. There would be no repeat of his undisciplined behaviour at the Guardia barracks. The *Capitán*'s features were set hard and he flashed Jack a glance that brooked no defiance, though the drama below had already begun to play itself out in any case. Some shouting. Then the first shot. Jack clamped his hands to the sides of his head, covered his ears. Yet he could not shut out the horror. And when the shooting finally stopped, he could not resist looking back down at the scene. The four victims, all men, being dragged into the trench, two of the Falangists shoveling soil over the bodies, the rest sharing cigarettes, laughing and joking. It was all so antiseptic. Just a piece of routine business.

'Who?' said Jack, when the men had climbed back into the truck and driven away. 'The dead.'

'In each concentration camp,' said the *Capitán*, 'they have lists. The lists have the names of all prisoners and the towns where they lived. From time to time, they send the lists to those towns. The *Falangistas* in the towns read the lists. They look for anybody political. Socialist. Communist. Anarchist. *Sindicalistas*. Then they go to the camp with a wagon. Come back with them. And then...'

'Always?'

'Always. And sometimes they kill because they think the people have helped units like mine. That they have helped the *guerrilleros*. Normally they are wrong. But they kill all the same.'

'How many? Killed like this?'

'Many, English. They say thousands.'

'Tell me about the others,' the *Capitán* asked him, more than a week later, as they climbed a ridge, back in the comparative safety of the mountains again. High in the freezing Sierra de Ayllón. Somewhere above Valverde de los Arroyos. 'The *Machados*. At Covadonga.'

Jack's Spanish improved every day now, as did the *Capitán*'s willingness to converse. But, even so, it was difficult to find the right words. For all manner of reasons. Yet he did his best to tell their stories.

'There are many groups?' he said, when the tale was told. '*Guerrilleros*? Like the *Machados*. Like your group.'

'The *Machados* are different. Anarchists.' The *Capitán* spat. 'Not part of the Fourteenth. You understand? We are the Fourteenth *Cuerpo* of the Guerrilla Army.'

'How big? The *Cuerpo*.'

'Three thousand, English. More or less. Four Divisions. In Andalucía. In Extremadura. In Aragón. And here, in the Centre.'

'And you have a General. General Lion. I will meet him in Madrid?'

'Yes. But in Madrid he is not the Lion. To us, here in the war, he is the Lion. There, he is General Kotov.'

And the *Capitán* began to sing, softly. The same tune that Bigote had given them in the hours before the raid. But the words seemed different now.

'*When you enter Madrid, the first thing you'll see…*'

He repeated the line.

'*Are the* chulos *with moustaches, sipping coffee and tea.*'

'*Chulos*?' Jack asked. 'What are they?'

The *Capitán* laughed.

'A man who is the *jefe* for whores, English. You understand? But the Lion is not one of those. Not really.'

Not really, thought Jack. *No, but this Lion — General Kotov. Russian, then?* No big surprise, he supposed. The *Capitán* and his men, like so many he had met, staunch members of the Communist Party. Many of the Internationals at San Pedro too, of course. Not all, but many. And Jack admired them. At least they were fighting the fascists. Yet the idea began to grow in him that there might just be some connection between Valerie Carter-Holt's work as an agent for the Comintern and this absurd effort to bring him all the way to Madrid.

'And how can we pass through the lines?'

He had been astonished that they had come so far and relatively so easily. There had been army patrols, of course. But far fewer than he'd supposed. And most of their tactics seemed determined by the need to avoid Falangists in the small villages, or barking dogs in farmyards. But the *Capitán* had warned him several times that they would soon need to cross the front lines separating Franco's forces besieging Madrid from the defenders' northern trenches. Jack imagined a version of Flanders, the Western Front, his father's traumatic experiences there. Yet, strangely, the nearer they came towards the Front, the more the *Capitán* appeared to relax, to make more frequent forays for supplies, even allowing Jack, on occasion, to accompany him.

'You will see, English,' he said. 'You will see!'

'And you, *Capitán*. How long in the army?'

His age was indeterminable. Forty, perhaps. Yet he could have been more. Or considerably less. But Jack wondered how his own face must look now: a lifetime away from the comfort of hotel rooms; these weeks in the mountains; the bruising that was only now finally disappearing from his cheek; the eye patch; and the beard he'd cultivated since Barcones – if it had, indeed, been Barcones – where the *Capitán* made it clear that all intimacies have their limit, in this case the line being drawn at sharing a razor.

'In the army?' said the *Capitán*. 'Since '24. They sent me to Morocco. To fight the Rif.'

Jack remembered the Rif Wars. From school. And university. Legendary tales of Berber tribesmen against the colonial armies of both France and Spain. Spanish military disasters had led, in part, to Spain's previous military *coup d'état*, in 1923, when Primo de Rivera had seized power. Yet it was still PC Wren's novel, *Beau Geste*, which gave him the most vivid images of the conflict.

'And now the Moors fight for Franco,' said Jack.

'Not all, English. There are still Moors, many of them, who want independence. There was a chance. For Spain. Weeks after Franco's rebellion. Negotiations. Between the Moroccan Nationalists and Largo Caballero. Imagine. A revolution in Morocco. What would Franco have done then? Robbed of his *Regulares*? In that case, he could not have won. Never.'

'What happened?'

'What do you think? Largo Caballero happened. The bloody Socialists happened. There are many in our government who are still imperialists. Colonialists. They did not want to lose Morocco. To give them independence. So the rest of us must lose Spain.'

'The war is not lost. Not yet.'

'Not yet. But our unit was at Teruel last winter, English. Then down on the Front at Córdoba and Granada. Then up on the Ebro. We've seen the way things are going. But, all the same, even if the Popular Front falls, the fight will continue.'

'And me, *Capitán*. Why am I going to Madrid?'

'Where else would you go, comrade?'

They lay on the lip of a low rise, looked out over a snow-smeared plain, a crumpled and unmade sheet between this bed head ridge and its twin. It was quiet. Extraordinarily so. As though both violator and victim had risen in the morning and simply slipped away to eat breakfast together.

Peaceful, Jack thought.

'Where is the Front?' He shivered, cocked his head to one side as he was wont to do these days. He thought it helped improve his limited peripheral vision.

'You're lying on it!' The *Capitán* reached into his haversack, took out his pair of ancient binoculars, scanned the horizon.

'It is not as I imagined.'

'English, nothing has happened here for many months now. Franco will have his army here and there. Around Madrid. But he does not need it everywhere. We cannot attack him from our positions. And if he keeps his men together, in blocks, he can feed them. He can guard them from sickness. He can make them warm in winter. But over there...' He nodded towards the opposite ridge. 'Over there it is different. Poor bastards.'

The drone of bombers. Familiar. They'd heard them every morning for the past week.

'And in Madrid,' said Jack, 'they bomb each day?'

'You will see. In a few days now.'

'When do we cross?'

'Soon,' the *Capitán* murmured, but he was focused on a small settlement down to their right. Mostly ruins. Shell-damaged. 'Perhaps.'

'Something there?'

'*¡Venga!*' The *Capitán* rose, unslung the machine gun, moved forward at a crouching run, diagonally across the slope and away from the ruins, into a famished gulley. It dipped down to cut a farm track, leading away to the settlement and, as their boots touched the sandy gravel, an engine roared into life from among the buildings. '*¡Puta Madre!*'

And Jack, stumbling behind, stole a glance towards the abandoned hamlet, saw an army truck lurch from its hiding place in a roofless barn. There were soldiers standing in the back, with rifles.

Crack.

The dirt and snow kicked up at Jack's feet, made him run faster, the lorry's engine screaming louder behind him. The *Capitán* leaping and bounding down the gulley, in a series of zigzags, keeping low.

Crack. Another bullet whined from a slab of slippery rock, inches from Jack's fingers as he used it to steady himself in his descent. He flinched, fell, picked himself up again. Saw the truck bouncing over the rough ground to his right, running almost parallel with him. And then he saw it slew to a halt. There were two more shots, though they seemed to go wide. Shouts. But, by then, Jack and his guide were out of the arroyo, sprinting across open ground until, without warning, the *Capitán* stopped, threw himself down, stared around him. Jack dropped too.

'*¡Joder!*' the *Capitán* panted, as two more shots barely missed them. But it wasn't the bullets that occupied him. It was the strange patches of recently cultivated land, the snow more sparse on the broken ground. Small patches, scattered at random around them. '*Minas,*' he said. And then he was on his feet again, dragging Jack behind him, running a serpentine path between the death-sown plots until they dropped into a trench, half-collapsed. Welcome cover though.

'Mines,' said Jack. 'Bloody mines.'

'Don't worry, English. Now they are *our* mines. Those bastards lay them down. We pick them up. Put them somewhere else. To stop their tanks. But don't worry, my friend. They will not trouble us unless you are heavier than you look! Still, best to avoid them, no?'

He began to clamber out of the ditch. Then was flung backwards. *Crack*. The sound only carried to Jack at the same moment as the *Capitán* was hit. Yet it had carried to him, not from behind, but from somewhere ahead. Somewhere distant. There was blood. The Spaniard coughing, gasping for air. The breath coming in bubbling bursts of agony. And Telford found himself grabbing the man's ankles, hauling him up the side of the trench, knowing that he was making a target of himself for whoever had taken that shot, as well as for the soldiers behind them. But that rage again. Mindless red rage as he pulled at the *Capitán's* lapels, ignored the bullets, heaved the man up onto his shoulder, staggered on towards their own lines where, he now knew, they could not distinguish between friend and foe. So he shouted the word *'Amigo'* over and over again. As loud as he was able.

He only looked back once. Just after he had raised himself upright – almost upright – under the *Capitán's* weight. The army truck still stood on the far side of the minefield, perhaps fifty yards back, the soldiers scattered around it, loading and firing as fast as they were able. But, standing on the bed of the truck, staring back at him, was an unmistakable figure. One that Jack would never forget. The Guardia Civil *Teniente*, Enrique Álvaro Turbides.

Chapter Fourteen

Friday 16th December 1938

It struck Jack that the Gaylord Hotel must be eminently suited to a Soviet propensity for intrigue and espionage. A discreet location, on a street with no traffic, Calle Alfonso XI, in a quiet but well-heeled district, yet very close to the Spanish War Ministry buildings, this latter, on the Plaza de Cibeles, heavily guarded, despite the Government itself no longer being in Madrid.

A couple of shaven-headed Slavic thugs, dressed like Chicago gangsters, stopped him just inside the opulent entrance, one of them carrying a machine gun very similar to the weapon Jack had used to take that second life. They frisked him, while Jack stared in wonder at the crystal chandeliers, the gold leaf worked into the oak paneling, the bas-relief semi-naked nymphs adorning the walls. It sounded like a party was in progress. Dance music drifted on cigar smoke. And he thought he heard champagne corks a-popping somewhere within.

'Telford,' he said. 'Jack Telford. To see General Kotov.'

But he had barely finished the introduction before a thickset man with carefully oiled hair marched to meet him, hand outstretched. The grip was cold and hard, as though the fellow's fingers had been chiseled from some Russian rock face, and his features carved from the same stone.

'Comrade Telford,' he beamed. 'Most welcome. You risk so much. To come here.'

Jack looked around, wondered if he had fallen down some Lewis Carroll rabbit hole.

'It feels remarkably safe, General. In Gaylord's at least.'

The General laughed. A charming laugh. It matched the ambience.

'Oh, we're too near the Prado for any harm to strike us here. Franco would not dare bomb the Prado. No, of course he doesn't know that it is empty but, for the time being – In any case, I meant your journey from Burgos. And across No Man's Land. What is it that our Spanish friends call it? *Tierra de Nadie.* Wonderful. Carrying poor Fidel Constantino on your back. Remarkable.'

Hardly on my back, thought Jack. *I had to drag the poor bugger by his leg most of the way.*

'The *Capitán* you mean? It was the least I could do. He saved me from the firing squad, didn't he?'

'The thing we need to talk about, comrade. And it seems that, now, you have saved his life too. But all that can wait. First, some vodka. Yes? You've eaten, I assume.'

'At the hotel. Thanks.' He'd heaved the *Capitán* through the Republican trenches without further mishap and in time to see some hapless sniper taken away for punishment – and Jack had carefully avoided any questions about the man's potential fate. But, from there, a makeshift ambulance had borne them through Guadalajara and into the northern outskirts of Madrid itself. To the converted hotel hospital where the *Capitán*, barely still alive, had insisted on telephone calls being made. 'And it seems,' said Jack, 'that I'm in your debt for picking up the bill there too.'

'Debt? We talk about that later, as I say. For now, the vodka.' An imperious flick of his wrist brought a scurrying waiter. A bottle. Two glasses, filled to the brim. 'Your health, Comrade Telford. *Na Zdorovie.*' The General opened his mouth wide, tossed the glassful to the back of his throat, swallowed in one gulp, while Jack sipped cautiously at the limpid firewater, unable to stomach the stuff. Part rebellion against the ostentatious surroundings. Something unethical about all this luxury. But, mainly, it was so many weeks of frugality. The effects on his system. And, when the caviar arrived, Jack thought he would be physically sick. But the General seemed not to notice, nudged Jack's arm before downing his second glass. 'Ah,' he said, 'here is somebody else who wants to meet you. Ilya! *Idi syuda, tovarishch.*' The newcomer was slim. Sharp Jewish features. Spectacles and a thatch of black hair. A pipe smoker. An attractive younger woman on his arm. '*Ilya, eto tovarishch Telford.*' Jack shook hands. 'Sadly,' said the General, 'Ilya's English is not good. But he speaks French. Well,' he swallowed another vodka, 'he says that he speaks French – though he almost got into a fight with

Hemingway because of it. Something lost in translation, I think. But look at you. Like Comrade Marx himself. The beard!'

Jack raised a self-conscious hand to his chin. Facilities at his new lodgings were adequate, though he'd still not acquired a razor.

'*Parlez-vous français?*' Ilya asked him, while the General slobbered over the young woman's fingers, called for more glasses, another bottle. And yes, said Jack, in his best Worcester Royal Grammar School French, he spoke a little. Asked whether Ilya was himself a correspondent, for he had the air of a journalist. 'Yes indeed,' Ilya told him. 'For *Izvestia*. But tell me about your own newspaper, comrade. They say it is one of the only socialist journals in England. The only one to consistently support the Republic. Apart from the *Daily Worker*, naturally.'

Jack explained. *Reynold's News* had been bought by the National Co-operative Press nine years earlier. A Sunday newspaper. But yes, radical. A voice for the Co-operative Movement. And its editor, Sydney Elliott, had worked tirelessly to support the Republic. The United Peace Alliance. The Milk for Spain Campaign. Funds to support the Basque Refugee Children.

'And the politics of your *Reynold's News*,' said the General, in English. Jack had assumed he'd been taking no notice, for he seemed so entranced by Ilya's attractive companion. 'You agree with it?'

'My editor sent me to Spain so I could research what he calls the Third Story. He thinks people don't give a shit any more about whether the Popular Front is fighting to defend democracy. Or whether Franco is fighting to stop the Reds. He thinks we should be writing this Third Story. The Popular Front gets elected in '36. Then Franco's military coup. And, at least in the beginning, it's the ordinary workers who organise themselves to stop him. Because, as Sydney Elliott says, Popular Front or no Popular Front, the people of Spain had started their own revolution. So that's our editorial line, General. How this is a war in which ordinary Spanish workers have defended their fight-back against a feudal aristocracy and a feudal church.'

Jack thought that he'd quoted Sydney correctly. But what had he said besides? Pulitzer stuff. Only Jack had still not written it.

'And you believe?' the General sneered. 'The issue is that we cannot tolerate yet another fascist state in Europe. They threaten us all, Comrade Telford. Our only duty is to destroy fascism. And all those who might hinder our efforts to do so. Wherever we find them. That is the Third Story. The one that counts.'

Ilya, the *Izvestia* correspondent, pretended to admire the ceiling decoration.

'Have a care, my friend,' he murmured in French, as though to himself. 'Dangerous ground. Dangerous ground.'

'Time for us to talk privately, I think.' The General snatched up the bottle, their two glasses, swaggered towards the flamboyant staircase.

'I wonder, General,' said Jack, 'did you ever hear of a Guardia Civil lieutenant called Turbides?' Even though it was only a couple of days, he had already begun to doubt the evidence of his own eye, wondered whether Turbides was now appearing to him as a vision, in the same way as his father and Colonel Telford, or even the *Jefe*. Though they, of course, were all dead and Turbides was, so far as he knew, still very much alive. And, anyway, a momentary glance, at some distance, while he was trying to shoulder that burden of the *Capitán*? It could have been anybody, could it not? Any oversized fellow in an army uniform.

'Is there reason? That I should have heard of this man?' There was not. But Jack told his story in any case, sitting in that empty first floor room, furnished with nothing but two dining chairs, one facing the other, across a simple card table. He even took a glass of vodka himself in the course of the tale's telling. 'Perhaps not so strange,' said the General, when it was done. 'You say that Constantino allowed you to go with him. When he was visiting the villages to find food. Safe houses, yes. But that was foolish of him. There are spies for Franco everywhere. Have you seen today's paper? A whole nest of fascist informers uncovered in the Catalan Zone. Two hundred death sentences to be carried out. How easy would it have been for somebody to see you? The eye-patch, Comrade Telford. Your very English face, even with the beard. It would not have been so hard to work out where you were both headed. Or perhaps this Turbides was simply a figment of your imagination. You must have felt, perhaps still feel, somewhat – Disorientated. Is that what you say?'

'Disorientated hardly does it justice, General. In fact, I was thinking of 'phoning home. Family. Friends. You understand? When I was in Burgos, they told me that my obituary had already been posted. I suppose they must be right.'

'I imagine so. I have only seen the obituary for Miss Carter-Holt. In *The Times*, naturally. Very moving. But no mention of you, I'm afraid. Swimming accident. Yes? Though your own newspaper, this *Reynold's News* – So, why not? We can arrange something, I'm sure. A call to London. Perhaps a little money too. But, for now, you must humour me, comrade. I should like to know something of your background. You went to Eton, perhaps?'

'Eton? God, no. The Worcester Royal Grammar School. Then university in Manchester. All very provincial, I'm afraid. But why are you asking me this?'

'Ah, Manchester. Very political town, they tell me. Engels. And Karl Marx again.' He leaned across the table to tweak Jack's beard. 'They worked there together, did they not?' Jack remembered a visit he had made to Chetham's Library. The table in the alcove where Marx and Engels had thrashed out their philosophies. Painful nostalgia once more. 'You must have been very political yourself, I suppose.'

'Editor for the college magazine, so I had to be a bit neutral,' Jack lied. 'President of the Esperanto Movement though.'

'Yes, I heard about your fluency with Esperanto. The language of spies, of course. Comrade Stalin has decreed it so.'

'Then I shall avoid using it to speak with him should we ever meet.' But Jack wondered precisely how General Kotov knew about the Esperanto. He hadn't used it since Covandonga. And the last time he recalled its mention had been during an interview after their release. An interview with the Military Governor of Asturias. And that strange fellow, Vice-Consul Harold Fielding. From San Sebastián. Jack had first met him when the diplomat was also sent to investigate Julia Britten's death. And then, later, when he had acted as negotiator at Covadonga itself. Something between him and Carter-Holt too. Something he'd never quite fathomed. She'd admitted sleeping with the man when they'd been in Santander. Old acquaintances, she'd said. *How deep does this rabbit hole go?* he wondered, his head spinning now.

'I'm sure Comrade Stalin would be more interested in why such an ordinary fellow as yourself – I mean no offence, of course, when I say that – should be held for sentencing by a Military Tribunal and with the certainty of a firing squad at the end of it.'

'You never told me how that should be such common knowledge, all the way here, in Madrid. Or why it should be so important that it took a special operation to get me here.' *Not to mention*, Jack thought, *the death of poor Bob Keith.*

'An innocent man, facing the firing squad? How could we let such an injustice stand, Comrade Telford? What is it your poet says? *"Any man's death diminishes me. Because I am involved in mankind."* We have our contacts, even in San Pedro de Cardeña. Word came to me that you were sentenced to death for your journalism. It intrigued me. And I thought we might have some use for you.'

Jack shrugged, wished he'd not downed that last glass. He wondered how many deaths already lay at this man's door. How many more would be piled there in future.

'That's what they said. At first. They'd intercepted an article I was trying to send back to England. And it's happened before. You know that, General.'

'Koestler,' the General smiled. 'Yes, we know all about the Koestler case.'

'Exactly. Working as a correspondent without authorisation. A capital offence just by itself. But then they found the gun.'

'Tell me about the gun, Comrade Telford. You had a gun?'

'I had this plan. To assassinate Franco. We'd been so close to him. At Santiago de Compostela. I couldn't believe how easy it was. To get close. It gnawed at me. The idea that I could play a part. Kill the *Caudillo*.'

'How original. And who put that idea in your head, I wonder? Miss Carter-Holt, perhaps.'

'I've no idea what you mean, General. And why should you think so? A rabid supporter of Franco, wasn't she?'

'You were with her when she died. And then you ran.'

'She'd been decorated by Franco. It seemed a fair bet they'd think I had something to do with her death. So I ran.'

'And did they accuse you of killing her?'

'They accused me of many things.'

'But did you kill her, Comrade Telford?'

Jack struggled to clear his head. This was it. Carter-Holt the Soviet agent. An assassin for the NKVD. And here he now found himself, in the lair of the NKVD itself. This General Kotov its head in Moscow. Wanting to know whether Jack had been responsible for their hired assassin's death. And the contact in San Pedro? He recalled the conversation with the German. Karlsen. *'You're certain, Herr Telford, that you were not in Fräulein Carter-Holt's confidence? She never mentioned Willi Müntzenberg, for example?'* What had he told Karlsen? *Oh, what tangled webs...*

'Not exactly. An accident, General. On the train back to San Sebastián, there had been certain – Intimacies. You understand, General? I hated myself for it. We were poles apart, after all. Hardly agreed about anything. Politics. The war. But then she suggested we go for a morning swim. I agreed. Couldn't really say no to her, truth be told. Plucked up the courage to tell her I wanted to end the affair though. I'd found out something, you see...'

'And that was...?'

'A rival, I'm afraid. Bloody British Vice-Consul from San Sebastián. Long story. Jealousy. Blind jealousy. But we argued, and I hit her. Too hard. She went under and the tide took her. I tried to get to her. But too late.'

'So you *did* kill her.'

Jack took a deep breath, took the plunge.

'Of course I killed her. Fascist bitch!'

The expression of stunned surprise on General Kotov's face, at the brutally frank admission, stayed with Jack all through that long afternoon in the cinema's cosy comfort.

He left Gaylord's with a fistful of *pesetas* and an instruction that he should return again the following morning, but should not attempt to contact England until then. First stop, a *papelería*. Notebooks, the best he could find. A pen. Some pencils. So he could begin recording his journey, his weeks since San Sebastián. An account of San Pedro de Cardeña, as he had promised Major Frank Ryan. And his first impressions of the city. They crowded his mind, begging to be released, to be spewed onto his new and precious pages, just as soon as he could find a table at which to write. Madrid, shrouded in the night fogs of winter. It would be a bad one, everybody told him. The worst. Warnings about the dangers of *sabañones* – chilblains, he now understood. The Madrid of grey, decaying plaster, peeling paintwork and slogan consecrations. The Madrid of owl-eyed women with gunmetal cheeks and threadbare rags.

The Madrid over which hung the constant pall of wood smoke, whether from cooking fires or timber beams, blazing in the bombsite gaps where houses once stood. The Madrid now surviving at the end of time itself, at the end of its tether, literally the end of the line. The Madrid of twisted tram rails, where the soot from incendiary fires turned to tar beneath your feet, and where the music of the streets was made by the constant tinkle of shattered glass. The Madrid of occasional stray rifle bullets, or the lottery game of navigating Shell Alley – that stretch along the Gran Vía and the Calle de Alcalá, with shells randomly falling all the way to Cibeles. The Madrid in which Franco's forces had held its salient in the University complex for two whole years, a short walk from the centre, and from which it could direct those artillery strikes, or call in the air raids that shook the city almost daily – raids by which watches could be set, sirens sending besieged citizens scuttling to their shelters, while the Junkers and Capronis overhead hummed their own twin-noted mockery of a song. *Give-in. Give-in. Give-in. Give-in.*

Second stop, an *estanco*, a long wait in a queue to buy his own cigarettes and a few spare packets for his intention to visit the *Capitán* in hospital. A copy of *ABC* – a Madrid version of the paper he had read so many times during the tour, back in September. Only *that* had been the edition printed in Sevilla, in Nationalist territory and under Franco's control. Still twenty-five *céntimos*, but the tone of this one obviously quite different. Here was the article mentioned by the General. The fascist spy network uncovered in the Catalan Zone. Here, too, a report of the reception given to International Brigade volunteers from Britain on their return home yesterday to London. Outrage, as well, about the Westminster debate on the extent to which Italy continued to provide troops for Franco; about the British Government's certain knowledge of that ongoing involvement; about Chamberlain's failure to challenge this at the Non-Intervention Committee; and about his refusal to do so during a forthcoming visit to Rome. Now, said the paper, Chamberlain would appease Mussolini in Rome just as he had appeased Hitler in Munich. It all felt very depressing. The Internationals supporting the Republic now mostly withdrawn. Those supporting Franco apparently multiplying. One question on everybody's lips. When would Spain fall?

Yet on the back page there were theatre and cinema listings. And it was these that took him to his third destination. The Madrid-Paris.

One of the picture houses on the Gran Vía. A song-and-dance show. *Roberta*. Randolph Scott. Irene Dunne. Fred Astaire. Ginger Rogers. The dialogue all dubbed into Spanish, naturally. But the numbers? All mercifully in the original. Jack snoozed through most of it. The effect of the vodka. His escape from General Kotov's clutches. But he woke for each of the songs. Loved them. *Smoke Gets In Your Eyes*. And *I Won't Dance*. In fact, he sat through the whole thing twice, arriving halfway through and leaving, more or less, two showings later, at the same point. For there was one more thing he had learned, at least, about life under siege in Madrid. It was this. That the Nationalist artillery, able to receive and read precisely the same edition of *ABC de Madrid*, honed their skills each day by targeting shelling upon the precise location, and the precise time, at which audiences would be filling the street outside a particular cinema or theatre.

In Madrid, Jack knew, only a fool waited until the curtain came down.

Chapter Fifteen

Saturday 17th December 1938

He was lying awake in the still-dark hour before dawn: wondering whether the General had truly accepted his tale; worrying about the precise use that the NKVD might have for him; and rehearsing in a thousand different ways the manner in which he might break the news to England that he was still alive. But then, outside in the Plaza de Santa Ana, there was a truck. Coming fast. Much faster than the other traffic that had passed beneath his window at regular intervals through the night. Grinding gears. And, as it blustered to a halt outside, Jack was out of bed, fumbling frantically for his clothes, living again the nightmare of the Hostal Toledo in Burgos. The same yelling and screaming below. The same clatter of boot studs on the pavement. Hammering upon the hotel doors.

Jack cursed himself for not having identified an escape route, a bolt-hole. And he should have done so. How could he spend so many sleepless hours contemplating the General's motives and intentions without playing through the worst potential outcome. But as he snatched up his meager possessions, the prized overcoat, the cigarettes, burst out into the corridor, reached the staircase, he realised that the commotion all seemed confined to the entrance lobby, three floors below. A dozen or more raised voices, each competing with the others. Impossible to disentangle the sense of it all. And edging his way down the stairs simply made it worse, the confusion more profound as it became louder. Yet, when he reached the top of the final flight, he saw one man trying to restore some order. A tall, thin fellow in his dressing gown. Domed forehead. Spectacles.

'Quiet! Quiet, please,' he was saying, and holding two of the Hotel Victoria's waiters from the assault they so plainly wanted to launch upon the armed and boiler-suited militiamen crowding in the doorway. The waiters seemed to share considerable support for their intentions from those other guests filling the lowest stairs. 'For the love of God,' shouted the man in the dressing gown, so slowly and deliberately that Jack could follow his Spanish perfectly, 'there's no problem here. I shall go with them. And be quite safe.' He turned to the militiamen, spoke sternly to them, forced them to lower their rifles, ushered them back out onto the pavement before a final admonishment to the excited waiters. Then he pushed his way up the stairs, smiling at Jack as he went past. 'Well,' he said, 'at least I am allowed to get dressed. Before they shoot me.'

An hour later, in the hotel bar, Jack was still trying to work out whether the man had been joking. He must have been, surely. For the Hotel Victoria had returned entirely to normality. One of the same waiters had taken his order, grinned politely when he asked for coffee, but nodded with enthusiasm at his request for bread, oil and salt. And as Jack contemplated the arrival of his breakfast, he glanced around the other tables, his eye caught by the same dome-headed man from the altercation. Without dressing gown, of course, but now sporting a clerical collar and a suit, originally charcoal grey wool but so worn at shoulders, lapels, elbows and knees that it gleamed like shot silk. The same smile.

'Good morning,' he said, in heavily accented English. 'Again. You want?' And he waved a hand towards the empty chair at his own table.

Jack accepted the proffered place.

'It's good to see you safe. Father...?'

'Lobo. Father Lobo. And you?' Jack introduced himself. He knew that *lobo* meant wolf in Spanish, wondered whether he'd heard correctly. 'There was no danger, *Señor* Telford. As you see.'

'Those *milicianos*. All Anarchists, aren't they? A reputation for shooting priests.'

'Even Anarchists have mothers, my son. And when a mother is dying, need a priest, they come for me. Curse themselves for doing it. Yet still come for me. But you. Why you here? Most internationals gone now.'

'A long story. I was in prison. Burgos. But I escaped and came to Madrid.'

Father Lobo examined him closely as the bread arrived. Then he examined the small pieces of toast with the same precision. He picked up one of the slices and blessed it.

'Twelve *pesetas* per kilo for flour. On the black market. The official price set by the *Junta de Defensa* is two. In Madrid we are starved and robbed at the same time. And your eye?'

'Lost that in Burgos too.'

'But not a soldier, I think.'

'No. A journalist, Father.'

'I have a good friend who is journalist. For a long time, he was our Voice of Madrid. Broadcast. Every night. Help us survive. Through all the death. All that madness. But not here now. He is gone to France. And, soon, to England. To work with your BBC. World Service. Spanish Section. He will be good. But I miss him.'

'Lucky man,' said Jack. 'That's my ambition too. One day. To work with the BBC.'

'Then when I speak him next, I give him your name. Who knows?'

'That would be good. But could I ask another favour, Father Lobo? I think I'd like to interview you.'

'Now, *Señor* Telford?'

'I have an appointment, Father. But later?'

'Of course. And your meeting?'

'At the Hotel Gaylord.'

'Then may God protect you, my son. For there is more danger to you in the Hotel Gaylord than for me in the company of those *milicianos*.'

Back at the Hotel Gaylord, yesterday's party spirit seemed entirely evaporated. More military uniforms in evidence. Russian uniforms. And those wearing the sandy green of the Red Army now included General Kotov, disentangling himself from the arm of a sinuous woman who flattered Jack with her best business smile, poppy-glossed, before sliding along the bar rail to another customer. But there was no private room this morning. Simply more vodka. Here. Sitting on the bar stools.

'How was your journey, Comrade Telford?'

'I walked over towards the Paseo del Prado. Picked my way through the bomb craters. Caught the tram to Cibeles. And then...'

'The Metro would be safer. Though they tell me there are more people living down there than ever before.' Jack decided that General

Kotov did not possess the air of somebody who would ever have ridden the Metro. 'But I can provide you with a pass. Why pay when you can travel free, eh?'

'That's kind,' said Jack. 'But you've already been generous. And the waiters at the hotel seem to have adopted me. Keep giving me advice about the safest way to get around. Directions. That sort of thing.' It was the waiters, of course, who had given him that tip about leaving theatres before the final curtain fell. Waiters all too old, too young or too physically impaired to be any use at the Front.

'Waiters? At the Victoria? All Anarchists. Dangerous people to know, Comrade. Dangerous. And you would not want me to change my opinion of you, I trust. There is a benefit of the doubt to be considered here. Miss Carter-Holt was something of an asset for us. Her death a significant loss. I would not expect you to understand – though I appreciate your frankness in the matter of her death.'

'An asset? No, I certainly do not understand, General. But her death sits heavily on my conscience. Fascist or no fascist. As you said, every death touches our humanity, one way or the other. And I'm a journalist. Not a killer.'

'Yet the pen is mightier than the sword, they say. And I agree. A more powerful weapon. You writers may rarely get more than ink on your hands. Physically. But how often do your words help shape people's views? How frequently do they incite men to violence?'

Jack needed no lecture on this theme. While working on his Diploma of Journalism he'd studied every critical word ever written about his chosen profession. Every example of news print warmongering propaganda, from the incessant lies of Hearst and Pulitzer, which stoked up the Spanish-American War, to the inflammatory articles by former-Socialist Robert Blatchford, employed by Lord Northcliffe's *Daily Mail* to fuel public sentiment against the Germans in 1909.

'Well, now I've seen the ink on my own fingers turn blood red. In reality. Not once, but twice.'

'Truly?' said the General. He filled Jack's glass again. 'And the second time?'

'The *Capitán* – your Fidel – attacked a Guardia Civil post. A diversion, I think. But I killed one of the Civiles there.'

Hardly the same as killing Franco, thought Jack. It still rankled him that his own modest assassination plan had gone so badly wrong.

'I suspect there will be far more killing to do before we're through. We might have done enough here to stop Franco joining Hitler and Mussolini in the next round though, don't you think?'

'The Republic still hopes for a better outcome than that, General. Surely?'

'You're an idealist, Comrade Telford. Now that *is* a rare quality in a journalist. So. Killer. Idealist. Whatever should we make of you? And a better outcome may have depended on your own country's position, perhaps.' Something else upon which Jack needed no instruction. He had, after all, written about that very theme in the last copy he'd managed to send to London, from Santiago de Compostela.

'You mentioned helping me make contact with England, General,' he began, but Kotov was reaching over the polished walnut of the bar top, careful to avoid the slops and abandoned glasses. His fingertips locked around the edge of a newspaper from just under the counter, and he sat down again heavily.

'Here,' he said. 'I knew we should be able to find a copy.' It was *Reynold's News*. The edition from Sunday, 2nd October. The familiar banner. Sydney Elliott's bold headline: *Munich Agreement or Munich Betrayal?* And Jack almost choked, quickly wiped away a tear that threatened to run down his cheek. The day he had set out from Pamplona, bidden farewell to Father Ignacio. *Hell*, he thought, *it feels like ten years ago.* But the General was turning the paper, licking his thumb as he went through the pages, back to front. 'Ach!' he exclaimed, and thrust the Stop Press obituary notice at him.

'*The Editorial Board of Reynold's News must report, with great sorrow,*' Jack read, '*the information received yesterday evening from San Sebastián in Spain.*' The swimming accident. Reuters correspondent, Valerie Carter-Holt. But concern also about Jack's own disappearance. A eulogy about the quality of his work as a journalist. Details of his latest assignment. Fears that he may have died while attempting to save Carter-Holt. And that final, heart-breaking sentence. '*But wherever you are, Jack… God speed. Sydney Elliott. Editor.*'

'Sentimental fool,' said Jack. 'My editor.' It was intended as a piece of bravado, though it almost stuck in Jack's throat.

'And a poor judge of character, it seems.' The General snatched the paper back. 'What is it he says? *"May also have drowned during an unsuccessful effort to save the life of Miss Carter-Holt."* But it was this piece that really interested me.' He turned more pages. 'This.' Jack found himself confronting that same article he had written, then wired to Elliott. A commentary on Britain's brokerage of the Non-Intervention Pact, and its failure to act against Italian and German bombing of innocent civilians, and especially their attacks on British merchant shipping. 'And particularly this section,' said the General. 'Let me read it. *"Worse, we have allowed the Germans to be rewarded by General Franco for these violations. A reward of minerals, raw materials and resources. All that Hitler could possibly desire for the completion of his re-armament programme. From this, loyal reader, there can be only one conclusion. That a further global conflict now seems inevitable. And, when the conflict erupts, we Britons will not be the innocent victims. We shall have been the instigators."* You believe that, Comrade Telford? Really? That Britain will be responsible for the next war?'

'Where did you get this?' said Jack.

'A friend. In the British consulate. Somebody there must admire your writing. But do you? Believe what you have written.'

'Yes, of course. It's not all been one-sided, naturally.' Jack recalled the pride he'd felt in the early part of the war. British skippers were trying to break the Nationalist blockade of Bilbao. But those had been rare incidents in what Jack now understood to be a catalogue of calumnies. The Madrid Embassy's apparent foreknowledge of the coup months before it had actually taken place, and its failure to act on the information. And then the involvement of the British pilot, Bebb, and the murky Major Pollard in helping Franco fly from the Canary Isles to Morocco so that he could help lead the insurrection. Carter-Holt's insistence that Pollard was directly linked to the British Intelligence Services. 'But yes,' said Jack, 'I believe it.'

'And there is much more that you don't know, my friend.' He filled their glasses again. 'For example, Franco needed to airlift his *Regulares* from Morocco to the mainland. He needed help. He needed to phone his friends in Germany. To ask for planes. But he couldn't use the official telephone networks. Of course not. So he asked his other friends, the British in Gibraltar, if they'd mind him using their exchange. And, of course, they agreed. And when those German planes left Morocco, they flew through British airspace, over Gibraltar itself. Nothing. It was your Royal Navy in Gibraltar, Comrade Telford, that willingly relayed intelligence on the Republican fleet to Franco's commanders. And then they helpfully assisted Franco's forces and base in Algeciras by anchoring one of your dreadnought battleships across the bay to prevent the Republic's fleet from shelling the place. What are we supposed to conclude from all that, Comrade Telford?'

'That Franco has more influence with the British establishment than the Popular Front does.'

'Or perhaps that your leaders, Baldwin and now Chamberlain, would rather be in bed with Hitler than Soviet Russia. Despite what that choice will cost them – cost the whole world. So, tell me. This reward that your country has so willingly allowed Germany to acquire, those minerals – the pyrites, the antimony, the tungsten, all the rest – what is your source?'

'You don't have one of your own?'

Jack saw a nerve begin to twitch in the General's jaw.

'What we know, Comrade,' Kotov said, with exaggerated deliberation, 'is that the man who was once political adviser for Rio Tinto is now in Burgos. At Franco's headquarters.' Jack felt the room spin. Those sealed left eyelids throbbed for the first time in weeks. His hand began to shake, spilling vodka down his trousers. 'And that reminds me,' the General smiled. 'We must do something about your clothes. But Burgos. Painful memories?'

'I was there. At the Muguiro Mansion.'

'Not to chat with Captain Charles from the Rio Tinto Company, I suppose.' The General smiled. 'Once Commercial Secretary for your Embassy in Madrid. Not him?'

'No. The Guardia lieutenant I mentioned. Turbides. And a man with the even more unlikely name of Merry del Val.'

General Kotov slapped his own thigh, the blue jodhpurs.

'A case in point, my friend,' he shouted. 'His father. Spanish Ambassador to London. Did you know? The family has the ear of everybody in England from your fascist Lord Beaverbrook to Chamberlain. The royal family too. But this man from Rio Tinto. This Captain Charles. We know he sends reports. Regular reports. To London. About iron. About the pyrites. All now flowing from Spain to Germany's arms industry. The reports come through Madrid. Coded.'

'Why not through the British Embassy at Hendaye?'

The Madrid Embassy itself, and the British Ambassador, Clinton, had scuttled off to Hendaye, just across the border with France, not long after the Civil War broke out. And Clinton had retired the following year, leaving Republican Spain without an Ambassador from Britain for the past twelve months. To Jack, that spoke volumes.

'It seems this Captain Charles does not trust the staff there.'

'But Madrid?' said Jack. 'You already said that you've a friend within the Consulate.'

'A friend. But not in a senior position. Not to access such information. No, Comrade Telford, for that we need a man with very special talents.'

Chapter Sixteen

Sunday 18th December 1938

'Normally, Sunday is quiet,' said Father Lobo. 'Fortunately, most of our enemies over there are good Catholics. Apart from the *Moros*, of course.'

They stood on the broken ramparts of the old Montaña Barracks, wrapped in their overcoats, looking down from the upper slope of the ridge, over the Parque Oeste, towards the Manzanares River, the Casa de Campo beyond – all of it resembling nothing so much as the churned devastation of the Western Front – and north to the ruins of the University. For Madrid, it had all begun here. The day after Franco's insurrection. The General's misguided belief that the garrisons of Madrid would rise in his support. But they had not. And when the fascists had seized this barracks, the *milicianos* and Republican Assault Guards had taken it back in just two days, destroyed the place in the process, left many of the defenders dead in its rooms and revetments, killed others later at the Modelo Prison.

'Quiet for you too then, Father,' Jack smiled. 'Sundays.'

'In one hour, I say Mass. In the chapel of the Santísimo Cristo de la Paz.' He saw the surprise on Jack's face. 'Yes, my son. I know the stories too. The Godless Reds of Madrid. But how do you say? Writing on the wall? Even Comrade Negrín sees the need to allow our people their faith now. Not that we ever lost it. I have a house. On the Calle de Tamayo. An oratory. I have said Mass there for the past two years. For those who wanted. But now it is official again.'

'Writing on the wall?' said Jack. 'You think the war's lost.'

'Munich destroyed our last hope, *Señor* Telford. We're not fools. Why would England or France risk conflict with Hitler over Spain now, when they have just sacrificed Czechoslovakia to appease him. All we can do is pray that, one day, there will be a new, free Spain. The war is terrible. But I believe something good will come from it. And perhaps those other Spaniards, over there, may pray for the same thing.'

'One people,' said Jack, 'divided by a shared religion.' It was a poor attempt at parody, some recollection of a quote from Oscar Wilde. About Americans and British being identical, except in their language. 'You must relish these moments of peace, Father.'

'Hard to imagine from here,' said Father Lobo. 'You can't quite see them. But still there. Still full of soldiers. The trenches. Along the riverbanks. And the thousands who died. At the beginning. Be grateful you weren't here two years ago. Franco's troops just down below. Five minutes from the Plaza de España. They were thrown back. But that close. In the *barrio* of Carabanchel, we had to fight them street by street. You can still see them over there, though.' He pointed to a hill in the middle distance. 'On Cerro Garabitas. That's where they've got all their heavy artillery. When you see the shells fall on Madrid, that's where they're coming from. We tried to dislodge them a dozen times, but never succeeded.'

Jack had just walked here with Father Lobo. They'd passed through the rubble of Plaza de España on their way from the Metro. He knew how close it was.

'The *milicianos* threw them back,' said Jack. 'And the Internationals. Durruti and his men.'

'Durruti? Yes, while the Government ran away to Valencia. He was shot fighting for the University. Did you know? He died later, of course. And his funeral in Barcelona. They say it was the biggest funeral Spain has ever seen.'

'But you weren't there, Father? In the University?'

'Of course I was there. On a battlefield, there are few atheists, my son.' Chilling, so similar to something that Merry del Val had said to Jack in Burgos. 'But I never want to be in a place like that again,' the priest went on. 'Not ever. Our *milicianos* fought them room by room. Corridor by corridor. Lecture hall by lecture hall. I remember blessing a boy. Dying behind a barricade. And that barricade was built from great mounds of *Encyclopaedia Britannica*. You know where? In the *Facultad de Filosofía*.' The University's Philosophy Faculty. 'You can't see it from here. But it's up to the north. All in ruins now. Just a mile away. Such ironies!'

'You know what terrifies me most, Father? It's the normality of it all. Those people living in the Metro stations. As though that's the natural place to be. The fascists just over here. We could almost throw stones at them.'

'Normal. I suppose so. People are resilient. They adapt. And the thing that terrifies me, *Señor* Telford, is that the people of Madrid will adapt just as quickly when Franco eventually takes our city. How quickly will they stop calling each other *compañero*. How quickly they will go back to using *buenos días* instead of *salud!* How quickly they will remember to wear collars and ties. How quickly the Falange will be on the streets once more. How quickly they will forget what this has all been for.'

Once again, Jack remembered how close he had come to killing the *Caudillo*. To maybe ending this thing. To sparing the people of Madrid from their agonies. And his shame burned his brain.

Jack had finally been forced to tell General Kotov that most of his knowledge about the minerals deal between Franco and Hitler stemmed from the boastful information given to the tour group by their fascist guide, Brendan Murphy. Murphy had been proud of the fact, and Jack had not questioned him very much. But yes, it would make an interesting article. Perhaps not his Pulitzer piece, but good enough. And it would certainly stir things up at home. Embarrass the British Government too, which seemed to suit the General's agenda perfectly. There was the danger, of course, that Jack might be putting himself in the way of becoming yet another asset for the NKVD. Yet he could see little risk. And the prospect of wheedling his way into the British Consulate here offered him not only the potential for a good story, but also a potential avenue for him to get home. And, more immediately, a practical way to make contact with London. Better, the General had said, than using his own lines of communication, through the Telefónica building and its censors. There would need to be another invention, of course. Another fable about Jack's experience in San Sebastián. About Carter-Holt. About his journey to Madrid.

Yet that was all for tomorrow. He would visit the Consulate then. For today he walked the shattered streets of the Argüelles district with Father Lobo, left him there on the Calle de la Princesa to say his Mass, and made his way down into the nearest Metro station at Santo Domingo on the Gran Vía. He bought a ticket for Banco de España. Twenty-five *céntimos*. Line Two. And an attractive clippie snipped his ticket at the barrier, directed him to the platform, direction Ventas.

Jack wondered again how the system worked for those who had apparently made their homes down here. Other people came and went through the barrier with impunity, exchanging greetings with the young ticket puncher as though she were the concierge for their apartment block. She recognised them, clearly. Exchanged banter with them, yelled at the noisy children playing statues, or an exuberant chanting and clapping game – something about stealing bread – while their mothers folded blankets, stowed them neatly in their allotted place alongside the suitcases, brocade cushions, cooking pots and woven baskets from which their lives were ordered. Jack stroked his fingers down the ochre ceramic tiles of the wall, felt Madrid's heart vibrating within, then picked his way past a small girl distributing copies of the Communist Party daily, *Mundo Obrero*; past two old men absorbed in a game of chess; past a lad absorbed in a collection of Lorca's poetry; past the general odours of unwashed bodies and damp straw; and past a smartly suited man, furtively selling his wares from a bottomless Gladstone bag. Always a profit to be made, somewhere, in a war, he thought, and attracted hostile glances from each and every one of those he, himself, had studied. The obvious outsider. And how could you be anything else, he decided, if you haven't been here since it all began?

On the train itself, he tried to decipher the shouting, the staccato Madrileño slang. It sounded like collective rage. But against whom? He could not tell. Yet when he alighted at Banco de España, took the stairs to ground level, he found his way blocked by an anxious crowd. The religious Sunday morning truce was ended and Franco's artillery was busy again, shattering glass and mangling masonry, at that point where the Gran Vía put its neighbourly arm around the shoulder of the Calle de Alcalá, almost the eastern extremity of Shell Alley. Half-starved children howled in their mothers' arms. Men screamed near-hysterical pleas for calm.

'*¡Tranquilo! ¡Tranquilo!*'

Two years, thought Jack. *Two bloody years.*

He pushed his way through, emerged onto the street in a grey pall wafting towards him from the right, and driven by the wind-whistle howl of incoming high explosives, the taste of brick dust thick on Jack's tongue his whole body shaken by the vibration, his head ringing from the blast, perhaps a hundred yards away but still so loud that it stabbed him painfully, deafeningly, somewhere deep inside his inner ear. He turned his back on it all, followed the smoke until it rolled across Cibeles, with its sandbag bastions, then he turned right, along the Paseo, until the palatial grandeur of the Prado loomed ahead, and Jack swung left, to find the museum's only marginally less ostentatious neighbour, the Hotel Ritz.

'They say Mata Hari once stayed here,' the *Capitán* told him.

Jack had found him, still weak from loss of blood, on a camp bed in the hotel's former dance hall, surrounded by scores of others, sick and dying beneath the crystal chandeliers.

'With a room of her own, I hope,' he said.

The *Capitán* looked around.

'It's not so bad. Durruti died upstairs too. And I was here after Brunete. There were ten times this many.' All the hospital stench of disinfectant, carbolic, human faeces, vomit, stale food, hit Jack at the same time. 'Better now,' the *Capitán* murmured. 'Thanks to the Americans. Did you know Goff, English?' Jack admitted that he did not. 'Good man. One of the best. I was with him when we hit the Albarracín Bridge. Then Teruel. Carchuna too.'

'I know about Carchuna,' said Jack, remembering a story told to him by that British Vice-Consul, Fielding, from San Sebastián. Something between him and Carter-Holt, his brain reminded him. Said she'd slept with the man when they'd been in Santander. Bitch! The rabbit hole. He shook his head to clear it. 'Carchuna,' he repeated. 'Three hundred prisoners. You made them free.'

'What a day!' The *Capitán* smiled. 'But the rest, they were hard, English. Hard days. Not like your writers say. Just pain. Blood. Hard. But Goff, the big American. Mother of God, there was a man.'

'One of the Internationals?'

'Yes. And a volunteer to join the Fourteenth *Cuerpo*, the Guerrilla Army. But gone now. Back to America. I never thought...'

'What?'

'That I should love an American so much.'

'An American communist,' Jack laughed.

'Yes. So many of them. To come all this way. For Spain. And to pay for all this. Thousands of *pesetas*. Hundreds of thousands.'

Jack knew about the donations. Some of them at least. The Medical Bureau and Aid Spanish Democracy committees in the States. But there were always two sides to the Yanks. Always two sides.

'But the others,' he said. 'Americans who send money to help Franco. To help Catholics in the Nationalist Zone.'

'There it is, English. The struggle between Communism and the evil of Fascism. Always there now.'

Jack remembered a discussion on the same theme. The Paris Exposition. July '37. With Canadian art critic, Angela Alexander. Gazing down from the Trocadéro towards the Eiffel Tower, and the view blocked by those two monstrous pavilions confronting each other – the Third Reich's Volkshalle and the Palace of the Soviets. The shape of things to come. And she had defined Fascism. "An autocratic and class-neutral system of government, normally reacting to perceived socio-economic problems through the forceful promotion of insular Nationalism." She had invited Jack to respond with his own definition of Communism. "An autocratic and worker-centric system of government," he had said, pleased with himself, "normally reacting to perceived socio-economic problems through the forceful promotion of international Marxism." But even if he had been able to fit the concept into his meager Spanish, Jack would not have done so now.

'Well, I bring you cigarettes,' he said, instead, and tossed a couple of packets onto the blankets. The *Capitán* picked one of them up, grimaced.

'*Superiores*,' he said. Not *Luckies*. That's a shame. But did you meet the Lion?'

'The General. Yes. Why do you call him the Lion?'

'A joke, English. His real name. Leonid. It is what we call him. The Lion. And you found out, why you are important to him?'

'Yes, I think so. Do you know?'

'That is a thing between you and him. I don't need to know. But you have work to do now, I think. For Spain. For the war.'

Jack looked around the converted dance hall, unsure how to answer, saw a set of bookshelves at the far end.

'The hospital library,' he said. 'Can I look?'

He picked his way between the beds, reached the shelves and ran his finger along the spines, relishing the smell of paper and print, at least some minor relief from the overwhelming odours of illness. Novels mostly. Spanish. A few German books. The majority in English though. Nostalgia. And he pulled out one in particular. G A Henty. *Under Wellington's Command.*

'Nothing is perfect,' the *Capitán* told him, as he returned to the Spaniard's bedside.

'Do you think I could take this?' said Jack. 'Read it, then bring it back?' No idea of the Spanish word for *borrow*, he realised.

The *Capitán* examined the book's cover, but was none the wiser.

'As you wish. But, like I say, you are in the war now. We are all in the war. We take sides. Then we do our duty. Our enemies must die. Or we die. And to kill our enemies, we do whatever we are commanded to do. Anything.'

'Anything?' said Jack.

'Yes, English. Anything.'

'I did not like Hemingway very much,' Father Lobo was explaining later, in one of the bars in the Hotel Florida. Jack admired the American's writing style and had suggested meeting at the Florida as part of his personal homage to the man. The place had once been majestic, then the haunt of celebrities and prostitutes, afterwards yet another hospital, now simply as worn by war as the rest of Madrid. 'Not enough interest in telling the truth. The whole truth.'

'Warts and all,' said Jack, then had to explain the adage.

'Ah, yes. The warts. There were terrible things done at the beginning. Not just by the *fascistas*. And the fight for democracy? Of course. But democracy is the first victim of war. No? Hemingway could never bring himself to write about that. The need, sometimes, to suspend democracy, simply so it can live again. Those are warts, I think.'

'It should be the task of journalists,' said Jack, 'to confront the uncomfortable. If we simply paint things in black, or white, we have no real credibility.'

'I have an example,' said the priest. 'I was in Barcelona. In July. I read an article in *The Times*. About religious persecution in the Republican Zone. There is a British Jesuit. Burns. He writes these articles for them. About the six thousand priests killed here. But I wrote a letter to *The*

Times. A response. And they printed my letter. I wrote that every priest killed in this terrible war has died because they were also politicians. Many of them were active members of political parties. Fascists. They had actively taken part in the distribution of anti-government propaganda. At the beginning, those priests paid a price for their political allegiance. As Socialists and Communists have done in the Nationalist Zone. Ignorant people, wicked people, took their revenge. Individuals. Yet not once – not *once* – have the Republican authorities issued orders for the persecution of priests, nor prohibited freedom of worship. And the fact is that Franco's rebellion could never have started without the assistance of the Church. If there have been innocent victims, it is the Church itself that must carry the blame. And while the Republic's government has never once sanctioned the murder of innocents, Franco does so every day of his life.'

And I came so close to killing the monster, thought Jack. *So close.*

'Perhaps,' he smiled. 'But isn't truth itself just another of those warts? We can only ever tell as much truth as the times can stomach. Tell too much of it and our enemies simply seize upon those parts that suit their own propaganda, play them back to us, corrupted and broken.'

'It's an argument I've heard many times, my son. Usually from comrades in the Communist Party. Some of my dearest friends are Communists, of course. But they sometimes forget that other voices are crying to be heard.'

'Not Franco's Fifth Column?'

'Of course not. Though even they are beginning to smell victory, I think. There were a few at Mass this morning. Men and women I've not seen for two years. But now feeling safe enough to venture out once more. In the open. But that is my point. If, God forbid, we lose this war, have to meet those people again in the street, how will we do so if we allow everything to be black and white? So, no. The men I'm talking about are those crying out now to be heard on Madrid's future. You must meet some of them. Interview them. For your newspaper.'

'Yes,' said Jack. 'Naturally.' But he found himself unable to look Father Lobo in the face as he made the promise, stared instead down the passageway between the mirror-image bars of the hotel's *Granja* drinking hole. The Farm. For Jack's time in the mountains with the *guerrilleros* seemed at least to have sharpened his sense of danger – and he had just felt the rabbit hole deepen again.

Chapter Seventeen

Monday 19th December 1938

'The blasted bomb came through just there,' said the Consul. There was planking and stretched tarpaulin where finely moulded plaster relief decoration had once graced the classical ceiling. One of the walls had been recently rebuilt but not in character with the elegance, which Jack imagined the room must previously have possessed. 'Straight down the centre of the Union Jack we'd taken so much trouble to paint on the roof. Germans, you know.'

The Consul was tall, early fifties, the British cinema's caricature depiction of colonial diplomacy. Robert Donat, though without the moustache. Measured Oxbridge voice, slightly breathless. But the name? Milanes. And Jack wondered whether he was, perhaps, foreign born. After his encounter with the impeccable English of Merry del Val, he'd never judge a man by his accent again.

'Anybody hurt?' he asked.

'A disaster, Mister Telford. The chef, Fernando. Out of action for weeks afterwards. And poor Mrs Norris too. Need to introduce you, actually. Left her to do some digging when you arrived.' He tapped the side of his Roman nose, led Jack out of the abandoned Embassy building itself and hurried across the windswept courtyard, past the guarded iron gates onto the Calle Fernando el Santo. 'And hopefully there'll be a cup of Rosie Lee waiting for us.'

But there was no tea in the Consul's office, over in the consular annexe, further along the street. Simply a steel-eyed feline fellow, perched on the edge of the mahogany leather-topped desk.

'Telford?' he said, before Milanes had even closed the door.

'I was about to make the introductions, Mister Telford. This is Major Edwin. Assistant Military Attaché. He has a tendency

137

towards the impetuous, I'm afraid.'

The Major took a cigarette case from his inside jacket pocket, tapped a Capstan on the polished gunmetal, then put the smokes away without offering them around.

'A strange tale you've been telling, Telford.'

'Such is life, Major,' said Jack. 'Fact is often so much stranger than fiction. Don't you find?'

There was a tap on the door.

'The char, I suspect,' said Milanes, opening the door to admit a middle-aged woman with an air of authority exceeding even that of Major Edwin. 'The admirable Mrs Norris I mentioned earlier, Mister Telford.' She offered a polite good morning and set the silver tray on the consular desk, poured two cups of tea, asked Jack how he liked his own.

'Fully recovered, I hope?' he said.

She looked puzzled for a moment.

'Oh, the bomb,' she smiled. 'Almost two years ago, Mister Telford. Excellent treatment, as it happens. The British-American Hospital. And might I just say how much I admire your suit? Very dapper. You're a navy man?'

'It's the beard, I suppose. But no. Only really comfortable on *terra firma.*'

She was right though. He'd bought the suit early that morning. Decent shoes too. From the Torrijos market, out beyond the Retiro. You could buy anything, the waiters at the Hotel Victoria had told him. Black market. Paid an absurd price. And Jack had not enquired too closely about the suit's provenance. But yes, dark blue, almost a uniform cut. It lent him an obvious nautical air. The beard. The patch.

'Yet you weren't so particular about staying on dry land in San Sebastián, I understand,' Major Edwin sneered when Mrs Norris had left them. 'Or have I got the story wrong?'

Jack had already given a brief summary of his new yarn to the Consul, when he first arrived, the details taken down by a silent shorthand typist with a neat centre parting to her dark hair. Jack hadn't been able to discern whether she was Spanish or not.

'It was foolish really,' said Jack, assuming that the Major must have read the transcript. 'But Miss Carter-Holt insisted on taking a swim. Before we caught the train to Irún. It seemed a bit risky. Because of the time, I mean. To be honest, we didn't get on too well. I explained to Mister Milanes earlier.'

'If it's not too much trouble, perhaps we could hear it again. It's quite a tale.'

'Major,' Milanes snapped. 'Mister Telford has been through a great deal. He's a British citizen, after all. Entitled to the normal courtesies, don't you think? And won't you sit, Mister Telford?'

Major Edwin ignored him entirely, but Jack accepted the invitation, settled himself onto the green Chesterfield.

'You were saying. "Didn't get on too well." What does that mean, exactly?'

'Political differences,' said Jack. 'One thing and another. It had been a difficult trip. You know about Covadonga, of course. And then the incident at Santiago. Does anyone know whatever happened to the Ketterings, by the way?' The question drew blank stares from both Milanes and the Major. He was forced to explain. Catherine Kettering. The woman who had spat in Franco's face when they'd been presented at Santiago de Compostela. Then hauled off to prison. Jack had no idea of her fate. Actually, he lied, no idea why she'd even done such a thing.

'I shall make every effort to find out, Mister Telford,' the Consul promised. 'About what's happened to them, I mean.'

'Political differences?' said the Major.

'Loyal supporter of Franco,' Jack told him. 'Carter-Holt, I mean. Fascist to the core.'

'You're aware that her father is Secretary to the First Lord of the Admiralty?'

'Sir Aubrey?' Jack smiled. 'I don't know the gentleman. And he may not share her beliefs, I suppose.' Actually, Jack was certain that he would not. 'Thankfully, not everybody in high office within our country is a Nazi supporter. Not everybody, Major. And I may not have had much sympathy for his daughter but at least I insisted on accompanying her, though she wasn't happy about it. She swam out a long way. My fault, perhaps. For being there. Maybe – Anyway, she swam out a long way. Right out towards that island in the middle of the bay. I saw her wave her arms. Thought I heard her shout. So I swam after her. And then the current took me. I didn't see her again. Like a nightmare. Thought I'd drown. Not a bad swimmer, truth be told. But that tide...'

Jack sipped at his tea. The first he'd tasted since Dover. Waiting for the Night Ferry train. Three months before. What if he'd simply changed his mind? Headed straight back to London? Told Sydney that he hadn't been able to face the journey?

'Heavens,' said the Consul. 'I've swum at San Sebastián many times. Before the war, of course. Never realised it was so dangerous.'

Somewhere in the building, a dog began to yap. A rare sound. Decadent, Jack thought. He couldn't recall having seen a dog since his arrival in Madrid. Certainly no cats. Not now. Still the occasional salted cod to be found on a menu or kitchen table. But no more *conejo*, the waiters told him. No more "rabbit", they would smile.

The door opened again, and a white Westie came scampering and slithering inside, claws trying to find a purchase on chequerboard tiles, followed by its mistress, a robust lady in a grey tweed skirt and autumn-striped cardigan. The gentlemen got to their feet, and the terrier barked up at Jack as the introductions were made. The Consul's wife, Mrs Milanes.

'Please,' she said. 'Call me Mabel. Mrs Norris just told me you were here. Poor man. Quite an ordeal, I gather. And poor Valerie. Such a blow when we heard about her death. I wrote to her mother, of course. Dear Ursula. But you were quite the mystery man. Famous international correspondent!'

'Hardly famous, I'm afraid,' Jack smiled.

'Oh, tosh!' said Mabel. 'Disappearance. That made you famous, didn't it, John?' She turned to her husband. 'Have we still got copies of the papers? We certainly had *Reynold's News*, I think.' Jack guessed that they might not find it. 'But your family must be delighted to hear that you're safe and well, Mister Telford.'

'Actually,' said her husband, 'the poor fellow's not had a chance to call home yet. We were chatting about that earlier.'

'Good gracious. But you must do so straight away. Your poor mother. She's still with us, I hope?'

'Very much alive and kicking,' Jack smiled. 'And my sister. Your husband has kindly promised to let me use the blower later.'

'Then you mustn't keep the poor fellow from his family one moment longer than necessary, John,' she told her husband. 'And what are you doing for Christmas, Mister Telford?' The question took Jack by surprise. Christmas? He had no idea. 'If you've no other plans, you must come to us. Nothing too elaborate, naturally. But it should be fun. Dinner. Twelve-thirty for one? And then we have a wee party arranged for the afternoon. Buster! Come on, darling.'

Keaton or Crabbe? Jack wondered.

The dog was now snapping around Major Edwin's shins. The contempt on the man's face was palpable. He would have kicked the creature, Jack was certain, if he'd thought he could get away with it. And the terrier, now to-heel, was still following Mrs Milanes from the office, when the Major resumed the interrogation.

'What time was this, Telford?' he said. 'When you were caught on that ferocious ebb tide?'

Jack sat again.

'Not sure now. Before ten though. We were due to catch the train to Irún at eleven-fifteen. But that tide! It carried me clear out of the bay. Exhausted. Could barely keep my head above water. And the next thing I knew, I was being thrown against the rocks. It ripped me up quite badly. Lost my eye there. And then there was a boat. I don't remember much about it, but they hauled me on board.'

'Fortunate they happened along,' the Major sneered.

'I believe Our Lady must have smiled on me that day.' Something about the fellow told Jack he might just be Catholic, tried to keep his face straight, self-satisfied, when he saw the Major's features soften for the first time. 'Anyway, they took me along the coast. To a village. And they kept me there. For quite a few days, I think. More than a week anyway. Unconscious most of the time. Woke up when they stitched the eye though. And again, when the Guardia Civil raided the place.'

'Stitched your eye?' said Milanes. 'My goodness. Is it permanently damaged?'

'I'm afraid so. It was the eye itself. They stitched the lid to prevent infection. I think that's what they were saying.'

'And the Civiles were looking for you, Telford?' the Major pressed him.

'No, not for me. Turns out they were smugglers. I suppose that's why they didn't tell anybody I was there. Just glad they picked me up though. But then, to my surprise, the Civiles didn't take me back to San Sebastián. Hauled me off to their barracks in Bilbao. Asked me all sorts of questions about my activities as a journalist. It seems they'd picked up a copy of an article I'd wired home from Santiago. Didn't like the content. Gave me a rough time about not being authorised.'

'Like Koestler,' said the Consul.

'Wouldn't allow me to contact London,' Jack told him. 'Nothing. Then sent me on to Burgos. More interrogation. And I ended up in a prison. At San Pedro de Cardeñas. Waiting for a Military Tribunal to hear my case, they said. Anyway, one day they sent a gang of us down to the river for a bath. Some of the Internationals were being exchanged for Italians. Did that happen, by the way? The exchange?'

'Yes, it did. And more to come, we're told.' Milanes smiled.

'Good, I'm glad. But one of the boys didn't get away, I'm afraid. Bob Keith. Some sort of argument. They shot him. The guards, I mean. And then all hell broke loose. An ambush. Some of the guards killed. A raid by *guerrilleros*. And I got caught up in the middle of it all, somehow. I managed to explain to them, asked them to take me east. But they said that was too dangerous. Brought me south instead. To Madrid.'

'Brought you south,' the Major snorted. 'Two hundred miles? Across Nationalist territory. You could probably sell the story rights to John Buchan.'

'Major,' said Milanes, 'I see no reason to doubt Mister Telford's word. Have you any basis for challenging his account?'

'Not yet. But you may be sure that I shall do my best to check the facts.'

'You might begin, Major,' said Jack, 'with Captain Constantino. He's an officer with the Republic's Guerrilla Army, Fourteenth Corps. You'll find him in the hospital at the Hotel Ritz. He was wounded as we came through the front lines. And he'd been with me every step of those two hundred miles. Is it only that far, by the way? It seemed much further.'

Always good to have the last word, he thought, as the Major slammed the Consul's office door.

'We've become something of a backwater here, I'm afraid,' said Milanes. 'All the real action's in Valencia. Makes some of the chaps a little tetchy.'

'I'm sure the Major's simply doing his job, sir. But now I'm rather stuck. No passport. Nothing.'

'We can issue an Emergency Certificate, of course. Need a photograph.

Itinerary for your journey. Some independent references for the evidence section of your statement. *Et voilà*. Have you home in no time.'

'If I could get to the coast, Valencia maybe, I could find a ship. And the references? If I could contact my family. My editor, perhaps. Get the process moving. Meanwhile, I think a friend of mine was due to visit Spain too. Frederick Barnard. You know him?'

'Freddie? That dear boy. Wherever did your paths cross, Mister Telford?'

'Yes, Fredddie. And his book, of course. Is he still in Spain, d'you know?'

'Something of a saga too, as it happens. Nothing like your own. But serious enough. Some bounder stole his passport. On the Camino de Santiago, of all places. And one of Franco's fellows too, it seems. Freddie was travelling with a woman. Mexican girl. Bit of a revolutionary, so far as I can gather. Ended up in prison herself, without Freddie's diplomatic papers to protect her. But we got her out, in the end. No bones broken, as they say. Did you know her too? Josefina something-or-other.'

'No, I didn't know the lady. But glad she survived the ordeal.' And so he was. Josefina's words were the only thing that soothed the pain of his failure to assassinate Franco. That it would have been a useless gesture. That the fascists would simply have thrown up a new *Generalísimo* in his place. That he may simply have created the worst of all martyrs. 'You must have pulled a lot of strings, sir.'

'Well,' said Consul Milanes, 'one does one's best. Now, about these telephone calls...'

Chapter Eighteen

Tuesday 20th December 1938

'Christ, Jack!' Sheila Grant Duff sobbed. 'Where…?' And then she couldn't continue.

Déjà vu, he thought. Like Santiago. He'd tried to get through yesterday. No connection. And again, today. His second visit to the Consulate. No answer again from Sydney Elliott's number. The temptation to call his mother direct. In Worcester. But he could not bear even the thought of her hysteria. He needed Sydney's intercession. She would take the news better from him.

'Sheila, listen to me.' He was shouting, above the tapping of typewriter keys behind him. 'We may get cut off again. And I need you to get word to Sydney. Please, I know this is difficult. But you have to listen.'

It was cold in the office. Ice-cold. He was glad he'd worn the overcoat today.

'We thought you were dead, Jack.' Sheila's words came slowly, broken by her tears. 'Your mother – She had a special service held at All Saints.'

Oh, I bet she loved that, he thought. *The drama*. And, for the first time in quite a while, he sensed his father's presence there, alongside him. The smell of his uniform.

'Sheila, I'm alive and well.' He paused. 'Give or take,' he said. 'But it's a terribly long story. And I need a couple of things doing. For Sydney to speak with mother, break the news gently to her.'

'Jack, you really don't know? God damn you. What happened? To Carter-Holt. And then to you.'

'She drowned, Sheila. Don't you read the bloody papers? I told you. A long story. Just about as strange as that book you lent me. *The Hobbit*.

Remember? Though I seem to still be trapped in the dragon's lair. But I promise I'll tell you the whole thing when I get back. But first, I need to ask you to speak with Sydney. The message to my mother. And then he needs to call the Consul here in Madrid. His name is Milanes. A decent man.' He glanced around at the young shorthand typist working at the desk behind him. She looked down quickly, back to her machine.

'Jack...' There was a long pause. 'It's your mother, Jack. She's dead.'

'Are you all right, sir?' said the young woman.

Jack realised she was the same secretary who had taken his details during his first visit to the Consulate, yesterday.

'Just you on duty today?' he said. There were three other desks in the room, three more Underwood typewriters standing idle.

'Only me every day. Now, that is. Mister Telford, isn't it?'

'Jack. Please call me Jack.' He offered his hand, and she fumbled with a fingerless glove before taking it.

'I wouldn't dare,' she said. 'We must observe all the proprieties here, Mister Telford, I'm afraid.'

She was bundled into an oversized brown cardigan, her face floating deep within its ample rolled collar. The face of a pixie, he thought, recalling a charmingly illustrated children's book he had, as a small boy, once possessed. Dark hair, naturally curled. And that neat centre parting.

'And do the proprieties work both ways, Miss...?'

'Apparently not. Among the Consulate staff I'm always Miss Waters. But, to the world at large, I'm Ruby.'

Definitely not Spanish then, he thought.

'Well, Ruby, thanks for your concern. Just a spot of bad news from home.' Jack knew that he should be experiencing something. Anything. Oh, he had made the correct noises for Sheila's sake. Told her what a great shock the news had been. Timid enquiries about what had happened. Listened to the details, as relayed to Sheila by Jack's sister. Devastated by the loss of her beloved son. Collapsed during the service at All Saints. Died in hospital a week later. It all seemed so strange. It had never occurred to Jack that his mother was even especially fond of him, let alone that she should be so overcome by grief at word of his death. Their relationship hadn't offered much warmth, and Jack had only discovered the truth of his father's suicide many years later – even then, not from his mother. She had pressed her pacifist views upon her son without once ever explaining the basis for her passion on that subject. So, after university, they had become even more distanced, his visits regulated. Diary commitments, rather than filial duty. Each second Thursday of the month.

The typing pool door opened and Mrs Norris strode purposefully to Ruby's in-box, deposited a fresh batch of work.

'Mister Telford,' she said. 'You got through, I hope?'

'I did indeed. But some bad news. My mother's passed away.'

'Oh, my dear.' Her hand went to her mouth. Ruby gasped.

'I'm so sorry,' said Ruby. 'And there was me, prattling away. I'm really sorry.'

'Our condolences, Mister Telford,' said Mrs Norris. 'I can't imagine what you must be going through. But I came down to give you some better news, I hope. The couple you were asking about. The Ketterings. Safely repatriated, we've been told. We heard from one of the consular officials in the north. Mister Fielding. He says they're none the worse for their experience. But Mrs Kettering spat in old Franco's face, I understand. How very strange. You must tell us the whole story. Perhaps on Christmas Day. You will be coming, I hope?'

'I'd be delighted,' he said, tried to fix a smile on his face. But Fielding again. The rabbit hole.

Jack walked down the Calle de Zurbano, crossed Génova and into the Justicia district, through all the kaleidoscope varieties of Madrid's deprivation. At the northern end, close to the Consulate, he could almost believe that the war had conveniently left the *barrio* unscathed. Bomb damage still, here and there, but the scattering of snow, fallen over the past twenty-four hours, softened the image, cast a shroud over the occasional mounds of debris. But then, finding himself at the Plaza de Chueca, the damage was suddenly more acute, less sparse. Entire houses and apartment blocks collapsed along the Calle de Gravina and Hortaleza. And, ahead of him, a man was trying to flog the final spark of life from a spavined donkey hauling a cart of salvaged furniture. The fellow beat the beast with a fury that Jack could barely believe. All to no avail. For the poor creature faltered in its traces, took two last staggering steps, and collapsed. The carter still plied his whip but, by then, a pack of women and children had appeared on the road, as though by some gift of prescience, knives at the ready so that, by the time Jack had closed the distance, the man's anger was dimmed to the weakest of protests. Blood mingled with the snow, ran into the gutter, and turned the street to a shambles of hacking, slicing and sawing.

He hurried past, found refuge in an *estanco*, bought a copy of *ABC*. He paid for the paper, skimmed the pages. Chamberlain's trips back and forth to Rome – and Mussolini's demands that Italy should be allowed to annexe Corsica and Tunisia. Signs that *Il Duce* wanted to turn the Mediterranean into a fascist lake. News from behind the Nationalist lines. *Can this be true?* Jack wondered. Report of a prison in León, converted by Franco to jail children – 4,000 of them – simply because they refused to give information about the whereabouts of their Republican parents. Visit to Barcelona by the Labour Party's Lord Listowel and Lady Hall, solidarity messages, and claims that opposition to Chamberlain was growing after Munich. And, finally, a reassurance that the National Lottery would be paying out as normal. He thought about his mother, her weekly flutter on Littlewoods football pools.

Near to nostalgia, Jack left the shop, still reading the paper, and almost immediately stumbled into the middle of a funeral cortège – though he did not, at first, recognise it as such. A crowd of people emerging from an alley. Hand-drawn cart. And, on the back of the cart, a long, sacking package. It was only the attire of those in the crowd that gave the thing away. Every scrap of best clothing still remaining, but oversized, hanging from torsos turned skeletally thin since the time they'd last been worn. *And in this Madrid*, thought Jack, *who the hell would waste good firewood timber on a coffin?*

He was glad to reach the Gran Vía, turned right past the Telefónica building – that soaring fortress tower – until he spotted the Café Zahara on the opposite side, the corner with Mesonero Romanos. A sheet of corrugated iron, rusted, daubed in scarlet painted slogans, covered one of its windows, but the place still smiled at him, modern and rationalist. Jack stopped, unsure whether to cross, uncertain whether he truly wanted to meet Father Lobo's friends, and he glanced around, a moment of paranoia, to see whether he was observed.

Across the street, folk queued outside a small store, the ground floor of a building leaning against the Café Zahara's flank. A lottery shop. *Doña Manolita*. Busy selling tickets for the big Christmas draw. To famine-eyed women. To their consumptive, emaciated children. To languid, shambling men. And Jack remembered the promise in the newspaper. Business as usual. Yet he began to wonder how a winner from this queue might spend their prize money. Share it across their neighbourhood? Purchase evacuation and freedom for their own family and those of friends? Feed the starving thousands? Or…

The air raid siren wound itself from bored beginnings to full-throated frenzy. People in the queue cowered, looked up and around, waited to see what their neighbours might do. Run for one of the shelters? Or keep their places for the winning ticket? A tram trundled past, men hanging from the back, eyes fixed on the sky. Other folk were running too now. In both directions. For there were Metro stations each way, equidistant from where Jack stood. The lottery queue was somewhat diminished, but not substantially. His father was with him. At his side. Watching the bombers thrumming into sight above the Gran Vía's canyon lip. *Give-in. Give-in. Give-in.* Junkers or Capronis. He'd still not learned to tell the difference. His father's ghost smiled at him.

'*Well, here it is, Jack,*' he seemed to say.

For the first time in his life, he wondered whether that life had any value, and he ambled across the street, hands thrust in his overcoat pockets. *A little flutter of my own, a lottery*, he thought, listening to the bombers roaring overhead, watching the other lottery gamblers huddle, crouched against the wall, heads down, a sure sign that, somewhere above, a deadly payload was now falling from the steel-grey sky. The engines were loud. Ear-shattering. Absurdly low, he thought, as he waited for the first whistling and explosions. Or the rattle of machine gun strafing. But they did not come. Instead, a new sound. Like hailstones. *Splat. Splat, Splat.* And he turned to see small balls, lines of them, bouncing along the Gran Vía towards him. Red and yellow bouncing balls. He dodged one of them, just in case, unsure whether it might be some new and deadly weapon. Yet, as it spun before him, finally came to rest in the road, he saw that the red and yellow was a paper wrapper, now ripped and opened to reveal the charge it contained. Bread. He stared at the thing. *Poisoned?* he wondered. And then, *Of course it's bloody poisoned. By the wrapper.* He picked it up. Red and yellow flag of Nationalist Spain on one side. On the other, its message. "*En España Nacional,*" it began. "*In*

National Spain – *one, great and free…*" Jack remembered that slogan. The yard at San Pedro de Cardeña. But he read on while the bombers passed into the distance and, around him, the lottery customers finally broke ranks. "*In National Spain – one, great and free – there is no family without a home, no home without a table, no table without bread.*" The queue was entirely abandoned now. Those who would risk bombs rather than lose the chance of a winning lottery ticket were not going to gamble away the chance of bread. For the moment, they had the street to themselves, ran around, frantic, gathering the small loaves into their arms, stuffing them into pockets, inside their clothes. Anywhere. While a *miliciano*, emerging from a building across the way, screamed at them to leave the things where they lay.

'*¡Veneno!*' he shouted. Poison! And Jack knew that the young Anarchist was right, though perhaps not in the way he intended. The fellow tried valiantly to wrestle the bread away from an old man but, as the all-clear sounded, as the street began to fill, as folk saw the bounty fallen from the enemy sky, as the clamour to collect it turned to chaos and fracas, the *miliciano* gave up his endeavours and stood, shoulders slumped, watching his country's fight for democracy, their long fight for Madrid, finally falling apart under this most wicked of weapons.

Father Lobo turned the small loaf slowly on the waxed tablecloth with his fingers. And the other two men watched him, silent, hands folded before them while, in the background, Reinhardt and Grappelli's *Belleville* celebrated the gift of bread with unashamed but entirely misplaced joy from the loudspeaker of the Café Zahara's Miami Bar.

'Franco's Christmas gift,' said the smaller of the two men. Dark suit, jovial face. Perhaps forty-five. Father Lobo had introduced him as Miguel San Andrés. Editor of *Política*, the newspaper of *Izquierda Republicana* – the Republican Left party. And an admirer of Sydney Elliott. Had met him once. A conference in London. 'This is how it ends, I suppose. With fascists bearing gifts.'

The conversation had jerked and jostled between Spanish and English, with Father Lobo having the best grasp of both, helping with the more difficult translations. It was sometimes tortuous. But the surroundings were interesting. The bar was well named, murals around the wall depicting scantily clad sun-worshippers on the imagined beaches of Florida. The circular column near the bar designed as a palm tree, its leaves spiraling around the ceiling.

'The reason that our work is so important, *Señor* Telford,' said the second man. 'And so sensitive. Leocadio says that you're a man of integrity.' Julián Besteiro. Little loved now for his reputation as a moderate, he'd admitted. Yet his story impressed Jack. Dean of the University's Philosophy Faculty. Stood as a candidate in the '36 elections. A record number of votes for the Popular Front. And he could have chosen to leave the city with the rest of the Government when war broke out. Declined the opportunity. Stayed. And yes, he was there. When Franco's barbarians destroyed his Faculty buildings. Burned his books. 'You cannot imagine how much I despise them,' he went on, spittle clinging to the gap between his teeth, slightly protruding, his old face long, equine, deeply sad. 'And I knew it was over when I went to Eden.'

Father Leocadio Lobo smiled, and Jack thought for a moment that it was a biblical reference.

'Julián was in London,' the priest explained. 'Last year.'

'Anthony Eden?' said Jack.

'I truly thought – truly,' said Besteiro, 'that he would help us. I was in London for the coronation. But I was invited to meet Eden. Nothing. After that, I knew we had lost. Just a matter of time. Something of a recluse ever since, I'm afraid. I think Eden wanted to help though. Do you know him, *Señor* Telford?'

'Not personally,' said Jack. 'Not a bad man, though. Not as bad as Baldwin. Or Chamberlain. Liberal – for a Conservative. And I think you're right. He would not have wanted a Franco victory. And Chamberlain undermined him because of that. So he resigned as Foreign Secretary. Whatever happened behind the scenes, maybe we'll never know. But his resignation speech was powerful enough. That we constantly give in to pressure from dictators. Hitler. Franco. They're all the same.'

'The Russian conundrum, of course,' said San Andrés. 'Without the Soviets we could never have survived so long. And here we are now. Contemplating the end of the Republic. Trying to work out a way to salvage something. Anything. To at least think the unthinkable. Reaching an accord with Franco. Saving more lives. Impossible, of course, while he – most of the world, in fact – identifies Spain so closely with Communism. You could help us a great deal, *señor*. Let the world know that there are still many democrats here. Seeking a democratic solution. A democratic future. For Spain. After all, if there had been no Soviet involvement, perhaps Britain and France would have helped us in the first place.'

'I'm afraid I don't believe that,' said Jack. 'Britain showed its hand long before Stalin did.'

If I'm going to tell anybody's story, he thought, *it will be the one General Kotov wants me to write. That's where the Pulitzer is! And at least he's willing to pay me.*

Chapter Nineteen

Sunday 25th December 1938

'I did not think to see you again so soon, *Señor* Telford,' said Miguel San Andrés.

'Me neither,' said Jack. 'But I should have guessed. You said you were on the Entertainments Committee. Just the man for a Christmas party.'

'The *Junta de Espectáculos*, yes. One of our cinema managers was able to find the films. For later.'

The atmosphere at the Consulate was quite a contrast to that at the Hotel Victoria. Just another day to the Anarchist waiters. Although they had made an effort last night. *Nochebuena*, they had told him. Christmas Eve, even though they didn't believe in all that religious nonsense – Father Lobo or no Father Lobo. Yet a fish stew – improbable, but there it had been. And not bad. A small portion of *turrón blando*, too. And a few roasted chestnuts. Even a glass of sparkling wine. From Cataluña, they'd explained. Then apologised. There would be no more, of course. Not for a while, at least. Not until they'd taken back the two hundred mile-wide fascist corridor, which now divided the Republican Zones. Pure bravado. And Jack loved them for it. Because the whole city had been paralysed, earlier that day, by the news that Franco had launched a six-pronged attack on Cataluña, with separate columns striking towards Barcelona everywhere from the Pyrenees to the Ebro. Of course, the papers reported the whole thing in a positive light. Brilliant counter-attacks. Heroic defensive actions. But everybody knew that there were no Republican reserves. Barely any ammunition. And when Prime Minister Negrín made a dramatic morale-boosting Christmas Eve radio broadcast – Jack had listened to it with Father Lobo in the Miami Bar – people had openly laughed, taking bets on where he might have broadcast from. Certainly not Barcelona, they had joked.

'Not with your family today?' said Jack. 'Christmas, and so on.'

'Christmas Day is not such a big thing for us,' San Andrés told him. And Jack smiled to himself, remembered that the man was supposed to be a moderate. *A moderate atheist then*, he thought. But perhaps San Andrés read his mind. 'Not because we aren't religious, you understand? Here in Spain, even our atheists are good Catholics. But we prefer to celebrate the birth of Our Lord at *Reyes Magos*. You know *Reyes*?'

'Kings?' said Jack.

'Yes, Kings. You call it Epiphany, I think. The adoration of the Magi. The Twelfth Night and Day. Sixth of January. That is the day for our families.'

Jack had been tempted so many times over the past five days to make contact with his sister, to phone Sheila, try again to reach Sydney Elliott. But he couldn't do it. He was angry with them. All of them, though the reason was quite beyond him.

'Oh, Mister Telford,' cried Mrs Norris, carefully manoeuvring a paper chain over the table, making sure that it wouldn't snag on the pots of flowers or the wine glasses. 'Would you mind taking this end?' She passed him the final fragile links. And a drawing pin. 'Feel free to stand on the chair. Yes, just in the corner there. A little higher? Oh, perfect!'

By the time Jack jumped down again, San Andrés had been collared by the Consul's wife, Mabel Milanes, who was already sporting a crown of red tissue paper.

Jack wasn't sure whether he was enjoying this collective festivity. Christmas, he always considered, was a day for solitary enjoyment. Too many years spent that way as a boy, he supposed. One of the few days in the year when the front parlour fire had been lit, and Jack dispatched there, to the unfamiliar realm of starched antimacassars, as soon as his porridge was eaten, to delve into the pillow-case of unfulfilled dreams. The boxed Hornby clockwork train for which he had prayed all year had turned out to be a Chad Valley games compendium. Then, next year, that William Britain Mountain Artillery set, which had lured him, week after week, in Russell and Dorrell's toy department, somehow transformed itself into a long tin of Walter's Palm Toffee. But there was always the dependable apple. And a book. A yearly salve to wipe away his ingratitude. By the time he reached Grammar School, it was *The Boy's Own Annual*. Maybe Henty, Bretherton, HG Wells, or Zane Grey.

'The Ghost of Christmas Past, Telford?' The unpleasant Major Edwin.

'I'm normally only haunted by my father on days like this,' said Jack. 'But now my mother seems to have joined forces with him. It's the very devil, Major.'

'Well. My condolences. Mrs Norris told me your news.'

Jack was about to thank him for his kindness, then stopped himself, knowing that kindness would be an alien concept for the man. So he mumbled something in its place, snatched a glass of sherry from an oriental platter as it was carried past.

'My own news seems to have been overshadowed entirely.'

'Cataluña?' said the Major. 'Shed no tears for them, Telford. Most of them have no affinity with Spain. A nest of anarchists, communists, freemasons and Jews. The very creatures who plunged Spain into this mess in the first place.'

'Wasn't that Franco and the other rebel generals, Major?'

'Oh, save that for the *Daily Worker*, or whoever it is that pays your wages. This damned country was about to commit collective suicide before Franco stepped up to the crease. Our Lady be praised! You're a good Catholic, Telford. Surely, in your heart, you must see what Hitler, Mussolini – and Franco, too – are doing for Europe. And it will be our turn one day. Mark my words. The same conspiracy. But Germany has the right idea. Particularly about the Jews. Though, with a bit of luck, we'll be standing with Herr Hitler, shoulder to shoulder, before long.'

Jack had almost stopped him. The point about being a good Catholic. But the idea of Britain becoming an ally of Germany? Had it gone so far? He had still been in the mountains when the growing threat to German Jews had finally hit the world's headlines. So bad that, when he arrived in Madrid, it was still front page news. Early in November, a young Polish Jew had shot a German embassy official in Paris. Revenge for the forceful expulsion of his own and thousands of other Jewish families from their homes. Just the excuse the Nazis needed, their leaders stoking up crowds across Germany itself, across recently annexed Austria, and across their new territories in the Sudetenland. Hundreds of synagogues burned to the ground. At least a hundred Jews murdered in their homes. Tens of thousands rounded up and sent to prison camps. Thousands of Jewish businesses destroyed, their windows smashed. The Night of Broken Glass. And only halted – at least for now – when Hitler and Göring became fearful of the crippling implications for German insurance companies. Non-Jewish insurance companies, naturally.

'How many good Catholics, d'you think, Major, might have been involved in those attacks against Jews in Berlin and Vienna? Or is that an unfair question? Perhaps I should have said, how many good Christians?'

'Oh, no bleeding-heart liberalism, please, Telford. These are infidels we're talking about. Unbelievers. People intent on destroying our very way of life. And they're at work in this very city. Do you know how many *chekas* there are in Madrid? Those little nests of Reds and Jews where they take friends of National Spain to eliminate them. D'you know how many? Dozens of them. Near the Atocha. Cine Europa. Dozens.'

He had been getting louder and louder. Heads had begun to turn.

'Good gracious, Major.' Mrs Milanes was suddenly at their side. 'Christmas Day. Good will to all men.' She was smiling angelically, but there was fire in her eyes. 'And I need to show Mister Telford my husband's OBE. John's very proud of it.' But as they threaded their way through the Consulate's guests, down the room towards the elaborately framed portrait of King George and Queen Mary, Mabel Milanes on his arm, Jack was certain he heard her mutter. 'Despicable little man.'

'Mrs Milanes was just showing me the OBE,' Jack told Ruby Waters when they were finally seated. But she merely smiled at him politely, while a white-coated waiter ladled onion soup into her bowl. Across the table, a loud young man with an adenoidal northern accent – a consular wireless operator, Jack thought – was shouting to another fellow further down the table. Liverpool beaten by Chelsea, it seemed. 4-1. At Stamford Bridge. Liverpool's only goal scored by Balmer. From a clever pass by right-half, Matt Busby. And, elsewhere, the chatter was mostly about the weather. Britain stricken by snow. The worst anybody could remember. But, for Major Edwin, it seemed that the big issue remained Jewish by nature. The news that another six hundred Jewish children had arrived in London. Part of the efforts made by the Movement for the Care of Children from Germany. These six hundred come from Vienna, it seemed, hot on the heels of two hundred from Germany itself, only a couple of weeks earlier.

'Mark my words, there'll be thousands of them before we know it,' he was saying to a fellow in naval uniform. 'A synagogue on every street corner.'

'I dread to think,' whispered the redoubtable Mrs Norris, seated just to Jack's left, 'of the fate those poor children may have faced if they'd remained in Germany.'

'You've been here long, Mrs Norris?' said Jack.

'Oh yes,' she told him. 'Ever since Delhi.' He wasn't certain of the reference, felt as though he'd missed something. But, by then, she was begging for his own story. He related it slowly, careful to use the correct version. Swimming accident. But he made sure to include the story of Catherine Kettering spitting in Franco's eye. Mrs Norris was enthralled, made all the right noises. 'And how are things at home now?' she asked, when he had finished.

'Terrible to have missed the funeral,' he said. 'But hopefully I'll be back there before too long.'

'Indeed!' she beamed. 'And the Consul has some good news for you, I think.'

They chatted amiably through one of the strangest Christmas dinners he'd ever eaten. After the onion soup, sardines pan-fried with radish, garlic and butter. A mousse of spiced carrot and other blended vegetables. Goujons of fried cod with fresh mayonnaise. And then quail, or possibly pigeon, with a red wine sauce and sautéed potatoes – which may, or may not, have come from a tin. Tiny portions, the meal's paucity reflected in reminiscences of memorable festive highlights long ago and far away. Not a word, though, about the rations upon which *Madrileño* families would be feasting that day – a single egg, a small piece of sausage, and a tiny lump of *turrón*. Yet, in the best tradition of British diplomatic siege adversity, Jack thought, those gathered around the table compensated for their own relative paucity with stiffened upper lips, an excess of bonhomie and nonchalance. But which of them, he wondered, could be responsible for the confidential reports to London which, according to General Kotov, would prove such an embarrassment to Britain? There seemed to be no Commercial Secretary among the team. And Jack considered it unlikely that such a duty would fall to amiable Consul Milanes himself. Not Mrs Norris. Nor young Ruby Waters. Nor the wireless operators. The Naval Attaché and his foppish assistant were possibilities, but both absorbed, just now, with their respective female companions: Spanish women; good-time girls, Jack assumed; and somewhat distained by the more respectable *Madrileño* guests – Miguel San Andrés and his wife, several other members of the Madrid *Junta de Defensa*. So, the Air Attaché perhaps, though he and Jack had not been introduced. And, anyway, wasn't it most likely to be within the remit of Major Edwin?

'And yourself, Miss Waters.' Jack took advantage of a lull in Ruby's long and fluently Spanish discourse with San Andrés about their favourite Spanish artist. Sorolla, they had both agreed. 'How long have you been in Madrid?'

'From the start, Mister Telford,' she smiled. 'Well, since before the start, truth be told.' He pressed her for more, discovered that her father had been on the consular staff in Valencia. Ruby herself had been born and educated there, private tutors, then sent to England, finishing school. 'By the time I came back,' she said, 'my father was about to retire. They went off to Suffolk, and I applied for the post here. Clerical Assistant, technically.'

'Excellent Spanish,' said Jack, knowing that it was trite.

'Spain's my home, Mister Telford. My mother's Spanish too. It helps, you know.' It was all very formal. But then her voice dropped to a conspiratorial whisper. 'And my name's not really Ruby. It's just easier for everybody.'

He was about to ask her to elaborate, but Major Edwin was waxing lyrical about refugees again. Jewish refugees.

'You have a short memory, Major,' the Consul was saying to him. 'How many refugees did we process here in '36? A thousand? More? And I don't recall that we delved too closely into their faith, or even their nationality. A refugee from death and destruction is exactly that. If those poor souls chose to call themselves English, we never saw it as our duty to challenge them too closely.'

'You wouldn't believe,' murmured Mrs Norris into Jack's shoulder, 'the number of people who suddenly remembered they'd been born on an English ship.'

'Or in Gibraltar,' whispered Ruby.

The Consul's wife made a diplomatic intervention, cutting through the raised voices at the farther end of the table with an announcement about Christmas pudding and, remarkably, the blazing beast duly arrived with great ceremony.

'And now just time for photographs,' Mrs Milanes explained, when the pudding was all devoured, 'before the real party begins.'

Coats were brought. But while Jack was shrugging into his own – he had kept the military greatcoat taken from the raided Guardia Civil barracks – the Consul tapped him gently on the shoulder.

'Mister Telford,' he said, 'I received a call yesterday. From your editor. Elliott, isn't it? Charming fellow.' Milanes passed Jack an envelope. Inside, an Emergency Certificate. Number 1397 (Madrid). 'He was very concerned about you, old chap. Asked me to make sure you give him a tinkle. Whenever you're able.'

Jack thanked him, studied the Certificate as he followed the other guests out into the jangling breeze of the Consulate garden. *Not valid for more than one person. Valid only for the journey to Great Britain, leaving Madrid-Valencia/Alicante via France.* A summary of the supporting statement from Sydney Elliott. The consular stamps. The Consul's signature. And no time limit. That was good. He took his place, as instructed by the photographer, on the right flank of those gathered on the steps, just behind Ruby Waters.

'I didn't realise we still had so many consular staff in Madrid,' he said to her.

'Far less than the old days,' she laughed. 'And when the Embassy was open – Well, my goodness.'

'And everybody with their office here?' he said. 'Inside?'

'Oh yes. We lesser minions on the ground floor. The Attachés on the first. The Annexe, of course.'

The various Attachés in question, their assistants, the clerical staff and assorted spouses had agreed to adjourn to the consular lounge. For a quick tipple. And Jack glanced at the wing behind them.

'Even Major Edwin, I suppose,' he murmured.

The corridor was dark, and Jack was nervous. Very nervous.

Downstairs, and in the Consulate itself, he could hear the raucous din of the party. A children's party. In the main reception hall, a Christmas tree. From whence it had come, Jack had not the faintest idea. And the neighbourhood kids – arriving after the dinner table was cleared, after the cheese eaten, after the port consumed – had gazed at the thing in wonder. An alien object. But worse, one that Jack imagined they must have viewed through terrible temptation. It would, after all, have kept any of their families warm through many days of that awful winter. But, beneath the tree, there had been small gifts for all. Each lovingly wrapped by Mrs Milanes in person. More than a hundred tiny packages. Modestly priced toys. But toys, all the same. Then chocolate. Hot chocolate. With some form of fried and sugared confection that Fernando the Chef had made. For the children to dip in the dark and viscous luxury. *Churros*, they called them. And while the children chewed and slurped, John Milanes had entertained them. Piano. His own composition, he'd said. And accompanied on guitar by a friend from the Madrid Royal Conservatory. Joaquín Turina.

Jack had taken down a few comments from the man, a brief interview at the Consul's insistence, then slipped away quietly when Miguel San Andrés announced that the Eastman Kodak Sound Projector was now ready and the first film due to begin. Mickey Mouse in *Plane Crazy*. The talkies version, of course. To be followed by no less than that modern animated miracle, *Snow White and the Seven Dwarfs*. Jack had seen it in London, back in April. But he would always associate it now with Max Weston, the clownish comedian who had been with them on the tour. It was Weston's absurd joke that Jack remembered.

'I got a good'un this time,' Max had told them. 'What did Snow White sing when she was waitin' for 'er snaps to be developed?' Nobody had known. And it was the first time he had shared a joke with them since everything went so badly wrong. Max had waited, a wide, beaming smile on his stupid face. And then the punch line. He had sung it. '*Some day my prints will come!*' And they had all joined in. A shared hysterical outpouring.

Jack spared a thought for Weston's flirtatious and domineering wife too. Marguerite. He wondered where they might be at this moment – as Jack groped his way along the corridor, sliding his fingers along the varnished paneling, sniffing the air for any hint of Major Edwin's Capstan cigarettes within the overall scent of stale tobacco, peering closely at each name plaque, ears straining for any sound apart from the overloud ticking of a grandfather clock, dimly outlined at the corridor's farther end.

159

What the hell am I doing here? he wondered. Even if he found the Major's office, then what? The fellow would have left the door conveniently unlocked? Incriminating documents on the desk under the helpful glow of a discreet lamp? It was ludicrous.

Squeals of childish laughter reached him from below. For today, at least, they could simply be kids again. But tomorrow? Daily life on the streets of Madrid, their lives cheapened once more, their innocence exchanged for the lottery tickets of Franco's bombs and artillery shells, or the equally indiscriminate bullets of the *Pacos* – the Fifth Column's snipers.

Jack saw all this as he'd done so many times before. Spreading. Today Madrid. Tomorrow? London, Paris, Brussels, Warsaw. And the task he had set himself – that General Kotov had set for him – regained its significance.

Just check the last couple of offices, he told himself. *Might as well. At least find out where fascist Major Edwin has his lair.*

Yet, as he edged carefully along the corridor's carpet runner, his eye adjusting to the gloom, he thought he heard muffled voices. He stopped, tried to separate the sound from the din downstairs, to work out whether his ears had deceived him. But, by then, he had spotted the name. *Major LT Edwin, Military Attaché.* He was drawn towards the door, the frosted glass upon which the Major's name and title had been sign-written. And, as he approached it, he was surprised to see his reflection in the pane. A distorted, shapeless reflection. Reflected how, when there was no light? His hand went to the knob. But before he could touch it, the thing turned of its own volition. Jack stepped back, quickly. The door opened. No reflection, but Major Edwin framed in the doorway, stepping into the corridor. An impression of somebody else with him. A uniform. Inside the room. The door closed again, and the Major's face no more than inches from his own.

'Telford! Something we can do for you?'

Chapter Twenty

Tuesday 27th December 1938

Elbert Hubbard, that eminent American anarchist and socialist, had written: '*When you grow suspicious of a person and begin a system of espionage upon him, your punishment will be that you will find your suspicions true.*' It had been a basic tenet of his journalism course. Beware reaching a conclusion and then moulding your investigations to fit the preconception. Check the facts. Ignore your obsessions. And Jack knew that Major Lawrence Edwin had become an obsession. Guilty without trial. Nameless crimes and frameless charges.

'I don't think I've got the makings,' he told the General. 'To be a spy, I mean.'

The Gaylord was busy, communiqués back and forth. And much busier again, of course, at the War Ministry, which he had passed, kicking through the snow, on his way. Reports from Cataluña, Jack imagined, then saw his own face reflected in the dining room's polished paneling. *Neither San Andrés nor Besteiro would be seen dead in here*, he thought. Partly the presence of the Soviets, partly the decadence. A relative decadence. For they had been served *Cocido Madrileño*. The soup first, a by-product of cooking the ingredients. And then the stew itself. Chickpeas. Something green and stringy masquerading as cabbage. Ham chunk impostors. Blood sausage, which also brooked no close examination. Suspicion and guilt each equally defeated by Jack's hungry belly.

'Tell me again,' said Kotov, for once nursing his vodka instead of knocking it straight back. 'The man who was in the Major's office. Describe him.'

'Just a figure, General. A uniform. No. I only *think* it was a uniform. It was dark. And the Major closed the door behind him. So I couldn't see.'

'He did it deliberately, of course. So, nobody from the Consulate. Let's assume that. Or else why should he hide him? Not one of your naval uniforms?'

'Ah, no. I see what you mean. Not a uniform I recognised. Lighter than any of ours.'

'Spanish then.'

'I suppose so. But I feel a complete fool. Ridiculous excuse about looking for the toilets. The bugger just laughed in my face. Marched me back downstairs without a by-your-leave. But at least I caught the end of *Snow White*.'

'Snow white?' said the General, and Jack apologised. For rambling.

'But here's a thing,' he said. 'They'd all been talking about refugees. At dinner. Refugees processed through the Consulate. Some of them would have been nationalists, I suppose.'

The General laughed.

'Of course. Though nothing of importance. Not through the British Consulate itself. But your Major Edwin's predecessor, now that was another matter. There was a cabal of Franco supporters in the diplomatic community. Schlayer at the Norwegian Consulate. A whole nest of them in the Guatemalan Legation. The Turks, naturally. Always the Turks, *da*? And your own Military Attaché. Up to their necks in supporting the Fifth Column. Helping to smuggle real fascist pigs across into the Nationalist Zone. Some prizes we would have loved to keep. Betancourt. Renedo López. And then the Fifth Column held together by a couple of senior army officers. Republican army officers. Traitors. With foreign help, naturally. Even masquerading as Party members. But we picked up the last of them in January. Since then...'

'Since then,' said Jack, 'I suppose they've had plenty of time to build up a new network. And you say that the Major's predecessor was involved with all that?'

'We caught him too. In Valencia. One smuggling trip too many. The last I heard, he was in Barcelona, waiting to be shot. But now, who knows?'

'A British Military Attaché?'

'Didn't you know? Your Government has been remarkably quiet on the matter. I sometimes wonder what game they really play, Comrade Telford. But if the new Military Attaché has taken up the work of the old one, he could well be the source of those reports to London. I think they would make interesting reading. Don't you? And at least you now know where to begin your search, my friend.'

'Like I said, General, I don't really think I've got what it takes.'

Kotov regarded him silently, a nerve beginning to twitch in his cheek.

'After we went to so much trouble? To save you from the firing squad? For poor Fidel Constantino to risk his life bringing you here? We still do not know whether he will live or die. And you want to make that all for nothing, comrade? That shows a remarkable lack of gratitude, does it not? The clothes. Your comfortable room at the Victoria. Your cigarettes, *Mister* Telford.'

Jack flushed, struggled for a clever response, found that his mouth was hanging open, ready to receive a spoonful of the Russian-sponsored stew.

Damn the man, he thought, and set the spoon back on his plate. *But he's right, of course.* He knew that he wouldn't be there except for the *Capitán* and his *guerrilleros*. And, to the *guerrilleros*, Kotov was their general. A debt to them was a debt to him, their Lion.

'You think they resent us being here, General?' Jack asked, finally. 'The *Madrileños*, I mean. Outside the hotel last night, I heard two women. Something about there still being too many foreigners. Even though most of them have gone. Had their fun, they were saying. Now gone back to their own comforts. Left them with this mess. With nothing. You think that's true? Is that what they think about us?'

'There!' beamed the General, doubtless reading the uncertainty that Jack knew must be written plainly on his own face. 'I knew you'd see sense. Those women? Simply the ingratitude of Franco's sympathisers. You reported them? No? Well, you should have done so.' The General spat a lump of gristle into the remains of his stew, pushed the plate away. 'These people want to be rid of us? For me, I'd leave them to get on with it. How I long for a decent borscht. But I have a gift for you.' He swallowed his vodka, fished in his tunic pocket and produced a worn leather case, a hand's span long. Jack thought of cigars, but it was too heavy. Inside, slender but robust tools, like larger dental probes, a couple with saw-toothed edges. And all attached to a single key ring.

'Lock-picks?' said Jack. 'You can't be serious, surely.'

'I realise that your education may not yet have stretched to using such equipment, my friend. But every man should know how to pick a lock, don't you think? We all think we're safe behind a locked door. But a few minutes of tuition in how to use these and you will understand just how fragile is our own security. Our personal security. Any fool can learn to use a lock-pick and, after that…' He snapped his fingers to illustrate the point, accidentally summoned the waiter, ordered another bottle of vodka.

'I've been here all these weeks,' said Jack, 'and never been to the park. It's good of you to show me, Miss Waters.'

'You should have been here before the war,' she told him, peering through the iron railings. 'But at least on this side, the trees still deaden it all. They hold back the war. *¡No pasarán!* Not past the trees anyway.'

Jack had been astonished that there were still any left standing. And Ruby had patiently explained that the poor people of Madrid had, of course, wanted to cut down the Retiro's trees. But the powers-that-be had stopped them. Closed the park. Appointed armed guards to protect it. Militiamen. They were still there. The guards. Though that hadn't prevented the more desperate from their clandestine activities. Thousands of the trees had disappeared and now, blanketed in snow, shrouded in fog, it was somehow the saddest of Madrid's ruins. But she hurried him onwards, down Menéndez Pelayo, past the writers' houses. Because she thought he'd like to see them. The fascist author, Agustín de Foxá. And Sender's place, where he wrote *Míster Witt en el cantón*.

'I've never read it,' Jack admitted.

'Oh dear,' she said. 'The British can be so insular, can't they? And his poor wife. He left her behind in San Rafael. They'd been on holiday there. And when Franco's men took the place, they shot her.'

A silence fell between them, until they came to an abandoned kiosk, plastered with old posters. '*Winter is one more enemy to be defeated in the fight against fascism.*'

'Back to work tomorrow?' he asked, by way of resuming their dialogue.

'I owe it all to the National Whitley Council. An extra day off in lieu of Christmas Day falling on a Sunday. Aren't I lucky? But yes, back to the grind tomorrow. And I'm sorry, Mister Telford. This is a very long way around.'

'Long way, safe way,' he reassured her. A childhood adage against the dangers of shortcuts. 'And is that all the staff? Tomorrow, I mean.'

'More or less. The Attachés come and go as they please, of course. Always important meetings to attend. So they say. Just a good excuse to go skiving off, if you ask me.'

No point pushing this, thought Jack. *Too soon. If I'm going to do this, I'll need to learn those bloody lock-picks first. Then work out the best time to use them. Step at a time, Jack. Step at a time.*

'It's good of you to show me the place,' he said. 'But you mustn't feel obliged to do the hospital too. I could easily put you on the tram when we get to the Prado, if you'd prefer.'

'Not on your life, Mister Telford! I could never afford to go inside the Ritz before the war. And never had a good enough excuse once they turned it over to the saw-bones. Just a peek inside. That's all I need. And I cope very well with blood and guts. On the whole.'

They turned along the park's southern extremity, with Ruby pointing out anything of interest. Anything with a British connection. Like the former office of the Rio Tinto company.

'That reminds me,' said Jack. 'When I was at San Pedro, the boys told me they'd had a visit. This one from a fellow from Rio Tinto. Captain Charles.'

'Oh, I know him. He used to come here quite a lot. Before the war. I think he went to Burgos, didn't he?'

'You still hear from him?'

'Gosh, no. Nobody bothers with us here any more, Mister Telford.'

Jack recalled the General's words. *'The man from Rio Tinto sends reports. Regular reports. To London. About iron. About the pyrites. All now flowing from Spain into Germany's arms industry. The reports come through Madrid. Coded.'*

'Nobody ever mentions him?'

'Why on earth do you ask? Sounds like you have a score to settle.'

They found the *Capitán* sitting up in his camp bed, reading reports in the morning papers of Doctor Negrín's Christmas Eve broadcast.

'English! I thought you must have gone home.' Jack apologised. In truth, he hadn't realised it was more than a week since his last visit – though Fidel Constantino was plainly more interested in Ruby Waters. 'But I see you have brought me a better gift this time.'

'I brought you some *Luckies* too,' Jack smiled, and threw down two packs of the American cigarettes, while Ruby and the *Capitán* exchanged formal greetings, kisses on cheeks.

'It's cold in here,' she said, and adjusted a blanket, which the wounded man was wearing like a shawl, pulling it up around his shoulders, the bandages that swathed his chest and shoulder. The stench in the room was still dreadful, though it seemed not to trouble her. 'Next time, I'll bring something warmer for you. Is it true that the Ritz won't allow artists or bullfighters to stay here?'

'There do not seem to be many of those here at the moment,' said the *Capitán*, looking around at the other beds, 'so I suppose it must be true, *compañera*. And you, English. Still having nightmares?'

'Even more since I came to Madrid,' Jack replied. It was a fact. That bastard lieutenant, Turbides, and Merry del Val still haunted him most times when he managed to sleep. They were usually accompanied by the Guardia Civil Jack had shot – an imagined face, for Jack could not remember his real one. But always the same. And Carter-Holt, of course. Usually all four of them, burning out his eyes. Or worse. And all those falling dreams, linked somehow to the torture.

'At least your Spanish is better now. This comrade *señorita* is teaching you? She is far too beautiful for you, English. What do you see in him, *compañera*? An ugly man. One eye. Big ears. Not particularly brave. Cries in his sleep. Like a woman. Beard like Rasputin.'

'Perhaps I see nothing in him at all, *Capitán*,' she said, 'beyond the things you have listed. Though I can't speak for his habits in bed. Why should I want to? On the other hand, he is liked and respected by colleagues who I like and respect in turn. He has made friends here in Madrid. Good people. And, as we Spanish say, Show me his friends and I will tell you about the man.'

A pretty speech, thought Jack. And he wondered about Ruby Waters. He had a terrible flaw – and he knew it. An absurd conviction that every woman with whom he came into contact must somehow feel attracted to him. To some extent. A largely harmless self-delusion that he, himself, saw as ludicrous and, thus, kept firmly under control. Yet it

166

suddenly occurred to him that he felt no such fallacy about Miss Waters. He wondered why. But, by then, Ruby and the *Capitán* were engaged in a fast and furious discussion about her background, the blood inherited from her mother.

The girl's normally so prim, thought Jack, astonished at how flirtatious she'd become in Spanish. He picked up the copies of *ABC* and *Mundo Obrero*, each of them carrying broadly the same front page. Verbatim report of Negrín's address to the people of Spain, his reminder that it was now four months since his open proposal to Franco's rebels that both sides should suspend the execution of political prisoners – an offer entirely ignored by Franco. Yet he struggled with one of the subs. He translated it, with difficulty, as: 'Only those who feel themselves secure and strong can offer to be magnanimous.' Presumably a statement that the Republic remained robust, stalwart, and therefore capable of magnanimity – while Franco's decision to reject the proposal showed him to be fearful, weak. But Jack doubted that many of those left in the two Republican Zones still believed that.

'And our English friend,' the *Capitán* was saying. 'You know that he had a plan to kill Franco?' Jack saw the disbelief on Ruby's face, the smile that showed she thought this was a jest. 'You don't believe me?' The *Capitán* made a pretence of being offended. 'Well,' he said, 'I was never sure that I believed it myself.'

'This sounds like a pretty tale, Mister Telford,' said Ruby. 'I'm intrigued.'

'*¡Joder!*' spat the *Capitán*. 'I have a big mouth. See, English? She looks at you with interest now. I am a fool and have lost my chance. But that is life sometimes.' The Spaniard studied his two visitors with mock consideration. 'And, you know,' he said, 'I believe that you may belong at his side, *compañera*.' Jack saw Ruby blush. 'Yes, I see it now, English,' the *Capitán* went on. 'This woman may just be your salvation.'

Chapter Twenty-One

Saturday 7th January 1939

Jack hardly knew where to begin. And Sydney Elliott wasn't making it any easier. Silence at the other end of the line. But Jack could picture him there, in London. The office would be swimming in smoke by this hour of the evening. He could almost smell them. Capstan Mediums. The windows would be filthy, yellowed from cigarette smoke within, grey-gritted from the smog out on the street.

'Is she ready yet?' he said, though he knew that, by now, the copy-cutters would already have divided the work, hoping for an early dart if they could get one. The hand-compositors would be sorting the heads, and the Composing Room on stand-by. Midnight print runs. Dispatch ready for circulation – that fine web of consignment trucks, milk train routes, pre-dawn delivery vans, newsagents' steps and Sunday morning paper rounds.

'Nothing much to shout about this week,' Elliott told him, at last. But it was a reserved Sydney Elliott. 'We're having another go at Chamberlain, of course. All this back-and-forth to Rome. And nothing to show for it except more appeasement.'

'I wanted to wait until I knew you'd be there. And some time when it would be quiet this end.'

'The Ambassador said something about your eye.'

'The Consul,' Jack corrected him. 'Milanes is the Consul. No Ambassador in Madrid any more, I'm afraid.' It seemed strange that Sydney didn't know that. Jack had always admired his editor's detailed knowledge of Spain, realised that their roles must now be somewhat reversed. But what was he going to say about the eye? 'And officially,' he went on, 'it happened when I was washed out to sea. The rocks. I lost my eye in the process. But the real story's a bit different. Can't tell you now though.'

'Is this call being monitored, Jack?'

'Welcome to Wonderland.' Jack hoped to lighten the tone. 'We'll have our very own censor listening in at the local Telefónica exchange. But I doubt they'll take much notice of us. It's just a long story. And we may get cut off. You'd better get used to it, though. If war comes to London. Censorship, I mean.'

It all went quiet, down the line.

'D'you know, I'd never thought of that,' said Elliott. 'And I'm sorry about your mum, Jack. I should have said earlier.'

'The Consul passed on your message. And thanks for 'phoning him. At least I've got papers again. I can get out of here. Soon maybe.'

'You should get out now, Jack. All this stuff about Barcelona. Franco's closing in. Once Cataluña goes…'

'Hey, that sort of defeatism can get you shot,' Jack laughed. 'According to the papers here, Franco's breaking himself on the solid rock of Cataluña's defences. And our new offensive in Extremadura – don't tell me you've not picked up the news.'

'It's not funny, Jack. And what's all this about you being thrown in prison? Threatened with being shot. Is that true too?'

'Great story, isn't it? *Reynold's News* has got its very own Arthur Koestler now, boss. Aren't you pleased?'

'You sound different. Sure you're all right?'

'Never better. But it would be a damned sight worse if I'd been jailed by our own side, wouldn't it? Not to worry though. I've got some good friends here. Going to arrange for me to be accredited. As a cor-respondent for the Republic. And I've got a few juicy stories for you.'

'Is it safe?'

'Perfectly. And anything that's sensitive, I can get to you another way.'

Jack had made good use of the past week. Daily lessons with the lock-picks at a grubby and sinister little place within the Mediodía Station complex, the Atocha *cheka* there – buildings whose furtive occupants sent shivers down his spine. There were dark stories: Nationalist prisoners killed there, taken off trains and shot; Kangaroo court executions. Then the New Year's Eve party at the Consulate, though Jack hadn't stayed long. Just a short conversation with Milanes. Another favour requested. Some personal correspondence that Jack would need to send to his sister. Didn't really want the censors to read it. Perhaps the diplomatic bag? Of course, the Consul had told him. Not a problem. So that Jack had begun to bury himself in his writing, spurning two separate offers from Ruby Waters during the *Reyes* celebrations that he might accompany her on short excursions. To have a look at the National Palace. And then to the refugee camp established within the cloisters of the Plaza Mayor. Polite refusals. No further invitations. Jack's guilt both at slighting her, and also at deceiving John Milanes about the real reason for needing the diplomatic bag.

'We printed the piece you sent from Santiago, Jack. Did you know? It was bloody good. Exactly what I wanted. The third story.'

'Somebody showed me.'

'In Madrid? Somebody in Madrid had a copy of *Reynold's News?*'

'Oh, we're very big here at the Consulate.' Jack couldn't quite bring himself to say that he'd actually been shown the article by a Soviet general. 'Though I think,' he said, 'they take it mainly for *Young Ernie*. But that third story thing. It looks very different again, here in Madrid.' Elliott agreed that anything fresh about Madrid would be welcome. All the big names had given up writing about the siege now. Old hat. So any new angle... 'And there's another thing,' Jack told him. 'D'you know about the kids? The children of Republican families taken by fascists to be re-educated.'

'You hear stories of kids taken away for conditioning, children of political opponents. Hitler's Germany. Stalin's Russia. But Spain, Jack. Are you sure? And money changing hands in those little arrangements?'

'Good question,' said Jack. 'I'll check. Always new ways to turn a profit from war though, I guess. And talking of money...'

'Don't worry, Jack. Already ahead of you. Will make arrangements on Monday to put you on the payroll again.'

Jack tried to keep the emotion from his voice. The ability to survive in Madrid without General Kotov's patronage. The chance to escape and finally put Carter-Holt's death behind him. The possibility to focus on his writing.

'And the back pay?' he said.

There was a strange mood in Madrid that night. Jack could sense it. Street lamps flickering yellow, flashing out a morse message that all was far from well. Snow turning to slush, seeping through even the best of shoe-leather. Cold feet, literally. Silence. Trams all halted for the night. The Calle de Génova empty of traffic. The few pedestrians nothing but grey ghosts moving among the shadows. And the taste of Madrid on his tongue. The taste of lentils. Lentils and fragments of dried cod, *bacalao*, reconstituted. And now, in the Café de las Salesas, lentils had done no good at all for the woman.

'Please,' she said, 'there is no need to worry.'

A waiter was fanning her face with a wine-stained cloth, and Father Lobo was patting her hand, while Julián Besteiro poured a glass of water, encouraged her to take a sip. She did so, rested her head against the wall-length mirror behind her, took the pin from her once-fashionable cloche hat, and gave the hat into the waiter's safekeeping.

'You should look after yourself better, Rosario,' Father Lobo scolded her. 'She works too hard,' he told Jack. 'And then forgets to eat.'

'I forget nothing, Father,' she snapped.

Jack liked her. Mid-forties, perhaps older. The demeanour of a school-mistress. But the sunken shadowed eyes ubiquitous among Madrid's women. And thin as watered milk. But, like Besteiro, she'd had the chance to leave the city and pursue her Press Office responsibilities in Barcelona, turned down the opportunity. To stay with her family.

'Perhaps you need some air,' said Besteiro. 'Shall we take a turn outside.'

'With you, Besteiro?' she sneered. 'That would not help my credibility on the street. Just a faint. It happens sometimes. Eating too quickly. And when did you become such a health expert? You were at death's door yourself a few weeks ago.'

'Death's door is permanently open here, *compañera*,' said Besteiro. 'Fortunately, I managed to avoid walking through. This time.'

'Father Lobo told me you used to meet Machado here, *señora*,' said Jack.

'You know him, *Señor* Telford?'

Jack shook his head.

'No. But I spent some time with a group of *guerrilleros* in the north. They called themselves the Machados, in his honour.' Jack had been reading *The Crime was in Granada* again, practice for his Spanish, but touched afresh by Machado's elegy in memory of Lorca's murder by Francoists. *"They killed Federico at the first glint of day."*

'I fear that Antonio is unwell too,' she said. 'And planning to get out of Barcelona as soon as he's fit to travel. France, of course.' She took another sip of water, a modicum of colour returning to her cheeks – probably as much as they ever carried. 'But then, these days, it's hard to find anybody who's not unwell. I hate to agree with him, but Besteiro's right.'

'It's the children,' said Father Lobo. 'Such diseases. Starved of vitamins. Tuberculosis. Pellagra. Dementia. Poor little things. And now, the chilblains. Frostbite too. I passed a woman today, beating her son's feet with a thorn branch. To make them bleed, she said. To cure the frostbite. Where do people get these ideas?'

'And then this,' said Besteiro. He picked up the still-damp leaflet from the table. More fascist propaganda. They'd been fluttering down regularly, along with the bombs and shells, ever since the pre-Christmas bread-wrappings. "*In National Spain – one, great and free – there is no family without a home, no home without a table, no table without bread.*" These latest flyers were about medicine. "*No child without a doctor. No doctor without medical supplies.*" That sort of thing.

'I'd like to write about the children,' Jack explained. 'Those here in Madrid. And those taken by the *facciosos*. By Franco's thugs. Those in prison for no better reason than belonging to Republican families.'

'Tomorrow,' said Rosario del Olmo, 'I will complete the authorisation for you to be accredited. It will need to be approved by Barcelona. But a mere formality.'

Tomorrow? thought Jack. *Monday. Everything happens on Monday.* On Monday, Sydney Elliott would put him back on the payroll, hopefully wire him some money. On Monday, Sydney would also phone Jack's sister, Sheila too, explain to them both the difficulties of calling, that Jack would be writing. Jack would do so, naturally. Bulky letters, so that Milanes might get used to his lengthy correspondence in the diplomatic bag. He had already scripted one, to Nora Hames, explaining that, for reasons entirely out of his control, the Nationalist authorities had confiscated many things previously in his possession, including Julia Britten's scrap book. He was mortified by its loss, naturally, and would make every effort to seek its safe return in due course, but… And, on Monday, Sydney would begin drafting the editorial which, the following week, would announce to readers of *Reynold's News*, to the world at large, that Jack Telford was, thankfully, still alive. Not too much detail. Just enough. Impossible to avoid, he knew, yet he'd hoped to dodge publicity. It troubled him. Too many sensitivities. Carter-Holt's family, for instance. They would be pestering him for details, surely. Maybe more than that.

'Formalities here can take some time, I've found, *señora*,' he said. 'How long, do you think?'

'Are you in a hurry to leave us, *Señor* Telford?'

'I feel like this is part of me now,' said Jack, and he gripped the table's edge with both hands, for emphasis, felt the sturdy Spanish oak seep into his fingers. 'But I have to go back to England some time. Quite soon.'

'Does General Kotov know that?' she said. 'He tells me you're helping him with some investigative journalism. Not the children, surely?'

Jack had assumed that the duties with which Kotov had charged him might be the subject of some secrecy, but he tried to maintain a poker face as he worked out a response. Rosario del Olmo was, after all, a prominent figure in Spain's Communist Party, herself a journalist for *El Heraldo de Madrid* and *Mundo Obrero*, now responsible for Foreign Press Liaison on behalf of the Defence Committee. *Obvious that she's got close ties to Kotov*, he thought. *But isn't this a bit loose-lipped?*

'I'd rather hoped the General might provide a reference. For my accreditation. But no, not the children. That's a different story. I'd mentioned to him that I was planning an article on Britain's role in the war. Its official *and* unofficial role, perhaps. He was very interested.'

'Naturally,' said Besteiro. 'The Soviets are sadly more interested now in their games with England, France and Germany than with the fate of Spain. Everybody has forgotten us.'

'Please!' snapped Rosario del Olmo. 'They're still here, are they not?'

'I owe a great deal to the General's *guerrilleros*,' Jack jumped in.

'*La guerrilla*,' smiled Father Lobo, almost as quickly, 'is a Spanish tradition.'

'Perhaps,' said Besteiro, 'but I'm still uncertain how much the Guerrilla Corps has contributed to the war.'

'Oh, my friend,' smiled the priest, 'you remind me of those many people who have witnessed Padre Pio's stigmata at first-hand but still doubt the evidence of their own eyes.'

'Padre Pio?' said Jack.

'Ah, the English.' Father Lobo shook his head. 'Was there ever a people who knew so little about so much?'

'That would make an interesting discussion, Father,' said Rosario del Olmo, 'but I think our business is concluded here and I am, as you see, a little tired. I shall process *Señor* Telford's accreditation as quickly as I'm able, and then...'

'And then,' Jack patted the priest's arm, 'I hope Father Lobo will put in a good word with your predecessor. About the BBC.'

'Barea?' she said, sneering dismissively as she untangled herself from the table.

Poor Spain, thought Jack, as they paid the bill. *So many divisions.*

Outside the café's front door, their farewells were formal and somewhat frigid. But Jack was struck, once more, by the hush on tonight's streets. Their voices echoed emptily between the buildings of the Plaza de las Salesas, and the streetlights still flickered. That warning again. And he was about to say his final goodbye when the door behind him crashed open.

It all happened too quickly. Jack was pushed brusquely aside. The waiter. The beginnings of an apology. Rosario del Olmo's cloche hat in his hands. A grateful smile leavening upon her lips. Jack's sudden sensation of his father at his side, the first time for quite a while.

Crack.

Jack's head turned towards the sound. From across the square. Somewhere high up. A loud, slapping impact. Suction sound. Wet splashes, gobbets of viscous moisture, sprayed Jack's face and neck. The waiter slamming back into him, knocking him through the doorway, glass shattering. Jack smashed through splintering chairs, cracked his head on the tiled floor, the waiter's heavy body pinning him down.

'Bloody *Paco* snipers,' said Besteiro, when the SIM secret military policemen had finished with them. 'Coming back out of the woodwork again.'

They had all agreed. Franco's Fifth Columnists scenting blood, gaining their confidence afresh. But then gone to ground again. The SIM's rapid raid, sealing off the street, house-to-house search, had revealed nothing but angry, frightened neighbours. Ambulance. The dead man taken away. Afterwards, a lengthy debate about the shooter's target. The priest? Besteiro? Rosario del Olmo? All with their enemies. It could have been any of them.

'Except,' said Rosario, 'the waiter – that poor man – it was *you* he pushed aside when he took the bullet, *Señor* Telford.'

Chapter Twenty-Two

Saturday 21st January 1939

Tarragona had fallen. Franco's armies now less than fifty miles from Barcelona. And a profound silence had wrapped itself around the city in the ensuing seven days. But, at the Teatro de Calderón, the matinée performance, it was hard to believe that anything was much amiss.

'I don't think I could bear to be here,' said Ruby, during the intermission, 'when Franco arrives in Madrid.'

They had already been entertained by the clown, Ramper; by a ventriloquist, the Yankee Balder; by tap dancers, Elsie and Waldo; and by the Republic's very own "Shirley Temple", Ana Mary. And there were still another dozen variety acts to come.

'To be honest,' Jack told her, 'I don't think I could bear to be here for the second half of the show. But it's the same thing, I suppose. Always get out before the curtain falls. Isn't that the idea?'

They worked their way along the row, apologising as they went, and collected their coats from the cloakroom. He helped Ruby into her tan gabardine.

'Do you never wear a hat, Mister Telford?' She tied the flower-printed headscarf under her chin, as he lit a cigarette in the foyer.

'Never. But with this duck-egg on the back of my head, I'd never find one to fit.' He rubbed the lump.

'You think I'm a coward? Running away?'

'From what, Miss Waters? I imagine the Consulate will enjoy the *Generalísimo*'s blessing – for all the ways Britain's helped him.'

'You should have had your head examined, don't you think, Mister Telford?'

Jack was no longer sure whether this was concern for the condition of his latest wound, or a commentary on his cynicism, but they plunged out of the theatre's main entrance into the dark and bitter depths of Madrid's early evening. Into an excited tide of *madrileños* too, flowing around the corner into the Calle de Atocha, where a convoy of wagons was grinding along the icy roads.

'Troops?' said Jack.

'No. Food donation,' Ruby shouted, pointing to the flapping canvas on one of the trucks. 'Orihuela. It's a town,' she told him, seeing his confusion. 'Not far from Alicante. Aren't you glad I persuaded you to come now.' Yes, he agreed. Very glad. And it was the truth. He had been summoned to see the General again, the previous day. What was the delay? Kotov had demanded. His patience was running thin. And, according to his reports, Telford had now mastered the lock-picks reasonably well. So here were two further pieces of equipment to help him. A flat angle-head military flashlight with a spare dry cell battery. And a slim-line miniature camera. Minox. 11mm film cartridges. Tiny. Expensive, the General explained. German – a pity, but... Jack knew that he should have been impressed by this wonder of modern technology, but he was back in the world of cameras and espionage, impossible that it should not have brought back memories of Carter-Holt. He was trapped by the woman, yet again, it seemed. He had still been trembling when he arrived at the Consulate, nervously made arrangements with Milanes to be there for another Saturday night telephone call to London. A front, of course, for his planned attempt on Major Edwin's office. So, when he had found Ruby waiting for him as he left, and she had mentioned this afternoon's variety show at the Calderón, he had accepted more from distraction than genuine enthusiasm. But during a sleepless Friday night, he had grown properly grateful, for it was the only thing that diverted his insomniac thoughts away from the impossibility of his mission, those recollections of his nightmare experiences in Burgos, and the nagging doubt that possibly, just possibly, Rosario del Olmo had been correct about him being the sniper's deliberate target. 'Well, thank goodness,' Ruby went on. 'I'd decided to give up on you entirely if you'd said no. It was your very last chance, Mister Telford.'

And, to Jack's amazement, she wrapped herself around his arm, gave it a small hug as they followed the crowd and convoy up towards the Plaza Mayor. Torches had been lit in the square, and loudspeakers mounted on the back of a cart, blaring out scratchy recordings of the

Republic's many anthems, the volume set high enough to drown out the terminus traffic of the *plaza*'s incessant trams. *Milicianos* pushed and prodded some semblance of order upon starving citizens, almost driven mad by the crates of winter oranges, flagons of olive oil, sacks of salt, rice and potatoes driven here from the Vega Baja coastal district. Too little. Probably too late. But that didn't matter much. Hungry hands stretched out for whatever small rations they could glean from this welcome but necessarily modest windfall.

'Christ,' said Jack. 'They can't have much to spare there either.'

'The Spanish idea of family runs deep,' said Ruby. 'And it runs wide. For those who belong to it, their family is the Republic. They'll share their last lentil. Until there's simply nothing left. They wouldn't know how not to.'

But around the loudspeaker cart excitement had reached fever pitch. A woman was being helped up to the microphone, her familiar face lit by the flames that flickered all about. Familiar, because he had seen it on a dozen newsreels, a hundred posters, countless newspaper images. And beautiful, Jack thought. Perhaps the most strikingly beautiful face he'd ever seen.

'She's back in Madrid,' he said. An entirely redundant observation, but he was surprised, believed she was still in Barcelona.

'There was a piece in Mundo Obrero,' said Ruby. 'But not much in the papers apart from that. She's supposed to be here to organise this year's Congress. You can't fault the Party for its optimism, Mister Telford.'

Indeed you cannot, thought Jack. Only the Communist Party of Spain could still be planning its regular policy conference when it faced such imminent destruction. Unless, of course, they knew something of which the rest of the world remained blissfully unaware – some Marxist equivalent of divine intervention. And there it was, naturally, in the short speech she delivered to the gathering. The people of Madrid still standing, unshaken by bombs or bullets, by the lies of the Fifth Column or the taint of counter-revolutionaries. The mothers of Madrid, women of Spain, become yet one more legend in the Republic's struggle to survive. The women of Madrid, no longer domestic slaves with no rights, standing firm in the path of fascism.

And the women hurled back at her the slogan that La Pasionaria, the Passion Flower herself, made her own.

'*¡No pasarán!*'

Jack knew that Dolores Ibárruri was now in her forties, but she looked at least ten years older, her features settling into sadness each time there was a natural break in her speech. The war may have taken its toll upon her in entirely different ways than the women who here hung upon her every word, but it was a considerable toll all the same. And he struggled to maintain some objectivity about the more questionable stories he'd heard. Her part in the destruction of the Marxist Workers' Party, the POUM. Her role in the suppression of Trotskyites. And her reported view that, when the life of a people is threatened, it's better to convict a hundred innocents than to acquit a single guilty person. But he could not deny that she inspired him, enflamed his need to strike a blow. For Spain. And somebody patted his back, as though it may have been congratulatory, so that he turned to find the *Capitán* at his side, in uniform once more.

'I would follow that woman into hell,' said the *guerrillero*.

'Yes,' Jack nodded. 'She has that effect on me too. But they let you out. Better now?'

'If I had been forced to spend one more day in that place, it would have killed me. Much quicker than this.' He thumped a fist to the sling wrapping his left shoulder and arm. 'And, besides, I wanted to see this beautiful *compañera* again. Has she saved you yet, English?'

'Have you had a chance to read any Kafka, *Capitán*?' said Ruby. 'I suppose not. The poor man. Died far too young. Anarchist, of course. But the Gestapo despise his work. Lots of it confiscated in Germany. He wrote an interesting thing. Something along the lines that even if no salvation should come, he would want to be worthy of it at every moment. I suppose he meant we should live our lives in a godly fashion, even though we may not believe in God. That's a wonderful thought, is it not?'

Jack struggled both with the Spanish and her meaning.

'She's telling you, English, that she lives in hope, I think.' The *Capitán* laughed, slapped Jack on the back again. 'But I need a drink now.'

They promised to meet later in the week and, for one moment, Jack was tempted to ask for his help. The *Capitán* would be so much better at burglary. Though with only one fully functional arm? And Jack with only one eye. The image was suddenly comical. In any case, the man had gone by then, vanished in the crowd, and Jack's sometimes sluggish brain was still churning an earlier exchange.

'Last chance?' he said.

'Do you find me too forward, Mister Telford? I meant what I said. I've no intention of being here to see Franco cheered along the Gran Vía. To see these same women, who've braved so much to defy him, feeling obliged for the sake of their families to stand on the street and give the fascist salute. It would break my heart. And you're clearly planning to get out sooner rather than later. When you leave, will you take me with you?'

'Are you certain you're not simply beguiled by my new-found fortune, Miss Waters?' It was a shared jest, for he had already told her about his back pay. The equivalent of just over three thousand *pesetas* wired to him by Sydney Elliott, most of it now securely stashed in the Consulate's main safe – but some of it already spent, at the local *papelería*, on better quality notebooks, a long and elegant Font-Pelayo fountain pen, spare nibs, and matched propelling pencil.

'No, it's definitely the eye-patch, I think,' she smiled. He lit another cigarette, and she stretched out her hand, palm upwards. 'May I have one?'

'You don't smoke,' he said.

'I may decide to begin. You don't mind, do you?'

He found that he had no idea what to make of her. Precocious, yes. Pretty? He supposed so. If you liked pixies. But he was never entirely easy in her company. And this suggestion of Ruby's. It felt a little like Carter-Holt all over again. He had been ready to head for home after all that mess at Covadonga. But Carter-Holt had begged him to stay on, to go with her on the rest of the journey. To Santiago de Compostela. *"Because I need you,"* she'd said. *"To protect me."* And, like a fool, Jack had believed her.

The Consul and Mrs Milanes weren't at home. And the Consulate's duty officer was that same foppish assistant to the Naval Attaché Jack had met on Christmas Day. Somewhere beyond, there was gramophone music, high-pitched, girlish laughter. But at least arrangements had been made for Mister Telford to use the telephone and, on his arrival, Jack explained to the sub-lieutenant that he might be there for some time, a lengthy conversation needed with his editor, plans to be made for his journey home.

'Oh, as long as you like, old boy,' the fellow told him.

But Telford had still been nervous, stammering out his excuses and lies, though the young man seemed not to notice, anxious only to resume his own entertainment. And, when Jack was finally satisfied that the coast was clear, the buildings silenced and dark, he crept across the yard, applied the lock-picks – tension wrench and scrubber – to the annexe's outer door, then trod carefully in the flashlight's feeble ellipse as it bounced along the hallway's blackness, made a shadow play up the staircase to the upper floor, where he quickly located the Major's office afresh.

Jack stood for what seemed a long time, outside, his ear pressed to the frosted glass, convinced there must be somebody inside. The hairs stood up on the nape of his neck as he forced his quaking hands to apply the lock-picks once more. Too easy. The levers and springs surrendered to him and he slipped inside. His heart was beating wildly, and he felt queasy, so he closed his eye, breathed deeply, clenched his fists to still them, before shining the flashlight around the room. On the walls, separate large-scale maps of Europe and Spain, as well as a framed photograph of the bizarrely abdicated Edward VIII – with Wallis Simpson, naturally. There was a large roll-top bureau, and a matching pair of roll-front filing cabinets. Bureau, he decided. It took a while, but revealed nothing of obvious interest. And neither did the first of the cabinets. But the second revealed far more than he had hoped.

Jack shook like the proverbial leaf all the way back to the Hotel Victoria. A mix of residual terror and a quaking sense of euphoria. The flashlight was bulky in one greatcoat pocket but, in the other, he kept his hand closed protectively around the Minox. It had been absurdly simple to use, the documents illuminated by the small lamp. After that, it had merely been a matter of sliding the body open, centring the image in the viewfinder and pressing the button – then closing and opening the mechanism again to advance the film. Eight exposures. So he had used both cartridges, wrapped them in a handkerchief.

In the hotel itself, the anarchist waiters seemed especially boisterous, turning chairs and arranging them, seats downwards, on the dining room tables. One of them shouted a raucous greeting, though Jack could not quite follow his jargon. Another grinned at him, an exaggerated wink too. And he was at the desk before the penny finally dropped. As usual, there was no night manager. Just the brass bell to summon service should it be needed. All very free and easy at the Victoria. But his key was missing from its pigeonhole. *Ruby*, he thought. *It must be.* Yet he wasn't sure what to do, sat down in one of the armchairs. It was just possible that he was jumping to all the wrong conclusions. Perhaps she simply had a message for him though, if so, she would be waiting down here, surely. He liked her, though his emotions were so raw just now that he dreaded confusing them still further. In any case, Ruby Waters was that one woman about whom he had made no silly assumptions whatsoever. But he was emotionally exhausted, drained. Or, perhaps more accurately, sated. As though he had no further capacity for additional feelings, complications. And Ruby Waters was in his room. Well, there was only one way to find out why.

He drove the rattling elevator to the third floor, and Jack forced himself along the corridor, stood with his hand on the doorknob while he composed himself. But it didn't work too well and, by the time he walked inside, he had become irrationally angry.

'Before you say anything, Mister Telford,' she snapped, 'I think I must make one thing clear.' She was sitting in the chair by the window, threw down Jack's book as soon as she saw his face. 'Have you any idea how difficult it is to get to the coast these days?'

'That's no way to treat a good book, Miss Waters.' He bent down, picked up the Henty novel he had borrowed from the Ritz hospital library, examined the cover for damage. 'And you've caused quite a stir down below.' He realised that this might be misunderstood. 'Those bloody waiters will be wallowing in this for weeks,' he added, hastily.

Her gabardine and scarf were draped across the bed, so he shifted them, sat as close to her as might be considered proper.

'You have sensibilities, Mister Telford. A rare quality in a journalist.'

'You're not the first person to tell me that, Miss Waters. But it's a cliché, all the same.'

'Life is a cliché, isn't it? And have you given it any thought at all? How you'll get there. What *is* your story, by the way? Valencia? Alicante? Cartagena? It makes a difference, you know.' He realised she was mocking him. But why? 'You can hardly go dressed like that, either,' she pressed on. 'You'd need supplies. Lots of things.'

'I managed to get here all the way from Burgos,' Jack laughed. 'Across enemy territory. Remember?'

'But you had that dear captain of *guerrilleros* to look after you. This time you'd be on your own. Unless...'

'It's out of the question, Miss Waters. I appreciate that the journey may not be easy. A damned sight harder if I had to keep an eye on you too, though.'

The words were out of his mouth before he could stop them. Surely there would be a riposte. About his eye. But her own dark eyes simply twinkled and she let the moment pass.

'Really?' she said. 'You know what I think, Mister Telford? I think you're not quite what you seem. That's a fine performance. Treating me like I'm the little woman. A masterful misogyny. But I've seen the way you are. You respect women, I think. It's a rare quality in a man. Perhaps you're somewhat afraid of it. And then there was that strange story about you having a plan to kill Franco. Wasn't that what the *Capitán* said, in the hospital?'

'He was joking, I think. Or delirious.'

'There! You did it again. Touching the eye-patch whenever you're nervous. Or telling fibs, perhaps. You're not going to the coast at all, are you? You've unfinished business with Franco. If so, I shall stop making demands of you.'

The last sentence almost choked her, and Jack saw that her eyes were damp. He wondered how his life could possibly have become so complex.

'Miss Waters – Ruby, it's a long story. It's true that I did have a plan to kill Franco. But the wheels came off that particular wagon. I botched it, if you want to know the truth. And then somebody persuaded me that there was probably good reason for my failure. Fate. Or something. That the upshot may have been even worse. For the Republic. For Spain. I don't know. I've no plans to go down that path again, though. I've only stayed in Madrid to pay something of a debt. To the *Capitán*. Or, rather, his commander. But that's just about settled now. Debt paid. So I'm going home. To England. As soon as I'm able.'

Now she looked disappointed. An illusion shattered. Her lips pressed tight together. And she stood, picked up the headscarf and raincoat.

'I see,' she said. 'Well, I'm sorry about the book.'

He tossed it onto the bed, opened the door for her, saddened by her resignation, wishing that she'd tried harder. For, in reality, he was far from certain that he wanted to make the journey alone.

'Perhaps we could talk about all this some more,' he said. 'In the week.'

'Yes, perhaps,' she replied, and stood in the corridor. 'Well, goodnight, Mister Telford,' she whispered, at last.

'Goodnight, Ruby.'

Chapter Twenty-Three

Friday 27th January 1939

At the Gaylord Hotel, a few days later, there was no vodka at the bar. Instead, Jack was ushered to the first-floor private room where he'd been interviewed by the General at their first meeting. But today they were not alone. The place was driven by all the dour determination of disaster. Barcelona had been surrendered. The papers had barely given it a mention. Nor the Government's relocation to Figueras. Disbelief, perhaps. Some vain hope that the situation might be reversed. But the people knew. The anarchist waiters at the Victoria knew. Yagüe's *Regulares* – Franco's Moroccan troops – were already rampaging through the Catalan capital, looting and burning, raping Spanish women, slaughtering anybody fingered by Nationalist sympathisers. And here, at the Gaylord in Madrid, the Soviets were finally packing to go home.

'How did you know what to look for, Mister Telford?' Kotov tapped the photos, enlargements of those Jack had taken, scattered across the corner table among the maps and mounds of other documents. 'These are carefully coded. It's taken four days to break them. Our best code-breakers.'

'But the files themselves were not, General. Astonishing. But I think Major Edwin must have felt pretty secure in his activities. They were neatly ordered, and I just went straight to the one marked *Río Tinto*. It seemed fairly obvious. Lots of uninteresting letters. And then these.' Jack selected five of the images. 'Coded, as you say. And, clipped to them, these reports. Carbon paper copies only, of course. But you can make them out?'

'It's an interesting story, my friend. These, the figures supplied by Río Tinto's man in Burgos. The money that the company's being forced to pay to Franco. Over two million pounds. And here, the tonnage of Río Tinto mineral production sequestered by the Nationalists for payment to Germany. Iron pyrites mainly. You see? They calculate the value at around five hundred million in pounds sterling already. Five hundred million pounds-worth of essential minerals, Mister Telford. Going to the German arms industry instead of to your own. Do you see the betrayal here? How much has Britain's ability to arm and defend herself been slowed by the loss of those minerals? And all because your leaders have deliberately chosen not to intervene in Spain while giving a free hand to Germany to do exactly that!'

'Major Edwin's reports to England confirm those figures?' said Jack. He was genuinely shocked.

'Not precisely. You see, Major Edwin seems to be playing a strange game here.' The General picked up a couple of blurred photos. 'His own reports, also coded. But two reports. Each very different. This one to your Board of Trade. For public consumption, we assume. The figures minimised. More than halved. And this one? The real figures. Sent to his superiors. For their eyes only. Or those of Hitler's friends in your Government, perhaps. The question is, how do we use this information, Mister Telford?'

'You still intend to? It looks like you're all ready to pull out. And me? I feel like I've fulfilled my side of the bargain.'

'I still have work here,' said the General. 'This may be the end of another contraction in the birth of New Europe, but the pregnancy has a while to run yet. Far more pains to come, comrade, before we see the infant itself. The delivery will be an agony. For all of us. A great deal of blood. And, of course, after the initial euphoria that the agony is over, the baby survived, that is when our troubles will truly begin.'

Jack had heard the argument before. A favourite theme of Sydney Elliott's. That the sovereign states of Europe had been struggling since the French Revolution to reconcile their various political systems. That the war to come, like the Great War, would be a European civil war, though fought on a global stage. And that, like the aftermath of the American Civil War, it would take generations afterwards before a new balance was restored.

'Until the time when we reach our dotage, General, and the child we've raised has reached maturity, takes care of us in turn. And you may still have work here, but me...'

'Perhaps you have a part to play too. You've crossed a line, have you not? Taken a risk or two. Because your own intelligence services would hardly see these as evidence of your patriotic loyalty.' He waved the photos at Jack, who looked in vain for any sign of humour on Kotov's rock-face features. 'Not that they will find out,' the General sneered. 'Of course not. But you have skills, Mister Telford. Skills that would be useful to us.'

'What I've done, General, is to contravene Section One of the Official Secrets Act, various Defence of the Realm Regulations, and several pieces of trade secret legislation. Whether I have the skills to turn this information into an article that my editor feels able to print remains to be seen. For now, I have to try and work out how all those reports can have been passing back and forth without the British arms industry itself commenting about the true scale of the damage it's been suffering.'

'I assume that your industries – shipbuilding, munitions, the rest – have all been told that overall ore production from Spain is simply down. Because of the war. Regrettable, naturally. A shame. Spain was such an important trading partner before this all broke out, your ministers will say. Twenty per cent of all Spain's exports were to Britain. Ten per cent of all her imports came from your country. But now – The war. World recession. Just another slump in the cycle of Capitalism. And your people will react the way the British always react. A few more hunger marches. Bury their heads in the sand. Accept the lie that Mister Chamberlain is securing peace through appeasement. Hitler and Mussolini not such bad fellows after all. So what will you do about it, Mister Telford? You and your editor? You and this *Reynold's News*. This "*socialist journal*" for which you work. You and your plan to kill Franco. A simple article in a Sunday newspaper seems like such a small thing by comparison.'

Jack felt his temper quicken, surprised to find himself offended by Kotov's poor opinion of his country. The sweeping generalisation. He had covered Jarrow, the other hunger marches, the demonstrations to drive Mosley's Blackshirts from the streets, and the Brigaders who'd come here to fight for Spain. You could never take Britain, as a nation, for granted. Never apply simplistic analysis to their reactions. But that was for another day.

'There are ways of writing the story,' he said. 'An "undisclosed source" and keep it simple. To start with, at least. The worst that may happen is that we'll have a D-Notice slapped on us. But I doubt it. Not for this. We are, indeed, only a weekly, General. I'm no spy, though, I'm afraid. Haven't the stomach for it. I may have got away with it once, but that experience simply convinced me I'm not cut out for this sort of thing. No, I'm heading for home as soon as I can.'

I promised, after all, he thought. In the letters he had finally written to his sister. To Nora Hames. And to Sheila Grant Duff. Explanations. Lies. Subterfuges. And sent them through the *Correos*, the postal service, knowing that the same half-truths would satisfy the censors. Sent them through the *Correos* because he'd also lied to Milanes and to Ruby Waters, told them that these same letters weren't yet written – for he still needed the diplomatic bag for the articles he was writing. *This* article.

'I understand,' the General was saying. 'But you could perhaps still be useful to us in England, my friend. I think you have little sympathy for the capitalist élite that runs your country, no? You British are good at the pretence of democracy, though you and I both know that it's a game, your country actually run by the press barons, a few captains of industry, the country house set with their inherited wealth. Would you not want to help change all that, Mister Telford?'

Hard to argue with that, thought Jack, *even allowing for the complexities of folks at home as a whole.* But this was hardly the future he planned for himself.

'Work for the NKVD, you mean?'

'I see that the idea repels you. Though I don't understand why. Mother Russia has lit a beacon for the working classes. I'm proud of that. My modest role. And I must try not to take offence. As you, Mister Telford, have tried so hard not to be offended by my abrasive portrayal of your country. In truth, I admire Britain very much. Of course, you must return to England as soon as you may. But, meanwhile, I have just one more job for you.'

'I think my debt is paid, General.'

'Not quite, comrade. I have a small confession to make. We already talked about your plan to kill Franco. Remember? And maybe you also recall that, when we first met, I asked whether Miss Carter-Holt had put the idea in your head.'

'Yes, I remember. I thought you must be mad.'

'Not so mad, Mister Telford. You see, Miss Carter-Holt was an asset. You understand what I mean by that?'

'For Russia, you mean? No, that can't be. The woman was a fascist, through and through.' There were moments when Jack felt he could have made a career in the theatre – a view which, he was shocked to learn, the General seemed to share.

'We are all actors on the stage, are we not?' said the General. 'And I assure you she was working for the Comintern. For the NKVD. For me, my friend. Fortunate for you that I believed your story. If I had not done so, Mister Telford, I assure you that the outcome would have been very different. Just another reason that we needed to bring you here. To clarify matters. And, because I believed your story, you may also be right about your capacity for espionage. The work requires a certain guile. Basically, I think you are a man without that quality. That's why I believed you. But you see my predicament. You owed me a debt for saving your life. Yet you still owe me an entirely separate one for killing such a valuable asset – even if you did so for what you considered the proper motive.'

'Have you ever read *Alice in Wonderland*, General? Yes? Well, I have to tell you that, since I arrived in Madrid, the story feels quite commonplace. As though that's the world I now inhabit. This thing about Carter-Holt, it's extraordinary. Unbelievable. Though I don't see how you can hold me accountable for your loss.'

'Please, my friend. The work is already half-done. These two other documents you copied. How did you find them?'

'Those? Oh, the same way. There was another file. Its tab said *QC*. Coincidence, I suppose. But a couple of weeks ago, I was involved in an incident. A sniper. One of the *Pacos*, isn't that what you call them? The Fifth Columnists? He fired at a café where I'd been eating. Almost took it personally. And then there was the file.'

'I'm sorry, Mister Telford, but *QC*?'

'Not at all, General. The advantages of a classical education, I'm afraid. *QC. Quinta Columna.* Latin. For Fifth Column. It stuck out like a sore thumb. Inside, there were just a few sheets of paper. Lists. Coded, as you see. But there were a couple of exposures left on the second film. I simply thought –'

'Perhaps guile is not the most important characteristic for a good espionage agent after all. You know what these are, Mister Telford? You should do, for we've already discussed some of them. Major Edwin's predecessor. His links with the Fifth Column. And those senior army officers at its heart, but posing as good Republicans, as Party members. Well, here are their names. Joaquín Jiménez de Anta. Rodríguez Aguardo. A dozen others. Here, times and dates. Meetings, we assume. And payments listed. Whether expenditure or receipt, it's hard to tell. But these are all 1937 transactions. While these…' He held up the second photograph. 'These are all for 1938. And the latest, my friend, just before Christmas. These are all Major Edwin's own transactions, naturally. Not those of his predecessor. Now, let me draw your attention to this name in particular. You know who that is? That man is the personal assistant to Colonel Casado. You know Casado, I assume?'

'I spent last Sunday evening watching him make his big speech at the Monumental.' The cinema had been packed. For Colonel Segismundo Casado – *de facto* head of the Republican forces in Madrid, regardless of old Miaja's formal responsibility for the city – rarely made public appearances. And news that he was going to speak seemed to herald some significant development. But it had simply been the normal lines. About Spain's fight for independence and justice. For a democratic Republic. Yet a great deal of stress on the democracy theme. And the anarchist waiters at the Hotel Victoria had seized on this, of course. '*That's it,*' they had said, '*the start of a divorce. From the Communists.*'

'Yes,' said the General. 'You have to be careful where your friend, Besteiro, leads you, comrade. You know that, don't you? He is more dangerous than he seems. For you, at least.'

It was Besteiro who'd invited him to hear Casado's speech. And he knew that Besteiro, Father Lobo too, admired Casado greatly. But in all his stupidity it had never occurred to Jack that Kotov would have been spying on him as well. He almost made the protest. About being followed. Yet he knew that it would simply dig his hole even deeper.

'And what is it you want, exactly?

'You heard the Passion Flower speak, I understand.'

'The *Capitán* told you, presumably.'

'Yes, of course. And he tells me that you had a charming young companion with you. You should cherish her, Mister Telford.'

It was hard to avoid the feeling that there was a moot threat in all this.

'What do you want?'

'Comrade Ibárruri was not here simply to welcome a food convoy from Orihuela. You see the way I take you into our confidence, comrade? But the truth is that there are rumours. Activities. And Doctor Negrín needed reassurances. That our good Colonel Casado is not in secret contact with Franco. Shall I tell you something? This Fifth Column of which we all speak. Have you any idea how many of Franco's secret police are operating here in Madrid? Right now. As we speak. SIPM agents. Over a thousand. Some of their names are here. But let us look, for a moment, at this final list. This one seems to be an exchange between Major Edwin and a man called Juan March. You've heard of him?'

'I think everybody's heard of him,' said Jack. 'Incredibly wealthy. Franco supporter. King of the Baleares, isn't that what they call him?'

'March is like a spider, scuttling between Rome and Majorca, other parts of the Nationalist Zone. It was his money that financed much of the insurrection. And now this. It seems to be – What do you call it? A promissory note. From Edwin to March. A list of potential payments. But all to Franco's generals. And even to Franco's brother, Nicolás.'

'Payments from Britain to Franco's brother.' Jack was incredulous. 'That can't be correct, surely.'

'We want you to provide us with the link, my friend. Between Major Edwin and Casado. There *will* be one. But, more important, about these promised payments. Bribes? For what? Oh, and one more thing,' said the General. 'This business about Miss Carter-Holt. You mentioned a rival for her affections. The British Vice-Consul from San Sebastián. Fielding, I assume.' *The rabbit hole again*, thought Jack. 'Yes, I know him, Mister Telford. Indirectly, at least. But I thought I should tell you. To avoid any embarrassment. That you may be meeting him again very soon.'

Fielding. Coming to Madrid. Why? And the news delivered to him not through the British Consulate but, rather, through the NKVD's representative in the city. Carter-Holt's liaison with the fellow had been political rather than simply sexual then. Jack had always thought so. Too many hints along the way. But, beyond that, Jack was unable to gather any new clues. Kotov became tight-lipped on the subject and simply told him he'd be informed when the time came. Meanwhile, he should get on with the task at hand. A link between Major Edwin and Colonel

Casado. An explanation for the promissory note to Franco's generals, with Juan March as the go-between.

It all swam around in Jack's brain as he skirted the north side of the Retiro and headed for the Torrijos market. He'd been intending to take the Metro, but he badly needed some fresh air, time to think. There was an easy solution, of course. He could pick up the things he needed for his journey, then head straight off. Just leave all this nonsense behind. But Ruby Waters was right. The journey *was* complicated. How wonderful if he could simply wander down to the station, catch the next train. Or a bus. For the coast. Anywhere on the coast. Yet, of course, that was an option he didn't have. Nobody did. Not just like that, here in Madrid. And Kotov seemed to know his every move. Looking around, Jack could see a dozen people who might be NKVD men. Or agents of the secret police, presumably also at the General's disposal. Besides, he'd invested a lot in getting this story, hadn't he? Pulitzer? Probably not. It was good though. And he thought Sydney Elliott would run with it. Elliott wasn't a man to run scared of an occasional D-Notice. So Jack just needed a bit of space to finish the thing. Maybe the article about the kids too. Get them in the diplomatic bag and then…

He reached the market almost before he knew it, picked up some woollen socks at ten times their true value, then a rucksack, military pattern. Patched, in two places, to hide – Well, Jack didn't want to ask. He managed to find a water bottle. An old army sweater too. A couple of rusted tins. Bully beef. Meagre supplies, though they would see him on his way. Yet, at every purchase, he was convinced that the same man was on hand to observe him. A weasel with sallow skin and an army overcoat not unlike Jack's own. And, sure enough, the fellow followed him onto the tram, back along the Paseo del Prado. Jack carried his new acquisitions up the steep, bohemian Calle de las Huertas, home to the Hotel Victoria, trying his best to pay Weasel no attention but, once he had dropped his shopping in his room, he took the stairs down to the ground floor, went out through the kitchen and took a circuitous route around to the Plaza Mayor. There, he spent a tortuous hour checking the timetables and prices for bus routes, through Cuenca, a mass of connections from there to Valencia or Alicante. Twenty-seven *pesetas* to Cuenca. But a journey that could take up to two days. Horrendous. So what was the alternative? He rode the Metro's Line One to the shell-pitted Mediodía

Station, the Atocha. Impossible to be there without feeling the ghosts of that place all around. Yet at least it was easier to plan the journey by train. Madrid to Albacete. Then the choice of whichever port he might prefer. The only complication? That heavy bombing raid just before New Year's Eve, and the first section of track, to Aranjuez, still under repair. So, a bus journey to Aranjuez, at least. But, after that, with a bit of luck, a mere nine or ten hours to the coast.

At a bar across the road, he bought a coffee, and mulled over his options while he puzzled over Fielding and worked some more on the arms industry article. It was coming along very well, but the forthcoming journey, the article, getting it into the diplomatic bag, all forced upon him thoughts of Ruby Waters many times during his deliberations. Had Kotov genuinely intended a threat to her? Or Jack himself? Had he truly crossed a line, put himself at risk? And then there was the conundrum. The temptation that he might, after all, want to give the General what he sought. A link between Casado, the Fifth Column and Major Edwin. Between Major Edwin and Juan March. He had come to the conclusion that he would love to give the Major a bloody nose. To see him brought down. Perhaps this was the blow that Jack was destined to strike.

He was beginning to relish the idea, wiped a hand across the steamy window of the café – and almost dropped his cup. On the opposite side of the road was the jaundice-faced Weasel again, though now engaged in a close quarters conversation with a much bigger man, a figure who sent shivers down Jack's spine, a man with his back turned, a man who was unmistakably Lieutenant Enrique Álvaro Turbides.

Chapter Twenty-Four

Sunday 29th January 1939

'But, Mister Telford,' said Father Leocadio Lobo, 'I am leaving Madrid. Tomorrow. It's a good time to leave, I think.' He passed a letter to Jack, then continued to fasten the buttons of his cassock. 'You see?'

'I'm rather dazzled by the robes,' Jack smiled. He'd become accustomed to the shiny suit.

'Will you stay for the service, my son?'

'Holy Mass? I don't think so, Father.' He looked around the sacristy of the Santísimo Cristo de la Paz: the vestments cabinet with Father Lobo's chasuble laid out on the green leather top; altar linen, folded carefully; and a golden chalice, silver cruets, all the other impedimenta. 'Should I be in here?' asked Jack.

'Of course not. But then, neither should I. You didn't know? The Bishop suspended me from my duties *a divinis* in December, two years ago. For my support of the Republic. Or, rather, my failure to support Franco. To denounce the killing of priests.'

Jack laughed.

'But you're still saying Mass,' he said. 'And all this – It's a strange world.'

'Well,' said Father Lobo, 'the Bishop did not make the resolution public. And he was no longer here, naturally. So I never received a copy either. And since our Republic seems to acknowledge the need for faith again, at last, I have assumed that the Holy Father would have wanted me to resume my duties. But what do you think?' The priest jerked his head, and Jack studied the letter, then whistled.

'New York!' he said. 'That's going to be quite a change.' The letter was an invitation from the Medical Bureau and North American Committee to Aid Spanish Democracy – the same American organisation that had funded the hospital facilities at the Hotel Ritz. Countless other medical establishments for the Republic besides. 'And you're going tomorrow? That's very sudden? What about your parishioners?'

'Already arranged, Mister Telford. My good friend, Father Eduardo, from Chinchilla, is taking over my duties here. And I'm not going straight to New York. Some business in France first. I'm hearing terrible stories. Refugees streaming from Cataluña over the border in their thousands. Thrown straight into concentration camps with no food, no shelter. In this weather! What are the French thinking of? Don't they know what's coming next? Well, I'll see what we can do. And, after that, to London. To catch up with my old friend, Barea.'

'The one who works for the World Service?'

'The same. And don't worry. I will, indeed, put in a good word for you. Give you his address, too, for when you get back yourself. Don't stay too long though, my son. Personally, I would rather remain here, with my parishioners. We've been through a lot together. But I'm not a brave man. And *El Caudillo* will hardly be forgiving, don't you think? Besides, a little bird has whispered in my ear. A rumour that, if I accept this invitation – a speaking tour across the United States about this sad conflict – some form of rehabilitation may be offered to me.'

'I hope so, Father. Though it's a bit of a blow. As I said, I was hoping to seek sanctuary from you.'

'There is no sanctuary from snipers, my son. Is that what troubles you? I think Rosario was merely being provocative. All that nonsense about you being the target.'

'I thought so too. But not any more. You remember, I told you I lost my eye in Burgos?'

'You never told me how. I always assumed it was something to do with the prison.'

'It was before the prison. Do you have time for it?'

Father Lobo hoped that it wouldn't take too long. But five minutes, perhaps? If it took longer, they could conclude later. Yet Jack had practised the story often enough – this version, anyway. The same version he'd told the General. No mention of Carter-Holt or the assassin's camera. Just his own plan to shoot Franco. His arrest for unauthorised journalism in the Nationalist Zone. Tantamount to spying. Their discovery of the old pistol he'd bought. The conviction that he must be far more than just a newspaper correspondent. The torture. His eye. Turbides.

'That's a very strange story, my son. On balance, I think I'm glad you failed. The assassination plan, I mean. For the sake of your own immortal soul, not Franco's. And you're certain? This man is now here, in Madrid?'

'General Kotov tells me there are hundreds of Franco's agents in the city. I don't suppose one more would attract much attention. Even one like this. I've not been out of my room for two days. Working, that's been my excuse. But, really, I have to confess that I'm terrified. And the room's not safe. I'd already been followed there. By a man I later saw talking to Turbides.'

'So you remembered that I'd told you about the house, where I used to say Mass before. The oratory.'

'On Calle de Tamayo, I think you said, Father.'

'And why not?' smiled the priest. 'After all, I won't be needing it now. Here, I'll write down the name and address of the woman who's looking after the place for me. I'd told her I would let her know what to do with it. Once – Well, after we see what happens here. But I'll send her a note. To expect you.'

'That's good of you. It makes me feel guilty. I never got around to interviewing you properly.'

'The more important thing is to make sure you get the stories of Besteiro and my other friends. Interview *them*, my son.'

'The men crying out to be heard on Madrid's future. Wasn't that how you described them? Besteiro and San Andrés. And what about Colonel Casado, Father. Him too?'

'Especially Casado. He may be the future for all Spain.'

'He's a popular fellow, isn't he? Kotov told me that the reason La Pasionaria has been in Madrid is to seek assurances of his loyalty. He seems to think that Casado's got links with the Fifth Column.'

'Kotov is a dangerous man, Mister Telford. One of Stalin's fanatics. Do you know about the swings? The roundabouts?'

'You're going to tell me I need to know the difference between them?'

'Of course. In this world, there is no black. No white. Simply shades of complexity. There are true Communists who believe in a better world. The sort of world that Our Lord, Jesus Christ, would have wanted.

A world of social justice. Like Rosario del Olmo. Many of my friends here. Negrín himself. La Pasionaria. Those who have defended Madrid for so long. Many of those who came here to fight. Your Internationals.'

'You can be a good Communist,' said Jack, 'but not love Stalin. Those I was with, in San Pedro, used to say they'd never lived their ideals as clearly as they'd done here in Spain. But then there are always the top dogs. The ones who cannot avoid growing fat at the food-bowl. Who need to destroy anything that threatens their privilege – Stalin's empire. The new Okhrana.'

'That's a strange comparison to make, Mister Telford. I met Orlov before he left Madrid. He was a little drunk, I'm afraid. But he insisted that Stalin himself had once been a member of the Okhrana. One of the Tsar's secret policemen. And that the thing which drives him is the need to wipe out any knowledge of his dark past.'

'Orlov?' said Jack. 'I'm sorry, but I don't...'

'Your General Kotov is one of those top dogs, my friend. A wolf pack leader. But how long do you think he's been head of the NKVD here? I'll tell you. Since August. Before that, he was just the Number Two. His superior then was Orlov. But Orlov got out. You know why? Because Kléber – the man who saved us, along with Durruti, when Madrid was attacked – had been recalled to Moscow. You know what that means? To be "recalled to Moscow." It means being shot.'

Jack had tried hard to wade through the treacle of articles about the Moscow Trials, wondering how so many journalists had been able to reach such a wide divergence of opinion about their veracity. Those who, like Walter Duranty and Harold Denny for the *New York Times*, had so glibly believed the confessions of countless Soviet leaders charged with plots to overthrow Stalin, or with working clandestinely on behalf of Nazi Germany. Or those who, like Crowther's correspondents for the *Economist*, regularly dismissed the trials as Stalin's answer to Nazi sports spectacles, a distraction from the woes afflicting the country's suffering masses. One way or the other, hundreds, perhaps thousands, of Russia's leading men had been executed. Certainly thousands of military officers had died that way.

'Or sent to a hard labour camp until you die, Father. Turned into a non-person. I've heard Kléber's story. Still alive, d'you think?'

'Who knows! Orlov guessed he was next, of course. Orlov, who received the Order of Lenin for successfully shipping all the gold from our Treasury to Moscow. Orlov, who boasted about how he was praised by Stalin for the number of Trotskyists and Anarchists he'd killed here. Orlov, who was responsible, they say, for the murder of Andreu Nín.'

'Tortured to death.'

'Yes, that was Orlov. But he knew. His own turn had come. So he got out. In July, it must have been. Defected. I hear he's in New York. Wouldn't that be strange? If I met him there again? But Kotov's task now is the same as Orlov's. To kill those who are seen as enemies of the Politburo. Regardless of whether those people are trying to work for the defence of Spain. Stalin doesn't control Spain. But your British newspapers like to believe he does. You must help tell the truth, my son.'

'I've no illusions about Kotov,' said Jack. 'And no doubt that your Colonel Casado wouldn't live too long if Kotov had proof of a link between him and the Fifth Column. With Franco's agents here in Madrid. But he set me a difficult puzzle. One I'd like to unravel. Some evidence he's found of a link between the Fifth Column and a Military Attaché in the British Consulate.' It was disingenuous, Jack knew, not to admit that he, himself, had provided this evidence. 'A man called Major Edwin.' Reaction to the name was instantaneous. The widening of Father Lobo's eyes. The open mouth, deliberately closed again. The pause in his preparations. Had Jack expected it? He wasn't certain. 'Kotov seems to think,' he pressed on, 'that this Major Edwin might be the link between Franco's agents and your friend, Casado.'

The priest looked as though the Holy Father in Rome had excommunicated him, rather than praise his initiative.

'I think, Mister Telford, that it's time for you to leave now. Use the house for as long as you like. But do not stay longer in Madrid than you absolutely need. Get out soon, my son. These are not waters in which you should wish to swim.'

Jack turned that piece of the jigsaw in every possible direction on his way back to the Hotel Victoria, desperately seeking somewhere for it to fit. Apart from anything else, he regretted parting from the priest on such an icy note. He'd come to think of Father Lobo as a friend yet now he knew he would never see him again. And he was still no nearer to making the links that the General sought. Well, he'd just have to think about it from a different angle. For now, he was more intent on finishing his own copy, so he walked a while, a circuitous route from Argüelles, through the Plaza de España, often looking back over his shoulder for pursuers, and uphill to Santo Domingo, where he caught the Metro to the Puerta del Sol. Then around the corner to the bar of the Hotel Biarritz. They still kept on display a signed copy of *Death In The Afternoon* from the time, not too long before, when Hemingway had been a guest. So it amused Jack to work at a table, Hemingway's favourite, ostentatiously scribbling away with that beautiful fountain pen, the Font-Pelayo, long and stylish, black celluloid but inset with gold, almost damascene, the matching gold filler lever cleverly set into the design. Yet he also delighted in spending some of his substantial back-pay buying drinks for everybody in the place. Coarse red wine. He had intended simple generosity, naturally, but achieved only a veneer of polite gratitude from the customers, thinly masking an underlying resentment, half-heard comments about foreigners with more money than sense. Yet he worked as long as he was able, passed the afternoon there on his article about the disappeared Republican children, and it was dark when he finally arrived back at the Victoria's reception desk.

The pigeon hole empty again. Well, the key was missing, anyway. But there was at least a letter for him. He tore it open and smiled. A note from Rosario del Olmo and, clipped to the note, an official and stamped form confirming his accreditation as a correspondent for the Republican Zone. He tucked the accreditation into his pocket and smiled, but not for long. No key. *Ruby*, he thought. *Dammit!*

She'd sent him a couple of messages over the days since their last meeting, but Jack had chosen to ignore them. So he carefully rehearsed the cool reception he intended for her as he pushed forward the lever, the elevator jerking and trembling its way to his floor. He stormed along the corridor, found the door still ajar. Surprise. Then, sudden caution. So he stood and listened. Nothing. Yet his hackles had risen and he did not quite understand the reason. All the same, he was irresistibly drawn to pushing it open, just as he might have been to touching the subject of a wet-paint sign. And, inside, he found that it wasn't Ruby waiting for him but, pistol in hand, Major Lawrence Edwin and, sitting in the chair once occupied by Miss Waters, the very diplomat mentioned to him by the General – Harold Fielding, Vice-Consul from San Sebastián.

'Planning a trip, Mister Telford?' That clipped Oxbridge English. Fielding had Jack's rucksack balanced on his knee and had been going through the contents. In his hand was an envelope. A bulky envelope, already addressed to Sydney Elliott and containing the arms industry article. One of the envelopes that Jack intended for the Consulate's diplomatic bag. The second was in his pocket – the article about the children.

'That's none of your damned business, Fielding.' Jack forgot about Major Edwin's pistol momentarily, filled with anger, strode over to the seated diplomat in his camel coat. The man's heavily scented pomade wrinkled Jack's nostrils, and he snatched the bag from Fielding's knee. But he didn't quite manage to also grab the envelope.

'Get away from there,' snapped the Major. 'Over against the wall.' There was no alternative except to obey and, meanwhile, Edwin positioned himself between Jack and any possible escape route, kicked backwards to close the door, then put his shoulder to it. 'And not going to ask why we're here?'

'I imagine it was the enquiry I made about the Ketterings,' said Jack. 'I knew it was stupid at the time. Serves me right for being sentimental.'

'It wouldn't have made any difference,' Edwin sneered. 'I checked the tide tables anyway. For the day of Miss Carter-Holt's so-called accident. You'd have been hard-pushed to be washed out to sea at low water slack. Not so bloody clever as you think, eh?'

'And then there was the theft of Frederick Barnard's passport,' Fielding smiled. 'That one came across my desk too. He's a friend. Did you know? And his description of the thief – Well, two and two, as they say. Though I'd hardly have recognised you now, of course. The beard. The eye-patch. But, by then, I already knew. My contacts in the Guardia. An interesting story about blood under poor Valerie's fingernails. They jumped to the obvious conclusion, naturally: you, the English Red, here to spy on them; and Valerie, the pride of National Spain, decorated by the *Generalísimo* himself. Obvious. You killed her. Political assassination.'

Jack recalled the conversation with Carter-Holt. And, yes, he'd been jealous. '*Have you shagged any other friends during this trip, Carter?*' he'd demanded. '*Fielding?*' She'd laughed at him. '*Harold?*' she'd said. '*In Santander. We are old acquaintances. Colleagues, you might say.*' Though she had refused to be drawn on whether he, too, worked for Stalin.

'Not the jealous lover story?' said Jack. 'What a disappointment. You had a starring role in that version, Fielding. Now, what the hell *do* you both want?'

'You're going to come for a ride with us, Telford,' Edwin told him, prodded him in the stomach with the automatic.

'Isn't this a slightly strange partnership, boys? The Military Attaché working with Franco's Fifth Column and Juan March, and the consular official working with one of Stalin's agents?'

'Really, Mister Telford,' said Fielding. 'Is life ever so simple? Your appearance may have changed. Yet it's the *naïveté* that gives you away. Same old Jack, Major. I'd know him anywhere.'

'And working with Franco's Fifth Column, did you say?' said the Major. 'That's imaginative, even for you. Now, collect anything that's not already in the rucksack and let's get going.'

There was no indication that Edwin had discovered the theft, and Jack wondered whether he'd make things worse by admitting it. Yet he quickly concluded that he now needed to clutch a straw or two.

'You're denying it?' he said. 'I've already seen the files, Major. In your bureau. In fact, there are photographs of the documents. My friend, General Kotov has copies of them. The links to the Fifth Column. The phoney reports on the Río Tinto situation. The bribes you're offering to Franco's generals. If anything happens to me, he'll leak them to all the right people.'

Major Edwin laughed. Not the reaction Jack had expected.

'Well, that's very enterprising of you, Mister Telford,' said Fielding. He stood, brushed some unseen dirt from his overcoat's expensive camel hair, and picked up a bowler hat from the bed. 'But I feel obliged to fill a few gaps for you. You see, I had my doubts. Continued to dig. And, finally, my persistence paid off. I spoke with our old friend, Lieutenant Turbides. He told me that a certain camera was found in your room.'

'That's not true,' said Jack. 'The camera never left Carter-Holt's room. And I think you know it.'

'You're splitting hairs,' snapped Fielding. 'You think anybody cares? The point is that you knew Valerie's little secret. Poor girl. Killing your lover, believing her to be a rabid fascist, that's one thing. Knowingly killing an agent of the NKVD, quite another.'

'Whose side *are* you on, Fielding?'

'And what d'you think this is, Telford?' said Major Edwin. 'A Margery Allingham novel? Get moving. You'll be dead soon and all the questions in the world won't save you.'

Dead, thought Jack, as the Major opened the door again, just enough to peer each way along the corridor. *Killed by my own people, after all this.* It was almost laughable. Almost. But not laughable enough to ease the nausea. He clutched the rucksack tighter to his breast, and Edwin was pushing him out of the room, the pistol now concealed in the man's coat pocket but still pressed into Jack's kidneys.

'Interesting what you say about Kotov though,' said Fielding, bringing up the rear.

'He said he was expecting you.' Jack kept his eye fixed straight ahead, calculating where he might make his break, wondering about shouting for help. Anything. He was having trouble forcing his legs to work.

'Met him this morning, as it happens,' Fielding murmured. 'He never mentioned the photographs, of course. Gracious, no. He was far more interested in my own tale by then. And incredibly angry. That you'd killed one of Comrade Stalin's agents so deliberately. Made a fool of him. Do you know what they did to Andreu Nín, by the way? Him and his pal, Orlov?'

'Tortured to death,' said Jack. A strange sense of *déja vu*, his conversation with Father Lobo. They'd reached the elevator, still waiting patiently, exactly as Jack had parked it.

'Tortured hardly does it justice, Mister Telford. I know a member of the Party who was there. They beat him until his face was pulp. Pulled out his fingernails. Peeled the skin from his flesh, piece by piece.'

'You're taking me to Kotov.' The simple statement was about as much as Jack's terror would allow him.

Major Edwin slid back the elevator's folding cage door, pushed Jack inside.

'We'd promised to do that already, Telford,' he said, gesturing for Fielding to operate the controls. 'You're a valuable commodity, after all. But now we'll change the deal slightly. Charge a premium. In addition to everything else, we'll now only agree to hand you over if we get those bloody document copies back. Something of a nuisance, but no more than that. We'll find out how you got them later. That little bitch of a typist, I'm guessing.'

Ruby? Jack knew that he should speak out. Yet a denial about Ruby's involvement was hardly likely to help and, anyway, Fielding had caught his attention.

'You see, Mister Telford, it would cause something of a scandal back home if you were allowed to squeak about the daughter of Sir Aubrey Carter-Holt being a spy for the Comintern. Secretary to the First Lord implicated with Russian agents? It simply wouldn't do. And much better for us if we let General Kotov tidy up the mess.'

'Won't this bloody thing go any faster?' said the Major, smacking his free hand against the concertina grille. 'And it's a pity your Guardia friend didn't do his job properly.'

'Turbides?' Fielding laughed. 'Oh, he tried. And I gave him as much help as possible. You see, Mister Telford, what an unpopular fellow you've become?'

It took Fielding a few moments, fiddling with the lever, back and forth, the elevator clanking up and down, until he finally positioned it so the folding grille door would open. All the time, Jack praying that somebody would come to his rescue. But only a couple of old men he didn't know, making their way to the bar. His captors pushed him out into the foyer and towards the entrance.

'Car's around the back,' said Major Edwin, then grabbed Jack's collar, dragging him to a halt and pressing the gun even harder into his spine – one of the anarchist waiters coming in, struggling under the weight of a wooden crate, rare clandestine supplies on which the Hotel Victoria relied so much.

'Mister English!' mumbled the waiter in his confusing Madrileño Spanish. 'Where have you been? And where are you going? It's cold as the Virgin's Tits out there.'

But he barely paused, too intent on shedding his burden.

'Hotel Gaylord,' Jack shouted, as they started through the doorway.

'You are joking, no?' the waiter called back, and Jack saw that he'd halted in his tracks, turned back towards them. Invoking the Gaylord to any self-respecting anarchist was like mentioning the Belfast Orange Hall to an Irish Catholic.

'Never mind,' snarled Edwin. 'Keep going.'

'What is happening, comrade?' the waiter asked, and set down his crate.

'This is official business, comrade.' Fielding smiled at the man. 'And none of yours, I'm afraid.'

The stocky little waiter scratched at his chin stubble. Then he whistled, a loud whistle, and started to move slowly forward.

'Mister English,' he said. 'Is everything good here?'

Major Edwin pulled the automatic from his pocket, aimed at the waiter.

'Stop!' he shouted, his Spanish badly accented. He waved the barrel a couple of times, warning the man to get back. But he didn't. He kept coming. And, now, two of his colleagues had also arrived in the foyer, shouting, wanting to know what was wrong. Edwin took aim. Jack saw his eyes narrow, swung the rucksack up and knocked the Major's arm towards the ceiling, the pistol exploding, deafening Jack and showering a plaster snowstorm down on all their heads. Cordite and chaos, the first waiter racing forward, tackling Fielding to the floor while Jack dropped his bag, grabbed for Major Edwin's gun hand, knowing that he was no match for his opponent. He pushed and pulled, the major pummeling at his head, only half aware of the two young lads in their greasy waiters' aprons now joined in the melee. Jack wasn't even aware of the blow that sent him sprawling on the chequered tiles, but he heard the automatic fire again. Twice. One of the young anarchists, slamming down beside him, his face half shot away. *Alfredo*, thought Jack. *That's Alfredo.* And he was rolling away, waiting for Edwin's bullets to find him, almost wetting himself. Feet pounding all around so that, as Jack got up, Major Edwin went down, finally at a disadvantage, but the pistol still waving, random ricochets whining about the hall.

Fielding, meanwhile, had fought his way off his own assailant, knocked him senseless and was up, dragging at one of the Major's opponents, tripping him, then kneeling on the fellow's chest and punching at his face. Fielding and Edwin might be outnumbered, but Jack had no doubt they'd soon have the upper hand again – the pistol was a great equaliser. And he knew he had just this one chance. Before he left, though...

Telford ran for the exit but, as he passed Harold Fielding's kneeling form, he couldn't resist taking a punt at the bugger's head. Vic Woodley couldn't have done it better, the running drop kick connecting squarely under Fielding's chin with the same satisfying slap as though it had been a soccer ball. And he didn't stop running as he reached down for his rucksack, crashed down the steps onto the Plaza de Santa Ana, hurtled past the statue of Calderón de la Barca, and lost himself in a crowd pouring from the Cervecería Alemana to discover the source of all this commotion.

Chapter Twenty-Five

Tuesday 31st January 1939

'How long has it been closed?' said Jack. He was wrapped in his army overcoat, looking out from the shuttered window of the old house on Calle de Tamayo y Baus, his eye aching. Two nights of insomnia, all the old flashbacks to the torture in Burgos, hallucination – ghosts of his father, mother and Colonel F C Telford – feelings of uncontrollable panic whenever he picked up an unexpected noise from outside. He'd come straight here after his narrow escape from the Victoria, but he was far from settled.

'Since the war,' replied the tiny, toothless and wizened housekeeper, wiping her hands on a stained pinafore. 'Better now. Then, it was all noise. Every day. Every night.'

The grey façade of the María Guerrero Theatre stared back at him across the narrow street, its walls plastered with propaganda posters, one of them just revealing an original billboard with the face of the famous actress herself.

He finished the letter, signed it, pushed it inside the envelope.

'There,' he said. 'Are you certain, *señora*, that you know what to do?'

He had given up trying to address her as *compañera*, for the old girl would simply not tolerate it. Insisted on *Señora* Moreno. A good Catholic, she kept saying. Wanted nothing to do with all this other nonsense. Jack wondered about her politics, her sympathies, unsure whether he could trust her. Yet she was plainly loyal and devoted to Father Lobo. Except – Well, he had started to ponder the priest's words. '*These are not waters in which you should wish to swim.*' If there was any sort of link between Major Edwin, the Fifth Column and Father Lobo's associates – particularly this Colonel Casado – could the priest himself be trusted? He hoped so, for no better reason than the priest's friendship with that fellow now in London. Barea. The man who worked for the Beeb. Maybe a good connection for the future. Still, here he was, for now, in Father Lobo's somewhat dilapidated house. On the ground floor, rooms converted to an oratory, now fallen into disuse, with a kitchen, an open yard and shed with occasionally functional toilet. Here, on the first, this modest, dark-furnitured living room and a solitary bedroom. On the floor above two more rooms, each filled with junk.

'You think I'm stupid?' shouted the housekeeper. She came to the desk, slapped her withered hand down on another envelope, much thicker than the one Jack had just sealed. 'This one for the man called Milanes,' she repeated, like a child practising that which she had learned by rote. 'A letter to your sister. Addressed to your friend in London. That one,' she pointed to the envelope still in Jack's hand, 'only to be put in the girl's hands. She is called Ruby.' *Señora* Moreno struggled with the name. But it was passable. 'Nobody but Ruby.'

'Very good, *Señora*. And you will be careful? Not to be followed.'

She tutted, snatched the second envelope, then headed down the stairs to collect her coat. Jack was far from sure whether he was doing the right thing but there, it was done now. He took a last glance through the window, checked the street one more time, then lit yet another cigarette, his hands still shaking. He'd lost count of how many he'd smoked since Sunday. Too many. But he was grateful for the relief they brought him. Those and the music too. Father Lobo's German gramophone stood on a small mahogany table, his record collection beneath. It was an eclectic mix. American jazz. Carlos Gardel's *tango-canciones*. Puccini's *Tosca*. And a Columbia recording of a song by a woman he'd never heard before – Brachah Zefira, a Hebrew song called *La-Midbar Sa'enu*, but with all the Flamenco melodies of Andalucia, a strong reminder of Spain's Jewish roots, the Sephardic tradition. It entranced him, helped him to think. And, goodness, did he need to think!

So, the theft of Frederick Barnard's passport had set Fielding on his trail. And Fielding had that bloody closeness to the Guardia Civil and Turbides. But how deep did that go? Was it possible that the arrival of Turbides in Madrid was something to do with Fielding? And then there was the sniper. Coincidence? Or had the waiter in the bar that night taken a bullet actually meant for Jack? Yet he had seen Turbides for himself. In Madrid. With the Weasel. And Turbides already wanted him dead. To obliterate the chance that Jack might expose Franco for a fool, duped by Carter-Holt, his award of the Red Cross of Military Merit to a Soviet assassin.

But he couldn't ignore the threats from Fielding and Major Edwin. The Major, he imagined, was the easiest of the pair to explain. A member of the British Secret Service. Wasn't that the usual clandestine role for Military Attachés? He recalled that conversation with Carter-Holt. About the beginning of this rebellion by the insurgent generals. It had come to mind again during an early conversation with Father Lobo. And, now, here he recalled it once more. The involvement of the English pilot, Bebb, and his friend Pollard. Bebb, she'd told him, had always insisted that his plane was effectively commandeered to fly Franco from the Canary Isles to Morocco – so he could help lead the revolt. Commandeered by the Nationalist conspirators. That Bebb had no choice – when, according to Carter-Holt's sources, the plane had actually been hired, by friends of Franco, weeks before the insurrection began. No coincidence, either, that Bebb happened to have Pollard on board. Because, she'd said, Pollard was also an agent of the British intelligence services. Was she right? He'd never doubted it. There were so many of the great and the good back home up to their filthy necks in admiration for Hitler and Mussolini – Franco too – that it was perfectly feasible for Major Edwin to be among them, clandestinely helping Franco's Fifth Column, doctoring reports, to play down how helpful the war was being for Herr Hitler.

If that was the case though, where did Fielding fit in? His liaison with Carter-Holt was more than simply sexual. Old acquaintances, she'd said. However they might first have met, it was plain that Fielding knew what she was. And he had involved her in his clever little scheme to get the tour group released at Covadonga. Why? *Because*, thought Jack, *he knew damned well that she had bigger fish to fry.* Her plot to kill Franco. Fielding must have known that too. Couldn't allow anything to stand in her way. So was he also working for the Russians? If that was right, what was he doing now? Side by side with Major Edwin – the man Jack had already concluded was with England's pro-fascist faction. Double agent, perhaps? The bloody rabbit hole again. Whatever might be the case, if he took their word for it, Fielding had already tipped off General Kotov about the real story. So that Kotov would want him dead too. Simple revenge for Carter-Holt's death, killing an NKVD agent.

Then there was Major Edwin himself – who didn't want to dirty his own hands, but was happy for the Russians to do the deed on his behalf. To avoid any chance of embarrassment for the British Establishment, the potential scandal if it became known that Sir Aubrey Carter-Holt's daughter was a Russian spy. On top of that, Edwin now knew that his own double-dealings were at risk of being revealed. In a nutshell, Edwin and Fielding wanted him dead as well.

How was this even possible? To be hunted not only by the Guardia Civil and the fascist Fifth Column, but also by the NKVD and, now, by his own country's intelligence services. It was four months since he'd killed Carter-Holt and here he was, back where he started. On the run. Still far from home. No. This was worse, of course. Much worse. His hands still shook. He was terrified. From Turbides and the General he could expect nothing but the most painful of deaths. Painful and lonely. Fielding he simply despised. Yet all Jack's hatred, his strongest emotions, were reserved for Major Bloody Edwin. If there should be another war, if Britain was condemned to lose yet one more generation of young men, men like his father, if her towns were going to suffer bombing – as Guernica, Barcelona and Madrid had done – then it would all be down to pro-Hitler traitors like Edwin.

Brachah Zefira's song had come to an end, the gramophone stylus scratching aimlessly on the central grooves until Jack lifted the arm from the record. There was no bathroom in the house, but there was a basin and ewer alongside his bed, and a mirror on the wall. He found his shaving kit, lathered up, and began the painful and unsteady process of scraping the beard away, wiping the hairy sludge on Sunday's copy of *ABC*. Lots of soul-searching in the paper, about how the Popular Front had managed to lose Barcelona – but still heroic fighting taking place elsewhere in Cataluña, rearguard actions north of Mataró. *¡No pasarán!*

Will this help? he wondered, as the pale flesh beneath the beard began to reveal itself. As a disguise? He cut himself a couple of times too, ripped corners from the paper to staunch his blood. Blood. The young anarchist from the Hotel Victoria, Alfredo, standing behind him, reflected in the mirror. Another one, he thought, come back to haunt me. One more death on his conscience.

And, finally, there was Ruby Waters to consider. Major Edwin's immediate assumption that she was somehow implicated in the copying of his precious files. Was she in danger too now? Jack's note to her had been simple. A brief apology for not being in touch. A promise to explain. An offer that, if she still wanted to head to the coast, she should meet him later, in the Plaza Mayor. Three-thirty, prompt. If not, he'd understand. But, if yes, she should say nothing to anybody. Certainly not to Major Edwin. Maybe leave a letter, he'd suggested, for Milanes.

Jack spared a thought for the Vice-Consul – and for Mrs Milanes too, naturally. They had been kind. Decent folk. Perhaps, one day, he'd have the chance to repay them. Which reminded him. He scrawled yet another note. This one to *Señora* Moreno. He thought he could trust her. And what the hell was he going to do with all these *pesetas* back in England anyway? Technically, his bill at the Hotel Victoria had been paid by General Kotov, but he stipulated in his note that five hundred should be sent to the family of the waiter, Alfredo; three hundred to be shared among the rest of the Victoria's workers; and two hundred for Señora Moreno herself – for looking after him, albeit briefly, and for taking care of his wishes. There were lots of mistakes in the Spanish, but he reckoned she'd understand. The rest of his back pay he divided up, put it in different pockets.

Major Bloody Edwin, he thought.

It was the thing he'd returned to, over and over, since he'd run from the hotel. What had the man said? That Jack was a valuable commodity now. '*We'll change the deal slightly. Charge a premium. In addition to everything else, we'll now only agree to hand you over if we get those bloody document copies back.*' Edwin needed the documents. Well, so did Jack. *If I'm going to do anything at all to bring the bugger down, that is*, he said to himself. Once Edwin got them back, Jack's evidence of his duplicity, his treason, would be gone. He'd already lost the article about Río Tinto – left it on the floor when he'd delivered that drop kick to Fielding's chin. He could always write it afresh. Not too much of a problem. But the document copies themselves could, he considered, be put to much better purpose.

He packed the rest of his things, checked that he'd left everything as he intended, then headed downstairs. A man on a mission. There was a coat stand in the narrow entrance hall, with a large black beret, left behind by Father Lobo, he guessed. Jack never wore hats, but the beret attracted him. *Might come in handy*, he thought, and tried it for size. It smelled strongly of hair cream, but it was roughly the right size. He burned the newspaper and the evidence of his shave in the toilet bucket and then, in the abandoned oratory, sitting on the table that Father Lobo had once used as a makeshift altar, he found his father. In uniform, of course, exactly as Jack had known he would be. There was rarely expression on the spectre's face whenever he appeared. Sometimes a wry smile, nothing more. But now there was concern, and it almost made Jack weep.

'Yes, I know,' he said. 'This is bloody suicide too.'

He turned left along Calle de Tamayo in a light and sulphurous drizzle and reached the corner just before all hell broke loose behind him. He watched as two trucks screeched to a halt and disgorged more than a dozen armed men, swaddled in their *capote-mantas* against the cold and damp. But Jack could see, here and there, from their caps, from evidence of the uniforms beneath, the blue and the grey-green, that this was a mixed force of Assault Guard urban policemen and *Carabineros*. Two cars as well. Leather-coated members of the SIM. And, from the second, Major Edwin, helping a tearful *Señora* Moreno out of the back seat, while the men's shouts filled the street. Their boots clattered on the paving and the front door of Father Lobo's house was kicked open. Was the old woman in tears through concern for her betrayal of him, or simply for the house? Jack neither knew nor cared. He simply gripped the straps of his rucksack, put his head down, and plodded through the back alleys down towards Cibeles.

As he crossed the square, he paid scant regard to the sandbagged bastions of ministry buildings, or the workers clearing rubble from another shell-hole that had appeared in the road during last night's artillery attack. It had been particularly violent though, and echoes of the bombardment seemed to remain, even now. Yet, in Calle Alfonso XI, only a few hundred yards away, almost perfect silence. Cold but quiet. Lots of activity further along, however, outside the Hotel Gaylord. Vans being loaded. But the whole thing muted, and Jack keeping his distance, watching and waiting. Partly, it was his way of plucking up courage. Partly, the total absence of a sensible plan. But the raid on Father Lobo's house had encouraged him. Major Edwin's presence. If there was, indeed, contact between Edwin, Fielding and Kotov, and the raid had failed to find him, might the phones not now be ringing?

Might that not help draw the General from his lair? But then, what? A diversion, perhaps? But, as his vigil went on, Jack's hope for such a miracle faded – and he was slowly freezing to death.

Time to move, he decided. Time to test his luck. The words Russian roulette filled his head. It was insane. And suicide might be exactly what he was doing. Visions of Andreu Nín's gruesome death. The concept of suicide had always been with him, ever since he'd discovered the truth about his father's death. About terrors so great that they could override a man's love for life, for his family, for his wife – for his son. But, ultimately, a selfish act, which paid no heed to the terrors it would bequeath to those left behind. Well, that was hardly a consideration for Jack, and death held no mystery or fears for him. It was simply the potential pain involved that he could not contemplate. Yet something else. Akin to euphoria. An end in sight. And audacity. This was the very last place on earth where his now numerous enemies would be looking, or expect to find him.

He marched into the street, pulling the beret down on his head, eye fixed on the Gaylord's entrance, the ant nest procession of cardboard suitcases, corrugated boxes and slatted crates being carried to the waiting vehicles with their armed guards, each guard wrapped in an olive-brown groundsheet, and the second line of empty-handed local workers shivering their way back inside for the next load. He timed it perfectly, the guards busy with the loading process. He murmured a brusque Spanish instruction to make way as he shouldered through the line. He marched up the steps, into the foyer, not even the usual shaven-headed thugs on duty today. No sign of Kotov or the other officers in the bar either, just the cigar-smoke memory of them, hanging around the chandeliers.

The line of porters wound straight to the first floor, and Jack went with them, though never part of the queue. He'd thought for a moment of joining them, but knew that would never work. Only audacity might save him now. And yes, he knew it was the Henty novel, borrowed from the Ritz hospital library that had inspired him. *Under Wellington's Command*. A boy's own adventure story, now left behind at Father Lobo's. The way Wellesley had forced the passage of the Douro at Oporto. Cool audacity. So he strode straight into the room where he'd last met Kotov, examined the documents with him. Would they still be there? Unlikely. Three more soldiers here, Soviet winter uniforms, supervising the dispatch. A steadily diminishing stack of packages and crates alongside them. But the table was still there, away in its corner. Two boxes balanced upon it, the top one open, rolled maps and charts protruding at all angles, the bottom one apparently closed, maybe sealed.

Jack lit a cigarette to give himself a chance to think. But one of the soldiers eyed him suspiciously. There were a couple of triangular badges on the red lapel flash of his overcoat, but Jack had no idea of the rank that conveyed. Well, in for a penny, in for a pound, he thought.

'You speak English, sergeant?' he demanded, strolling towards the man with his cigarette packet extended before him.

'*Da*,' said the soldier. Yes. And he and accepted one of the proffered *Luckies*. 'Little.'

'*¿Español mejor?*' Was Spanish better?

'Yes. Spanish. Better.' But Jack was doubtful. The man's Spanish was appalling.'

'You know me?' he said. 'Lieutenant Hemingway. Remember? Part of *Capitán* Constantino's unit.'

'Unit. Yes. Constantino. Good man.'

'But me,' said Jack. 'Lieutenant Hemingway. Remember?' The man looked doubtful, but Jack went on regardless, raising his voice, feigning impatience, even though his stomach was now completely knotted. 'Good. I come from the General. From the Lion. General Kotov. He needs papers. From that box.' Jack pointed to the table.

'General say he come back for box,' said the soldier. 'Only General. Where is General? Now.'

'I just told you,' shouted Jack, reverting to English. 'He's with the Captain. They sent me for the papers. Those bloody papers.' He dropped his cigarette, stubbed it out under his boot. 'What is your name, sergeant?'

'Name?' said the soldier. 'Me?' And doubt clouded his eyes. A flash of fear. 'I help you.' He smiled, weakly, led Jack to the table, helped to move the boxes, cut the strings binding the lower one. It took a few minutes to find the photograph copies in their manila folder – perhaps the hardest minutes of Jack's life as he strove to steady his hands, resist the temptation to constantly look around, to maintain a pretense of superiority and nonchalance.

But at least I've got them, he thought, as he dismissed the sergeant back to his other duties and made for the stairs. *All I need to do now is work out how to use them – bring down that bastard, Edwin.*

He continued to play his new role as he pushed through the removals men once more, hurrying now, and almost collided with the fellow coming up the stairs towards him.

'English?' The *Capitán* shook his head. 'It's you? By the Host, what the hell have you done? The Lion has men out looking for you.' Fidel Constantino's glance fell to the manila folder under Jack's arm, and his hand fell to the flap of his pistol holster. 'What the hell have you done?' he said again.

Hidden among the colonnades around the Plaza Mayor, with their temporary shelters for Madrid's homeless war victims, a little before 3:30 pm, and pretending to watch the passing trams, Jack replayed the encounter over and over. He had stammered for a story. About how the *Capitán* should trust him. About this English major. Major Edwin. A traitor to Spain. But, by then, Fidel had drawn the gun. The men coming and going around them had run for cover, panic and shouting, pushing and shoving. Jack had been jolted from behind, fell forwards, knocked against the *Capitán* in the crush and the two of them bowled down the stairs, arms and legs everywhere, more of the porters entangled in the confusion – and the manila folder slipping from Jack's fingers.

He had landed on his back. Rather, on the rucksack, struggled like a stranded turtle to turn himself over, scrambled to his knees and back up a few stairs to pull the folder free from beneath some wide-eyed man who was shouting for the Holy Virgin to save him. He picked up the beret too. But, by then, Jack's sergeant and his two mates from the room above were at the top of the stairs, yelling in Russian, pointing their rifles. And, below him, the *Capitán* was back on his feet, clutching his wounded side, but with Jack firmly in his sights.

Jack had raised his hands, very slowly, shook the folder.

'I have evidence,' he'd said.

And the *Capitán* had called to the soldiers.

'*¡Tranquilo!*' Relax! And then, to Jack. 'I don't know what that is, English. But here, it's all over now. You'd better go. And go fast. Because I think that if we ever meet again, one of us must die.'

Jack hadn't even thanked him. He just ran, didn't stop running until he reached the Plaza Mayor. To wait for Ruby Waters. But she'd not appeared. And the bus was due to leave, from just along the street, in less than ten minutes.

She won't be coming now, Jack, he told himself. But he checked the square one more time in any case. He gave out cigarettes to those who asked for them, and he picked his way between the tarpaulin tents, sank his fingers into the cold and ancient Spanish stone of the colonnade columns. He wondered where Turbides might be hiding. Then, incongruously, he wondered about Sister María Pereda, about what she might think of him now. And he wondered why, instead of all this business with buses and trains, he hadn't simply hired somebody with a truck, a car, to take him to the coast. Well, one way or the other, he was going. No chance any more to make the link between Major Edwin, the Fifth Column and the Republican Colonel, Casado. Nor these bribes apparently being offered to Franco's generals. But he suspected that the whole thing would unravel, here in Madrid, before too long. By then, Jack would have caught the bus to Aranjuez, the train to the coast and, hopefully, be well on his way back to England. But he would miss Spain. Miss it very much.

Somebody touched the sleeve of his greatcoat, and Jack spun in surprise, in fear.

'Mister Telford, I didn't recognise you.' Ruby Waters. Shock turned to delight, delight turning to disappointment when he saw the stiffness of her bearing, the formality of her greeting. 'The beret,' she said, though without any feeling. 'And without the beard.'

'I can't do much about the eye though, eh? But Ruby, where are your things? You'll need clothes.'

There was no smile, no warmth from her.

'I can't come with you. You must know that, surely? Much as I'd like to get out of Madrid.'

He was determined to hide his disappointment. And it surprised him that he should feel so deeply downcast. But he unslung the rucksack, rummaged for the envelope to Sydney Elliott, and for the folder too.

'I think you're in danger. From Major Edwin. Look, I took some documents from his office. He's a traitor, Ruby. But he thinks you helped me. And he's a dangerous man.'

'I have no idea why I came here, Mister Telford. I don't really know who you are, do I? But certainly not who you say. I might not like Major Edwin very much, but all the evidence tells me you're far more dangerous than he is.'

He's spun her some sort of story, thought Jack. *But no time to sort things out. Not now.*

'Then will you do a couple of things for me?' She began to shake her head, looked uncertain. But he pressed on, regardless. 'First, there's this article. It's about the Republican kids taken from their parents by Franco. Can you make sure it goes in the diplomatic bag for me?'

'How am I supposed to know what's really in this?'

'Open it, if you like. Read it. Then seal it up again.'

'I suppose I can do that,' she said. 'For the children.'

'And then would you deliver this to Milanes? Thank him. And show him. It's very important, Ruby. Look, I've written some notes on the back. But it's for his eyes only.' She scanned his penciled handwriting, trying to make sense of the information. 'One of the documents,' Jack explained, 'proves that Edwin's got secret links to the Fifth Column here. But the others are much more important. He's been receiving reports. About the amount of war materials going to Hitler from the Nationalists. From British firms like Río Tinto. Then he's been doctoring the figures. To hide the speed with which Hitler's re-armament programme's going ahead. Something else too. Seems to be in touch with Franco's generals, through that fellow, Juan March. Edwin's a traitor to Spain. But worse, he's a traitor to his own country as well. And I really do wish you'd come with me. To the coast, at least.'

'I can't come with you. You're a wanted man, Mister Telford. I don't know what's going on here, but I can't be part of it. I just wanted to see you again. God knows why. I shouldn't be here though. Don't you know, Mister Telford? What you've done?'

'I know I've managed to get three different enemies chasing me. And they all seem to want me dead, Ruby. I know there's a young waiter from the Hotel Victoria who's dead because Major Bloody Edwin shot the poor bugger. Goodness knows what else happened after I got out. But Edwin obviously survived all right. I've seen him. Tried to get me arrested by the *Carabineros*. Or shot, maybe.'

'No. You really don't understand, do you? It's Mister Fielding. You killed him.'

Jack froze.

'That can't be,' he said. 'It's Edwin again. More lies.'

'He says they were trying to question you. About a possible murder. That you set a gang of thugs on them at the Hotel Victoria. And that you waited until Mister Fielding was down, then kicked him. Like a coward. You broke his neck.'

'Did Edwin explain the waiter he shot? In cold blood, Miss Waters.'

'You didn't kick Mister Fielding?'

'I –' Jack was struggling, had reached that point where he knew that any further attempt to justify himself would simply dig him into a deeper pit. But he had no doubt that she was telling the truth. Fielding dead. The world closing around him.

'I think we've said enough, Mister Telford. Don't you?'

He agreed. Nothing more to say. Not much.

'Ruby,' he gripped her shoulders, 'I don't expect you to believe this, but I could explain. Only there's no time now. I have to catch that bus. To Aranjuez. Then the train to Valencia. But will you at least check that letter? And pass the file to Milanes? It might help me start to straighten all this out. Will you?'

'I suppose so,' she promised, and then he hurried her to one of the Plaza Mayor's many tram stops, made sure she saw him head for the Aranjuez bus in the Calle de Atocha. He looked out of the dirty window as they passed the Calderón Theatre, where he'd watched the variety show that afternoon with Ruby, ten days earlier. It was closing time, people spilling out onto the street. In Madrid, Jack knew, only a fool waited until the curtain came down. But, for him, it had already come down. With a crash. The NKVD. Turbides and the Guardia Civil. Major Edwin. That was all bad enough. Yet now? Accused of murder? The murder of a British diplomat. Telford was alone, a fugitive from his own police force, or from the International Police Commission. Alone, and on the run once more. His new papers, the Emergency Certificate he'd so painstakingly acquired from Vice-Consul Milanes, suddenly worthless. Return to England impossible, unless he could somehow clear his name. *But how can you clear your name*, he thought, *when you know you've committed the crime?* Through his panic, guilt and fear, the rational part of his brain told him he needed a new plan. So, when the bus pulled into the next stop, at the Mediodía-Atocha Station, he grabbed his rucksack and jumped off.

Chapter Twenty-Six

Tuesday 7th February 1939

He'd spent the night among the bombed-out ruins of the Argüelles district and then, next morning, almost a week ago now, made his way carefully back into the centre, to a bookshop he'd seen in the Puerta del Sol, its windows all sandbagged. He needed a map, yet didn't want to draw attention to himself. And the Librería San Martin provided pretty much what he needed – something to help him with the general geography of the Levant. So he picked up two publications there. The first was a battered copy of Baedeker's 1908 *Spain and Portugal*. He'd picked one up in London, but only bothered with the sections about the north coast – never dreaming that he'd need the rest of it and, consequently, hadn't even taken it on the tour. The second was a brochure, *Folleto Turístico: Aspectos de España*. It was richly adorned with photographs of the Escorial, the aqueduct at Segovia, the Alhambra – and, more darkly, the beaches of San Sebastián and the cathedral at Burgos. Yet there was a decent map inside, and Jack had taken time working out possible routes against the information he already possessed about transport to the east.

There was, indeed, an alternative way of reaching the coast. Bus to Cuenca, just over a hundred miles away. Tortuous but feasible. Then the local train to Arguiselas. And a series of further bus or train journeys until he reached Valencia. After that? Well, perhaps he needed to see which way the wind was blowing. France, maybe. Would they look for him in France? He supposed so. But he figured that he could hide there, if necessary. He'd mentioned Valencia to Ruby, though. Would she tell? If so, it wouldn't take a genius to work out that he might choose the Cuenca route. It would take several days too. More days during which he'd be at risk of being spotted. Whereas, Ruby had seen him go for the bus to Aranjuez and, if she'd spilled the beans, they'd already be looking for him there, probably decided by now that he'd given them the slip. So why not head for Aranjuez anyway? Lay low there. Until he was sure the station wasn't being watched, and then try for a fast train. Not Valencia though. No, better to try the more southerly ports of Alicante or Cartagena.

He had pored over the brochure's crude map in particular, remembered what he'd learned about the mainline trains, and his finger had found the place. *Albacete*, he'd said to himself. *Where the line splits. That's it. I get to Albacete and then decide. Alicante. Or Cartagena.*

Aranjuez almost made him weep. After Madrid, it was relatively peaceful. Only thirty-odd miles south of the city, just on the opposite side of the Nationalist salient, the ground they had won but never been able to extend, during that fateful Jarama offensive in February '37. A town that had grown around − and purely for the purpose of serving − the springtime royal palace and gardens there, on the banks of the Tagus. A sense of comfortable isolation, despite its proximity to Franco's Front Line. Something to do, perhaps, with the temporary breach in the rail line between Madrid and Aranjuez itself. Yet that just made the road even busier, that one main road, which crossed the river and thumped into the Plaza de Santiago Rusiñol's daily congestion. Congestion by the standards of Aranjuez, at least. Though, even there, it seemed like the trucks themselves merely whispered past, in deference to the artist for whom the square had been named while he was still alive, and as though the great man was still sketching, still sipping at his Pernod in the Green Frog restaurant, just opposite.

Jack had arrived by road, having hired a taxi to take him there. A rare commodity, Madrid cabbies, most having had their vehicles converted to water bowsers, the *taxistas* themselves retrained as tank drivers. But there remained a few for hire.

He had found a room easily enough, just across the street from the San Antonio market. An easy walk to the station each day or, rather, to the smoky bar on Calle Toledo from which he could observe the richly ornamented Moorish-style train station of the Madrid to Zaragoza and Alicante Railway Company. He watched. And he listened. While the old men argued. Loud and violent. About anything and everything.

'Only bloody Mexico could allow women in the ring!'

Conchita Cintrón, the Chilean girl, was making a name for herself in the bullrings of Mexico City.

'Well, she certainly won't be appearing here. And what about this new lad? In Córdoba. Manolete? It's a crying shame. Good bullrings standing idle. What's so different here than in the Faccioso Zone? Spain's the home of bullfighting, when all's said and done. If we don't have bullfights, it stands to reason we can't be Spanish.'

'Don't talk bollocks! One less bullfighter, one less fascist.'

'¡Hombre! Have you seen this? Now we're going to ask the bloody English and French to broker a peace deal for us.'

'Some chance. It's all the French can do to set up a few poxy dressing stations for the refugees. And the English? Don't make me laugh.'

'Refugees? They say Figueras is just one big cemetery now.'

'Fascist bastards! Bombed hell out of the hospital there. The station too. Three hundred dead. Women and kids. Women and kids.'

'The river's choked with bodies – that's what I read. The roads littered with them. The Fritzes bombed shit out of the poor bloody refugees.'

'And where's Azaña, eh? I bet he got over the border safely enough. Sodding liberals.'

President Azaña, according to *ABC*, had now left Spain, gone to France, to Perpignan, leaving Prime Minister Negrín and the government in Figueras itself. And, in *ABC* too, Jack had read an astonishing account, taken from the *Daily Mail*, of all places. The same *Daily Mail* that had been solidly pro-Franco from the very start, reported with glee on what it had described as the Red Terror in the early days of the war. And yet, here was their Spanish correspondent in Barcelona, reporting in great detail about the unspeakable horrors he'd witnessed since Franco's army had taken that city. Cruelty and mass-murder on a scale worse than anything he'd seen since the war began. Yet, while Jack was pondering all this, the talk in the bar had returned to a matter which, to them, was equally crucial. Football.

'What the hell are we going to do? Now, we haven't even got the Cataluña League.'

'And poor Barça.'

Franco's forces had only been in Barcelona for two weeks, though already there was a proscription against them using the Catalan language for the club's name, and they'd been forced to remove the Catalan crest from their insignia. Worse, Franco now had control of the *Selección*, the Spanish national team. Spain had been absent from last year's World Cup, but *El Caudillo* was so certain of victory that he'd established the team afresh in the Nationalist Zone – and had immediately forced another change. No more red shirts. Now, the colours would be blue and white.

'Sod Barça! I'll just be happy when we get our own team back.'

Jack guessed that the men were talking about Real Madrid. The war had been difficult for the fans in an entirely unexpected way. The club's President, and former player, Santiago Bernabeu, was some-where among Franco's army, fighting for the fascists. Under the Republic, the club had been forced to drop the word *Real* from its name. Now they were simply Madrid Club Futból, the royal crest removed from their shirts. With Bernabeu's defection to the rebel generals, he'd been replaced by Communist Colonel Antonio Ortega.

'What, in the name of hell,' said the men, 'did Ortega ever know about managing a team, eh?'

At the same time, *La Liga* had been abandoned and two new championships established – the Mediterranean League and the Free Spain Cup. But, as the regions of Spain had fallen to Franco, one by one, the regional football leagues had folded too, and there were unanswered questions about why Madrid seemed to have been excluded from the Mediterranean League in any case. As it happened, Atlético Madrid had fared little better. Strangely, the situation had served to unite both sets of fans.

'It's poor bloody Madrid,' they'd say. 'Every bugger's got it in for Madrid.'

That evening, Jack ventured through the portico of the fine station head-building itself, kept to the shadows, made a circuit of the crowded colonnade wings and, finally, bought a ticket for the 10:00 pm *nocturno* sleeper. It seemed to him that the ticket attendant spent far too long scrutinising him, an excess of vigour, but that was possibly because Jack had to explain three times that, yes, he wished to pay for both bunks in the first class compartment. Two bunks. And the fellow peered out of his tiny window, looking for Jack's invisible companion, any sign of additional luggage apart from the rucksack. He was then subjected to a similar level of scrutiny as he bought a copy of *Mundo Obrero* and when, to his surprise, he found a food vendor selling pieces of garlic sausage. He suspected them all, looked frantically back over his shoulder many times as he pushed his way through the miasma of onion, tobacco fumes, sweat and coal-smoke clinging about the bustling beggars, the wounded war veterans, the loitering lottery ticket touts and the perplexed passengers. The place was busy, noisy, and filled with the unique odour of train station, but Jack pushed his way through the crowds, found his platform and, somewhere in the steam, also found that haven of tranquility provided by the two first class sleeper carriages in the orange livery of the Madrid-Zaragoza-Alicante railway. There was even a conductor, looking in vain for Jack's cases, who showed him to the compartment – all varnished wood and white cotton linen, everything emblazoned with the MZA insignia. Back in third class, there was an accordionist, a sing-song taking place but, here, there was peace.

Jack tested the dickey seat beneath the window, tried the switch on the bakelite table lamp with its frilly shade, then slung his rucksack on the upper berth. It was quite a change from the second class he'd shared on the *Sud Express* from Paris to Irún in September, and a long way from the wooden third class bunk on the overnight sleeper, which had carried him, and Valerie Carter-Holt too, back from Coruña to San Sebastián. The end of that fateful tour. The night before he'd killed her. The night when he had finally started to piece the puzzles together. And when he pulled down the door blind, settled himself, still fully clothed on the bed covers, but with his greatcoat for a blanket, it was hard to push back the memories. Of Carter herself. Her acerbic humour. Sarcasm. Sharp wit. Intelligence. Eroticism. Duplicity. Her final moments. So he reached up, pulled down the rucksack, rummaged until he found the newspaper, scanned it without any real interest. More defeats softened by tales of heroic defence, in the now abandoned Extremadura offensive, and the fall of Girona. Yet, as the locomotive lurched forward, out of the station and into the darkness, his head filled with other thoughts. The journey, naturally. His own less-than-successful life – thirty-one soon, no real family life, no prospect of long-term love and affection, still towards the bottom of his career ladder, the labyrinth of disasters and horror into which he'd spun since arriving in Spain. But three further recurring conundrums.

First, why had the *Capitán* let him go, there on the staircase of the Hotel Gaylord? Had his plea convinced Fidel Constantino that he should, indeed, trust Jack? Had his mention of Major Edwin struck a chord? Or their tumble, and the *Capitán's* wound – had it disorientated him? Jack had promised him evidence – evidence that he no longer possessed. And there had been that untypical defeatism. '*But here, it's all over now.*' The threat. The promise. '*If we ever meet again, one of us must die.*'

Then, second, was Ruby truly at risk from Major Edwin? Jack had left her in a terrible predicament if, indeed, the Major believed she had been his accomplice. So now, what? Had she succeeded in passing the photographed documents to Milanes? If so, what would he have made of them? And where would Edwin be now? Still on his tail?

But when he eventually drifted into a sleep assisted by the train's rhythms, it was with nightmare images of Lieutenant Turbides. Pain and torture.

He woke again with a start, the table lamp still lit and the locomotive snorting to an unsteady halt at another station. Jack flicked the switch, darkened the compartment and peered through the soot-smeared glass, looking for a station sign. Alcázar de San Juan. He dug into the rucksack, found the Baedecker, checked the tourist brochure map, the light now flickering once more. There it was. But with the scale so small it was hard to calculate the precise distance they'd travelled. A hundred miles? More or less. He settled down: wrote some notes, random impressions of his travels; wondered whether there was time to get off, stretch his legs; and later scribbled on a blank page – hasty sketches of folk going about their business on the platform, even at this ungodly hour. By the station clock, it was 1:15 am when they pulled out and, by then Jack was beginning to doze – yet suddenly disturbed by a voice, a loud Spanish voice, out in the corridor. Jack was at once alert, afraid, as the catch on the compartment door rattled, clicked, and the door itself slid open. He jumped from the bunk, hoping for the ticket inspector, but finding instead a swarthy man in a raincoat and homburg, thick spectacles, struggling with an oversized suitcase.

'Excuse me,' said Jack, trying to block his way. 'This is my compartment.'

'No,' said the man. 'Mine. And he fished in his coat pocket, produced a ticket, consulted it. 'Look!' He thrust the thing at him, peered over Jack's shoulder. 'Only you, comrade?' he said.

'I paid for both bunks.'

'English?'

Is that a problem?'

'The English and their money,' he said, shaking his head, pushing past, hefting the case into the luggage rack, puffing and panting. 'Greedy people, the English. Greedy.'

Jack watched his every move. He was stocky, a fighter's physique. But an old fighter, fallen out of condition, gone to seed. Could he be a threat? If so, how had he found him? A telephone call from the Aranjuez ticket office? Possible. But working for which of his enemies? Or was this just paranoia? *Yes*, he thought. *Paranoia. Except, the only problem with paranoia is...* Threat or no threat, Jack was determined to complain and, as the train picked up speed, sparks in smoke and steam, clouding and scudding through the blackness beyond the windows, he swayed down the corridor in the hope of finding the first class conductor.

He negotiated his way across the shifting plate of the connecting vestibule and into the second sleeper coach, then realised that he'd stupidly left his greatcoat and rucksack back in the compartment with a total stranger who, only minutes before, he had suspected of being a mortal foe. His Emergency Certificate was in the pack, and one of his cash bundles was deep in a pocket of the coat. Jack stopped, undecided whether he should go back, to collect them before continuing his search. And, in that hesitation, that distraction, he failed to properly heed the two men coming towards him, opening and closing compartment doors.

There was a moment of mutual recognition. Jack at one end of the corridor, a leather-coated Turbides, the Weasel behind him, at the other. Jack had rarely seen the lieutenant smile, he realised. Yet the bugger smiled now. Predatory. It chilled him, filled him with panic and recollected terror. The Guardia's hand went into his pocket, pulled out an automatic pistol as he advanced along the jolting corridor. Jack turned to run. Fight or flight? Flight, of course. No idea where he was going. Anywhere. But, as he finally forced his legs to action, he ran straight into his stocky fellow-passenger, hauling the heavy case.

'My mistake, comrade. Right compartment, wrong carriage. I should be down here somewhere.'

But Jack didn't give a damn, frantic to get past the obstacle now blocking his escape.

'*¡Facciosos!*' he screamed, pointing back at Turbides. 'Fascists. Fifth Column, comrades!'

Compartment doors were opening, faces appearing, vanishing again when they saw the gun. But Turbides was now waving an identity card in his free hand, holding it aloft. Even from this distance, Jack could see the initials printed large across the document. SIM. The Republic's Military Information Service. False papers, naturally. And the train seemed to be slowing again, the *clickety-clack, clickety-clack* of its wheels over the rail joints becoming more pronounced. Another station? Surely not so soon. But if the train stopped, if Turbides could take him off...

'That man is an English spy,' called Turbides. 'A traitor to the Spanish Republic.'

'*¡Hostia!*' the stocky man swore, as Jack gripped his coat's lapels, swung him around with all his might, the suitcase slamming against wood paneling, spilling open, the contents scattering about them. Packs of nylon stockings. And women's shoes. Heeled shoes. Jack almost laughed, caught a glimpse of Turbides, the lieutenant's eyes transfixed by the footwear now littering the corridor. Jack let go the lapels, gave the man a shove, toppling him over the open case. And then he was racing back through the connecting vestibule, jumping over the swaying floor-plate, crashing into his own carriage. Doors opened along this corridor too, but Jack didn't stop. He found his compartment door open, snatched up the greatcoat, the beret, the rucksack. Out again, as Turbides appeared behind him, the Weasel in hot pursuit. Only one way to go. Forward. But to where? No more carriages this way.

Crack, crack. Bullets ripped wooden splinters from the carriage wall, a foot from his ear. Turbides was screaming at him. And Jack didn't care. He'd rather be shot than taken again. So he dodged and ran, hugging his possessions to his chest, praying. *Sweet Jesus, help me.* He thought of Merry del Val. '*No such thing, old boy, as an atheist when the garrote's screw is tightening at your neck.*' The prayer again. *Sweet Jesus, help me.* And now, Father Lobo. '*On a battlefield, there are few atheists, my son.*'

Crack, crack, crack. But, by then, he'd turned the corner, reached that farther vestibule. A vestibule that foreshadowed nowhere at all. Nowhere but the emptiness outside the boarding door. His father was there, naturally, inviting him to jump. And, for the first time in their long and strange relationship, Jack decided to follow his filial duty. He levered the handle down, kicked the door open and, slower speed or no slower speed, he still felt the sucking blast of coal-smoke wind.

Then, with the vague awareness of Turbides in the space behind him, just breathing down his neck, reaching for him, he pressed his face into the greatcoat, into the rucksack, and he launched himself out into the gut-wrenching blackness of La Mancha's night.

Chapter Twenty-Seven

Wednesday 8th February 1939

Jack hit the ground long, long before the image of his old Physics teacher fully formed in his mind. Something about vertical and horizontal velocities, torque and drag. By then, the lesson had hammered every ounce of breath from his lungs – the bizarre thought that the engine had hit him, such was the impact. Bone-shattering impact, his teeth jarring in his skull. The gravel, Spain itself, embedded deeply and painfully into the backs of his hand, his knees, his thighs, his shoulders, his buttocks. The strange sensation that his legs were locked in one place, on some downward embankment, while his body was catapulted forward, spinning over and over, the train lights like tracer fire alongside and above, whenever his face came free from the rucksack, the earth below him trembling with the locomotive's passage. The smell of smoke and sewerage wrapped around his fear, his helpless, endless tumbling. Every fresh jolt brought another stab of abrasive agony in his race with the train. Onwards he went, and down he went, bouncing through scrub and spiny plants that scourged his wounds, spiked his skull with a crown of thorns. He thought it would never stop. *How far? How far?* On and on. *Oh, Christ, how far?* Until he slammed and splashed into a bank of foetid mud, lay on his ripped and burning back in a freezing sludge. Yet it was his hands and knees that made him weep, crying like a child in need of his mother, somebody to simply bring soothing. To make it all better. And it was an age before he took a grip on himself, shook himself free of his puerility, remembered that he had survived. That he had not been shot. That he had not collided with anything, which might have killed him. That all he needed to do, now, was to assess the cost of his survival.

He sat upright, though the process made him wince and cry out, to wring from him every foul swear word in his possession. He was sitting in some sort of shallow ditch, an irrigation channel, maybe. From his left, there was a vegetable smell. Cabbage? Sprouts? Jack clawed his way up and over the lip, pushing the coat and rucksack ahead of him. Yes, a field, dimly perceived footballs planted in rows, running away into the pitch dark. There was a cold wind blowing over the ground, catching at his face. Something unfamiliar. He lifted his hand to that scarred ruin where his left eye had once been, found that he'd lost the patch somewhere in the chaos. But he was alive. He dug his fingers into the gritty soil of this harsh land, peered at the backs of his hands. A stinging mess of trickling wetness, a few sparse threads of paler skin around the dirt-dark trembling knuckles. He reached tentatively towards his knees, felt the tattered shreds of his trousers, damp and sticky with his blood. And, God, they hurt, those knees. His thighs too, as if he had climbed a mountain. They screamed at him. His sides as well. His ribs. Broken? He could barely touch them. His buttocks, however, were completely numb. The icy sludge, he supposed. His back was the same, and he knew he had to move. The greatcoat. Jack lifted it from the ground, gingerly worked a wounded hand into one sleeve, then the other. The beret was gone, maybe still on the train, but he managed to hug the rucksack again, began to limp and haul his way back up towards the tracks.

First light. Jack had staggered, crept towards the source of those few beckoning lights he'd originally seen when he finally made it to the railway line. Nothing to the east except an ebony curtain. To the west, the lights. No idea, of course, whether they represented any form of settlement, but his only option. No idea, either, how long it had taken. But first light? February? It must have been four hours. Five maybe. Fighting the exhaustion, resting whenever he'd been overcome by fatigue.

First light. Calculations to be made. Would his pursuers have assumed that the jump had killed him? No, not Turbides. Jack was fairly certain that the next scheduled halt for the train would be Albacete, though he wasn't entirely sure. And, in his new guise as an SIM agent, might he not have the power to stop the express somewhere nearer? If so, and he'd commandeered a vehicle, he could already be back in the area.

First light. A lane, which climbed the gentle slope towards a half-ruined church. A more significant village than he'd expected and, around the outskirts, on the rising ground, windmills. Lots of windmills. Houses on each side of the track, ancient white houses, tiled, almost Arabic in appearance. Wood smoke, and the tantalizing smells of baking bread. Cockerels in competition with each other. Somebody shouting within one of the dwellings. A baby crying.

First light. Jack hid behind a corner, listening for any sign of pursuit, anything beyond the ordinary. But there was nothing. Just a donkey, with empty basket panniers, being hauled from a barn by a black-clad old woman, her face wrapped in a scarf. Jack hobbled towards her.

'Pardon, *señora*,' he said. 'Is there a doctor?' She grinned at him. Toothless mouth, cratered lips, mummified face. But yes, she told him. A doctor. Three streets up on the left, then straight on. Straight on. First on the right. Jack thanked her, repeated the directions, then remembered to ask where he might be.

'This?' said the woman. 'By the Grace of Our Lady, Campo de Criptana.'

'What, in the name of all the saints, happened to you?' said the doctor, fingering the splinters embedded in Jack's scalp.

He was still wrapped in the dressing gown he had worn when he'd finally answered the door, angry at being disturbed.

'The train from Aranjuez to Albacete, doctor,' Jack explained, picking through his expanded vocabulary carefully. He was still far from fluent, but conversations like this were much easier for him now. 'A cigarette in the corridor. I opened the window. Then, I think, I touched the handle. I fell, through the door.'

Jack was leaning against a table, peeling off the greatcoat, feeling like death.

'Well, you were lucky.' The doctor's Spanish was deliberate, easy to follow, though his manner was abrupt, curt, a very different proposition from the ministrations he'd received at San Pedro de Cardeñas from poor Bob Keith. Jack needed to remember. To look up Bob's family, explain how he'd died. 'It must have been at the curve, before the Córcoles,' said the doctor. He gave Jack's hands and arms a cursory glance, then pulled up a wooden chair and began to examine Jack's buttocks through the torn trousers. 'The express slows down there. Otherwise, you'd be dead. Lucky you were carrying the rucksack. When you went for your smoke. And please remove these filthy trousers.'

Jack ignored the cynicism, his own embarrassment too. His trousers pooled around his ankles, revealing undershorts that were equally mud-soaked and shredded. Turbides would know all this about the train too. He'd ask the conductor, find out how fast the train was travelling as it slowed for the Córcoles curve, calculate the chances of surviving a leap from such a speed. Thirty-five miles per hour, say. Or forty.

'What time does that express arrive in Albacete?' said Jack.

'The *nocturno*? About four, I think. Why?' He glanced at the wall clock. 'It'll be almost in Valencia by now. Did you leave luggage on the train?'

'No luggage.' Jack winced as the doctor probed the deep abrasions on his knees, used a pair of tweezers to pick the debris from inside the wounds. 'But I have to get to Valencia too,' he lied. 'Quickly.'

'Leaving Spain? Don't like it here, I suppose. You're English, aren't you? There were Englishmen here last year for a while. Some of your international volunteers. Come to help us protect our democracy. Are you one of those? Comrade...? What should I call you?'

'My name is Telford,' Jack told him, while the first piece of gravel tinkled into the doctor's surgical tray. There seemed no point in disguising his identity any more. Quite the opposite. If Turbides came looking, it would be good to make things easy for him. Telford. On his way to Valencia. 'And no, I'm not one of the internationals. But I was in prison with some of them. For a while, in Burgos.' The doctor didn't seem to hear. 'You think they should not have been here, doctor?'

'What I think doesn't matter, *Señor* Telford. I'm a doctor. Doing my best to keep the half-starved children of this village alive, with their illnesses, their infections, for which I no longer have enough medicines. Perhaps with more medicine in Spain, less soldiers, that might have helped the cause of democracy better.'

Jack wanted to tell him about Sydney Elliott's work with the United Peace Alliance, the support groups, the Co-op. About the medical supplies, nurses and ambulances. He wanted to tell him about men like Bob Keith. But it all seemed too little, too trite.

'How long will this take to heal, doctor?' he said.

'These? A couple of months. There seem to be no broken bones, at least. But Spain? A lifetime. Maybe longer.'

They fell into silence as the wound excavations continued; as the burning iodine was applied – diluted iodine, naturally, for it was too precious to waste; and as the bandages were bound expertly around Jack's knees, elbows and hands.

'And the next train?' said Jack, when the bandaging was almost complete. 'For Valencia.'

'There's only the mail train that stops here,' the doctor told him. 'It gets in at nine-thirty. If you're lucky, it'll get to Albacete in time for you to change onto the express from Aranjuez. Otherwise, you'll be stuck on the mail train until late tonight. But it'll get you to Valencia eventually.'

By nine-thirty, thought Jack, *Turbides will be here. It'll only take him two minutes at most to find me on the slow train.*

'That sounds fine,' he said. 'Nine-thirty. Perfect. Is there a bar that opens early, perhaps? I think I need a drink while I'm waiting.' Yes, the doctor told him, gave him directions. Not far from the station. And he put up no argument at all when Jack insisted on paying him for his services. A hundred *pesetas*. Enough, Jack hoped, for him to buy some medicines. For the children, whenever supplies might become available again.

'Speaking of children,' said the doctor, rummaging in a desk drawer, produced a flesh-coloured eye-patch. 'Here,' he said. 'It's a bit small, I'm afraid. For kids with lazy eye. But the string should be long enough. And it might stop you frightening too many folk with that scar. I assume it was no surgeon who sewed you up.'

'No,' said Jack. 'Not a surgeon. But a good man. English too, as it happens. Died here, doctor. Far from his home. Perhaps he didn't need to come – though he believed he did. And yes, he also believed it was all for Spain and Spain's democracy.' The surgical tray was on the table now, and Jack managed to pick up some of the blood-sticky grit between his fingers. 'You think I don't like it here?' he said. 'You're wrong, doctor. I love this bloody country. But didn't Cervantes say something about love that's not returned? About that often being the nature of things. That's how it is for me, I'm afraid. However much I may love your country, it will certainly kill me if I can't leave.'

The bar had suited his purposes admirably. The brandy. The owner's willingness to sell him a pair of over-sized work trousers – at an exorbitant price, of course. The man was a natural bandit. Yet he accompanied Jack to the crumbling yard of his good friend, Luís *el Loco*. Crazy

Luís, who was now, complete with flying goggles, at the controls of this death trap, Jack squashed alongside. He had seen the occasional four-wheeled cyclecar, but he'd never ridden in one. And this Izaro, with its crank handle, its evil-smelling 700cc engine, was no more than a box on wheels. No windows. A canvas roof on a flimsy frame. And Luís justifying his name by veering and skewing along the concreted *carretera local*, past the last of Criptana's windmills.

'Those,' Jack pointed. 'Don Quijote?' He doubted whether Crazy Luís was likely ever to have read Cervantes, but he was curious.

'For sure,' bellowed the man, over the engine noise. 'Quijote, Comrade English. He lived here. For real. He lived here.'

There was more nonsense, but Jack remembered that chapter of the novel. The decrepit knight's first sight of the thirty or forty windmills rising from the plain. His oath that he would fight the giants. The confusion of his servant, Sancho Panza. *'Giants? What giants?'* Those, over there, with their long arms. *Tilting at windmills*, Jack thought. *How very appropriate*. He smiled, and then the smile froze. Crazy Luís was still prattling away, hardly noticed as Jack shrunk himself down into the seat and shadows of the Izaro, huddled behind his rucksack, winced as he smacked his knees against the dashboard, while a black limousine thundered towards them, almost drove the cyclecar off the road. Luís stopped his chatter, leaned out of the open window, bellowed at the dust trail now behind them, speeding towards the village.

That was close, thought Jack, sure he'd seen Turbides in the other car. But now what? He'd paid Luís to take him to the next stop along the mail train's route, at Socuéllamos. There'd been a great deal of bartering, then a delay while Luís shook a succession of fuel cans until he agreed there was enough to get him to their destination, and then back again. Would the ruse work? Jack had no idea. But he was pleased with the plan. He imagined Turbides driving back from Albacete, through the early hours of the morning, checking along the roads around the spot where Jack had jumped. Not finding him, knowing that his prey must surely be injured. So, heading where? Surely to Campo de Criptana. He would approach from the east, exactly as Jack had just seen him. He, too, would ask for the doctor, be pointed in the right direction. And the good doctor would tell. Yes, he would say. I treated the Englishman. Told him about the train times to Valencia. Yes, Valencia. He would be certain about that.

Turbides would then be in time to search the station. Then the train itself when it finally arrived. The nine-thirty. They would have to search somewhere else. By then, Jack would be in Socuéllamos, waiting to catch the train that Turbides had already searched. The weakness? That bloody bar owner. Jack had paid him well to be forgotten. But it was a weakness, all the same. Jack painfully looked back over his shoulder, though the limousine had long disappeared from sight.

'Luís, are there many *facciosos* in Criptana?' It was Jack's way of beginning to probe whether the bar owner could be trusted.

'I think we got them all,' the driver shouted. 'The priest. A dirty priest, you know what I mean, English? A couple of bastards from the Falange. A few more when the *milicianos* came back from Cáceres. That's when they blew up the church. Boom! They rounded up another bunch too. Sent them to Ciudad Real. And one of the lads told me that when the *milicianos* went off to fight in Madrid, they had a list. *Criptanenses* who'd run off there to hide. Yes, I think we got them all.'

'I thought the church had been bombed,' said Jack. But he was trying to work out how many people had been killed for supporting Franco. Or maybe just being accused of the crime.

'The other churches. Yes. The bastards have bombed us plenty. But the Parish Church, that was dynamite my friend. Boom!'

Jack remembered his conversations with the *guerrilleros* at Covadonga. Their stories. The young woman, Encarna, who'd been raped by Franco's soldiers back in '34, in Asturias. Scores to settle and driven by fear to brutality as soon as she'd heard that he was back, the rebellion begun. Or the others, those who'd been threatened by the priests with terrible retribution as soon as Franco got there – and who'd got their retaliation in first, killed the priests. Or those who were simply out of control. Blood-frenzied, madmen. And, by then, most of them had picked up the stories of what happened in the zones first captured by the Nationalists. The official lists of those to be shot. The poets and the Left politicians. It hadn't stopped either. Like Barcelona, right now. Today, Jack imagined. How many being put against the wall and butchered like dogs by Franco's henchmen?

'How will it all end, Luís?'

'Like it always ends. With us poor bastards getting shot too!'

Jack knew he was right. But how long until then? Until the

summary executions, the mass graves in the cemeteries? He tried to shift in the cramped space, his body just a solid mass of aches and pains, and he switched his attention to the cyclecar itself. The engine roared and spluttered like a motorbike, the speed controlled by a lever on top of the steering wheel, and a gear lever – Jack assumed it was the gear lever – on the outside of the vehicle, along with a handbrake. He'd driven Sheila's Austin Ten-Four a couple of times and kicked himself for not forking out the five shillings for a voluntary licence before it all became compulsory – and more expensive. Sheila had nagged him about it often enough, but he'd always got along just fine with the buses and trains.

'You don't seem like the sort of man, Luis, who'll wait around to get shot.'

'No, I'm working on that, comrade.'

Perhaps the smile should have given him away, but Jack didn't notice. Too busy easing his bruised buttocks into a more comfortable position, and only half aware of the countryside slipping by. Yet there was little enough to distract him. It was flat, featureless for the most part. From horizon to horizon. Vines hugging the earth for protection. Fields of orphaned vegetables. Ravaged stubble. A vulture or two wheeling across the dreadnought sky. An occasional truck. And, on a particularly straight and barren stretch, with not even a ruin in sight, Crazy Luís worked his way through the three forward gears and brought them to a halt at the roadside.

'Is there a problem?' said Jack.

'Like you say, English, no point in waiting around if there's another way.' He pulled from inside his jacket a revolver. It looked fairly basic, neglected. But lethal. 'Let me see your money again.'

Jack leaned away from him, managed to get his bandaged left hand into the greatcoat pocket, took out the roll of banknotes from which he'd paid Luís back in Criptana. But how did this play out? At best, the old bandit would take these *pesetas* and leave Jack abandoned in the middle of nowhere. At worst, he'd shoot him and search his body for more. And there *was* more, of course. Two more rolls of cash hidden in other pockets.

'Luís,' he said, 'you can have all this if you drive me to Socuéllamos.'

Yet he'd not finished the sentence before Luís had snatched it from his hands.

'All this I can have,' he smiled at Jack, 'for doing nothing at all, Comrade English. The question I have to ask myself is, might there be more?'

'If there was more, Luís, why would I be travelling like this?'

'That is the same question I've been asking myself, *señor*. Why are you travelling with Crazy Luís at all in this poor excuse for a car? And who were the men in the Hispano-Suiza you did not want to be seen by? Oh yes, I saw them. With this much money,' he waved the newly-acquired *pesetas*, 'you could have travelled so much more comfortably. Without the need for this little detour to Socuéllamos. Now, get out. And leave the rucksack.'

Space in the Izaro was limited, to say the least, the cyclecar having only one door, on the passenger side – the driver needing to clamber in first if he was carrying a second person. So Jack reached behind him and clumsily levered the handle up, then began the difficult, even more painful task, of extricating himself from the vehicle.

'Oh, Mother of God,' he cursed, as he banged his knees again, part in and part out of the car.

'Over there,' said Luís. 'Go on. Move away.'

Jack hobbled backwards, just a couple of steps.

'Have pity, Luís. You can't leave me here.'

'Can I not?' Luís lifted the rucksack from the passenger seat, shifted across to that side, set his gun hand on top of the door, the other, still clutching the money, on the metal roof support. Jack's only chance and, difficult as it might be, he started forward, ready to use his boots. He'd killed Fielding that way, after all. But then the revolver came up. 'That would be stupid, English,' Luís snarled. 'Really stupid. Now, move.' Jack limped away, looking around for anything that might serve as a weapon, a distraction, an escape. But there was nothing. 'Pockets,' said Luís. 'All of them. Show me.'

A glimmer of hope. *If he meant to kill me*, thought Jack, *he'd have shot me first and searched the pockets later. Wouldn't he?* Now he wasn't so sure. So he reached into his coat pockets, gripped the linings with the tips of his fingers, turned them inside out.

'You see?' he said. 'Nothing.'

Luís shook his head, began to push himself up and out of the vehicle, turned to stop the engine, lost eye contact in the moment Jack needed to drop into a crouch and roll, feeling every cut and bruise, towards the back of the Izaro. The revolver fired, but merely kicked up dust several yards away, by which time Jack was pressed low against the sloping trunk.

'English, don't make me shoot you.' Jack heard the man's own boots on the gravel, stepping back, he guessed, giving himself space. But, sooner or later, Luís would have to shift his ground to get a clear shot. One side or the other. And there it was, the sound of his movement just off to the left. Jack had his back to the car, slipped around so that he kept the vehicle between himself and the bandit. 'I told you, *señor*, it is a poor excuse for a thing. Too small for you to hide. Why don't you come out now? Save yourself some pain.'

The voice was coming almost from the rear of the Izaro now, so Jack edged carefully towards the front, stopped when he got to the small grille through which the starting handle was inserted. He tried to pull it free without making any noise, but that was impossible, and the damned thing clanged like a monastery bell as he wriggled and turned it, finally held it in his hands. At the same time, Luis broke into a run, along the road, while Jack turned again, like a spinning top, seeking the cover of the front wheel arch, keeping his head down. He knew very well that Luís could have finished him. But the man, for all his faults, was plainly reluctant to kill. Or perhaps a little unsure of himself. Or his opponent. It was Jack's only edge.

'Luís,' he called, 'you've got most of my money. The rest is in the rucksack. And the rucksack's in the car. Look, I trust you, Luís. Take the money and let me walk away. Seriously, the men you saw, they want me alive. Very badly. They'll hunt you down if you kill me. I promise you. The rucksack is on your seat. Look inside for yourself.'

There was no answer but, after a moment, he heard Luis moving softly towards the driver's side. *Wait, wait,* Jack told himself, straining his ears for the moment when the old bandit must reach for his treasure. There. The passenger door was still open and Jack dived through. Luis was peering inside, his left arm stretching for the rucksack. Their eyes met. Luís started back, lifted the revolver. Then he smiled, thought Jack was going for the rucksack too, reached for it again. And Jack gripped the man's sleeve with everything he had, yanked it towards him, slammed Crazy Luís into the side of the car. The revolver went off again but

236

Jack didn't wait. He was back outside, rolling over the bonnet as Luís clambered to his feet. And, as he swung the revolver around one more time, Jack slammed the starting handle down on his wrist. There was a sickening crack, a scream of pain. Jack lifted the handle again, would have smashed the fellow's skull, but Luís had dropped the gun and was on the ground, writhing, swaddling the damaged wrist to his chest.

'Bastard,' he swore. 'I would not have killed you, English.'

'Is that right?' said Jack, collecting the revolver and stepping away from him. The Spaniard still sat, wincing with pain – something that gave Jack guilt-ridden pleasure, some compensation for the tortures he had just inflicted on his own body. 'Take off your boots, Luís,' Jack told him.

'Why, English? You're not going to shoot me if I refuse. I don't think so.'

'Luís, you need to listen to me. You remember all those questions? About why I'm travelling this way? About why I didn't want those men to see me? It's because, in the last four months, I've killed three people.' He could see disbelief etched upon the bandit's grinning face. 'That's why they're looking for me. If I don't get away, Luís, I die. So no, I don't want to shoot you. Well, more precisely, I don't want to kill you. But shooting you? That wouldn't bother me one bit. In your leg, your knee, your foot – that would be a small thing for me if it means I can escape.' Jack held the man's gaze steadily, coldly, until he saw the scepticism evaporate. Luís unfastened his bootlaces, one-handed, to reveal a pair of socks so badly holed that they were almost redundant. 'Now walk,' said Jack. 'That way.' He waved with the revolver, back towards Campo de Criptana.

'But, señor, you cannot drive the car.' Luís stood with difficulty. 'You don't know how.'

'I'll work it out, Luís. Just go. Now.'

Jack watched him until he'd disappeared from sight, then went back to the front of the Izaro, picked up the starting handle and after a few turns got the motor running again. Driving it, however, was a different matter. The throttle, the handbrake and the footbrake were simple enough. But the gears? Each time he depressed the clutch pedal and tried to engage forward drive, the uproar of grinding metal was horrendous, and the gears refused to engage. It took a half-hour of trial and error before he realised that operating this particular machine was counter-intuitive, required that the clutch pedal be kept to the floor while driving, released whenever he needed to select a different gear.

Yet, in the end, he mastered the art, was weaving his way to Socuéllamos – and, he hoped, to freedom.

Chapter Twenty-Eight

Thursday 16th February 1939

According to the Baedeker, the name Albacete originated from the Moorish *Al-Basita* – the plain. It was appropriate, Jack considered, both for its location and its architecture: the upper town, with its important rail junction – Jack had come to think of it as Castilla-La Mancha's answer to Crewe station; the medieval heart, possessing some interesting buildings; several fine streets, trapped in the centre of a mystifying labyrinth of narrow alleys filled with crumbling houses – and those houses only marginally less care-worn than their relatively more modern counterparts in the lower town, the *ensanche*, which clustered around the Palacio del Conde de Pino-Hermoso. 14,200 inhabitants. Or, there had been back in '08. It must have risen significantly since then, of course. More recently, the population had been swollen enormously by the arrival of the International Brigades, which had used Albacete and its outlying villages as their base. Thousands upon thousands of volunteers had come here to be equipped, organised into military units, sent to the various fronts to fight for Spain's Republic. Volunteers from more than fifty countries, they said. Yet now they were all gone. Mostly gone, anyhow. And Albacete had all the atmosphere of a once-bustling spa town, closed and windswept for the winter.

Jack had been here a week already, contrary to his original plan. He had managed to drive the Izaro to the outskirts of Albacete, then dumped the infernal contraption into a scrub-filled *arroyo*, walked the rest of the way to the station there, with time to spare before the day's stopping train arrived. He'd found a clothing shop where he bought another beret, then waited until the last possible minute before boarding, satisfied himself there were no obvious enemies in sight, and concluded that it would have been searched back in Campo de Criptana. But the tedious onward journey had kept his nerves on edge as they trundled through the snow-smeared landscape, paroxysms of fear every time they pulled into the stations. Villarrobledo. Minaya. La Roda. La Gineta. Finally into Albacete itself where, he'd convinced himself, there would be a reception committee awaiting his arrival – some strange grouping of the Guardia Civil, the British Intelligence Service, the Republic's secret policemen and agents of the NKVD.

There had, of course, been nobody but, by then, Jack's wounds were plaguing him and he'd lost confidence in what he should do next. He had dithered, then decided to find somewhere to rest, and had walked the streets until he came across the Hotel Francisquillo in Calle del Progreso. It had all the atmosphere of an old staging inn, but he liked it. He had weighed the possibility of pursuers tracking him here, though he thought it unlikely that any of them would think him stupid enough to break his journey this way. So he had settled into the Francisquillo, initially for just one night. But here he was, many days later, still in residence. Even so, on his arrival at Albacete he had done his best to set something of a false trail, making a nuisance of himself at the ticket office. A ticket for Valencia. And, when that train had eventually arrived, he had boarded and similarly annoyed the conductor, along with a couple of passengers, so they'd all remember him, before slipping back onto the platform at the last moment.

In the hotel room, he toyed with his latest acquisition. The revolver. There was a maker's mark, Eibar, and the year 1927, on the butt while, on the barrel, it carried the information Cal.32.20 CTG. So, a Thirty-Two, in the common parlance of the movies, of Jimmy Cagney and Edward G. Robinson. He knew that much, at least, but absurdly found himself clutching the gun between his awkward hands, muttering lines from *The Public Enemy* – an exceptionally poor imitation of Cagney.

His nervous laughter soon abated, though. Only four bullets left. Hardly enough to protect himself, he realised, should that be necessary. He thought about Eibar, for that was one of the towns they had visited on the north coast. The tour bus. Carter-Holt. All those confused images. And he thought about Crazy Luís. What would the fellow have done? Walked all the way back to Criptana? Jack doubted that. But he would have reported Jack, one way or the other, wouldn't he? Reported the wanted man, maybe hoping for a reward. Well, if they came looking for him in Albacete, they would pick up his clever false trail, surely. A long and wild goose-chase to Valencia. According to the Baedeker, Valencia looked enormous, the sort of place where a man could be lost for a very long time – that is, if he was there at all.

But I won't be, thought Jack, flattening the map on the Spanish tourism brochure. Albacete. More than halfway from Madrid to the coast. Excellent. *So, time for a decision. Alicante or Cartagena?*

'Good morning, Don Alberto,' said Jack to the bent and bespectacled fellow, sketching at a table window in the Francisquillo's small dining room. Jack draped his overcoat over the back of a chair and sat down, without needing an invitation, and eyed the sketch: a caricature of Hitler, with Franco and Chamberlain each licking one of the Führer's boots. 'That's very good,' Jack told him with genuine admiration. Don Alberto had talent and a huge amount of local respect, despite being only a few years older than Jack himself. But he seemed to be Don Alberto, rather than Comrade Alberto, to just about everybody in town. A cartoonist, yet also a local journalist and one of Albacete's official archivists. A regular, each morning, at the Francisquillo. 'And what's for breakfast this morning?'

'Oh, the usual,' said Don Alberto, picking up the *Defensor de Albacete* and a copy of *ABC*. 'Let me see. What would you like? You could begin with this Roosevelt promise to sell arms to any country fighting totalitarianism – any country except Spain, of course. Or maybe this promise by Chamberlain that any threat to France will bring Britain immediately to her defence. That's excellent news. But why, then, has Spain been hung out to dry?'

Jack hadn't hidden his own identity when they first met, several days earlier, nor his profession.

'I'm ashamed of my own country, Don Alberto. We seem to accept that Franco is only winning this war because of Italy and Germany, but we do nothing about it.'

'Well, too late now in any case, I think. Have you heard the rumours from Madrid?'

Jack admitted that he had not, and Don Alberto didn't really enlighten him.

'Well,' said Jack, 'happy anniversary, in any case.'

'Three years,' Don Alberto smiled. 'You remembered.'

Three years since the General Election, which had brought the Popular Front to power. But Jack had only remembered because of an article in yesterday's paper.

'And what's the latest on the Alicante line?' said Jack.

Word had come through yesterday. Italian bombers had strafed and de-railed a train. Few casualties, it seemed, but it couldn't have happened at a worse time, just as Jack had finally decided to continue his journey.

'Nothing in the papers,' Don Alberto told him. 'Why? You're leaving? And how are the cuts?'

The backs of Jack's hands were still a mess, but he'd got rid of the bandages, let the air lick at the wounds. They were starting to form scabs at last, to dry out, but they looked horrendous. His left knee and both elbows were the same while, around those abrasions, there was bruising in all the colours of a thunderstorm, and even bigger bruises on his thighs and backside. His limbs had been stiff as boards for almost the whole week.

'It was a nasty fall,' Jack replied. 'But on the mend. And yes, time for me to be moving on, I think.'

'I wish we all had that choice, *Señor* Telford. Such a mess. I just thank God that more weren't hurt on the train. A hundred of our people have died here in Albacete alone. Did you know? From the bombs. In Valencia, over eight hundred. And now this.' He slapped his hand on the copy of *ABC*. Jack had already studied the article. More atrocities by Franco's men against the people of Barcelona. 'Animals,' said Don Alberto. 'Filthy animals.'

Jack remembered Crazy Luís, his story about how the Falange supporters in Campo de Criptana had been rounded up and summarily shot. Wrongs on both sides, he knew.

'This isn't just some individual madmen taking the law into their own hands, is it?' he said, for he had been appalled at the scale of executions allegedly taking place now in areas newly-taken by the Nationalists.

'Are you still trying to be even-handed, *Señor*? The journalist in you, I suppose. But no, this is very different. And if the stories of killings by the so-called Reds still trouble you, let me tell you a different yarn. I spent a lot of time searching for the truth myself, in the beginning. Then, one day, I met this *campesino* from a village very near here.

I interviewed him. A literate man. Literate in his thoughts, at least. He told me this. That, somewhere deep inside him, there was a joy of simple pleasures, an animal instinct for his family. But he used to come out through the door of his shack every morning, onto the little patch of dirt he tried to farm. This particular patch of dirt was on a hillside and, from there, all he could see, from one horizon to another, was the land owned by the Duke of Alba. Or the Duke of This-and-That, I don't remember. This patch of dirt was part of the Duke's land. And the Duke paid him two *pesetas* a day to farm for him.'

'Two *pesetas* a day?' said Jack. 'What is that – Just enough to keep you from starvation but to trap you in malnutrition?'

'If you are a woman,' Don Alberto replied, 'you don't even receive the two *pesetas*. It's your born duty, after all, to break your back fetching wood and water, to scrub and mend and cook. You have no education. Why? Because the Church says you do not need one. Just a few months. Enough for you to learn how to make your mark and learn the names and history of the Saints, through some stupid little rhymes. Maybe enough for the priest to have fun with your arse too. But why complain? You're no different from a full three-quarters of Spain's entire population. You will be lucky to reach the age of fifty. But in that time, the Church will encourage you to have many children. Too many to feed. But, what the hell? Half of them will die while they're still babies anyway. They'll die and go to Heaven. If you work hard, and don't complain, when you die too you'll be rewarded, see your babies again.'

'And then along came the Republic.'

'Yes,' said Don Alberto. 'One day, the *campesino* heard that something had changed. Men came to his shack. The Duke of This-or-That had gone, they said. The people owned the land now. The *campesino* and his neighbours. You can work it together, they told him, and share the money you make. All that joy, all that passion for his family came pouring out of him. He danced and he sang. But not for long.'

'I think I know this part,' Jack told him. 'Because the priest had not really gone at all.'

Don Alberto smiled, but it was a weary, careworn thing.

'The priest said that a great General was coming, to take back the land for the Duke of This-and-That. He told the *campesino* that if he didn't give back the land willingly, the General would say he was a Red – whatever that meant. He said that the General would shoot him and that the Church would cast him out so that, when he'd been shot and was dead, he wouldn't go to Heaven and wouldn't see his babies again after all. What do you do, the *campesino* asked me? Maybe, he said, you just shrug your shoulders and do as the priest says, like you've always done. Maybe you decide that you will join the army that's fighting this General. And then the old *campesino* looked me in the eye. Oh, fuck it, he said, maybe it's just easier to kill the damned, dirty priest. I knew that's what he'd done, and I couldn't blame him. After that, I realised it was pointless to try and be rational about any of this.'

Jack smiled.

'That's a very clever story,' he said. 'I might use it one day.'

'Be my guest,' said Don Alberto. 'But you certainly won't be leaving today, *Señor* Telford. So will you come to the meeting tonight?'

A public meeting. There were posters all over town.

'Where is it again? The Teatro Circo?'

'Talayo's speaking,' Don Alberto reminded him. 'Yes, at the Circo. An excellent comrade from the Socialist Women's Collective. Another from the Women's Antifascist Movement. They'll put some fire back in our bellies. You'll enjoy it.'

Jack had rather been planning on the Albacete Women's alternative entertainment for the evening – one of their regular amateur variety shows at the Cine Capitol.

'Well, we'll see,' he said. 'But I'll walk up to the station anyway. See when they expect the Alicante line to be open again.'

'No breakfast, after all?'

'Say nothing,' Jack whispered, standing and pulling on the coat, 'but the coffee's much better over at the Matchbox.'

The Matchbox – the *Caja de Cerillas* – seemed to be so-named because of its long, white marble-topped tables, at the far end of which was a series of bright red divans. It was almost directly opposite the hotel, across the Calle del Progreso, an elegant snow-frosted boulevard with its tree-lined central *paseo*. It was also right next to the Town Hall. And it wasn't simply the coffee that attracted Jack to the place. It was the girl, Estefania. Attractive. Auburn hair. In conversation, during his first visit, it had transpired that she'd been born and raised in a village just south of Pamplona. A point of common contact. Had he seen this? Had he visited that? Jack had to admit that his time in Pamplona had been short, not much opportunity for seeing the city's many sights. Still, she had flirted with him outrageously and Jack eventually enquired whether there might be a man in her life.

'Only you, *guapo*,' she had told him. But they were obviously attracted to each other and, as Jack liked to think of it, one thing had led to another. Two nights before. A great deal of subterfuge: Jack given her address and instructions on how to find the place; hushed voices when he'd arrived; no lights; but a great deal of passion, which had helped to clear Valerie Carter-Holt largely from his mind.

This morning, as had now become routine, his coffee and a piece of barely buttered bread were waiting for him as he entered the Matchbox, though Estefania's greeting was tepid, to say the least. Yet the place was busy at this hour and she seemed unusually flustered in her work. So, while she looked after her other customers, Jack made a real effort to concentrate on something other than the girl's obvious virtues. He was more than a little besotted, but he dutifully read through the other local daily, the *Diario de Albacete*, and watched the town's civil servants and military officers coming and going. Nothing new. So, when he was done, he called brightly to Estefania for the bill.

'There's a variety show tonight,' he told her, as he sorted through some coins, 'at the Capitol. Would you like to go?'

'No way!' she snapped at him. 'Don't you know there's a meeting, at the Circo?'

She went to fetch his bill, while Jack nursed his rejection.

'Hey, Estefania,' he heard one of the old men at the bar shout to her, 'any news from that husband of yours yet?'

She cast a hard-faced glance in Jack's direction.

'No,' she said. 'Not for months. Still somewhere on the Guadalajara Front, I think. But the bastard never writes, so how would I know?'

Should he have felt angry? He wasn't sure. Just sad, hollow in the pit of his stomach, despite the breakfast. He'd known, of course. A willing participant in the game. And she hadn't needed to spell it all out, nor rub his face in it. He threw fifty *céntimos* on the table, turned left out of the café and headed for the station, chewing over his grubby dalliance with Estefania as he went – thoughts that were too obvious to be in any way profound. He crossed Peral, with its arched portico for the Teatro Circo, where tonight's meeting would take place. Posters advertised the event, partially concealing those of movies recently shown there. *The Sailors of Kronstadt. Shanghai. Tiger Shark.* But, beyond Progreso, the side alleys grew steadily more shabby: small workshops; hungry children; smell of rotten vegetables; metallic ring of tools, all along the length of Calle de la Estación; and street vendors, mainly trying to sell the knives and daggers for which Albacete was famous. Jack stopped to consider them, but most of these seemed to be poor quality, despite the lurid slogans etched onto their blades. *No me saques sin razón ni me entres sin honor.* That sort of thing. Draw me not without reason, sheathe me not without honour. It made Jack think of Estefania again. Her husband too. His own dishonour. Then about whether such a weapon might be useful to him on his travels. But he decided not, and he moved on without accepting any of the many invitations to barter.

Before the station itself, he stopped, looked at the railway traffic stacked in Albacete's extensive sidings – several trains now prevented from making the onward journey to Alicante. An armoured troop train closest to the fencing, its hollow-faced soldiers with nowhere to go except along the tracks, squatting beside their cattle wagon accommodation. There was a strong stink of shit; small fires lit to boil mess tins; unhappy, defeated faces. He had a pack of cigarettes in his pocket, shouted to one of the men and handed over the *Superiores*, told the soldier to share them around.

'Where have you come from?' Jack asked, and the soldier looked at him as though he was stupid.

'From the Front, comrade,' he said. 'Where else?'

Jack nodded, wished him good luck and walked on towards the long, brick bulk of the main station building. He spotted a notice board, thought there might be news there about the Alicante line. But he recoiled in horror when he focused instead on the poster. A good hand-drawn likeness of himself. Two likenesses, in fact, side by side. One showing him clean-shaven, the other with him sporting a beard and beret. Both of them with the eye-patch.

'Shit!' he said, looked around quickly, then back at the poster. *Se busca*, it read. Wanted. *Para el asesinato de un diplomático inglés.* For the murder of an English diplomat. There was a good description of Jack too. And a reward. Five hundred *pesetas*. Instructions to report any information to the relevant authorities. Where else might they have posted the notices? He imagined them on every street corner. But why? Had he not covered his tracks? It took him a few moments to realise that, with few options for destinations – really only Cartagena, Alicante or Valencia – it would have been relatively easy for his various enemies to post watchers at each of those stations and, if he hadn't yet been spotted at any of them, he must logically therefore still have been somewhere between those ports and Madrid. And there was the guilt, of course. The feeling that he had been slapped by bad luck, brought upon himself, the retribution for his night of sin with Estefania. *Make sense, Jack – think*, he told himself, and almost instinctively stepped behind the nearest tree, decided to cross back over towards the city, grab his belongings and lose himself for a while, try to work things out. Yet, as he did so, his eye was caught by a figure coming from the opposite direction – the way Jack himself had walked not long before. The neat and busy figure of Ruby Waters.

Jack's heart literally leapt. He almost ran into the road, then realised the risk. *What the hell is she doing here?* he thought. She knew he'd killed Fielding, of course. But following him? She couldn't be. And then, further back along the Calle de la Estación, he saw somebody else. A man who moved like a cat, strolling nonchalantly, yet on guard at the same time, past the street vendors, stopping to chat with them though, now and then, making sure he also kept Ruby always in sight. Major Edwin. Jack's conclusion? That Edwin was using Ruby to help pursue him; that they'd somehow resolved their differences to form this alliance; that they'd tracked him to the Francisquillo; and that they'd followed his trail to the station. He pressed his back to the plane tree's trunk, watched as Ruby disappeared into the station, then observed that the major had remained partly hidden among the vendors' carts.

After a few minutes, Ruby emerged again and retraced her own steps. Interestingly, Major Edwin disappeared entirely, seemingly making sure he stayed out of sight. Then, when she'd walked a long way back down the street, he began to slowly follow her again. *Why?* Jack wondered. *If the girl's working with him, why is he staying hidden from her?* It was then that Jack noticed a third familiar face, coming out from a seedy local bar just after Edwin had passed. And this fellow sauntered off behind the major, just as the major had shadowed Ruby. Almost farcical. But far from funny. For the man pursuing Major Edwin, and therefore on Jack's trail too, was the Weasel – the creature Jack had last seen on the train from Madrid with Lieutenant Enrique Álvaro Turbides.

Chapter Twenty-Nine

Friday 17th February 1939

Money talks, thought Jack, *even among anarchists*. It was early, not yet seven. He'd spent a restless night holed up at the Francisquillo, the revolver never far from his hand. And, this morning, he had quietly checked out and found the service entrance for the Gran Hotel Albacete, just off the Plaza del Progreso's formal gardens and naked trees. Inside the hotel, room-staff were preparing fresh bed linen for the guests, the waiters preparing breakfast.

'*Mi novia*,' said Jack. My girlfriend, fiancé. 'She arrived yesterday.' It was a reasonable guess, made after he'd followed those who, in turn, had followed Ruby here, and he had observed Major Edwin himself enter the hotel just a few minutes after her. The Weasel, however, had taken up his observation post in the square opposite. 'I'd like to surprise her.' Jack slapped the side of his rucksack for emphasis. 'But I don't know her room number.' The old waiter with the red and black neck-scarf looked doubtful, but Jack's brace of crisp twenty *peseta* notes seemed to bring a change of heart.

'Name?'

'*Señorita* Waters,' said Jack, and slipped him a piece of paper on which he'd written Ruby's name.

'You fiancé, comrade?' The old man's face set hard.

'Yes,' Jack told him, knowing from the fellow's demeanour that something was seriously amiss.

'I understand, my friend.' The waiter nodded slowly, solemnly. 'Room three-one-four. Do what you must,' he said, and handed the money back. 'No need for this either.'

Jack took the back stairs, climbed to the third floor, then tapped quietly at Ruby's door. Time for a confrontation, and he was reasonably certain that he understood the waiter's inference. An affair of honour to be settled – though perhaps not that which the old anarchist had assumed. It was several moments before she opened, only a few inches, then astonishment and a few inches more.

'Mister Telford, my goodness.' A quick glance back into the room, but no invitation to enter. Jack's hand dropped into his greatcoat pocket, to the Eibar Thirty-Two.

'He's here, isn't he?'

'Who, Mister Telford?'

'Don't play games, Miss Waters. Your friend, Major Edwin, that's who.'

'I haven't seen Major Edwin since – well, for several days. And he's finished. It seems that way, anyhow. Mister Milanes read those coded reports. He's passed it all upstairs, to people he trusts. But there was a furious row. The major said that Mister Milanes had no jurisdiction over him. That he only answers to his own superiors.'

'Then what's he doing here in Albacete?'

As though he had uttered some pantomime portal spell, the door flew open and Jack's right arm was gripped so tight, as he was dragged through, that it was impossible to draw the revolver. He found himself face down on the carpet, somebody kneeling on his back, the gun taken from him, and every still-bruised sinew screaming against the violation.

'Shut the door,' hissed a Spanish voice, one that Jack knew well. 'And find me something to tie him. There, the belt. From your coat.' Then the same voice, closer to Jack's ear. 'Didn't I tell you, English? That if we ever met again, one of us must die.'

'I thought you were just being dramatic,' Jack wheezed. 'And no need to tie me. I've got nowhere else to go. Besides, you've got my gun.'

But it made no difference. The *Capitán* was soon trussing Jack's hands behind his back, binding them tight, rasping those fresh scabs from his wounds. Jack cried out – the pain almost as bad as the original injuries. Then he was hauled to his feet, thrown down into an armchair opposite the double bed.

'I gave you a chance,' said Fidel. He was holding the revolver in one hand, an automatic pistol of his own in the other. 'Because of her.' He nodded towards Ruby. 'But you seem to have a death wish, English.'

'In English,' Jack winced, 'we call that a bad penny.' He used the words *penique falso*, as he'd heard others say the phrase. 'But I don't understand. You let me leave because of Ruby?'

'I had grown fond of her, though I knew she liked you too. But my general, the Lion, had given orders that you should be shot. Well, he was on his way towards the coast by then, to Alicante.'

'Prime Minister Negrín's there, Mister Telford,' Ruby explained. 'In Alicante. He crossed into France with Azaña. But now he's back. Perhaps he'll be able to negotiate a peace after all.'

'Either peace or we fight together until the end,' said Fidel. 'That's now the policy decision of the Party in Madrid. Anyway, I figured that, if I killed you, it might be for the wrong reasons. Killing a rival. You know what I mean? An affair of the heart.' He laughed, but was suddenly serious again. Deadly serious. 'Instead of executing a traitor. Besides, she told me you'd only stayed in Madrid so long to pay a debt. To me. For bringing you from Burgos. Understand, English?'

Jack looked at Ruby. Her cheeks had flushed and the prim, pixie's face looked anguished. He liked Ruby. But there was nothing between them. Was there?

'Rival?' said Jack. 'I don't follow. And I stayed in Madrid because of my debt to your General Kotov. He wanted to find out from me what happened to the agent Comrade Stalin had sent to kill Franco. That's why he sent you to rescue me, wasn't it?'

'Never mind,' Fidel snapped at him. 'You said that this Major Edwin is here. In Albacete?'

'Last night,' Jack replied. 'He followed Ruby to the train station, then back again.'

'He threatened me, Mister Telford. After his confrontation with the Consul. Convinced that I'd somehow helped you to acquire the copies of his reports.'

'He did not believe, English, that you were clever enough to do it alone.' The *Capitán* smiled at Jack's humiliation.

'His inference,' Ruby went on, 'was that he could have Mister Milanes silenced through diplomatic channels. His superiors in the Intelligence Service would see to that. But he couldn't have a rogue reporter running loose or going back to Britain with the contents of those reports. Nor the rogue reporter's snitch. That was the word he used. He meant me, of course. I told the Consul, and he suggested that

251

I should get out of Madrid. Go home. For a while, at least. Things aren't good in Madrid, in any case. Not just now. And Fidel – *Capitán* Constantino, I mean – agreed to escort me. It's something of an irony, is it not, that I'd assumed you already gone from Spain?'

'Milanes is a good man,' said Jack. 'Is he in danger from Major Edwin?'

'Only professionally, he thinks. Poor, dear man. But he's due to retire. He'll be bound by the Official Secrets Act in any case.'

'Then why doesn't Major Edwin think you'll be bound by it too?'

'Oh, the lower grades of the Diplomatic Service are far more difficult to threaten. Far less to lose. So we seem to both be in the same proverbial boat, do we not? I can't believe that the major would genuinely harm me. While you, Mister Telford, seem to be in an entirely different predicament.' She turned to the *Capitán*. 'Fidel,' she implored him, 'you can't be serious. About needing to kill him? I won't allow you.'

'I have my orders,' said the *Capitán*. 'But perhaps I can get new ones. In Alicante. Turn him over to the authorities there.'

'You've still the death of Mister Fielding to account for, Mister Telford,' Ruby said to him. 'It might help if you told me the truth, perhaps. The whole truth.'

So he did. Told them both. About Carter-Holt. About the siege at Covadonga. About Fielding's part in bringing the siege to an end – though for his own and Carter-Holt's ulterior motives. About the consequences for the Machado *guerrilleros*, there in the mountains of the north. About her plan and attempt to assassinate Franco but place the blame on Jack. About their confrontation back in San Sebastián and his conviction that Carter-Holt intended his own murder. About his act of self-defence and Carter-Holt's own death. About Burgos. About his torture by Turbides. About his eye. Then about Fielding's appearance at the Hotel Victoria, along with Major Edwin – their plain intention to dispose of him. Fielding's part in giving General Kotov his own warped version of Jack's reason for killing Carter-Holt, as well as the man's murky relationship with Turbides. He hadn't intended to kill Fielding, of course, but self-defence too?

'You promised me evidence,' said Fidel. 'About those reports you stole from the Lion.'

'I stole the reports *for* the General,' said Jack. 'He knows what Major

Edwin's been doing. Providing false reports, which mask the way Hitler's been able to build so many tanks and planes. At the cost of our own defence programme. Tanks and planes that will be turned against Britain and Russia both. And there are people in high places, in Britain and Russia, my friend, who don't care very much about that. People who would rather see all of Europe under Hitler's boot-heel than disturb their own vested interests. I can't answer for Carter-Holt. If you want my opinion, I think she genuinely believed in what she was doing. As I genuinely believed I had no choice except to kill her, to save my own life. A true believer in the Communist cause. A principled cadre of the Party, as you are, *Capitán*. But Fielding? Playing for both sides perhaps. Certainly up to his neck in Major Edwin's games – whatever they might be.'

'And Mister Milanes,' Ruby told the *Capitán*, 'certainly believed the reports were genuine.' Then she touched Jack tenderly on the shoulder. 'He'd have to report Mister Fielding's death, of course. But I'm certain that you'd be acquitted of any wrongdoing, Jack. In the circumstances. Though, if Major Edwin's followed us here, that frightens me.'

'Not just Edwin, I'm afraid. The Guardia lieutenant, Turbides – those scum from Franco's Fifth Column – they're here too.'

'Turbides?' said Ruby. 'Wasn't he the one who...?' She raised plaintive fingers towards her own left eye.

'Yes, my dear. The same man.'

'That evil creature. Oh, Jack. You remember Christmas Day. The story you told us at dinner about losing your poor eye on the rocks. That was bad enough, but this...'

It occurred to Jack that, in all this time, he had only told three people the truth about the eye. Well, more or less the truth. Bob Keith, of course. Then General Kotov. And Father Lobo. But he sensed real concern in Ruby's words and began to wonder whether the *Capitán* had, after all, been serious. Rivals? Did she perhaps have some divided affection for them both?

'Evil barely does it justice,' he said. 'And now his men have been following the major, presumably thinking he might lead them to me as well. They still have the same problem. Franco doesn't want me spouting about Carter-Holt either: about how the *Generalísimo* awarded National Spain's highest honour to one of Stalin's top agents. Of course, Fielding was responsible for spilling the beans to them on that one too. But you

253

said things aren't good in Madrid, Ruby. In what way?'

'We picked up news two days ago,' Fidel replied, rather than the girl. 'The Lion, he talked to you about our Colonel Casado, I think?'

'Yes, of course.' Jack recalled, too, the way that Father Lobo's eyes had widened at the mention of a possible link between Major Edwin, Franco's agents and Casado. He wondered whether the *Capitán* had shared that snippet about the major with Ruby Waters also.

'Two days ago,' the *Capitán* continued, 'Madrid agents of Franco's secret police delivered terms to Colonel Casado. We don't know the full details but it looks like Franco wants nothing but an unconditional surrender. After that, the way they get treated will depend purely on how much they lick the arse of National Spain. You know what that means? Those of us who forget our beliefs, all that we've fought for, prove ourselves to be good *fascistas* – those may go free. The rest, even if we surrender, will spend the rest of our short lives rotting in one of his stinking concentration camps. Can you imagine that, English?'

'Only too well,' said Jack. 'And Casado? Will he accept?'

'Betray the Republic? We think so. Though the Party itself will fight to the end, whatever happens. But it seems Casado has been told that delay will be fatal. There are many around him who will persuade him to surrender. Some of those same men with whom you spent much time in Madrid, comrade. Besteiro. San Andrés. Your friend, the priest. Is it any wonder that so many people want to kill you? And, for me, I'm still not sure whether it would not be easier to just let them. That's what the Lion would want.'

What an awful bloody mess, thought Jack. All those discussions he'd had with them. About finding some way to bring this bloody war to an end, to save further mayhem. They were good people. He knew they were good people, Besteiro and his friends. But was this what they intended? To save Spain at the collective sacrifice of so many who had already given so much for the Republic?

'You can't do this, Fidel,' Ruby was saying. 'I won't let you. And if you leave Mister Telford behind, like a lamb to the slaughter, you'll have to leave me too. But I feel like I'm missing a piece of the jigsaw. The Consul knew about Casado too, didn't he? He was very clear. About Madrid becoming a more dangerous place. Not just the risk of Franco taking the city. Something else. Is Major Edwin mixed up in all that as well?'

'Whether your Consul's intelligence is as good as our own, I don't know. But if Casado tries to surrender on Franco's terms, Madrid will rip itself apart long before Franco can get there. And it was the task that the Lion had set for our friend, *Señor* Telford. To find proof of a third-party link between the Fifth Column and Casado. We believe that link is the British Secret Service. Specifically, the link is Major Edwin. The reason that this major wants *Señor* Telford dead is not simply because of those reports, but because he also thinks *Señor* Telford might just possess the evidence of such a link. Proof that he's a traitor to his own country.'

'It would be easier if you untied me,' Jack protested as the *Capitán* pushed him along the corridor towards the lift.

'Just imagine how much I would profit by shooting you, English,' whispered Fidel. 'I've seen the posters now. So, I could claim the reward. Five hundred *pesetas* would be very welcome. Then I would have the gratitude of the Lion, of Moscow, of the Party. I could probably do a deal with your Major Edwin too – your head in exchange for him forgetting all about Ruby. Finally, I could use your body to set a trap for this Turbides and his Fifth Column friends – kill those bastards. So you should not tempt me, my friend.'

He had already taken from Jack a detailed description of the Weasel and, from both Jack and Ruby, a similar thumbnail sketch of Major Edwin – more difficult, this one, since neither of them could identify many distinguishing features apart from his trench coat and slicked-down hair. After that, the *Capitán* had paid one of the hotel maids to go out and reconnoitre for him, deliver some messages, bring back one of the reward posters. And then Ruby had been sent off to the station with her Gladstone bag.

'But this is damned awkward,' said Jack, as his own rucksack dangled from his tied hands and banged constantly against the backs of his knees. 'If we're going to go all the way to the station like this.'

'Not the station, English. Not yet. With a bit of luck, this Major Edwin and any of those other pigs will follow her, while you and I are going in another direction entirely. For now.'

'Why not straight to the station?'

'Because we have no idea how many of them are out there. I could get help from our own people. Maybe they'd catch Edwin, maybe they wouldn't. Maybe they'd round up a fascist or two. But then what? We end up on the train. And it only takes one killer, my friend. One sniper. One man with a knife, or a piano wire. No, we need another way of getting to the coast.'

At the service entrance to the hotel, the old anarchist waiter with the red and black neck-scarf gave Jack a look of sheer disdain, and then they were out in the alley, Fidel Constantino checking that the coast was clear before pushing his prisoner in entirely the opposite direction from the station.

'Where are we going?' said Jack.

'To see a friend of mine.' Jack knew none of these streets, and they seemed to weave their way through an endless maze of single-storey houses, bomb sites and neglected orchards, until they came at last to a square with a large water tower in one corner. Rag-doll children were playing around its base and, just next to the water tower, there was a tall brick chimney. A sign on the street corner announced that this was the Plaza del Pozo de la Nieve. The chimney, Jack knew from those he'd seen elsewhere, was a ventilator shaft for the air-raid shelter which must lie underground here, though there was no other evidence of its existence. Across the square was a workshop, really a small repair garage, for motorbikes. 'Did you know, English, that Albacete was famous as a racing circuit? Before the war. Through the streets.' A one-legged man emerged from the workshop's darkness, a pair of goggles hanging from the armpit pad of his crutch. The fellow stopped beside a bike with a sidecar attached.

'This one?' shouted the man.

'Beautiful,' Fidel Constantino called back, his voice echoing around the *plaza*. 'My friend, Lorenzo,' he murmured to Jack. 'He was big here. Before the crash.'

'We're going in that thing?' said Jack.

'Just get in.'

'Like this?'

'Like that.'

'Who is he?' asked Lorenzo, as the *Capitán* forced Jack into the sidecar, his hands still tied behind him by Ruby's belt. Almost impossible and excruciatingly uncomfortable. '*Faccioso*, I suppose.' Lorenzo spat on the ground. 'But you'll look after the bike?' he said.

'Where the hell did you get it?' said Fidel, and he patted the polished green petrol tank admiringly. It bore the legend *Sokół* 1000 on a white background.

'Don't ask,' Lorenzo told him, handed over the goggles. 'And why don't you just shoot this bastard here.'

'No, we need him. For now.' The *Capitán* cocked his leg over the tank, settled himself on the wide leather seat, switched on the fuel, checked the gears and stood on the kick-starter.

'Careful,' said Lorenzo, 'she kicks back like a bitch.'

And so she did, but the *Sokół* started first time, roared into life, as the kids all came running around, shouting and laughing. The *Capitán* gripped the long, back-swept handlebars, twisted the throttle a couple of times, shouted something to Lorenzo that Jack couldn't catch, then off they sped, throwing up stones and dirt, the children running behind until they finally gave up the chase.

'What about Ruby?' Jack screamed at the top of his voice, as they seemed to head out of town, between some small factory buildings and warehouses. But Fidel ignored him, swung the motorbike in a tight left-hand curve as they neared the railway line, and followed the road alongside until they were heading back towards the station. Another sharp left-hander in front of the station building, the sidecar lifting perilously as they made the turn, and then they were speeding along the Calle de la Estación once more. Jack's eye was watering from the speed and he could barely make out the struggle that was taking place near the street vendors' stalls, but there were milicianos there, fighting to bring down a man who, Jack was sure, must be the Weasel.

Yet they didn't stop. On past the town hall, slewing to a stop outside the Matchbox, but Fidel still revving the engine.

'Where the hell is she?' he shouted, and he looked around wildly.

There. She'd been sheltering inside the café, ran out now.

Crack.

The now familiar sensation of being shot at. A bullet whistling close to Jack's ear and whining as it hit the café's wall. Major Edwin appearing from the Francisquillo's main entrance, to the left, leveling his revolver again. Ruby ramming the Gladstone bag down into the too-small space of the sidecar's well, already filled by Jack himself. A second shot, one that went wild because somebody was struggling now with Major Edwin. It was Don Alberto. And then Jack was distracted by

257

Ruby's undignified mounting of the bike's pillion seat, a glimpse of pink bloomers, stocking tops and alabaster thigh. The motorbike slammed into gear, as she gripped Fidel Constantino's own rucksack shoulder straps to steady herself, and Jack caught a final glimpse of Estefania's astonished beautiful but gaping mouth as she pushed her way through her customers to see what the commotion was all about. She saw him, and he thought she smiled, half raised a hand to bid him goodbye – a gesture, of course, which Jack could not reciprocate.

Chapter Thirty

Saturday 18th February 1939

The following morning found them just outside Jumilla. The town itself lay immediately below them, an old Moorish castle up on a rocky ridge to their left, and here a jumble of hovels on the outskirts, where Fidel had paid for them to stay in a crumbling barn, huddled in their coats. They had bounced along the rugged, twisting roads from Albacete – through Pozo Cañada, Hellin and Nava de Campaña. Somewhere, they had crossed into the Murcia Region, the weather improving marginally as they went, and grape vines growing profusely again all around them. The *Capitán* had also managed to procure a set of overalls for Ruby, to help cover her modesty, so that she now looked liked a true *miliciana*.

A shame, thought Jack, whose only pleasure during that eye-watering journey had been the proximity of Ruby's shapely, silken legs and the temptations occasioned by her suspender clips.

'How far have we come?' said Ruby.

'From Albacete?' said the *Capitán*. 'Sixty miles. More or less.'

'Sixty?' Jack grimaced. 'Is that all? Look, I can't feel my arms at all now.' Apart from a couple of occasions when he'd had to beg temporary freedom to answer calls of nature, he'd been bound for over twelve hours. 'And I certainly can't go any further like that. What do you call it, in Spanish, when a man promises not to run away? To stay voluntarily as your prisoner?' He was reasonably certain that any mutilation of the word *parole* would not serve him.

'In Spanish, we call it conditional liberty,' Fidel Constantino replied. 'But how can I trust you, English?'

'For goodness sake, where is he going to go?' Ruby opened her arms wide, used them to encompass that whole empty landscape.

'Perhaps when I get back,' said the *Capitán*. 'First, I'm going down into town, try to find us something to eat. Some bread, at least. See how the land lies.'

The *Capitán* jumped back on the *Sokół* 1000 and roared off down the road.

'You're fond of him,' said Jack.

'By that, you mean to imply some amorous connection between us – presumably because we seemed to be sharing a room in Albacete.'

Well, it crossed my mind, thought Jack.

'Is there an alternative I should consider?' he said.

'Mister Telford, you may recall that, just a few weeks ago, I asked you whether, when you left Madrid, you'd take me with you. You didn't even deign to give me a reply.'

'Yes, I thought you were just after my back-pay.' He laughed but, this time, Ruby didn't share the joke. 'And you settled for a cigarette instead, as I recall.'

'I didn't enjoy it. Neither the cigarette nor the fact that you couldn't take me seriously.'

'Of course I took you seriously. That last night, before I caught the bus to Aranjuez, I asked you to come with me. And that wasn't easy for me. I've become something of a curmudgeon, I'm afraid. To do with Carter-Holt, I think.'

'It certainly didn't sound like you meant it. And then you made such a thing about taking the Valencia train. Yet you plainly didn't do so. Did you ever have any intention of going to Valencia? No, you don't need to answer that. You just need to understand that it's difficult for me to consider any other scenario than one in which, first, you simply refused to assist me and, second, you fed me a line, as one might say, about Valencia, so that it would help muddy your trail. And I'm gratified that this amuses you.' Jack realised he was smiling foolishly, embarrassment really, and he bit his lower lip to control it. 'But, in truth,' Ruby pressed her assault, 'your own conclusions don't trouble me a great deal, one way or the other.'

'Perhaps I'd be on safer ground if I enquired after the redoubtable Mrs Norris.'

'She is, as you say, still redoubtable. And, before you ask, yes, I read your article, as you requested. You're grinning again, Mister Telford. An affliction I don't recall troubling you so much in Madrid.'

'The article?' said Jack.

'The one about the children. It's one of the best things I've read. It moved me a great deal. How many, do you think? How many of those poor mites stolen from their parents?'

Hard now, for Jack not to smile, when the praise gratified him so enormously.

'I don't know, Ruby. Thousands, I suppose. And what's next? For you, I mean.'

'Oh, I expect I shall marry *Capitán* Constantino, bear him many fine children, and settle down somewhere peaceful. A pretty little place. Dorset, perhaps. Cottage garden. Wildflowers everywhere.'

'It's not dignified to poke fun at a man when his hands are tied behind his back.'

'You don't believe me?'

This was precocious Ruby Waters again, and Jack liked it – strangely, now, more settled in her company.

'No, I don't,' he said. 'I think you're a young woman who's wedded, first and foremost, to her career. Whatever your feelings for the *Capitán* may be, I think you'll be back at your desk like a shot as soon as this all blows over. And, when that happens, will you speak with Milanes for me? Tell him the whole story. He'll know what to do. I'm seriously hoping that nobody in the Establishment will want too much fuss about Fielding *or* Valerie Carter-Holt.'

'I abhor violence, Mister Telford. I understand it, yet I abhor it. I find it very hard indeed to understand how one human being can deliberately inflict injury on another – even if, in Fielding's case, you were fighting for your life. But that woman in San Sebastián. You drowned her. With your bare hands.'

'You think your precious Fidel's any better? I've seen him do his share of killing too.'

'He's a soldier, Mister Telford. Rightly or wrongly, we ask him to kill on our behalf. To keep us safe from even worse evils.' Three young women emerged from one of the houses, carrying empty pitchers. They headed down the hill, chattering like sparrows. 'They look so cheerful,' said Ruby. 'So full of life in the middle of all this grief.'

'My mother raised me as a pacifist,' said Jack. 'She'd no more be able to understand any of this than I can.'

'Then where will you go? To work it all out. Or while Mister Milanes deals with the Establishment for you. France, maybe?'

At the mention of France, Jack realised that his father was once again standing next to him, smiling benevolently upon Ruby Waters. It was unlike any previous manifestation, for his father had almost always been a harbinger of some doom or tragedy. And then Jack heard the motorbike's deep-throated warning, the urgency of its gear changes, the fearful scream of its tyres.

'Untie me, Ruby. Now.'

And she obeyed without question so that, by the time Fidel squealed to a halt, they had grabbed the Gladstone bag and rucksacks, and were running down to meet him.

'Quickly,' shouted the *Capitán*.

'Turbides?' Jack yelled.

'Could be, English. The place is crawling with men claiming to be SIM agents. And they're all after you, comrade.'

There'd been a madcap race back down the hill, thrown from side to side with each hairpin bend, a sharp left-hander that took them in-to Jumilla's narrow streets. Poor houses. A church. A tree-lined square, which Jack had barely been able to see for the wind-blasted tears. Then a crossroads, the blare of a car's horn as Fidel threw the *Sokół* hard to the right, swerved in front of a huge black limousine. Familiar. The Hispano-Suiza in which Jack had seen Turbides outside Criptana. They had swung right just afterwards, Jack, worried, looking back over his shoulder, though no sign of the car by then. On, past the final few houses of the town's outskirts, out into open countryside again. Olive trees, vines, the wide, empty plain stretching east. Hills and mountains on the horizon.

The *Capitán* himself chanced a backwards glance.

'You saw them?' he shouted to Jack.

'Yes. Give me one of the guns.' But Fidel Constantino shook his head. Ruby had wedged her own bag, and Fidel's rucksack, between herself and the *Capitán*, and she was gripping the sides of his greatcoat, holding on for dear life, holding herself on the raised pillion saddle. Yet her face was turned towards Jack and she seemed to be considering him carefully. Jack, on the other hand, was more interested in the road behind. For there it was again, that same black car. And catching up fast. 'Here they come!' Jack yelled.

Fidel gunned the throttle, all that it still had left and, for a moment, Jack thought it might just be enough for them to pull ahead. But no such luck. His optimism oozed into concern when, for the next ten miles or so, pursuer and pursued seemed evenly matched. And then it plummeted into despair when he finally realised, with every additional mile that passed, the car was slowly gaining ground. A quarter-mile still between them, but a steadily diminishing gap.

Jack thought about lightening the load, certain that, without the sidecar and passengers, the bike could easily outstrip the limousine. But the bags would make only a negligible difference. Not enough. And he prayed that the *Capitán* had some sort of plan – some scheme to save them before they simply ran out of road.

They had passed some traffic, coming and going, where the road permitted. A couple of trucks, the occasional car, two buses. And now they hammered through a village, making enough noise to waken the dead from the neat cemetery of family mausoleums. A roadside *taberna* next, with local *campesino* customers waving and shouting at this passing spectacle. Then the road climbing, up the flank of a steep ridge to their north. Over a rise, and down, the Hispano-Suiza now less than two hundred yards away. Yet Fidel was steering some strange zigzag course, which was helping the car to shorten the distance still quicker. Jack tapped the *Capitán*'s knee, urgently, but the wind taking his breath away, preventing him from speaking. So he made chopping gestures with his hand. *Go straight!* Jack screamed to himself. *For Christ's sake, go straight.*

'Shooting at us,' screamed the *Capitán* and, sure enough, as Jack turned his head, there were puffs of smoke coming from the Hispano-Suiza's passenger side window, a head and arm sticking out.

The motorbike took the next bend at speed, Jack convinced that they'd be flipped over, so he leaned far out of the sidecar to help bring them flat again. Ruby, he saw, still seemed quite unperturbed, but Jack was terrified. He raised his hand, futile gesture, as they took another curve and there, ahead of them, where the road narrowed to cross a bridge, was a farm cart, almost blocking the way. He hadn't seen where any of the previous bullets had gone, but he saw this one. A spit of dirt thrown up just alongside him. He looked back, saw Turbides plainly now.

'For God's sake, give me a gun,' Jack shouted, realised he'd called out in English. Ahead, the cart was looming up, a drainage ditch to each side of the road, not enough room to pass. Surely not enough. But Fidel squeezed the ball of his own bulb horn, over and over, dropped down a gear, then another. The cart's driver stood, turned to see what was happening, began yelling, then dragged his reins sharply to the right as the *Sokół* went through the gap and over the bridge with literally inches to spare.

Behind, there was the car's horn too, screeching brakes, smoke billowing from the tyres, and the Hispano-Suiza slewing sideways into the ditch. Fidel Constantino was laughing into the wind.

'Well, there we go!' he cried.

Out of the frying pan, thought Jack.

The sun had come through, strong and bright, so they were stopped in the shade of some roadside olive trees, taking sips of water from Fidel's battered metal canteen. Ahead of them, the way had seemed peaceful enough: an occasional vehicle, crawling through the emptiness; vultures, high in the ice-blue heavens; the tart animal smells of Spain's rust-red earth, carried on a light breeze, which brushed their faces; and silence – perfect silence.

'Can you make them out?' Jack asked.

They had turned in, under the trees, before they spotted the wagon but, now, all their attention was concentrated there. Still a good way distant and seeming, for all the world, like an innocent and battered farm lorry, parked just next to yet another bridge. Not even real bridges, these – merely sections of road over culverts for the area's many dry *arroyos*, and graced with low, crumbling sidewalls.

'No.' The *Capitán* lowered his field glasses, rubbed his eyes. 'Three of them, I think. Maybe four. But staying in the shade, or out of sight, on the far side.'

'Siesta?' Ruby suggested.

'Too early, isn't it?' said Jack.

'Farmers would be working now,' Fidel told them. 'Finishing up before they eat.'

'Probably nothing though.' But Jack had a bad feeling. *Into the fire.* Yet, if they were working with Turbides, how could they possibly be here? 'Maybe a good idea to let me have a gun now, all the same,' he said, trying to sound as if he wasn't really too bothered, and ignoring the look of approbation on Ruby's face.

'I remember the last time,' said the *Capitán* but, as he put the binoculars back in their case, the case into the rucksack, he pulled out the automatic, careful that Ruby shouldn't see, slipped it into his greatcoat pocket. 'Right, *compañera miliciana*,' he said to her, 'let's go. Nothing to worry about, like the English says.' She was tying her hair back again, continued doing so as she mounted the pillion. 'Can you smell it?' Fidel whispered to Jack, while Ruby settled herself in the saddle. 'Out there. Waiting.'

'Yes, I smell it,' Jack replied, and the *Capitán* slipped the automatic to him.

'Remember the safety,' Fidel murmured, and Jack turned his back on Ruby, gave the gun a quick check, then had it in his own pocket. 'And, English,' hissed the *Capitán*, 'you don't use it unless I tell you. But if I tell you, for the love of God, shoot straight.'

They came out of the trees and bounded onto the road like a rampaging bear, the throttle wide and Fidel working the tank-mounted shift lever back and forth, up and down the gears to squeeze every last ounce of power from the machine. There was a strong smell of exhaust smoke and hot oil, Ruby giving him a quizzical look, knowing something was amiss, gripping the *Capitán*'s coat even tighter than usual.

'What's up?' she shouted, in English.

He shook his head. Nothing. Why? Though, by then, they'd passed the halfway mark towards the lorry and Jack squinted through an almost closed eye at the flurry of activity occasioned by their approach, by the motorbike's roaring charge. Three men. One running around to the driver's side and climbing into the cab. Two more racing for the bridge, one of them carrying a light machine gun.

Oh shit, thought Jack.

'What are you waiting for?' Fidel yelled. 'Shoot the driver.'

Jack fumbled in his pocket, swore when the fabric caught on those re-opened and bloodied cuts, saw that the driver had started the truck's engine and was backing, bumping towards the road. Jack's fingers found the automatic, and he leaned forward, resting both elbows on the sidecar's upper nose panel, gripping the pistol's butt in both hands.

How many bullets? he wondered, and squeezed off a shot, saw it bounce harmlessly off the bonnet, as the lorry lurched still closer to cut them off.

'The driver,' screamed the *Capitán*. 'The bloody driver.'

Jack aimed again. Three shots in quick succession, and the satisfaction of seeing the cab window smash, the driver slump over the wheel. But the truck didn't stop. And the two men at the bridge were shooting back now. There was a hammer blow to Jack's left. A neat hole low in the fuel tank, below Fidel's knee, fuel pouring out over the *Capitán*'s leg, onto the engine fins, the exhaust manifold. An image, in Jack's mind, of them exploding in a fireball.

'Petrol,' he shouted.

'Kill the bastards,' Fidel shouted back, heading straight for the truck, which had now run up onto the road itself, the driver dead at the wheel, but somehow… At least, it now blocked the line of fire from the fellow with the submachine gun, but not the third man. He had a rifle. He was kneeling. Jack fired, missed, saw the rifle recoil. Ruby's hands came loose from Fidel's coat, went to her head, blood between her fingers and, in that moment, she rolled backwards. Jack tried to grab her, barely touched the leg of her boiler suit – and she was gone, hitting the road, bouncing like a rag doll, keeping pace with the motorbike for one, two, three seconds, then falling behind. 'Shoot, English, shoot.' Fidel was keeping his head low, almost at the level of the handlebars but steering a course straight for the rifleman. Another bullet hit them, the wheel spokes, ringing like the notes of a xylophone. The truck was still trundling on, in reverse, a gap opening across the bridge.

Jack fired again. Another three shots. The rifle flew in the air and the man was thrown backwards, smacked onto the parapet, then over and down into the *arroyo*, while the *Capitán* jammed on the brakes, leaned sideways to stop them spilling over as they swerved to a halt. From behind the opposite parapet, the submachine gunner stood, his line of fire now clear, with the lorry rolling past. He lifted the weapon as Jack shakily brought up the automatic, no idea how many shots he had left. But, by then, Fidel was pushing him down into the sidecar and, in his hand, the *Capitán* held the revolver – the one Jack had taken from Crazy Luís.

Chapter Thirty-One

Thursday 2nd March 1939

Ruby Waters still lived, yet Antonio Machado, Spain's foremost poet, was dead.

'"*Wanderer*,"' Ruby quoted, solemnly, '"*your footsteps are the path and nothing more.*"'

'That's very apt,' said Jack.

'Of course.' She smiled at him from the bed, still too weak to do very much. 'But it's the only one I can remember all the way through. "*Wanderer, there is no path. The path is made by walking. Walking makes the path and, turning to look behind, you see the path that you will never tread again.*" Sad, isn't it, Jack?'

She had taken to calling him Jack more often over the last few days.

'I don't recall reading that one. But there can't be much wrong with your head if you can remember it. That's the main thing.' He tapped the newspaper, the last one they'd bought, a couple of days earlier. 'It says here that, after he died, they found a new poem in his pocket. They only give the first line though. "*Estos días azules y este sol de infancia.*" These blue days and this childhood sun.'

'Does it say how he died?'

'No, just his age. Sixty-three. In a French refugee camp, somewhere near Toulouse, I think.' He recalled Rosario del Olmo's concerns about the poet's health, the likelihood of him escaping from Barcelona to France. He remembered the nights in Madrid when he had used Antonio Machado's poems to help improve his Spanish – massively better now, though frequently deserting him entirely when he was fatigued. And he thought about the *guerrilleros* in Covadonga, who had taken Machado's name for their own, as a symbol of freedom.

'That's not very old, is it?'

'It's a bit sobering,' said Jack. 'On that basis, my life's already half over.'

'While I feel like I'm born again.'

'If I'm honest about it, we thought we'd lost you a few times. The first couple of days, when your eyes didn't even open, the doctor was convinced you wouldn't make it. And then you started crying. You remember that?'

'No, Jack. Nothing much. The first thing I remember is you turning me over.'

'You're heavier than you look, Miss Waters.' He decided not to impinge on her dignity by mentioning the times they'd had to clean her. Or try and make her take some water, some thin soup, when she couldn't even swallow. 'And how are the hands today?'

She lifted them with difficulty, the splints and bandages stretching from elbow to fingertips.

'You think I'll ever play the piano again?' An old joke.

'The doctor seems confident he's reset the wrists just fine. But it may be a long while before you're back at that desk of yours.'

'And how do I look, apart from that?'

A single curl of her beautiful hair had escaped from the bandages still swathing her head.

'As stiff-necked as usual,' said Jack. 'But those turbans are all the rage again in London, I'm told.'

'You must be pleased, Mister Telford. I suppose you'd be in custody somewhere by now, if this hadn't happened. Poor Fidel, I've rather messed up his plans.'

'Strangely, I don't think he minds too much. Oh, he's still determined to hand me over to the authorities. But he doesn't seem too sure who's in charge right now. It stopped him in his tracks a bit when he found out Negrín was back in Madrid last week. Inspecting the troops on the Front Line. Though he's no idea where his own unit might be and the barracks in town hasn't been able to help. He's picked up mixed messages. About General Kotov being in Madrid with Negrín, then word that he's in Valencia. And now, it looks like he might have headed home, to Moscow.'

It had been a strange week for news, all round. Lots of excitement in the papers about France and England making very clear statements, despite Chamberlain's continued friendship with Hitler and Mussolini, that they would respond immediately and militarily to any aggression towards Hungary or Poland. It was a direct warning to Germany. The world on the brink of yet another war. Yet, for Spain, was there not an implication that a European war against Germany must also mean a European war against Hitler's allies, against Franco? If only the Republic could hold out for that day. And wasn't that Negrín's message? To that end, the papers had also been full of the promotions Negrín had made. Colonel Casado in Madrid, promoted to General and even greater responsibilities for Madrid's defence. *Yet it's Casado*, thought Jack, *that Kotov believed may be in league with the Fifth Column.* Casado, trusted by those with whom Jack had become close in Madrid – Father Lobo and Julián Besteiro, the groups they represented, seeking an end to Spain's bloodshed and suffering above everything else, at all cost.

'He wanted to head straight back to Madrid, didn't he?' said Ruby, her voice filled with guilt.

'The *Capitán*? Yes. But he wasn't sure whether it would help. And he was never going to leave you like this. Besides, I don't think he could quite bear to hand the motorbike back to his one-legged friend Lorenzo without getting it repaired properly. You're at least lucky you don't remember the journey here. He stuffed the bullet hole in the tank with a bit of rubber. The front wheel was in a bad way though. A bullet had buckled some of the spokes, then damaged the forks. We literally hobbled all the way here.'

With you, dear Ruby, lashed to a bench seat from the back of that bloody lorry, and then your uncomfortable stretcher tied lengthways on top of the sidecar.

'And now?' she said.

'And now we wait. Your Fidel seems happy that we've shaken off Turbides, at least. They will have found the lorry, their dead killers. Decided that we're long gone. Maybe in Alicante by now. And, Ruby, I owe you an apology. About deceiving you. The Valencia thing. You were quite right. I did it deliberately. Trying to muddy the trail, as you said.'

'Apology accepted. I don't suppose it matters much now, in any case.' He'd hoped for a little more. Perhaps an acknowledgement that, while she still abhorred violence, Jack had at least taken down two of the men who'd tried to ambush and kill them. But he was disappointed.

'In the larger scheme of things,' she said. 'After all, we wouldn't be in this mess, and have people trying to murder us, if it hadn't been for you, Mister Telford.'

Jack waited outside, wondering what had kept the *Capitán* while, inside, the dapper doctor was making his daily visit to Ruby. It was a peaceful village, Encebras, a million miles from the rest of war-torn Spain though, in practice, no more than five miles from El Pinós and the Alicante road. It nestled under the terraced slopes of Monte Coto. But Fidel Constantino had chosen it with care. Friends here. The doctor had looked grim when he arrived and was still the same when he emerged.

'How is she?' Jack asked him.

'Oh, the girl? She's doing very well. The advantage of youth. But a black day in other ways, my friend. You've not heard? Comrade Lenin's widow has died. Poor Krupskaya. She was his rock. All through the revolution. Then nursed him during his illness. Dear creature. How precious it must be, to have the devotion of a woman like Nadya Krupskaya.'

And off he went, carrying his leather bag.

'Did he tell you anything?' Ruby demanded, as Jack came through the door. 'He frightened me. So glum.'

'It's not you, my dear. He's upset about Krupskaya.' Jack explained. 'But with you, he seems more than satisfied.'

'What about you, Mister Telford? What's your own prognosis?'

'Does my opinion matter? After all, this is all my fault.'

'No self-pity, please. It doesn't become you, Jack. And I'm sorry if I was harsh. I'm still in quite a lot of pain, as it happens.'

'Did the doctor give you anything for that?'

'He offered. But I don't respond very well to medication. In any case, some of the pain is self-inflicted. I fear I may have been playing the harlot to some extent. With poor Fidel's affections. I'd not intended that.'

'He's very fond of you.'

'Yes, I know. But it won't serve, will it, Jack?'

He supposed not, but he could feel doors opening ahead of him, and he pulled back, not wishing to commit himself, to one path or another.

'I'm not sure I can possibly comment, Miss Waters. After Albacete...'

He remembered afresh the scene when he'd knocked on her bedroom door, found the *Capitán* within.

'I fear you have a poor opinion of my morals, Mister Telford. Might you not have done me the courtesy of a direct question, not to mention a benefit of the doubt? But no. You jumped straight to a conclusion. As most men would have done, I suppose. Yet you were quite wrong. Fidel spent the entire night in the hotel lobby. Keeping guard. He only arrived in my room moments before you, yourself.'

Jack groaned inwardly, struggled to find some way to extricate himself but, at that moment, he heard the motorbike, newly repaired and refueled, its familiar song ringing through the village streets.

'He's somewhere here,' said Fidel. 'Alicante Province. The paper doesn't say where, exactly, but looks like we're going the right way.'

'That's good, isn't it?' Jack was struggling to know why the *Capitán* had returned so ill-humoured. Fidel brought back the local newspaper, and a copy of the previous day's *ABC*. And there it was, Prime Minister Negrín and his Ministers now established in that part of the Levant with Alicante as its provincial capital. It was a big region though, and no clue to wherever the Republican Government may be settled. But not Alicante itself, that much was certain. The city was being bombed to hell, even now. More raids over the past few days. The port. The factories. The city centre. 'And I see we've got a new President too,' said Jack.

'We?' Fidel snapped. 'I'm sorry, English. You think you've earned your place in Spain too, I suppose. But yes, with Azaña run off to France, a new President. *¡Viva el Presidente!*'

It was a big announcement. Something to celebrate, Jack imagined. But not in Fidel's eyes, that was plain. Don Diego Martínez Barrio.

'What's he like?' said Jack.

'Calls himself a revolutionary. And he's been President before. But he's close to that worm Azaña. Both skulking in Paris or somewhere now. He's only been named President because Azaña's resigned and he's next in line. You seriously think he's going to come here and get his hands dirty? No way. But you'd know all about that, English. About not getting your hands dirty.'

What's the matter with him? Jack wondered. The *Capitán* was occasionally prone to mood swings, but he was rarely so acerbic.

'I sense,' said Ruby, 'that it's time we were on the road again. Your duties call you, *querido*?'

Jack wished she wouldn't call the bugger that. It was just too intimate, and he knew she only did it to annoy. But the *Capitán*'s response to the girl was no less abrupt than his comments to Jack himself had been. Why so vexed? Stupidly, Jack thought about the death of Lenin's widow again. Krupskaya. Was that the reason?

'Better news, depending on how you look on it, of course,' said Fidel. 'The town councils have all been asked to send any available ambulances to Alicante. You know what's been happening there, I suppose? Yes? That's good. My people are dying there too. Hundreds of them. Well, I've asked whether we can get a ride. For you, *compañera*, at least. Perhaps not as comfortable as you'd like, but still, beggars cannot be choosers. Isn't that what you say? Your people?'

'You and me on the *Sokół*, I suppose?' said Jack. He was keen to lighten the mood, but he found himself simply becoming angered.

'Not good enough for you, English? You are the beggar here, are you not? The prisoner of Spain. Republican Spain, naturally. Not your friends among the *facciosos*. Or perhaps I should just hand you over to them. To this Turbides.'

'Have you had word of him?'

Fidel shrugged.

'I made a report at the barracks when we got here. They sent a patrol to pick up the truck, try to identify those *pistoleros*. They found nothing. No trace of them. They say Franco's secret police have been active in the area for a while though, so no big surprise. But then, there *are* no big surprises any more, are there?'

'You're talking in riddles, *Capitán*,' said Jack. 'You think he's still out there, don't you? Turbides. But I don't understand why. Franco's hardly likely to be much bothered, at this stage, by any revelations about Carter-Holt.'

'At this stage, English? No, you're right. But you don't understand too much, eh? For creatures like Turbides – this Major Edwin too – these things become personal. There's not much logic to it. A killer's just a killer.'

'And you, *Capitán*. Where does that leave you?'

'Where I've always been. With a war to fight. While you two? Back to England. Together, I guess. Where you can laugh some more at our expense.'

Jack felt the hairs stand on the back of his neck. Had the bloody man been spying on them? Impossible. He'd heard the motorbike coming back, had he not? He looked at Ruby, saw her cheeks redden.

'Fidel,' she began, 'I don't know what's angered you, but I can assure you…'

'Assure me of what, *compañera*? You will go back to your perfidious country and spit on my memory. Why do you look surprised, English? Too busy reading that nonsense about Presidents and Prime Ministers to see the most important news. Oh, they've only given it a couple of small paragraphs. Of course they have. No point in making too much of it. Many of us expected it all the time. That pig, Chamberlain. Hitler's friend. Here.' He stabbed his finger hard at the relevant section of the paper, and Jack read it afresh.

Three days earlier. Britain and France had officially recognised Franco's government.

Chapter Thirty-Two

Sunday 5th March 1939

They travelled in convoy, though Jack could not understand why that should be. German and Italian planes were in the air more frequently and it seemed a vain hope that those who had already bombed and strafed so many innocents might truly baulk at the idea of attacking a line of trucks simply because they carried red crosses.

The sidecar was attached once more, but loaded now with rucksacks and Ruby's travelling bag, while Jack perched on the pillion seat, gripping the front of the saddle, not daring physical contact with the *Capitán* as she had done. He may have carried a wounded Fidel Constantino a long way to reach Republican lines, but the man's righteous anger changed everything. An icy silence had fallen between them all, broken only by an occasional grunt, snarled instructions designed to make clear that Telford was, again, nothing more than the *Capitán*'s prisoner.

'We're still going to Alicante?' shouted Jack.

'Perhaps. You'll see.'

That was all. But it was plain that the *Capitán* had received orders before they left the barracks that morning at El Pinós. Yet Jack had no idea what they might be and, as they headed east, he was left to ponder the aching in his guts, the feeling of sickness which, he had known for the past couple of days, was simply the outward and visible symptom of his guilt about Britain's latest betrayal of the Republic. Something inside him screamed that there was a link here: between Major Edwin and his messages for the Fifth Column; or between Edwin and these strange promises of gold to that murky figure, Juan March. Yet he could find no answers, and they drove on. Through increasingly arid lands, which surprised him almost as much as the lush greenery of Spain's north. Through Culebrón, El Xinorlet, Manya and Pedrera, and halting at last in Monóvar, where they were supposed to eat – and where Jack went forward to help Ruby from the ambulance to which she had been allocated.

'Well,' he said, as he helped her clamber down onto the road, 'it looks like the cottage garden may be on hold a while.'

'I'm sure he'll come around,' she replied, leaning heavily on him for support, and her legs shaking from the effort. 'And you can hardly blame him, Jack. What a despicable thing to do. I feel filthy.'

It had been their most regular topic of conversation.

'Ashamed to be British,' said Jack. 'The idea that we'd simply walk away.'

'We abandoned Czechoslovakia, didn't we? I suppose this is no worse.'

'Are you supposed to have opinions of that sort, Miss Waters, given your position?'

'I thought I might risk falling upon your integrity, Jack. Not to snitch.'

'In that case, you should probably have told me beforehand that the conversation was off the record. That tends to bind me, as a journalist. Hippocratic oath. Seal of the confessional. That sort of thing. But I could let you have this one *gratis*, I suppose. The least I can do, given my own frequently unacceptable conduct.'

'Is that an apology, Mister Telford?'

'You know why, I assume?'

That stupid gaffe he'd made. About Ruby and the *Capitán* in Albacete. He wished the ground would swallow him as he spoke. And, in Albacete, there'd also been Estefania, scrambling his thoughts even now.

'Of course I know,' Ruby laughed. 'So I'll consider my secret, my temporary lapse of loyalty to the Service, as safe in your hands. And have you any idea where we're headed? Not straight to Alicante, I gather.'

'Maybe we'll find out over lunch – whatever's on offer here. Doesn't look too promising, does it?' The square was all dusty gravel, darkened by a leaden sky, mean streets running down to it on three sides, an abandoned church on the fourth. But as he helped her from the parked and guarded vehicles to an ancient *mesón*, across the way, Jack stopped in his tracks, jolted as though by an electric shock, jarring his brain. 'It can't be,' he groaned. 'My God, that's impossible.'

Yet not impossible at all, naturally. It had already happened, how many times? In the alley, east of the church. Almost entirely hidden in the shadows. The bonnet of a large, black Hispano-Suiza limousine.

Fidel had refused to believe him, accused him of playing some game. Ruby hadn't helped, couldn't confirm that she'd seen it. It could, after all, have been any black motorcar. And when the *Capitán* reluctantly agreed to come and see, there'd been nothing. Just more anger. A refusal to even say where they were going next, though Fidel plainly now knew their immediate destination. Yet, despite all that, despite Fidel's disbelief, Jack saw him, many times, turning to look back along the road behind.

So they had pressed on, left Monóvar behind, picked up the railway track to their left, a dry rock-strewn river bed to their right as they roared into the town of Elda, stopped briefly at an army headquarters – lines of trucks bringing supplies to be unloaded. The other vehicles peeled off here, left behind, with only the motorbike and Ruby's ambulance carrying on through the further outskirts, along the road marked Villena. A couple of miles, no more, and then onto a rutted track, which plunged into thick forest. It ran straight and true, bringing them to the gates and outhouses of a palatial property, nestled in the woodland. There were guards. A lot of guards.

They stopped before the wide staircase and balustrades climbing up to the front doors, the scent of pine forest heavy in the air. And, there, Fidel gave instruction to the ambulance driver before summoning Jack to follow him. The *Capitán* produced his identification papers for inspection, told the Assault Guard sergeant his name, rank and army unit. Yes, Fidel confirmed, the Englishman was his prisoner, and he told Jack to hand over his own papers, all of them, said that he needed to see General Kotov. The sergeant laughed.

'The Russians?' he said. 'Virgin's Tits, who told you there were any still here?'

But Kotov's name and Fidel Constantino's rank seemed to be sufficient at least to gain them admittance. A beeswax polish and dark oak reception room, also guarded. And there they waited.

'What arrangements did you make for Miss Waters?' said Jack.

'Obvious ones,' Fidel replied. 'That a medical officer should examine her, make sure she's not suffered from the journey.'

'Why not send her straight on to Alicante? At least there'd be a hospital there.'

'She's safer here.'

'Here being...?'

'In Monóvar they told me the house is called El Poblet.'

'It's very grand,' said Jack, and he strolled around the room, inhaling the strong smell of furniture polish, running his finger along pristine, dust-free edges of a writing desk, examining the pictures that graced the papered walls. A Sorolla. An Andreu. A Blanchard. *Genuine?* he wondered.

'We could hardly house the Prime Minister in the stables,' said Fidel, with exaggerated sarcasm.

Negrín? thought Jack but, before he could pose his next question, the door opened and a man entered. He ignored Jack entirely, gave Fidel the merest of acknowledgements, and sat behind the desk. He was well dressed, though his face looked as if it had been smashed by a shovel.

'*Capitán* Constantino?' he said. 'We have no idea why you should be here, but I'm instructed to hear your story. Captain Orca, SIM.' The *Capitán* told his story. His unit dispatched by their commander, General Kotov, to assist the escape of a prisoner in San Pedro de Cardeña. A journalist, imprisoned for the death of a woman close to Franco's heart – but a woman, unbeknown to the *facciosos*, also acting as an agent for the Comintern. General Kotov needed to discover what had happened, but also believed this prisoner could be useful, help unravel some of the clandestine dealings between Britain and Franco's Fifth Column. 'And the eye?' said Captain Orca, and flicked an imperious finger in Jack's direction. 'Was that in San Pedro?'

'No,' Fidel told him. 'They tortured him. In Burgos. It's how the General found out about him, I think. One of the guards, perhaps.' Then, as bidden, he continued his story. The escape successful, and the prisoner brought to Madrid. There he had provided valuable service – among other things, evidence of payments being considered by the British as offerings to Franco's brother and generals. Purpose? Unknown. Yet, as a result, the prisoner was now pursued by agents for both the British Intelligence Service and Franco's secret police. In addition, General Kotov had discovered that the prisoner had killed the woman, in San Sebastián, knowing that she was working for the Comintern. The

General had therefore ordered the prisoner's capture.

'And execution?' asked Captain Orca.

'If necessary, yes.'

'But you brought him here instead. Why?'

'I didn't expect to find him, Comrade Captain. It was pure chance. And by then I was already in Albacete, escorting a young woman. You know about her, I imagine. British Diplomatic Service, in Madrid. '

'This was an official duty? Escorting her?'

'No, not official. I'd been separated from my regiment and from my commander. I was told he was here, in the east. I needed fresh orders.'

'You could have got those in Madrid, *Capitán*, could you not? Ah, but no. You're part of the Guerrilla Corps, of course. Different rules from the rest of us. Isn't that what you think?'

'Not different, Comrade Captain. But General Kotov, the Lion, he had given me certain responsibilities. When I found the prisoner again, I believed he might be useful to us. The girl too. She was badly wounded helping us to get here.'

'Can I say something now?' said Jack.

'No, you may not,' Captain Orca snarled, turned again to the *Capitán*. 'And you allow him to wander around like this? No restraints. Free to escape.'

'Conditional liberty,' Fidel told him, and Captain Orca shook his head in despair. 'But there's one thing you should know, Captain. The *facciosos* who've been hunting him, they've been posing as members of the SIM. They've got phoney credentials.'

'And your point, *Capitán*?'

'His point,' said Jack, in impeccable Spanish, 'is that I saw the bastards again in Monóvar. At least, I think...'

Orca slammed the table.

'*Capitán* Constantino,' he shouted, 'I know your reputation. Your so-called exploits. But they do not impress me much. If this Englishman is your prisoner, I trust you will treat him as a damned prisoner. Whatever nonsense he may have put in your head, this is now the seat of government for the Spanish Republic. Here. Elda. This is our Yuste Position. You understand?' Fidel nodded, though the muscles in his face were taut as iron. And the reference to Yuste was lost on Jack. 'Our security here is impregnable,' the Captain continued. 'So take your prisoner, lock him in one of the storage rooms. We'll decide what to do with him later.'

The door to the storage room was thrown open, and Fidel stood silhouetted against the yellow light beyond. It was late. Very late.

'I'm to tell you that you're being honoured by sharing dinner with the Prime Minister, English.'

He seemed entirely dispassionate about the news, Jack thought.

'I'm free? What took so long? It must be almost bloody midnight. And dinner? Now?'

'Not free. I had to wait two hours before Orca could tell your story to Cordón, show him your papers. Then I had to wait three hours more until Cordón found time to interrogate me in person. Negrín's been in conference all evening. But they're just breaking. To eat. And yes, it's almost midnight.'

'Cordón?'

'Negrín's Under-Secretary of Defence. And no need to thank me, by the way, for making a fool of myself. Repeating that nonsense about Turbides.'

'I'm sorry, Fidel,' said Jack, as the *Capitán* escorted him out of the makeshift cell, led him to a bathroom.

'Here,' said Fidel, 'you'd better make yourself a bit more presentable.'

They stripped off their greatcoats' leaving Fidel in his battle dress blouse and Jack in his less-than-spotless shirtsleeves. But there was little Jack could do concerning his appearance, and he was still troubling about the stubble on his unshaven chin, the new scabs that covered his hands, wanting to ask why, in God's name, he was supposed to be eating dinner with the Spanish Republic's Prime Minister, when he found himself ushered into the dining room. *That bloody rabbit hole again*, he thought, as his befuddled, weary brain struggled to make sense of all this. A comfortable room, polish again, cigar smoke – a scent which he had once savoured but which now reminded him only of torture and pain. But the men gathered around the table were already at their food: red and green chopped tomato, base-layered with amber olive oil, washed with golden brown partridge, and textured by scented onion and toasted garlic. There was wine too, and Jack's tight belly ached for just a taste.

He looked around for Fidel, unsure what to do, found him standing, stiff and formal, back at the door, with another armed guard while, from the table, he heard his name spoken.

'*Señor* Telford.' Jack turned again. A man had stood up from the table, and though Jack knew him at once, it occurred to him that he had rarely seen photographs of Negrín. It had always been Azaña, the former-President, in the limelight, rather than the Prime Minister. It seemed stupid, but Negrín appeared larger than life, not quite the image of the eminent physician he had once been; more boxer and bruiser than doctor. 'I fear,' he said, 'that you've not received the hospitality due to one of our accredited correspondents.' *So*, thought Jack, *he's read my credentials*. 'Come,' Negrín invited him towards an empty chair, 'please join us. It's simple enough, but exceptionally good. The best cooks in Spain, you know, the Alicantinos.'

'But not your main reason for being here, sir, I imagine.'

Jack sat, accepted a helping of sweet tomato, finely sliced onion, deeply green olives and tiny slices of cold *bacalao*.

'No, hardly,' Negrín replied. 'But it does have something to do with the fact that Alicantinos are also among the Spanish Republic's staunchest supporters. And your *Castellano*, it's excellent.' Jack accepted the compliment with good grace, while the Prime Minister turned sleep-starved eyes to his other companions. 'What do you think, *caballeros?*' There were a couple of smiles, but several of the men seemed nervous, edgy, as ill-at-ease with Jack in their midst as Jack found himself to be in theirs. Introductions, and Jack struggled hard, making mental notes that he knew would desert him long before this night was through. But a suited, broad-faced, balding man called Paulino something-or-other. A soldier, a general whose name Jack knew, Matallana – cursed with a permanently sly grin. A Minister of Education, with a suitably thin and intelligent face. And others, Ministers of Communication, Justice, and the fellow Fidel had mentioned, another general, Antonio Cordón. 'Antonio,' Negrín said to him, 'explain to our guest, if you please. It's the least we can do.'

Cordón was perhaps the youngest there, older than Jack, but not by much. One of those perpetually youthful faces. *If I was going to trust any of these characters*, thought Jack, *it would probably be Cordón*. For the rest, half of them reminded Jack of mobsters in a hideout, planning their next heist. Or maybe, more precisely, mobsters waiting for their current boss to be gunned down, to find out which of them might take his place. *And I wonder how many of them Negrín himself can trust.*

'Where to begin?' Cordón was saying, and he began to arrange plates, condiments, pieces of fruit, cutlery for his tabletop map. 'Well, perhaps with yourself, *Señor* Telford. Had we known earlier that you were with us...'

'Can't we just get to the point?' groaned the other general, the one with the insincere smile, Matallana.

'You brought us important intelligence,' Antonio Cordón pressed on. 'This business of Britain considering payments to Franco's brother and the rebels' most trusted generals. Important, though perhaps we received it just too late.'

'It's true then?'

'It seems,' said Negrín, 'that the purpose is now clear. There've been responses from Franco's people. Favourable responses, so far as your country is concerned. Those closest to Franco are broadly happy with the idea that, should a war with Germany erupt, they may accept some bounty from your generous nation and persuade the *Caudillo* and Spain to remain neutral. Naturally, no such payment would be ethical until a state of war actually exists. But they were keen that there should be some down payment. A gesture of good faith.'

'Recognition of Franco's government.' Jack sighed. He should have guessed.

'Correct, *Señor* Telford.' Negrín knocked back half a glass of red wine in one swallow. 'They've used Azaña's resignation as their prime reason, of course. But you see what this means? That the thread by which the Republic's final strategy had hung is now snapped.'

Jack remembered the book he'd borrowed from the hospital library at the Ritz. The Henty novel, *Under Wellington's Command.*

'You planned to build a defensive last line here?' he said. 'Like Torres Vedras, around Lisbon.'

'The Comrade Prime Minister is an avid admirer of your Wellington,' said Cordón.

'And then hold out until war breaks out with Germany,' said Jack. 'Just a matter of time.'

'Just a matter of time, as you say,' Cordón agreed. 'A great plan. We hold out. Then offer to take care of Hitler's great ally, General Franco, if only Britain and France will give us the arms to do so. Only now your country has found a cheaper option. Keep Spain out of the war in any case. A few bribes here and there. Simply let the Republic go to hell.'

'And Madrid,' said Jack. 'A defensive line around Alicante simply means selling out Madrid, doesn't it? Surrendering the place, after they've held out for so long.'

'An orderly retreat, no more. Evacuate everybody who's at risk. Bring them all here, to good ground that we can hold afresh. Let Franco have Madrid itself. That's probably the kindest thing to do for those that are left in any case. There may not be much by way of food and medicine in the National Zone, but it's a lot more than we've got in ours.'

'And now?' said Jack.

Cordón shrugged.

'The first part of the plan still holds good. We evacuate our best people from Madrid. Slowly, slowly. Bring everybody here. To Alicante Province. That's why we've called this the Yuste Position. You seem puzzled, *Señor*. Just a code name. Yuste was the monastery to which Carlos the Fifth retired, with the intention of devoting the rest of his life to prayer. His own last stand for his Faith.' Jack saw Negrín smile. 'Yes,' said Cordón, 'our Comrade Prime Minister hasn't quite lost his sense of humour. But with the numbers we can pull together, Franco will never be able to remove us. Not from the mountains of Alicante.' He shifted his plates and condiments around to illustrate the point.

'And, if Britain and France go to war with Germany,' said Negrín, 'Hitler will at least have to pull out his bloody planes. Mussolini too, maybe. Then there'll be stalemate. And I can negotiate a settlement.'

'So it all depends on an orderly retreat from Madrid.'

'Yes, *Señor* Telford. Like it always did. It all hangs on Madrid. A few other things too. Our Anarchist comrades. The Fleet at Cartagena. But mainly on Madrid.'

'Thank you, sir,' said Jack. 'You've been very frank. But, if you'll forgive me, I have to wonder why. I now know the reason you're here, but what about me? Why would you share all this with a nobody from the country that's just betrayed you?'

'You underestimate yourself,' said Negrín. 'When I was in Barcelona, I made sure I held regular briefings with our accredited correspondents.

With Matthews, Forrest, Sheean and the others. Oh, Capa too, of course. It was always important to me. And, regardless of what happens next, we still need the world to know what we're doing here, that the struggle still goes on.'

Jack was about to reply, but there was an urgent knock on the door. It burst open and an orderly almost fell into the room.

'Sir,' he stammered at the Prime Minister. 'Radio Madrid, sir. They say there's going to be an announcement. At midnight. From General Casado, sir.'

'Announcement?' said Negrín, while Jack looked around the table, saw a few puzzled expressions. But others, like Matallana, were simply furtive, staring at their plates, knowing what was coming.

'Yes, sir,' said the orderly. 'About a new National Defence Council. To replace – Well, sir, to replace your Government.'

Those for whom this was genuinely news howled with rage, stood, shouting, thumping the table.

'Bring the damned wireless in here, man,' shouted General Antonio Cordón, as Negrín slumped in his chair. Jack stood too, edged towards the door, towards Fidel. The blood had drained from the *Capitán's* face.

'No,' said Fidel. 'Those bloody traitors. Your damned friends, English. They cannot...'

The wireless had arrived, the dials adjusted, whining and whistling around the airwaves until Radio Madrid was coming through the speaker mesh. Midnight, and a voice that Jack Telford recognised immediately. The nervous but unmistakably lugubrious tones of his friend, Julián Besteiro.

'My Spanish fellow citizens...' Besteiro was saying, and Jack almost collapsed against the door frame, his knees turned to jelly, the recently consumed *ensalada de capellán* rising back up into his gorge, as Besteiro announced General Casado's coup – a coup against those who had fought so hard, so long, after that other military coup, almost three years before.

Chapter Thirty-Three

Monday 6th March 1939

Telephones. In the gloom. Something, for Jack, of that rabbit hole world again, as Negrín tried so desperately to maintain his composure, the Prime Minister in rational debate with the man in Madrid who had overthrown him.

'General, I've just listened to the statement you made. I think what you've done is sheer madness.' A pause. 'Your duty? I hope you'll reflect further on your duty. Because perhaps we can still come to an arrangement.' Another pause. 'No, it's not all arranged. At least send a representative to discuss some separation of powers. Or I can send somebody to Madrid.' The silence in the dining room was broken by a babble of angry voices. Negrín placed his hand over the mouthpiece. 'Please, my friends,' he said. 'Please.' And then back to the telephone. 'You're wrong, General, we *do* still hold powers. And we've never abandoned them.' The Prime Minister raised a despairing hand into the air. 'You won't obey my orders? Then consider yourself stripped of all military rank. All responsibility.' He listened for a few moments more, then held out the telephone's handset. 'He's stubborn. Paulino, you speak to him, for God's sake.'

The telephone was taken by the man with thinning hair, broad features, good suit.

'Who is he again?' Jack whispered to Fidel.

'Paulino Gómez Saíz,' the *Capitán* replied, in a low voice, anger barely constrained. 'Minister of the Interior. Socialist Party. Do you know nothing, English?'

Clearly not, thought Jack, *but good choice*, for Besteiro's broadcast had been scathing, accusing Negrín of encouraging the people to fight when the Prime Minister himself was simply preparing to run. In that case, Jack had wondered, why on earth would Negrín have come back from France in the first place? And all these preparations to make a defensive wall of the mountains surrounding Alicante. Besides, in complete contradiction to the claim that Negrín was getting ready to run, Besteiro had accused him of planning a coup of his own, a Communist coup, leaving General Casado no alternative except to forestall this sinister plot. *Yes, good choice, getting a Socialist to try and talk sense into him.* And Jack looked around the table. He couldn't name all these men yet, but their comments had identified their politics pretty plainly. Not all communists, by any means. That one, Álvaro de Vayo, another Socialist. Segundo Blanco, the Anarchist. What about the rest? He wasn't sure. But something kept playing through his brain. A comment of Sydney Elliott's when they'd been discussing the start of this awful conflict after watching some Pathé News coverage. *Milicianos* in Madrid, chanting their slogan. '*¡El pueblo unido jamás será vencido!*' The people united will never be defeated.

'You know, Jack,' Sydney had remarked, very casually, with untypical cynicism, 'that's really only true of the Right. Haven't you noticed? That whatever their internal differences, the Right always comes together in a crisis. The Left always finds it easier to rip itself apart.'

Jack shook the memory away, with difficulty.

'Fidel,' he whispered, and gripped the *Capitán's* arm, pulling him out of the dining room, 'if Negrín wants me to write this up, I'll need my notebooks, my pens. Can I get out of here? And where's my rucksack?'

Fidel pulled his arm free.

'Your friends, English,' he spat back. 'How much did you know about this?'

'The coup? Nothing. Nothing at all. The last time I spoke with Besteiro, it was also in the company of Rosario del Olmo. She's in the Party too, isn't she? And I had the warnings about Besteiro loud and clear, from your General Kotov. From you too, Fidel. You knew how close he's been to Casado. Better than me, as a matter of fact. Did I like him? Yes, I did. But then, as the whole world seems to know, I've always been a bit naïve in my choice of friends. So what now? Haul me off to a *cheka* and bump me off? Isn't that what you do, you and your NKVD pals?'

'When you're angry, English, I sometimes almost like you. Come on, let's find your damned notebooks. They should be with Ruby. She's in one of the estate workers' houses. In the grounds.'

He led Jack towards the front doors, where Captain Orca rose to meet them.

'Now what?' said Orca.

'It seems he's not a prisoner any more,' said Fidel while, outside, there was the sound of a car, skidding to a halt on the gravel. Orca's hand went to his holster. Footsteps running up the stairs beyond the double doors, but women's shoes, surely? The *clack, clack, clack* of high heels. Hammering on the doors themselves, and Captain Orca cautiously opening to examine these late-night visitors. Two women and a man. The first woman, Jack knew. He'd last seen her in Madrid's Plaza Mayor – that last night, with Ruby Waters. Dolores Ibárruri. Spain's Passion Flower. The man seemed vaguely familiar, and the woman at his side was astonishingly beautiful. Even more beautiful than Dolores herself.

'Is it true?' said Dolores. 'About Casado?'

The three of them looked like they'd been at some celebration. Incongruous.

'The Prime Minister's very busy, comrade,' said Orca. 'Can I give him a message?'

Further inside the house, teleprinters had begun to rattle, and it seemed as though every phone must now be in operation.

'To hell with you, Orca. Tell me what's happened.'

'Forgive me,' said Fidel, 'but I'm *Capitán* Fidel Constantino Sánchez, formerly under General Kotov's command. Fourteenth Corps. I was with the Prime Minister when the broadcast from Madrid came through. And when he spoke with General Casado. I'm afraid it's true. There's been a coup, in Madrid. A self-proclaimed National Defence Council. But it's not good in there at the moment. Perhaps if you'd take a seat for a few moments in the reception room and I'm sure Captain Orca will let the Comrade Prime Minister know you're here. Won't you, Orca?'

Orca opened his mouth to speak but, by then, Dolores and her two companions had pushed past and into the waiting room, fulminating about Casado, about counter-revolutionaries, about so-called bloody socialists, about traitors, about their palpable and inescapable pain.

'Did you know she was here?' said Jack when they were outside, making their way towards the cluster of *campesino* houses at the end of the stable block, and across the gritty courtyard from the main house itself.

'What do you think I was doing all that time earlier?' Jack heard the grief in his voice for the first time, saw him drag the sleeve of his tunic across his face. 'Of course I knew. The whole of the Party leadership's here. Thought they had something to celebrate. At last, a strategy that might have given us a solution. A fighting chance. And if we were to make a stand, we'd all be in it, the Passion Flower included. They've got their own place, the party cadres, just the other side of town.'

'And the man?'

Fidel looked astonished.

'For an educated type, English, you know very little. Rafael Alberti Merello. You'll tell me now that you've never heard of him.' *Alberti the poet*, thought Jack. *A legend. A true legend.* 'And his woman, of course,' said Fidel. 'María Teresa León. Does she not stir your blood, comrade?'

Jack was initially too shocked to speak. He'd read her literary magazine, *El Mono Azul*, The Blue Overall, many times while he was in Madrid. As for stirring the blood, he would have given Fidel a very frank answer indeed but, at that moment, there was a shot, somewhere in the grounds, and all the lights in the house and gardens suddenly went out.

The hour that followed played itself out like a nightmare, details difficult to recall, or folding into each other like sand, cement and aggregate mixed with a heavy shovel, all bonded together by waters of self-deception from the rusting bucket of Jack's brain. But these were the things that Jack remembered for as long as memory remained to him: the depth of that black night; he and Fidel bursting into the dusty stone and baked-brick house of the old *campesina* estate worker, to which Ruby had been allocated; Fidel yelling at the old woman to douse the candle she had just lit; Ruby demanding to know what was happening; Jack himself, scrabbling in his rucksack, stuffing a notebook into one baggy trouser pocket and, uselessly, his precious fountain pen into the other; the *Capitán*, just visible in the gloom, checking his automatic and flinging the old revolver of Crazy Luís onto Ruby's bed; and his strident instructions that they must turn the bed itself over, form a barricade, then stay hidden. But then the old woman grew hysterical, ran screaming through the door. There was a burst of machine gun fire, the screams silenced, and a short symphony of other shots, mostly single shots, echoing from different directions, some close, some further away.

'Just stay here, and stay hidden,' Fidel told them both.

'What is it, Fidel? What's happening?'

'There's been a coup, *precisosa*,' he said. 'I think – Well, I don't know what to think. But I need to go. The English, he'll explain it all.'

'No, wait,' said Jack. 'Fidel. At least if we all stay here, together. That's safer, isn't it?'

Jack fought with his own terror and, in that darkness, *Capitán* Fidel Constantino Sánchez gripped his arm.

'Don't worry, my friend,' he said. 'You English always manage to survive somehow.' And then he slipped away, out of the room, into the darkened passage, and out into the night.

'Another coup, Jack?' Ruby whispered, and he could hear her terror too.

'We met Negrín. And then there was a radio broadcast from Madrid. Our friends, Ruby. My friends. Besteiro. They've gone mad. Think they can do a deal with Franco. But the whole Communist Party's here, Ibárruri, and others. Casado's basically called them all traitors, and these must be Casado's men, I'm guessing. Or...'

They touched each other's arm at precisely the same time. Some scraping sound out there, beyond the upturned straw mattress. Jack leaned over, peered around the edge of their flimsy barricade but could see nothing, just the vague outline of the doorway. *But where the hell did that revolver go?* Jack wondered. He couldn't remember, began to panic. It had been on the bed. Yet now?

Two quick, hobnailed steps out in the corridor, the doorframe suddenly filled and Jack shouting, in his own language.

'Don't shoot. We're English.'

And, alongside him, the small room erupted: the flash, which illuminated Ruby's clasped and splinted hands, the revolver between them; the ear-shattering percussion as the .32 Eibar went off; the muted slap and grunt as the bullet blasted their intruder to hell, whoever he was; and the clatter of his weapon as it fell into the room.

'Oh, may God forgive me, Jack,' Ruby sobbed. But then there was a moment of pure hysteria, her mimicry of his own cry. *'Don't shoot. We're English.* What was that about? And shouldn't we get out of here?'

Jack picked up the fallen rifle and they stepped carefully over the *campesina*'s spread-eagled corpse, then stopped at the front door and glanced outside. More shots. Two stabs of light from the big house. Yet, otherwise, nothing but a star-filled ebony sky and, in the courtyard, tall palm trees with their fronds wafting and rustling in a cordite-scented wind. Jack realised that he'd never, in his life, fired a rifle. But how difficult could it be?

'Jack, can you take this?' whispered Ruby and held the revolver's handgrip towards him.

'Where did you learn to shoot?' he said, and took the weapon from her.

'Father,' she replied. 'He insisted. Never know where you might be posted, that sort of thing.'

'You're enjoying this, Miss Waters?'

'I'm terrified, Mister Telford.'

'That's not what I asked. But I can't see anybody.' There was a terrible commotion from the house though. 'Let's make for the palm trees.'

He made an effort to keep within the deepest shadows, Ruby hobbling behind, her fingertips gripping a fold in his shirt. They reached the nearest of the palms, pressed themselves painfully against the sharp-edged remnants from decades of dead frond stalks that made up the trunk. He had a sense of needing to protect Ruby yet, for himself, Jack didn't feel very much at all. *If I die*, he thought, *I die*. It didn't move him, one way or the other. *But where the hell are Negrín's guards?*

Another blast of machine gun fire, behind them. Then two figures, dancing together in the dark, round and round, before falling to the earth. Jack set the rifle against the tree.

'Stay here,' he hissed. 'I mean it. Stay. No heroics.' And he edged towards the two men, revolver leveled in front of him. One must be friend, the other foe. But which was which? It was a bizarre sight, the first fellow on his back, the second apparently attached to him at head and feet, but his back arched impossibly, like a bent bow – though not for long. There was a ghastly gurgling noise, then the sound of something popping, followed by a gentle susurration, such as a scythe might make when it cuts through grass. The bow collapsed, and the man beneath extricated himself from the tangle.

'English,' he panted, 'it's me.' And Fidel was at his side, a long strand of metallic ribbon dangling from his hand. 'Cheese wire,' he boasted. 'Found it in the kitchen earlier. Always useful, cheese wire.' But, from the house, came more shots. 'Come on,' he said, 'you're with me.'

*

Ruby was left sheltering among the palm trees, but when Jack and Fidel got back to the front doors, now wide ajar, they found Captain Orca sprawled dead down the steps. They crept inside, two more corpses in the dim vestibule and hallway, the stink of blood, pale light spilling from the half-closed dining room door, and a voice within.

'Let's get this piece of Red shit outside, then you can finish the others. And make sure you leave a couple of calling cards.'

Jack tried to control the shaking, which had overtaken his limbs. Pure terror. He couldn't move. Not even when, inside, somebody began to sing. A woman's voice. The *Internacional*. Not even when Fidel quietly pulled back the slide on his own gun and edged towards the door. Not even when a third figure materialised from nowhere, from the passageway's inky depths, pressed the barrel of one pistol against Fidel's neck, pointed another at Jack.

'Bastards,' said the man. 'Drop your weapons. Drop them now.' Jack had watched scenes like this a dozen times in the cinema, knew with absolute certainty that Fidel, the hero, would now spin around, and disable their attacker in a dashing display of unarmed combat. But the sudden appearance of Jack's father made him realise that this scene would have no such ending. Only death lay ahead in this particular finale. Fidel bent a little, dropped his gun on the carpet, and Jack did the same. Inside, there was a shot, and the singing faded away. *'Teniente,'* shouted the man through the open door, 'two more of this scum.' He kicked the door wider, waved a pistol at his prisoners and, as the feeble light of a night lantern caught his features, Jack saw that this man was his Weasel. He understood, then, the panic that had gripped him. For, as the door opened fully, there was Lieutenant Álvaro Enrique Turbides.'

'These aren't Casado's men,' Jack murmured.

'*Señor* Telford,' Turbides sneered, his own pistol held to Negrín's head. The Prime Minister seemed unharmed, though his hair, his shoulders and the table were sprinkled with plaster dust, a hole in the ceiling overhead. 'An added bonus. I did wonder, when we saw the motorbike. And I would have caught up with you before too long. But this is even better.' At the farther end of the table, the other Ministers, as well as Dolores Ibárruri and the Albertis, were being held under guard by a man with a Thompson gun. They looked defiant, even though the lieutenant's warning shot had plainly silenced their singing. In some ways, their guard was the strangest man Jack had ever seen – a dwarf in reverse, oversized head, but set on an impossibly tall and skeletal body. Yet not quite *all* the other guests were gathered there. General Matallana seemed to be kept apart, his fellow-general, Antonio Cordón, watching him with a look of sheer contempt. *If looks could kill*, thought Jack, as Turbides continued. 'Even better,' he said. 'This whole devil's brood shot by the Reds' own secret police – at Casado's personal command, the world will conclude. And with Britain's notorious press correspondent, a double-murderer, caught up in the process. Dead too, naturally. Neat and tidy. And this filth,' he tapped his automatic against Negrín's chest, 'comes with us. We have something special in mind for him.' Then Turbides pointed at the *Capitán*. 'That one, over there with his friends. But the Englishman, bring him here. We have some unfinished business to discuss too.'

Fidel was forced to join the group at one end of the table, while the Weasel pushed Jack along to the other, and Turbides, still keeping Negrín covered, slipped his free hand inside his leather overcoat, took out a cigar, bit through the end.

'*Teniente*,' said the Weasel, 'there can't be much time.'

'There's enough,' Turbides told him, bringing out a lighter next, flicking the Zippo into life and puffing on the cigar until it was glowing, red-hot. 'You!' he called to Matallana's guard. 'Forget him and come here. Watch this traitor.' He motioned towards Negrín. 'And you,' he said to the Weasel, 'hold the Englishman. And hold him tight.'

Jack struggled, but the Weasel was stronger than he looked, pinioned his arms while Turbides gripped Jack's face in his vice-like fist, blew smoke into his good eye, let the cigar tip waver near his cheek so he could feel the heat of it, remember the last time, the agony, in its entirety.

'Son,' said Jack's father, 'you were really only ever blessed with one gift, you know?'

Jack didn't understand, tried to concentrate on the riddle, knew he was weeping from both the smoke and the dread, wanted to resist, but he could not. Somebody was shouting at the other end of the table. Fidel maybe. Then La Pasionaria, calling Turbides a coward, a disgrace to Spain. And, finally, there was Ruby, standing in the doorway.

'Excuse me,' she said, in her perfect, Anglo-accented Spanish, 'I'm with the British Diplomatic Service…'

It was the problem with that hour, the difficulty of total recollection. How can you properly remember a scene in which so many things happen at precisely the same instant? The oversized dwarf turning to stare at Ruby; Fidel kicking the Thompson gun from his hands and producing the cheese wire from his pocket; the quick circular movement with the small handles that wrapped the wire around the man's throat to garrote him; the Weasel, releasing Jack and groping for his gun; the youthful General Antonio Cordón seizing a carving knife from the dining room table and launching it like a throwing dagger straight into the distracted Weasel's heart; Negrín, using the advantage of his own guard's confusion to throw a jaw-crunching right jab that pole-axed the man; and Jack's father, once again.

'Only one gift,' he repeated. 'You should really use it. Now, Jack, my boy.'

Turbides had shifted his grip to Jack's throat, dropped the cigar and spun him around like a human shield, choking him with the crook of his elbow, pulling the automatic from his pocket again, aiming at Negrín. Jack clawed at the lieutenant's arm with one hand, reached into his own trousers with the other. Where was the damned thing?

'Stop,' shouted Turbides. 'All of you. Or that bastard dies now.' He still showed no fear, simply steadied his aim at Prime Minister Negrín, so that the blur of actions across the room slowed, then flapped to a halt, like a reel of film reaching its end.

There, thought Jack and, one-handed, slowly, fumbling, unscrewed the top from his Font-Pelayo fountain pen. He managed to turn his head just enough to see the face of Turbides with his own remaining right eye, measuring those cruel pig-like eyes as they, in turn, scanned the room. Jack took stock, also, of his torturer's thin and oily moustache, the absurdly flared nostrils above.

He brought up the pen in one sharp movement, wild and well wide of his mark. He'd hope for an eye but, instead, the nib plunged into the side of that hawk-hooked nose. The man's head kicked back in spontaneous reaction, he screamed and the automatic fired, then fell, and the grip on Jack's throat dropped away, allowing him to turn. Turn on the attack, a red mist of anger and loathing filling him. Turbides lifted a hand to remove the pen, but Jack's hand was faster. A writer's hand, the pen his weapon. And this pen was long, slender, sharp. Jack gripped the end of the celluloid case, forced the steel nib up through the lieutenant's nasal cavity. He hoped it would travel straight into the creature's brain though that, of course, was impossible. Yet Turbides crashed back against the wall, slid down the patterned paper, bellowing in agony, while Jack stooped, gathered up the pistol, and emptied its magazine into his enemy – emptied it slowly so that, with each angry shot, a little more of his innocence was drowned by instinct.

Reinforcements had arrived from Elda itself. More generals from the Communist Party's new headquarters, south of town, code-named the Dakar Position. Bodies had been identified, friend and foe, Jack confirming the identity of the Guardia Civil Lieutenant Turbides, and the attackers' Republican Shock Police identification papers exposed as forgeries. Negrín had sent one last futile message to Madrid once he had restored his composure, and Jack had still been present, around dawn, when the Prime Minister had begun to think more positively again.

'Never mind,' he'd said, 'we can still fall back on Alicante.'

'I'm afraid not, sir,' an orderly had replied. 'Even there, the rebellion has spread. We just received word that your Military Commander for the city has been arrested by Casado's supporters.'

Around the same time, Negrín found out that the Republican fleet had abandoned Cartagena. And, worse, that while this night's attack on El Poblet was plainly the work of Fifth Column *facciosos*, there were already reports of Casado's own men factually setting up roadblocks, looking for him, in the local towns.

'That's the end then,' Negrín had told his friends. 'Nothing left for us. Time to leave, I think.' And he had ordered transport planes to be sent from the airfield at Los Llanos, outside Albacete.

The whole situation was too dismal to afford any true recognition for the defence of El Poblet, and nor was there any real opportunity to consider how the attack had been orchestrated so well. It was clear that some of Negrín's guards had simply disappeared. No trace of them. Officially listed as missing in action, but an obvious suspicion that they had been bought by the Fifth Column. But Jack had plenty of time to chew over the events as they drove the ambulance, to the tiny hamlet and airstrip at El Fondó. It could not be pure coincidence, surely? That Turbides had followed him all the way to and from Madrid, and then, by pure coincidence, arrived in Monóvar and Elda with sufficient time available to discover Negrín's secret whereabouts, then plan the raid. Yet the missing guards suggested that there were enough traitors around the Prime Minister to have made the attackers' job easy for them. And then there was General Matallana. Fevered phone calls from Casado supporters in Valencia, insisting he be released – though it was news to everybody in Poblet that Matallana considered himself a prisoner.

So, thought Jack, *Matallana involved in this conspiracy too?* Maybe but, for now, they'd arrived at El Fondó, with Fidel instructed to join the other fighters brought there by Generals Lister and Modesto to form a final guard for Negrín. Twenty of them. And they included an old friend of Fidel, Sergio Sifre. The two men embraced each other like old lovers, swapped stories, expressed wonder at the way they had each ended up here while, in the single row of houses on the airstrip's edge, just across from the air-raid shelter's entrance, in a modest kitchen, the Spanish Communist Party's Executive held its last meeting. It was eleven in the morning, and three planes – two DC-3 transport planes and an older passenger biplane – had arrived from Los Llanos. Then a taxi turned up. A taxi. How odd that seemed. And, from the taxi, Dolores Ibárruri emerged with a couple of her friends. She waited a few minutes, while the first of the planes was made ready and taxied up the packed earth runway. It was a DH89 *Dragon Rapide*.

'Isn't that strange?' said Jack, as he watched La Pasionaria climb aboard.

'Strange?' Ruby had been settled in the shade of some trees, just opposite the houses, relishing the rest and sniffing happily at the wood smoke drifting across the road. Fidel had been told that he could be released, and their journey to Alicante continue, just as soon as the Prime Minister was safe.

'The plane,' said Jack, remembering the stories he'd learned about how Franco had been airlifted from the Canary Islands, to start his bloody insurrection, by British pilot, Cecil Bebb. 'Just an irony,' he said. 'That the Spanish Civil War should begin, and end, with a De Havilland *Dragon Rapide*.'

Not quite the end though, for Jack was still there when, later in the afternoon, more taxis arrived. Negrín. And his Ministers. But Jack saw that, even now, as they stood waiting for their planes, Negrín was left a little apart, staring out over the flat, desiccated farmlands, the misty mountains beyond, his broad shoulders shaking gently.

'I never had the chance to thank you properly, *Señor* Telford.' He hadn't even looked around.

'Can I offer you a smoke, sir?' Jack extended his pack of *Superiores*.

'And you'll write about this, won't you? Write about these last days of our poor Republic?' He accepted a light from Jack's match, sheltered in his cupped hands.

'Perhaps without mentioning last night's little débacle, though.'

'Maybe for the best,' said Negrín. Then he reached inside his jacket, to an inner pocket. 'But whatever you decide to write, you'd better have this. I owe you that much, at least.' It was Negrín's own fountain pen, less elaborate than the Font-Pelayo but, to Jack, worth more than its weight in pure gold.

'I don't deserve this,' Jack told him. 'You don't understand, sir. In Madrid. Some of those men, Besteiro and his bunch, they were friends.'

'Don't worry, *señor*. I thought they were mine too. We all make mistakes.' Negrín took a long drag on the cigarette, blew out the smoke. 'No, not mistakes. We set aside our personal principles for what we believe is the common good. Just a shame that we — those that poor Spain has chosen to lead her — seem to have no consensus on what that common good might be. Well, at least there's no tobacco rationing in France. You think they'll still welcome me there though, my friend? Yesterday, I would have felt at home there. Yesterday, I belonged to Spain also. To the world. But, today, I don't really belong anywhere, do I?'

Chapter Thirty-Four

Wednesday 22nd March 1939

The water in the wide bay was ice-cold. But the sun shone upon golden sands and Jack had been unable to resist a dip. Now, he huddled in his towel, at the thatched beach shack bar, fishing boats hauled up alongside, and their catch recently unloaded – the catch upon which he was already feasting. Fresh sardines, grilled over a wood fire, shared with Ruby Waters. At the waves' edge, where a wooden bathing pier ran down into the murmuring sea, Fidel Constantino Sánchez and his comrade-in-arms, Sergio Sifre, were reading Lorca. Sergio was sketching too.

'I wish we could stay here forever,' said Jack.

'Buy one of those, maybe?' Ruby smiled, and pointed to the row of bungalows – recently built as holiday homes by the province's wealthy merchants, but currently occupied by refugees from the war. The *casitas*, and the two-storey Hotel Moñino, ran in a line just behind them, this side of the dunes, the *esparto* grass, the pine trees, edging a stony road leading up to the village and its castle, a half-mile away.

'What happened to the cottage garden in Dorset? And having lots of children with Fidel?'

'I may have got that part a little wrong. Perhaps using it as something of a weather vane, anyway.'

What? thought Jack. *Just being precocious?* But he decided not to take the bait.

'They say this stretch of Alicante's coast has the best all-year-round climate in Europe.' *And the best cooks*, Jack remembered Negrín saying. *And the most loyal supporters of the Republic.* 'But I think the war would catch up with us before too long, even here.'

Jack could have bitten his tongue for, as he spoke, he saw the formation of tiny black specks circling beyond the Cabo de Santa Pola, just away to the north, where the city of Alicante itself lay hidden, immediately beyond. There were anti-aircraft guns on the headland but no sign of them firing, though it was hard to tell. They had made an excursion, yesterday, up to that prominent ridge and, from there, Negrín's thwarted plan had become clear – almost the whole of Alicante Province laid out before them: its fertile crescent, some of the best growing lands in Spain all around them and stretching into the middle distance; and, beyond, the rock ramparts of those mountain ranges that separated this region from the rest. The passes through those mountains, Sergio insisted, would have been the killing grounds within which Franco's advance could have been halted. If only...

'You see them?' Fidel shouted, pointing to the planes. Italian planes, of course. Germans too, maybe. The city had been bombed many times during the war, the worst when, ten months earlier, the market had been their target, hundreds of innocents killed. But the attacks had intensified over the past two weeks, since El Poblet. They had got away just in time, Negrín's final rearguard. Loyal fighters like Fidel and Sergio being given leave to consider themselves demobilised, warned to take care as Casado's anti-communist faction began its pogrom. Within hours, Communist commissars in Madrid were being arrested, Communist commanders relieved of their posts. At the same time, pro-Communist brigades had marched into Madrid and yet another civil war within the civil war erupted. Street fighting between Communist supporters on one side, Socialists and Anarchists on the other. Two thousand dead, according to rumours reaching them here in this haven.

'Yes, I see them,' Jack replied. But he was looking at Sergio Sifre. Alicante was the young man's home, and the pain written on those tanned and shaven-headed features was emotional to behold. 'Which one are you working on, Sergio?'

Slowly, the two *guerrilleros* picked themselves off the sand, brought the book and Sergio's sketches back to the table.

'*Canción China*,' Sergio replied. Lorca's poem, the *Chinese Song for Europe*. And Fidel began reciting it from memory.

'"*La señorita del abanico, va por el puente del fresco río.*"'

The young lady with the fan, crosses the bridge over the cool river. And there was Sergio's beautiful drawing, a Chinese girl, the arched, oriental bridge. More pictures.

'You have a gift, Sergio,' said Ruby, turning the pages of the young man's pad, careful not to soil them with fishy, oil-smeared fingers. 'These pictures are exquisite.'

'They teach you many things,' Sergio smiled, 'at Jesuit College.' Then he laughed, when he saw the shock on their faces. 'Where do you think I learned about Marxism, my friends? The words of Christ and the words of Marx are only separated by a thread. And the practitioners of those two faiths are not so very different either. Good and true believers on the one hand, hypocrites on the other.'

To Jack, he seemed very young, much younger than Fidel, for example.

'Is it possible to follow both paths?' said Jack. 'Marx and Christ?'

Sergio shrugged.

'In my *barrio*, in Sant Joan,' he replied, pronouncing the word *jo-anne*, in the way, Jack had learned, that local Valenciano speakers did, 'the fisherman's brotherhood, the *confradía*, is very strong. Hard men, shaped by the sea. Many of them are communists. Strong believers. Yet, on any of the holy days, when the *paseos*, those floats and statues of Christ or the Virgin have to be paraded through the streets, those same comrades are usually among the first to carry them. Tradition? Yes, I suppose so. But it's deeper than that. *España profunda*, my friends.'

'You saw the light then?' said Ruby. 'Sergio, on the road to Damascus.'

'Something like that, *Inglesa*. There was the election. In '36. Seems so long ago now. Another lifetime. And I'd seen the way the Church was already behaving, all the time I was at the seminary. Priests sowing terror into the hearts of the people. Real terror. Week after week after week. About what would happen to them unless they stayed loyal to their masters. Threatened them with terrible things. And I couldn't stay. We knew what was coming. So I joined the army instead. The army and the Party.'

That was all he'd told them on previous occasions. About how he'd enlisted just before the war began, then transferred to the Guerrilla Corps, where he'd met Fidel. Sergio had been promoted as well, in his case, to the rank of lieutenant.

'And when the war's over,' said Ruby, 'what will you do? Become a famous artist?'

It seemed to Jack that a cloud suddenly darkened the sun. He almost looked up, then saw the way that Fidel put his hand to Sergio's shoulder, squeezed it gently, each of the men's faces set hard for a moment.

'And you, English,' Fidel broke the silence. 'How is the writing going, with that fine pen of Comrade Negrín?'

'You're correct, *Capitán*. It's a very good pen. But I'm still riddled with guilt every time I use it. If I'd done things differently, maybe asked Besteiro and Father Lobo more questions, talked to them properly – I don't know, but it just feels that I should have seen what they were planning, done something about it.'

'You take too much on your shoulders, Mister Telford,' Ruby scolded him. 'And the truth, Fidel, is that he's been writing some very good pieces. I've seen them. They're excellent.'

It hadn't been easy. Because they had, all at once, fallen back out of the rabbit hole. The world they had known so intimately from inside – bizarre as it may sometimes have been – now seemed closed to them. Friends still arriving in Alicante had brought them eyewitness word of the chaos in Madrid, the slaughter there. But the papers, now largely under Casado's censorship, had only given that an obtuse reference. They had been assisted in doing so by the darkening international news: Hitler's invasion of the rest of Czechoslovakia; Britain and France posturing in the aftermath; fractures appearing in the British Parliament with dire warnings to Chamberlain about the consequences of appeasement, and Hitler's long-term ambitions towards the Ukrainian oilfields.

'Then you must help those pieces reach the outside world, *preciosa*,' said Fidel. 'When do you go back to Alicante?'

'Tomorrow. The next day. I'm not sure.'

'When did you decide this, Miss Waters?' Jack was shocked. Hurt. Filled with dread. 'And when you say you're going back to Alicante, you mean so that you can get away, I hope?'

'Jack,' she said, 'it reminds me of the beginning. In Madrid. When we arrived in Alicante, Mister Donald was very kind.' Donald was the Acting Vice-Consul in Alicante, operating now from temporary offices in the Vistahermosa district. The former Consul, Scotsman Gabriel de Callejón had been killed the previous August when a 500lb bomb, dropped by an Italian Savoia, had destroyed the old consular building. But Mister Donald had wired Ruby's family, let them know she was safe, then made arrangements for her to come here, a local spot that he loved, so she might recuperate a while. And, with no other plans, plus a more than obvious desire to remain at Ruby's side, Jack and Fidel, Sergio too, had tagged along. 'But you saw all those people, didn't you?' she said. Even then, there were streams of refugees pouring into Alicante, funneling towards the city because there was nowhere else to go – and many of them crowding into the British Consulate.

'All those people pretending to be British?' said Jack.

'Can you blame them, Jack? And I don't really care. If I can help just a few of them. It's important to me.'

'Mister Donald told you to do this?'

'Lord no, Jack. He thinks I should have left already.'

'That's good advice, Miss Waters. Very good. You remember the Anarchist waiters? Never hang around until the curtain falls.' Then Jack remembered Fidel and Sergio. 'I'm sorry, *compañeros*. What about you two? Ruby's right. You need a plan.'

Fidel laughed.

'We're relying on the fleet coming back to pick us all up,' he laughed again.

The Republican fleet, which had abandoned Cartagena during Casado's coup, was now lying in Bizerta harbour. French Tunisia.

'And, meanwhile,' said Sergio, 'we still have Lorca. For now.' He looked wistfully at the book. 'You know,' he said, 'what will happen? When this is all over and Franco has won, they will assassinate poor Federico all over again. Ban his poems. Burn his books. Maybe that will be the worst thing of all.'

'There are the peace talks,' said Jack. 'You never know.'

'We've already had word.' Sergio looked at him. 'The papers won't say so, but Franco's given his answer. "Negotiation is inconsistent with unconditional surrender." He means it too. That's our death sentence, *señor*.'

Fidel put an arm around the young man's shoulders.

'Chin up, *Teniente* Sifre,' he said. 'Time for a walk, I think.'

The two soldiers drifted off along the shoreline, each talking at the same time, loud, their hands carving patterns in the air for emphasis. *España profunda*, thought Jack.

'How can such beautiful people have been caught up in all this?' said

Ruby. Jack had never thought about the *Capitán* as being particularly beautiful. *Strange choice of words*, he thought. 'And will it ever be right for them?' she said. 'Ever?'

He picked up a handful of sand, hot Spanish sand, let it trickle through his fingers.

'The whole country's been caught up in it, Ruby. It's what happens when you feed people a diet of propaganda for long enough. Like Germany. You create a scapegoat, and you build fear. The fear turns to hatred and anger. It's frightening, but you have to put it in perspective. I never studied astronomy, but I know this. That there are more suns and planets in the universe than grains of sand on this beach. Everything that happens here, or on the entire planet, it's no more than the flutter of a butterfly's wing. Vitally important to those of us living it in this snapshot of time, but meaningless, really.'

'If it's meaningless, why do you spend so much time writing, trying to explain it?'

'Selfishness. Because, when I write, for a short while I can escape the futility, persuade myself there is some order, some justice, some value to those sacrificed lives, some purpose, after all. But it never lasts long.'

'You need a plan too, Mister Telford. For your life. Instead of all this self-pity. Settle down somewhere. Find yourself an intelligent wife, Jack. A good wife. A best friend.'

'Are you offering? Obviously not, since you've apparently decided to return to your desk – broken wrists and all. It would have been nice to know, of course. The rest of the world seems to be up-to-speed. But not me.'

'Now you're being petulant. I told you, it's my duty, Jack. When that's done, I'll be away from here. And, meanwhile, I just have to look after myself, do I not?'

'How do you plan to protect yourself from falling Italian bombs, Ruby? For goodness sake...'

'Then make me a better offer, Mister Telford. Persuade me that we could make a difference some other way. Where are *you* planning to go?'

'That depends on how successful Milanes has been in persuading the authorities that Fielding's death was either an accident or justifiable.'

'Your enemies have a habit of meeting unfortunate accidents, Jack.'

'Apart from those I kill in cold blood. Is that what you were thinking?'

Because it's what I think, Jack raged inside. *I used to have repetitive nightmares about being tortured by that bastard. Now I daren't sleep for fear of the nightmares from killing him.*

'I told you once before that I can't conceive of inflicting unnecessary cruelty on another living creature.'

'I'm sorry, Ruby. But was that not you at El Poblet, with the revolver?'

'I was saving your ungrateful skin, for goodness sake. And my own. That's a long way from the pleasure you so obviously derived when you killed Turbides. I don't think I can ever get that out of my head. Not the killing. He deserved to die. But the horror of it. The look of euphoria on your poor face. And if Mister Milanes persuades the authorities that you're not guilty, where will you go? To escape all that. Because you'll need to, Jack. Need to find somewhere you can reconcile things for yourself.'

'In the end?' He shrugged. 'Home, I suppose. England. Or France. I can't stay here, not with Franco's people still looking for me – maybe others too. Though I'd take a gamble on all that, if a certain young lady in the Alicante Consulate wanted me to stay around.'

He wondered from whence that little speech had come, because it was very far from what he wanted to say. His intention had been to speak with her, open his heart: about salvation; about how those deaths, a whole chain of deaths now, weighed upon his soul; about his guilt, his non-Catholic guilt; and about how much he believed, deeply believed, that this young woman's affection was truly the only destination and refuge he sought. But this was him, of course. Still Jack Telford. Lonely Jack Telford. For God's sake, even his father had abandoned him again – saved his life at El Poblet and now simply vanished like a snuffed candle.

'Jack – Mister Telford – I could not ask you. I wouldn't. Entirely futile. Disingenuous of me.'

'Still got your heart set on the cottage garden, and Fidel's offsprings?'

She laughed, looked along the beach, shaded her eyes so that she could make out Fidel and Sergio. They were a long way distant, splashing bare feet in the gentle waves lapping at the foreshore, each of them, Jack noticed, with an arm around the other's waist.

'Jack,' she said, are you entirely blind?'

Chapter Thirty-Five

Monday 27th March 1939

I have taken life, thought Jack, *and am now condemned to endlessly repeated reels of silent self-reproach with never a scent of absolution.*

She would have told him it was pitiful. Of course she would. Yet Ruby did not have to suffer the torment. And now, there was this. He stared at himself in the mirror of his room. A decent room, high on the seaward side of the Gran Hotel – still known by everybody in town, it seemed, as Iborra's. Morning sunshine so strong that, even with the wooden shutters half-closed, its fingers filled the room with light – bright enough to highlight those thin slivers of silver, which had appeared from nowhere, at his temples. And there was the blasted hand, too. The right one. He rubbed at it, tried to massage away the slight paralysis, the trembling, before he lit his first cigarette of the day.

He crossed to the window, drawn by the clank and rattle of the trams that trundled around the Plaza Joaquín Dicenta outside. In the centre of the *plaza* stood that Monument to the Martyrs of Liberty – those shot in the 1844 Boné rebellion; early revolutionaries seeking a more liberal and enlightened Spain. The monument marked the northern end of Alicante's promenade, its *malecón*, across from the entrance to Alicante's harbour.

It must be beautiful, he imagined, *under all that*. For the promenade was, today, as it had been for many days past, entirely choked with all manner of temporary shelters, assemblies of canvas and corrugated iron, of palm frond and sacking, smoke still rising from whatever fires had been lit during the night, or for cooking. There were scenes like this all over the city, which seemed to groan permanently under the weight of its influx of refugees. This sanctuary of last resort.

Beyond the road, the inner wall of the harbour itself stretched around in a semi-circle, crowned with cargo cranes, like wading birds, and sheltering just a few merchant vessels. Between the inner wall, with its berthing quays, and the outer breakwater – nothing. Not a single ship in the fairway because, beyond, in the offing, somewhere out there in the robin's-egg waters of the Mediterranean, were the Italian submarines, waiting and watching, making sure the blockade of Alicante was impenetrable. Yet there was still hope in the city, hope that the Republican fleet would, at any moment, return from Bizerta to carry all true loyalists away. To exile? Yes, but also to freedom, to survival. Though today there was still no sign of the Republic's destroyers and battleships. In the harbour nothing but seagulls sweeping and screeching around empty fishing boats. A couple of small coastal colliers too, and those British merchantmen, the *Stanbrook* and the *Maritime*. A few others had already sailed, carrying only a few hundred passengers between them, such a pitiful number compared to the tens of thousands waiting to escape the closing jaws of Franco's army.

Jack had been drinking the previous night with some of the *Stanbrook*'s hands, around the corner at the Bar Lepanto. Her skipper was taking himself off to Madrid, they'd told him, looking for instruction from the ship-owners.

'Why all the way to Madrid?' Jack had asked them, between raucous choruses of *Yes Sir, That's My Baby*, and *Alexander's Ragtime Band*, and *Danny Boy*, or any of those songs that sailors croak and slur when the wine and the beer and the smoke hacks their voices to sodden shreds.

'Beats me,' the Steward, Billy Clark, had growled. 'Couldn't get orders no other way, that's what we was told. But he's not a bad 'un. Not as skippers go. Knows his business.'

'There's a lot of folk in Alicante would pay a pretty penny to be on board when you sail, Billy.'

'Not goin' to 'appen, mate. Orders. No bleedin' passengers. Too risky.'

'Risky?' Jack had said. 'Then what the hell are you doing here?'

'We 'ad cargo to offload.'

He'd spoken as though Jack was an idiot.

'Weren't you warned not to come into port? Not past all those bloody U-boats. But you came anyway.'

'Yeah, well… They told us that at Bilbao. Christ knows 'ow many times.'

One of the other hands, Oskar the Swede, was draped on his back over the next table, amidst the food slops and broken bottles, hairy belly bursting from his open shirt and pumping like a bellows to the rhythm of his raucous snores. They were all rough as old rope, Jack had concluded, as Able Seaman Ramón staggered outside to piss in the street. Another, a Lascar, spewed in a corner, while yet one more, the Second Engineer, started an argument with a bare-foot, threadbare Spanish soldier over one of the gypsy-looking street girls. Neither had understood the other's insults but it had turned nasty, others pushing themselves into the jabbing and shoving that quickly developed – until Billy Clark had stood on a table and begun to sing *Red River Valley* in a deep baritone, of which Paul Robeson would have been justifiably proud. It had become something of an anthem, the tune borrowed by the International Brigades, adapting grumbling soldiers' lyrics for their own song, *Jarama Valley* – and the Spaniards in the bar, now with yet another version, and recognising the rhythm, joining in, accepting the thing as a peace offering, whether it was intended, or whether it was not.

'Have you seen Fidel?' Ruby shouted. 'Looks like you had a wild night, Mister Telford.'

The temporary consulate, around the corner from the Cathedral, was swamped with refugees, and a table had been set up, in the alleyway alongside, to try and help process the queue. Some seemed wealthy, packed suitcases, all their worldly goods on handcarts, or carried in their arms, an out-of-place birdcage. They seemed well fed, these folk, professionals with their wives and tidy children. But the rest looked half-starved: women with babes in arms; people of all ages, tiny infants, ancient folk, cripples, poorly dressed; and, among them, some remnants of the Republic's defeated forces. There were thousands more, Jack knew, out in the *barrio* of San Gabriel, around the area they called Twelve Bridges. Fidel and Sergio were there, doing their best to help.

'I've not seen them,' he said, just a little too quickly. 'I was trying to establish diplomatic relations with the crew of the *Stanbrook*.'

'We may have a few more customers for you, then,' she said, looking around at the simmering crowd. 'Have you ever witnessed anything like this in your life? Ever? And, Jack, you will make sure to find a place for the boys, won't you?'

It took him a moment. The boys? Fidel and Sergio, of course. But the truth was that since they'd arrived back in Alicante, he'd not spent much time in their company. The shock of realising Fidel's homosexuality so late in the day had rather rocked him back on his heels. Jack considered himself a modern fellow, progressive. At university, he had fought hard to confront snide comments about "pansy clubs" and "buttercups" – or much worse. But Fidel? He'd spent all that time with him. Never had a clue. He felt somewhat deceived. And yes, there were all those images of Ancient Greek warriors and their lovers within the ranks. Yet that was another world, was it not? Like that academic, artistic or theatrical world, which allowed the tendencies of the rich and the celebrated to be accepted so readily. Ivor Novello. Benjamin Britten. Noel Coward. Siegfried Sassoon. E M Forster. And, in San Pedro de Cardeña, among those poets and philosophers within the International Brigades, of course there were men who, at home, may well have been accused, like Oscar Wilde, of "gross indecency." But Jack would never have imagined it here, in Spain's own Republican army, with all its traditional *machismo*. Why not? He had no idea, and it simply confused him.

'I'll speak to them again later,' he said. 'They're expecting the *Stanbrook*'s skipper back from Madrid tomorrow morning at the latest. Should be able to find out something then. What does the Consul say?'

It took her a moment to reply, while she helped a member of the consular staff study some filthy and crumpled document which, the owner claimed, proved that his father had been an English sailor.

'Oh, Mister Donald's quite clear,' she said, at last, remembering that Jack was still there. 'Policy. No British-registered vessels to put their crews at risk attempting to run the blockade.'

'What does he expect the *Stanbrook* to do? Sit here until the war's over? Or until the Italians get bored?'

'My goodness,' said Ruby, 'this is quite impossible.' She shaded her eyes, studied the alley, the crowd simply growing by the minute. 'Would you like to help, Jack?'

'I'd prefer to buy you dinner,' he said, then saw that she wasn't even listening to him. It had been the one saving grace of that business with Fidel and Sergio, an end to the jealousy he'd not even realised was within him – the birth of renewed hope that she would now view Jack himself in a more favourable light. Frustrated hope. 'No, thanks,' he shouted, a little louder. 'I simply came to see how you were getting along. Find out how the wrists are holding up. But you seem fine.'

'Far from fine. The atmosphere's awful. Much worse than Madrid. And, last night, when it was dark, there were gangs of louts. You could hear them. Shouting, "We're coming for you." Other dreadful things too. I was really frightened, Jack.'

'Then, for God's sake, come with me, Ruby.' But she did not hear that either.

At the end of the alley, out on the main street, a taxi pulled up.

'Let's hope this is some more help,' she said, and then her mouth fell open.

Jack turned, squinted into the light, saw that it was not, in fact, help arriving. It was Major Lawrence Edwin.

Jack ran, faster than he remembered ever running before. And, behind him, a couple of patrolling Assault Guards responded to Edwin's call for him to be stopped, joined the chase. They pursued him down and across the *paseo*, where Jack collided with a barrow, pain shooting through his hip, yet the collision spilling stacked oranges onto the paving, where they bounced and splattered, with Jack dancing through the debris, the *campesino* cursing, screaming, hurling some of the homegrown produce after him. But there the Assault Guards gave up the hunt, leaving Jack to pound through streets which, away from the chaos at the Consulate, now seemed strangely empty. His chest was heaving, a stitch developing in his side. A backwards glance, Major Edwin still there, jacket flapping like sparrowhawk wings. And he was closing the gap.

For God's sake, leave me alone. The words rattled around and around in Telford's head.

A siren began to wail.

For me, thought Jack, stupidly, as he ran on. *The siren's for me.*

The siren grew louder, its whine rising and falling, drawing folk from their hiding places, from bars and apartment blocks. They were running with him now, mothers dragging or carrying their children, old men and women, couples, hobbling along. Individual fugitives.

He heard the bombers too, as he'd heard them in Madrid.

Give-in. Give-in. Give-in.

Ahead of him was the concrete bulk that marked an entrance to the local shelter, the air-raid refuge, and Jack ignoring every civilised convention, driven by his double-jeopardy panic, shouldered and elbowed his way through those already jostling to enter, forced his way through the darkened doorway, looking back over the swell of angry faces, to see Edwin also pushing towards him. Down the steps, two at a time, into the gloom, flickering overhead light bulbs. A central passage, small cubicles on either side, stretching away into the shadowy distance, Jack shouting apologies in English, again and again, as he clambered over blanket rolls, cushions, crashed into families looking for vacant spaces. And Major Edwin almost panting down his neck.

Then the bombs above. Immediately above. Two explosions, one after the other, each of them felt rather than heard, the walls of the refuge and everything, everybody within, shaken to the very roots, dust dropping from the ceilings, lights flashing off and on again, a crack opening in the roof. There was a small pram, empty, and Jack swung it around by the handle, hoping to trip his pursuer, but the action only slowed Jack himself, distracted him. The woman, the pram's owner, screamed. Major Edwin vaulted over the obstacle with ease and, in that instant, he caught Jack's coat with one hand while, in the other, a knife appeared from nowhere, a switchblade, the wicked stiletto flashing open in a conjuring trick.

The major slammed into him, both of them tumbling into the cubicle, into the mother, the infant she carried, the toddler twins at her side. Jack grabbed for the wrist, as they fell, managed to clamp all his fingers around the major's cuff, tried to push that deathly steel away from him as he crashed backwards onto a crate, a basket, agony searing through his spine. Yet he still held the wrist. *Anywhere*, he thought. *Anywhere away from me. Oh, Christ...*

The major's reptilian eyes inches from his own.

'Treasonous little shit,' Edwin gasped, as they rolled over onto the cold concrete. His left hand was up, clawing at Jack's fingers, the right with the switchblade, and Jack's grip slowly loosening. He looked around, desperate for help. Nothing. A blur of people, shouting, the mother and her young brood being dragged away from the fray, one of the twins caught in the pram wheel. Major Edwin's hand came free. The blade flashed. Jack couldn't look, heard a child's high-pitched, piercing squeal, felt wetness splash upon his cheek. When he opened his eye, the major was on his knees.

'Fuck,' he said, his gaze wild. From the knife, to the hysterical child he'd slashed, and then to Jack. 'You shit,' he spat again.

My fault too? thought Jack. *The kid?* But he'd no intention of hanging around to persuade himself, one way or the other. He scrambled to his feet, pushed himself through the crush of Spanish humanity squeezing itself down the passage, into the cubicle to help the distraught mother, the bloodied, injured child, and the child's stricken siblings.

Jack crashed blindly down the corridor, almost losing his footing each time the entire structure was shaken, like a marrowbone in a terrier's jaws, each time another bomb fell above. *How much further?* The thoughts raged. For the refuge seemed endless and, right now, he'd rather take his chances with the bombs. And he didn't need eyes in the back of his head to know that Edwin was close behind again. He could hear him. Smell the hair oil. Taste the garlic breath.

Steps. Going up. An old accordion player sitting on the lowest stair, easing the first couple of wheezing notes from the instrument. Shock, then anger on the fellow's face as Jack sprang past him, caught his foot on the discordant keys, almost fell through those folk funneling into this other entrance-exit. Glare of sunlight, fresh air, and a second flash, blinding. But then the world fell apart, the collapse coming almost before he felt and heard the blast. It seemed that he was tossed aside, turned upside down while, at the same time, somebody had taken masonry nails and hammered them through each ear-drum, alarm bells peeling through his skull, lumps of concrete pierced by lengths of reinforcement bars smacking at his body. Smoke, dust and silence. Purely momentary silence. Before the muffled yelling and sobbing of the entombed began. He looked up and saw the sky. A plane droned and banked across the blue circle above him, and disappeared from his view.

He shook himself, tentatively shifted each limb. His back hurt, but he blamed that on the basket, back in the cubicle, and it wasn't going to prevent him from climbing clear. The bomb, he saw, must have hit the shelter. A direct hit, which had somehow left both Jack and the entrance wall intact, yet scooped out a crater immediately behind. He crawled to the edge. Below, the refuge's corridor gaped open. *Rabbit hole,* he told himself. There was the accordion, intact, untouched, not even a coating of dust, though there was no sign of the old man himself. Beside the instrument, a slab of concrete had collapsed into the passageway and, beneath it, Major Lawrence Edwin was trapped, his legs crushed. He was moaning softly while, above his face, another block, round, the size of a moderate boulder, hung swaying, almost by a whisker, slowly sliding down a length of armature bar. All Jack needed to do was give it a good kick.

'Do it,' Major Edwin groaned, though Jack barely heard, his ears still ringing. 'Go on, Telford. Do it.'

Your wish is my command, Jack thought, and he clambered down the rubble, tested just how easy it would be to shift.

Beyond the major, there was darkness, the tunnel blocked, those trapped still calling for help.

'I always imagined you'd want my death to look like an accident,' said Jack, and he gave the lump of concrete another casual shake.

'Nine lives, Telford,' murmured the major, though he seemed to be hallucinating. 'But running out of road. Nowhere to go now.'

'You're a bloody fool, Major. Milanes has all the reports. Your dirty little deals with Franco's generals. It will all come out anyway. Nothing to gain by killing me. And now look at you.'

Jack felt the slab begin to give, to slip down the steel rod.

Let it go, Jack, a voice told him. *Just let it go.* But he was curious. About lots of things.

'Milanes?' the major snorted, then shook with the pain. 'Can keep that fool quiet. Easy. But you. Meddling bloody paper...'

'Well,' said Jack, 'you just lost your chance. And, for the record, Major, the girl had no part in it. Just me. With a little help from my friend, General Kotov. There's another thing, too. If any of this blasted vendetta's about Carter-Holt, you need to know that her secret's safe with me. I don't bloody care whether you believe me. But it should be obvious, even to the British intelligence services, that I can't say anything about her without incriminating myself too.'

More bells. This time, the fire service. Getting closer.

'Do it,' the major said again.

Jack squeezed his eye shut, cursed himself for an idiot. Major Edwin alive would, he was certain, go on pursuing him for as long as he was able, legs or no legs. The shadow of Fielding's death left hanging over Jack's head. But he put his shoulders under the concrete boulder anyway, held it there, sobbing, even when the *bomberos*, the fire fighters, arrived to relieve him of his burden, to deliver him into some sort of redemption – though, in truth, he was not entirely sure that he'd not saved Major Edwin out of malice rather than mercy.

Chapter Thirty-Six

Tuesday 28th March 1939

In later years, Jack would always remember the scene in monochrome but, that late-afternoon, the traitorous sun was smiling happily on the sandstone and scrub prominence, as well as the pale castle walls along their high summit while, below, and as far as the eye could see, it gleamed upon the grey, metallic or tiled cupolas of Alicante's white and ochre waterfront elegance.

'Where is he now?' Ruby asked. He'd joined her at the temporary consulate again, found her helping some of her flock, as she now described them, on their way here, to the quayside Customs House where the refugees must await a decision on whether one or other of the British ships would agree to take a few of them as passengers.

'Provincial Hospital,' said Jack. 'He was still calling me a traitor, even when they carried him off to the ambulance.'

'I suppose, in his eyes, he's right. British military attaché, working under orders from his superiors. Working in the interests of national security, he would say. People in government, some of them at least, see war coming with Hitler. In that war, we'll need Gibraltar. And as few enemies as possible. So a few bribes to Franco's generals will seem like a fair price to pay, to keep Spain out of the fight.'

'A few bribes and the freedom of Spain, Ruby. Look where we are, for pity's sake.'

There must have been a thousand in the queue already, and more arriving all the time. That strange mingling of the permanently destitute, the suddenly stripped middle-class, and the desperately defeated, threadbare remnants of the Republic's army – a few of them still with their weapons. Yet Jack saw only Ruby Waters, the petite little figure in her blue *miliciana* overall and a red headscarf keeping the unruly hair from blowing in her face. He loved her for all this. For her devotion to the refugees. For being Ruby.

'Spain's freedom was already lost, my dear. It was lost at the Ebro. Maybe much earlier.'

'Because Britain and France stood by and watched it happen. I'm just so ashamed. So deeply, deeply ashamed.'

'Is that why you're not going back?'

'If there was a choice, maybe I would. I don't know what's waiting for me there, do I? But I can't stay either. That's clear. If Turbides was still pursuing me, I must be on one of Franco's lists, the same as many of these poor devils. Spain's in my blood now, but if I don't get out, Spain will be the death of me. There's no way out except from here. And neither the *Stanbrook* nor the *Maritime* is heading anywhere except Oran. From there, I can get to Gibraltar, I suppose. Lisbon, perhaps. We could both get there, Ruby.'

'I can't say it's not tempting, Jack. Let me talk to Mister Donald. Do you mind?'

There, thought Jack. *Thank goodness. She's coming around to it. And once we're on a ship together...*

'He'll tell you the same as me, I'm sure.'

'I'm sure he will as well.' She touched his arm, smiled kindly at him, filled his heart with hope. 'And the child, Jack? You never told me about the child – the one that Edwin stabbed.'

'Fine. So far as I know. Bad cut, but they got him out through the other entrance. He'll be in the same hospital, I imagine. Bit of an irony, don't you think? But look, that must be the skipper.'

At the top of the passerelle, several uniformed figures had gathered. At their centre, in the middle of the gangway gap in the *Stanbrook*'s guard rail, a cheerful and animated fellow, mid-forties, his officer's cap having seen better days. Dickson, wasn't that what Billy Clark had told him? Jack saw him point down at the cargo, scattered alongside the wharf, most of it netted and ready for hoisting aboard. Casks of saffron. Hundreds upon hundreds of wooden packing cases – oranges. Valencian oranges. Hogsheads of tobacco too. Jack could smell it. All of it. The tranquil but muted spice aroma. Tangy citrus. Sweetness of the leaf. Essence of oak barrels. The creosote of hemp and cordage. Oil and grease, iron rust and pungent paint from chain and crane, winch gear and hoisting boom. *How much room will be left,* Jack wondered, *when this lot's all loaded?*

'She's not very big,' said Ruby. 'Not when you get up-close.'

She was right. Two hundred feet maybe? A bit more. Crew complement of twenty, according to Billy. Twenty-four at a push. Not big. And, over at the *Maritime,* no activity at all.

'Any word from Madrid?' Jack asked.

'You don't want to know. There was a broadcast this morning. It will be the last, I think.'

'Besteiro?' He assumed it must have been, though he wasn't sure why.

'Yes. It was very moving. He said he could see white flags at people's windows, all over the city. Casado's flown to Valencia, it seems, and then going into exile. Besteiro said something strange. That he'd been invited to go too. It was the word he used. Invited. As though to a dinner party. But he'd decided to stay. Apparently Casado's been on the radio as well. Advising everybody to come here. To Alicante. Says there'll be boats.'

Jack stared out towards the harbour wall, then back to the open dock gate, where trucks and buses, trams and taxis, were arriving by the minute, more and more soldiers or families swelling the huddled masses.

'That's got to be a lie,' he said. 'About the boats.' It was monstrous.

'Not the worst of it, Jack. We were getting word all morning. Provincial capitals everywhere, swearing allegiance to the Nationalists.'

At the gate, a second crowd had been steadily forming. Young men mainly. Chanting. *Franco! Franco! Franco!* A few scuffles but in the main the refugees, the soldiers included, largely accepting this humiliation with bowed heads, as though they somehow felt they deserved it. More singing from the Falange supporters. And they had taken down the enormous photographs of the Republic's heroes, which had once adorned the promenade, the *malecón.* Pictures of Miaja, Rojo, Modesto and Lister. They were burning them. Oh, how they must have longed for this day, hiding themselves away, like cockroaches, even here in this most loyal bastion of Republican Spain.

'*The ships won't come!*' came their serenade. '*The ships won't come! But Franco will! But Franco will!*' Like a soccer crowd.

All hope lost. Jack glanced back at the *Stanbrook.* There were Assault Guards now, at the foot of the gangplank and, halfway along its length, four suited officials in matching homburg hats, deep in conversation with Captain Dickson. Behind them, the cranes were already in action, a cargo net of orange crates swinging into the air, and the ship's deck busy, her hands waiting eagerly at the open hold hatches.

'Can he survive, d'you think?' said Jack. 'Besteiro, I mean. I liked him, you know. Despite everything, I liked him.'

Would it have made a difference – if good men like Besteiro had not so readily encouraged Casado's coup? And, not for the first time, he glimpsed how it must be, as a leader, having to make those choices between two impossible options, to sacrifice one section of your people to save the rest – how it must feel when you know you got it wrong. Then Ruby touched his arm again.

'Jack, I need to get back.'

'I'll come with you. It's dangerous, Ruby. With those thugs on the street. And you, dressed like La Pasionaria.'

'It'll be fine,' she told him. 'And anyway, you've got more important things to do. Arrange a passage. Find the boys too, Jack. Bring them here. I'll get back by – What time? Eight? I mean it. I shan't leave without them.'

He'd had to take a tram all the way to Twelve Bridges before he found them. But they were almost invisible within that tide of humanity – once the pride of Republican Spain and now a shambling procession of khaki-clad vagrants. And it was they who'd spotted Jack.

'Where are they all going?' said Jack, as they embraced him, Fidel and Sergio. 'It's a lie. Tell them. Casado's lying. There are no ships.'

They laughed.

'You think we're stupid, English? And are you so innocent? There are never rescue ships for soldiers. Only for generals. Only for the *políticos*. Well, that's the way it is.'

'Then where are you going?'

'You mean, where are *we* going, no?' said Fidel. 'Did you forget? About the conditional liberty?'

'You're mad. Who the hell cares any more if I'm a prisoner or not?'

'It wasn't me,' Fidel snapped at him, 'who murdered one of Comrade Stalin's favourite agents, and then lied about the circumstances. Or killed one of your own diplomats.'

'There was almost another,' said Jack. 'Yesterday.' Puzzled glances. 'It doesn't matter. Not really.' They had joined the plodding procession, heading along the coast road, towards the port, towards that useless castle which, now, couldn't protect any of them. There was a railway line, heading out towards Elche, then south to Murcia. Beyond the tracks, low sand dunes, stretches of sand. More abandoned fishing boats, whose lateen sails could still have carried them to the North African coast. Though not today. And, along the beach also, this side of the port, there were shacks, with reed-covered roofs, bars, with long tables and benches, all empty too. 'But I think we've found a ship. An English ship,' Jack told them. 'I know some of the crew.'

'Is that why you came?' Sergio smiled at him. 'To look for us?'

Jack didn't have the heart for honesty any more. Would he still have been there, he wondered, if Ruby hadn't made their passage to safety so provisional upon her own?

'Of course,' he lied.

The two men laughed again, and somebody started singing. *¡Ay, Carmela!* Then a tune he remembered from the *guerrilleros* in the cave at Covadonga. He could only remember the chorus, and the song's name, *Santa Bárbara Bendita*. How apt, as they picked up the step, with the Santa Bárbara Castle before them. By the time they were in the castle's lee and reached the harbour, it was La Internacional, naturally – the tatterdemalion horde almost a battalion once more, remembering the fights they'd made: at Córdoba, Badajóz, Bilbao, Toledo, Madrid, Jarama, Guadalajara, Brunete, Belchite, Teruel, and all along the Ebro. Good God, how they'd fought.

'You see, English?' said Sergio 'That's where we're going. To the end. Together. It's what soldiers do.'

It was about eight in the evening and, at their approach, a gang of fascist *bravos*, even bigger than before, simply evaporated. At the quayside end of the Stanbrook's gangplank, there was a table, a couple of Assault Guards, two officials processing papers and the queue of refugees now snaking from there, back to the Customs House. The cargo net of oranges still hung from the crane, precisely as it had done when Jack left.

'Is that your ship?' said Fidel.

'Our ship,' Jack corrected him. But he saw the look that passed between the two men. 'What?' he said.

'My dear friend,' Fidel gripped his arm. 'I used to wonder at the old men in my village, in my family. Each of them would say the same. "The world's not the place it used to be." But, to me? It always seemed that the sun shone, that life was good. Getting better, too. Slowly, but better. The wheel turns, and sometimes, as it turns, it faces back in the direction from which it's come. But, overall, its progress is always forwards. And then I came to understand. That those old men were just getting ready to die. Convincing themselves that life wasn't really worth living any more. We don't want that, English. Not to die in desperation. Not separated and alone. Not with our dreams and hopes for Spain's eventual freedom stolen from us. Better this way, English. Truly.'

'What way?' said Jack. He felt stupid. 'Stay here, you mean? Go into hiding?'

'Hiding?' Sergio smiled. A sad smile. 'Yes, I suppose so. One day, it will all change. Spain will be happy again. Somehow we need to still be here. So that maybe we'll be part of that. A small part, perhaps.'

'They'll find you.' Jack was appalled. It was a stupid plan. 'Wherever you hide, they'll find you. And Ruby,' he said. 'Think of Ruby. She'll never leave without you two.'

'No,' said Sergio, 'they'll not find us.' He spoke the words with such conviction that Jack couldn't help but believe him.

'Your hand, *compañero*,' said Fidel. 'It troubles you?' Jack was rubbing at the blasted thing again, hadn't even noticed he was doing it. But yes, he admitted. It troubled him. 'Then perhaps you should go home, English. We don't need you here. Not any more. Find peace in your own land, while you can. Leave us to find some sort of peace in ours. And Ruby? I think she needs to discover peace in a place of her own choosing. Go and find her, my friend. Consider yourself freed from your conditional liberty too. Now, you're just free. To go where you will. As we must do.'

'Where the hell have you been?' Jack shouted, as he and Ruby Waters waded towards each other through the milling crowd. 'And where's your bag.'

It felt like the Plaza Mayor, in Madrid, all over again. She had changed, at least. No more blue overall and headscarf. A simple tweed jacket, comfortable trousers and a cap, which made her look just a little like Dietrich.

'I appreciate your concern, Mister Telford. But not your manner. And, if it comes to probing questions, where are the boys?'

'I was worried about you. Didn't you hear the shooting?' It had been sporadic. Occasional shots over the past hour. 'Are they here already? The Nationalists?'

'Mister Donald says it's probably Fifth Columnists. Falange support-ers. The word is that Franco's army – the Italians, at least – will be here tomorrow.'

'All the more reason to get away tonight, Ruby.'

'On this?'

She looked up towards the *Stanbrook*'s deck. Refugees filling every available space, pressed against the guardrails, lining the ladders and upper sections of her superstructure, clustered around the bridge. Like 'photos Jack had seen of railway journeys through India, thousands more passengers than the trains were designed to carry.

'I managed to speak with the Captain a while back,' he said. 'Decent man. Cardiff. He's had instructions not to take anybody at all. Not unless absolutely necessary.'

'He's plainly decided that must be the case. But, Jack –'

She didn't finish, her eye caught by some ripple of movement in the waiting lines, raised voices, kids responding to the tensions with tears, with howls of confusion. Jack saw it too.

'He came down among them,' he murmured, though he knew they'd both lost track of the conversation now, each of them intent on the crowd, the palpable thickening of the atmosphere. 'Humanitarian disaster, that's what Dickson said. Kissed a few babies' heads, then – '

It happened all at once, the ripple swelling to a surge. He heard the words *ataque* and *bombarderos*. Air-raid. Bombers. Repeated time and again, heads turned towards the town, towards a fading twilight sky that framed Alicante, a sky already black to the east, beyond the green and red harbour lights.

'Jack, the guards.'

He glanced back at the canvas-sided passerelle, where the Assault Guards and the Customs Officers were pushing their way upwards, almost trampling those in their way, so that the queue upon the quayside followed their example. Screaming, cursing and shouting. And the skipper, up on the deck, bellowing orders to his crew, a couple of sailors beginning to work loose the lines holding the gangplank in place.

'No,' Jack yelled. 'You can't. For Christ's sake, they'll all be killed.' There must have been a hundred on the passerelle alone, many of them women and children. He started to push his way towards them, unsure what to do, but determined to try. At least to try. Yet, when he arrived at the gangplank's foot, jostled and shoved aside by those he sought to assist, he stared up into Captain Dickson's face. The fellow had removed his battered old cap and was scratching his head, speaking calmly to his men, the order belayed, and the lines safely back in place.

'Does he mean to take them all?' said Ruby, who had fought her way to his side.

'Twenty hours to Oran, they reckon. Give or take. I suppose he must know what he's doing. And when I spoke to him, told him about your predicament, he was happy to give up his cabin for you, my dear. But now he doesn't need to, does he?'

The words were out before he even knew they were forming. And yet they poured forth with such a terrible anguish that he thought he must surely choke. An intolerable pain in his chest, and an abject sense of loneliness, of abandonment. *You must not lose her*, howled his inner voice. *Fight for her, man. Fight.* But there were Ruby's stubbornly set features. His pride. His weariness with it all. *Almost thirty-one*, he wanted to tell her. *And nothing. Nothing.*

'I have to stay, Jack.' She gestured towards the crowd. They were still anxious, still fearful of the rumoured raid, but steadier now, moving in a more orderly fashion up the gangplank. No more papers being checked. 'This is nothing, my dear,' she said, simply. 'Imagine what it will be like tomorrow. When the Italians get here. All the people who'll need help.'

'Then I'll stay too. With you.'

'No, Jack. You know that's not possible. You're on one of their damned lists. You said so. Somewhere. On a list. You, Fidel, Sergio. But especially you, Mister Telford, my dearest friend. And imagine the grief, the unbearable guilt, if you remained for my sake, and then I learned – Well, I couldn't bear it.' She stood on the tips of her toes, threw her arms around his waist, and buried her face, her tears, into his chest. 'Find them, Jack. Keep them safe. And God bless you all.'

Then she vanished, like a wraith, into the night.

319

'You have thirty minutes, Mister Telford,' Dickson had told him. 'And then we sail.'

Jack had thought of going after her, trying to work out another solution. For there had been more shots and he was almost beside himself with concern for her. Yet she was right. He knew she was right. She may be at some risk, but his own fate, if he remained, was absolute. And she would be protected, to some extent, by this newfound friendship between Britain and Franco. No, he'd decided, even though his leaden heart already ached for her, he would go to Oran, wait there until it was safe to track her down again. It would be the easiest thing, wouldn't it? Through the Diplomatic Service. *And, after that*, he thought, *my goodness, what a reunion we shall have*. So he had set off to search for Fidel and Sergio, his stupid head filled with all those visions of Dorset, tranquility and cottage gardens.

Stupid. Stupid.

Because, when he had picked his way among the soldiers and their equipment scattered all along the harbour wall, followed it to that point where the northern section ended, its green light flashing in harmony with its red companion, over on the farther side of the entrance, he saw men gathered around the light's base and he knew what he must find there. His father. And, at his father's feet, within the circle of soldiers, the light caressing those bloodied features with a clockwork wash of viridian, lay the sprawled body of Sergio Sifre.

'What happened?' Jack yelled, forced his way through, knelt at the lad's side. 'Tell me what happened,' he raged.

He took Sergio's poor head in his hands. Through this left side there was a neat bullet hole. Too small, too tidy, too clean to have killed him, surely. But, on the other side, Jack's fingers sunk into a mess of wet pulp. A foot or so away, on the cobbles, an automatic pistol. Beyond that pistol, another.

'*Hombre*,' said one of the soldiers, shrugging as though it was obvious, 'they shot each other.' Jack saw that the man was holding something. Sergio's sketchbook. Lorca. *La señorita del abanico...*

'Give me that,' said Jack, and snatched the book.

The soldier shrugged again.

'They won't be the last,' he said.

Jack looked around for Fidel, then stood and peered over the edge, down into the dark, lapping waters of the outer harbour. Something was there, floating, shapeless, and Jack remembered the words he thought forgotten. '*If we ever meet again, one of us must die.*' But he remembered these words too. '*Not to die in desperation. Not separated and alone. Not with our dreams and hopes for Spain's eventual freedom stolen from us. Better this way, English. Truly.*'

He had no tears left. Not yet. And he saw his father walking away, down the quayside. Then he stopped, turned to face him. He imagined that his father spoke, though he knew it was merely his own voice, his own words, in his own head. *In life, there may sometimes be a need, as well as the opportunity, to select the manner of our exit carefully, rather than merely wait until the curtain falls.* The figure of his father waved, just once, smiled, happy that his son understood him at last, then strolled on. And Jack knew that this was the last time; knew he would never see that spectre again.

The *Stanbrook* sailed beyond the breakwater in almost total darkness, her lights dimmed, even her navigation lights. And almost two thousand people on board held their breath. The decks were packed, Dickson's officers trying to persuade the refugees down into the holds. But they would not go. And Jack didn't blame them. Somewhere, all around them, were the Italian U-boats. If they struck, he wouldn't want to be caught below decks either.

He leaned on the stern rail, watched the ship's wake roiling away behind, and he thought about Ruby, prayed that she was safe. Yet, as he prayed, the wail of a siren carried to them across the water, and he heard the bombers again, saw the flashes as they unleashed their payload on the sleeping city.

No, he thought, *Fidel and Sergio will not be the last.*

Postscript

Sunday 30th April 1939

'You sail tomorrow, Captain?'

Jack stood at that same stern rail, though the *Stanbrook* sat now at her moorings, only the dull vibration deep inside her as a reminder of their passage, red ensign flapping in the breeze from the flagstaff, and the breeze tugging at the letter in Jack's hand.

'A month in Oran is enough for anybody, don't you think, Mister Telford?'

He sniffed at the rancid air.

'This particular month, anyway,' said Jack.

The last of the refugees had finally been disembarked, marched off to the concentration camp established by the French authorities on the Avenue de Tunis. But it had been a long haul.

'Might I enquire if that letter is from the same young lady – the one you thought might have needed my cabin?' Dickson asked him. 'If so, perhaps it's just as well she didn't sail with us after all.'

The *Stanbrook* had not even been allowed to enter the port for a couple of days, forced instead to anchor in the bay. Two thousand souls on board, two toilets, no food. Dickson had sacrificed his own cabin, and every other available inch of cabin space, in an effort to marginally alleviate the suffering of the women and children, hundreds of them. Then, when finally allowed to berth in the harbour, the authorities would still not allow anybody to go ashore.

'She would, I think, have beaten down the door of every French official in town to help you.'

And so she would, though Jack doubted whether even the stubborn Miss Ruby Waters could have affected the situation very much. It had been left to local Spanish residents, coming alongside in rowing boats, to deliver fresh water, some modest supplies of food and, by the time the French authorities softened to some extent, at least allowed the women, children, the sick and the injured to land and be herded into the concentration camp, they'd been on the ship for six days already. But the men would have to suffer another three weeks of confinement in those most unsanitary conditions, almost starving, nowhere to sleep, exposed to the extremes of heat and cold, riddled with fleas, and a level of sanitation far worse than anything the soldiers among them had ever experienced on the battlefield.

'Diplomatic Service, did you say? Your young lady? That could have been useful.'

My young lady, thought Jack. *What a quaint turn of phrase. And hardly accurate.* He had grown progressively more angry at Ruby over the intervening weeks. He still suffered nightmares. About Burgos. About Fidel and Sergio. About the dark depths of Alicante harbour and the additional tragedies they must conceal. Reports had been smuggled out quite regularly: the Italians arriving in the city on the day following the *Stanbrook*'s departure; fifteen or twenty thousand Republican troops trapped there, and now imprisoned in concentration camps, in Alicante's castles and bullring, or simply sentenced to death; more suicides in the hours before the final fall; and, the day after that, Franco himself had entered Madrid in triumph. All over. So how much was Ruby's decision to stay actually worth? She could have been here, with him.

'You think so?' he said. 'Doesn't it make you ashamed sometimes, to be British? Our own people here have been worse than useless, after all. The French have been enough of a disgrace. But at least understandable. There they are, with hundreds of thousands of Spanish refugees pouring over their borders. Thousands more here in Oran. Colossal problem.' For the *Stanbrook* hadn't been alone in the port. The *African Trader*, the *Lézardrieux* and the *Campillo* had arrived before her with their own cargoes of human misery. And the *Maritime* arrived not long after. 'And dear old Britain crows about the few hundred she's taken. No wonder French attitudes are so hard.'

'Politics, of course,' said Dickson. 'Britain and France have their relationship with Franco to consider. He's now Spain, after all. I suppose it's some small blessing that these poor devils haven't simply been packed off back there.'

'Small consolation indeed.' But Jack was thinking: *I could have killed the bastard. In Burgos. I could.*

'Well, at least I've got my vessel back. The owners will be pleased. I think. Though heaven only knows whether we'll ever get her clean again.'

'How do you endure it, Captain? The French impound your ship as surety for the cost of running the concentration camp. And our own government, the owners too, leave it to Negrín's Refugee Committee to stump up the money for her release. What was it? Two hundred thousand *francs*?'

'A quarter-million, in the end. And yes, it's a disgrace. But the old girl played her part, did she not?' Captain Dickson slapped the *Stanbrook*'s handrail affectionately. 'And you, Mister Telford. What's next, for you?'

Jack looked at the letter. Ruby was safe, at least. Still in Alicante and unsure about her next posting. But he could write to her at the Alicante address and they would, she was sure, forward any correspondence to her. For she would like to stay in touch. *How polite*, he thought. *How bloody polite.* What had she said? "*Mister Telford, my dearest friend.*" And the tears. Those heart-breaking tears. Yet here they were, back to the formalities. She would like to stay in touch. And the finishing sentence. All her love to Sergio and Fidel. How in God's name could he ever tell her? Well, he would not, of course.

'I'm not sure, sir,' he said. 'I've sent off all the pieces I'd promised to my editor. Hopefully they'll arrive safely.' It was good copy too. Jack knew that. Eyewitness accounts of those last few days in Alicante. He'd sent them on his birthday, the Twenty-Fifth. Then: 'Oh, and I've resigned.'

'Really?' said Dickson. 'The paper won't be the same without you, Mister Telford. I always look forward to my Sundays with *Reynold's News*, when I'm at home.' Sydney Elliott would be furious, Jack supposed. But it seemed entirely wrong, to remain on the payroll when he was still out here. 'Ah,' the Captain observed, 'here comes Henry with some good news, I hope.'

The First Engineer, Henry Lillystone. *He must be seventy, if he's a day*, thought Jack. But a good man. Brilliant mechanic. Jack had bunked with him, since the ship emptied. Lillystone waved to him.

'Sailing home with us, Jack?' he shouted.

'No – But you have a safe journey, Henry.'

And then Jack was alone again. He lit a cigarette. Where *would* he go? Or would he stay here? He'd made some friends among the refugee families, and there was still much work to be done. Conditions were appalling. Not quite so bad here as in the many other camps in North Africa, they said, but bad enough. Few opportunities for work. Some of the men seriously considering the offer made to them – if offer it could truly be called – for enlistment in the French Foreign Legion. Others had already gone off, to the work camps on the French trans-Sahara railway, the stretch now under construction way down near Béchar. Maybe there was a story here, somewhere. To make sure these survivors of Spain's Republic weren't forgotten. Maybe he'd do something with Sergio's sketches. Maybe the bloody Pulitzer.

Yet, who would he write it for? The BBC, perhaps? He remembered that friend of Father Lobo's, Barea, the man now working for the World Service in London. It was a possibility. Jack would drop him a line. No need to go home. Not yet. And wasn't that strange? He had begun all this with only one goal – to get away after Carter-Holt's death and return safely to England. He knew there would be no repercussions on that front now. Perhaps a difficult interview with her father, simply to offer his condolences, repeat the fictional account of her last moments. And he doubted there'd be any charges arising from Fielding's death either, though he couldn't be sure. Not until he heard something definite. It was more that, the way being now open to him, after all these months, to take a passage to England, he had somehow lost the will to do so.

And keep in touch? he asked himself. *Is that all there ever was?* He had thought – Well, it didn't really matter what he'd thought. He'd been wrong. Again.

Telford opened his fingers, and the letter from Ruby Waters floated away on the winds of Africa.

The End

Historical Notes

Much of this novel is rooted firmly in fact. Some is pure fiction. And most sits in that murky netherworld between the two. It is, of course, a sequel to *The Assassin's Mark* and, as a reminder, that story is set in September 1938. By then, the Spanish Civil War had already been raging for more than two years and the outcome still hung in the balance. It had all begun when four Spanish generals, including General Franco, decided to overthrow the democratically elected Republican government in July 1936 and Franco established an "alternative" Nationalist government, based in Burgos – which introduced its own currency, the Burgos *peseta* and, soon afterwards, extraordinarily, a National Tourism Department. His reason was that he badly needed a sophisticated propaganda plan to convince the world at large that his own side, and not the legitimate government, were the "good guys." So, among many other propaganda strategies, they began to organise bus tours, attracting thousands of international travellers, between 1938 and 1945, so that people could hear the stories and visit the sites of Franco's victories, then return to their own countries and "spread the word." It was remarkably successful, and I therefore decided to set *The Assassin's Mark* on one of those tour buses across Northern Spain and, as it happened, during the same week as the Munich Crisis.

This novel, *Until the Curtain Falls*, picks up the story where *The Assassin's Mark* left off. I was keen to follow the Spanish Civil War to its end. It's a novel, of course, basically a work of fiction, but many of the characters that appear in its pages are real. As such, I apologise in advance if I may have depicted them incorrectly or unfairly. Naturally, any conversations in which they engage with fictional characters are inventions, but they include the following individuals.

In Burgos: Josemaría Escrivá de Balaguer (Father Josemaría), who founded Opus Dei in 1928; Pablo Merry del Val, head of Franco's Foreign Press Office – and Franco's headquarters, of course, still there and never visited, in the Palacio Muguiro, also known as the Palacio de la Isla, on the Paseo de la Isla in Burgos.

In San Pedro de Cardeña, 8 miles south-east of Burgos: the Basque chaplain, Francisco de la Pasión (Victor) Gondra Muruaga, commonly known to the other prisoners as "Brother(s) Mine", but more famously known, within the Catholic Church, as "Aita Patxi", freed in 1939, died of leukaemia in 1974 and beatified in 1989; Hyman Wallach, Polish-American, freed in 1939, died 1999; Edgar Acken, American, prisoner exchange, late 1938, died 1978; Bob Steck, Jewish-American, freed in 1939, died 2007; Lou Ornitz, American, prisoner exchange, late 1938, died 1983; Bob Doyle, Irish, British Battalion, prisoner exchange 1939, died 2009; Chen Agen, Chinese, released 1942, died – unknown; Joe Norman, English (Salford), released 1939; Frank Ryan, Irish, released 1940, died in Dresden, 1944; and Clive Branson, English artist, exchanged, late 1938, died in Burma, 1944.

In Madrid: General Kotov, the alias for Soviet NKVD Chief, Leonid Eitingon, who had helped forge the Spanish Republic's XIV Guerrilla Corps and who later (and more famously) employed his protégé, Ramón Mercader, to assassinate Trotsky in Mexico; at the British Consulate, John and Mabel Milanes, plus the redoubtable Mrs Angela Norris – and yes, they really held that Christmas Party, though on 27th December 1938; Jack Telford's friends in Madrid – Julián Besteiro, refused to go into exile after General Casado's coup failed to achieve a negotiated peace with Franco, and died in a fascist prison in September 1940; Miguel San Andrés was also imprisoned and died in June 1940; Rosario del Olmo Almenta, died in Madrid, January 2000; and Father Leocadio Lobo, who remained in Madrid throughout most of the siege and given the position, late in 1937, by the Republic, as Head of the Technical Section for Confessions and Religious Congregations, remained in exile in New York until his death in 1959.

In Elda and Alicante: Prime Minister Juan Negrín (his official title was President of the Government, whereas Azaña was President of the Republic) remained an exile in France for the rest of his life, and died in Paris in 1956; Dolores Ibárruri, of course, *La Pasionaria*, remained in exile until 1977, died in Madrid, 1989; Rafael Alberti, remained in exile until 1977, died in Cádiz, 1999; María Teresa León, remained in exile with Alberti until 1977, died in a sanatorium near Madrid, 1988; General Antonio Cordón García, died in exile, in Rome, 1968; Julio Álvaro de Vayo, died in exile, in Switzerland, 1975; Segundo Blanco González, died in exile, in Mexico, 1957; General Manuel Matallana Gómez, part of Casado's conspiracy and possible Fifth Colum connections, though later imprisoned by Franco's fascists, and died in Madrid, 1952; Paulino Gómez Saiz, remained in exile in Colombia until his death in 1977; and the *Stanbrook*, whose skipper, Archibald Dickson, along with Ship's Steward William Clark, Able Seaman Oskar Johansen, Able Seaman Ramón Charlín, First Engineer Henry Lillystone and the rest of her mixed 20-man crew of British, Spanish and Moroccan sailors, was sunk by a German U-boat in the North Sea, with the loss of all hands, on 18th November 1939, and plaques commemorating the vessel's action can be seen both in Alicante harbour and her skipper's home port, Cardiff.

What about those characters that are fictional but based on real people? Frederick Barnard was inspired by Bernard Bevan, British diplomat, who wrote the seminal *History of Spanish Architecture* (1938). Major Edwin, similarly, was loosely inspired by Captain Edward Christopher Lance who, in 1936, was a military attaché at the British Embassy in Madrid and allegedly became some sort of "Spanish Pimpernel", helping Franco supporters trapped in the Republican Zone to escape – and narrowly avoided a firing squad when he, himself, was caught undertaking those activities in Valencia.

Finally, I should confirm that suicides among Republicans trapped in Alicante in the final days of the war are well documented. And so, too, are the almost countless executions, tens of thousands of them, ordered by Franco's régime in the aftermath of the Spanish Civil War and detailed in Paul Preston's *The Spanish Holocaust*. Preston's figures record 200,000 soldiers killed in battle, on both sides; another 200,000 killed by death squads during the conflict – around 150,000 killed in Nationalist Zones, and roughly 50,000 in Republican Zones; but then a further 20,000 executed by Franco in the aftermath – although some sources put this figure as high as 100,000, to include the unknown numbers who died in Franco's concentration camps.

Acknowledgements

My list of thanks for the sources on which I based this book is enormous, so apologies if, as inevitably must be the case, I've omitted anybody. I've tried to group them under main subject headings so that anybody interested in a particular element of the story might more easily find those references. And I decided to begin with an acknowledgement to the main inspiration for this novel's prequel, *The Assassin's Mark*, since so much of that obviously spills over into this story too.

So, on Franco's Battlefield Tourism: Sandie Holguín's paper for the American Historical Review entitled *National Spain Invites You: Battlefield Tourism during the Spanish Civil War*, and for the University of California's Mandeville Special Collections Library for allowing me "fair use" of the relevant materials.

For relevant background to specific aspects of the Spanish Civil War: Paul Preston's *We Saw Spain Die*, plus Franco and *The Spanish Holocaust*; Antony Beevor's *The Battle for Spain*; the Spanish Ministry of Justice site: *mapadefosas.mjusticia.es*; the brilliant website of the Spanish newspaper, *ABC* (www.hemeroteca.abc.es) which allows you to search for and read every daily edition for the entire Spanish Civil War period, and for the various editions published respectively by the Republican side in Madrid, and by the Nationalist side in both Sevilla and Córdoba – an astonishing way to get a "contemporary" picture of how the conflict was reported from different perspectives but also a rich source of trivia detail, everything from retail prices to theatre listings; Baedeker's 1908 edition of *Spain and Portugal* (still pretty accurate in 1938-39); and *The Life and Death of the Spanish Republic*, Henry Buckley's eye-witness account.

For the Camino de Santiago in 1938: Fernando Lalanda's *El Camino de Santiago, de izquierda a derecha* (1930-39); and Carlota Bustos

Juez's paper on *The Bernard Bevan Enigma*, about the mysterious British diplomat, his seminal 1938 *History of Spanish Architecture*, with its links to the even more famous *Codex Calixtinus* – a 12th Century hitch-hiker's guide to the Camino.

For British Involvement in the Spanish Civil War: Angel Viñas, *La Conspiración del General Franco*; Peter Day's *Franco's Friends*; Graham D. Macklin's paper, *Major Hugh Pollard, MI6, and the Spanish Civil War*, originally published by the Historical Journal in 2006; *The Spanish Pimpernel* by C E Lucas Phillips (1960); Julio Ponce Alberca's *Gibraltar and the Spanish Civil War, 1936 – 39*; and the paper by Angel Viñas: *Los Sobornos a Generales de Franco y Juan March – Una Operación Supersecreta (The Bribes to Franco's Generals and Juan March – A Highly Secret Operation)*. There is, of course, no evidence that the bribes to Franco's generals, in order to keep Spain out of the Second World War, had been offered as early as I suggest in the novel.

For International Brigades and Spanish Concentration Camps: Richard Baxell's *British Volunteers in the Spanish Civil War: The British Battalion in the International Brigades, 1936-1939*; Nacho Eli García's blog, *The Jaily News*; the 1997 paper by Javier Bandrés and Rafael Llavona, *Psychology in Franco's Concentration Camps*; the International Brigade Memorial Trust pages on *Prisoners at San Pedro de Cardeña*; George M. Wheeler's *To Make the People Smile Again: A Memoir of the Spanish Civil War*; David Convery's chapter on *The Memory of British and Irish Prisoners in San Pedro de Cardeña* in Anindya Raychaudhuri's book, *The Spanish Civil War – Exhuming a Buried Past*; and for Richard Baxell's very helpful personal e-mails.

For Republican Army Guerrilla Units: Barton Whaley's paper on *Guerrillas in the Spanish Civil War*, September 1969; and Hernán Rodríguez Velasco's paper, *Las guerrillas en el Ejército Popular de la República (1936-39)*, February 2011.

For the Siege of Madrid: Carlos Menéndez-Otero's paper, *Linguistic Pluralism and Dubbing in Spain*, May 2013; Arturo Barea's three-part autobiography, *La Forja de Un Rebelde (The Forging of a Rebel)*; Fernando Cohnen's *Madrid 1936/1939: Una guía de la capital en Guerra*; *El hambre en el Madrid de la Guerra Civil (1936 – 1939)* by Laura and Carmen Gutierrez Rueda; Doctor David Mathieson's web pages, *Spanish Sites: Madrid and the Spanish Civil War*, as well as the magnificent day that we spent with

David, in June 2016, walking many of the locations in Madrid itself; the website *Guerra en Madrid*; José Luis González Gullón's 2010 paper on *Leocadio Lobo, Un Sacerdote Republicano*; and *The Spanish Pimpernel*, by C E Lucas Phillips.

For the history of Spanish Civil War Soccer: Timothy J. Ashton's *Soccer in Spain – Politics, Literature and Film*; and Matt Pottinger's paper on *Football in the Spanish Civil War*.

For the Last Days of the Republic: José Ramón Valero Escandell's SBHAC 1981 paper on *El Final de la República: La Posición Yuste*; the Alicante Vivo page on *La Posición Yuste*; the brilliant guided tour of Elda, Petrer and El Fondó, organised by the International Brigade Memorial Trust, in conjunction with Lorraine Hardy from the Labour International Costa Blanca Branch in February 2016; Luis Martínez Mira's *Alicante 1936-1939 – Tiempos de Guerra*; Captain Archibald Dickson's letter from Oran, 2nd and 3rd April 1939, to the Editor of the *Sunday Dispatch*, London, about the escape of SS *Stanbrook* from Alicante harbour; and the paper by Juan Martínez Leal, *El Stanbrook: Un Barco Mítico*, published in the contemporary history magazine, *Pasado y Memoria*, in 2005. There are many accounts of the *Stanbrook's* exploits but I naturally preferred the skipper's own version of events. Generally, the *Stanbrook* is attributed with carrying around 3,000 souls to freedom, though Captain Dickson, who counted them, after all, gives the number as 1,835 in total – still a very significant figure. In addition, I read relevant sections of *Los Invisibles: A History of Male Homosexuality in Spain, 1850-1939*, by Richard Cleminson and Franciso Vásquez García, as well as various contemporary accounts of suicides on Alicante's waterfront, on 28th-29th March 1939.

Then, two special mentions for this book. First, I want to thank the people of Pamplona. We were checking out locations and writing sections of the story, in some of Hemingway's favourite haunts, in company with my sister and her husband, when she fell and fractured her femur. A spell in Pamplona's very fine public hospital, and in the care of Spain's excellent Health Service, meant an extended stay in the city – during which we were made to feel like family and treated with exceptional affection. Second, it was nothing short of a tragedy when, as the book was in its final stages, we lost our dear friend, José García Quesada (Chamorro), who had so inspired the story and, over thirty years, taught me so much about Spain and its culture. It is some small consolation that his daughters, Mónica and María García Irles, as well as his brother-in-law and lifelong companion, Blas Andreu Gilabert, have been heavily involved in the editing process for the Spanish edition – the edition that, to my deepest sorrow, Chamorro will now never read.

None of that, of course detracts even slightly from the acknowledgements I must make, for their own huge contributions to... Kelly Thornhill at the fabulous Adventures in Spanish (Spanish translation); Jo Field (overall editing); Cathy Helms at Avalon Graphics (cover design); Helen Hart and her team at SilverWood Books (publishing and distribution processes); Ann McCall (my "ideal reader"); Pablo Fernando Zarate (additional help with the Spanish editing process); plus authors Elizabeth Buchan and Doctor David Mathieson for their brilliant endorsements.

And a particular acknowledgement here to those who contributed to the crowd-funding project and promotional work that made this publication possible. Thanks to all of you!

Joan Roberts; Lee Conrad; Steph Wyeth; Joe C. Dwek CBE; Kelvin Ling; Sharon Powell and Kim Withers; John Haywood; Peter Booth; Ian Berry; Gary and Charo Titley; Ian Stewart; Tony Norbury; Beverly O'Sullivan; Anne Brown; Adrian Weir; Judy and Bob Jones; Liam Davies; Chris Remington; Julie Tift; Lord Ray Collins of Highbury; Solène Leti; Stuart Howard; Sharon and Nick Povey; Saras Anderson; Phil Burrows and Cath Roberts; Paul Cosgrove; Tony McQuade; Brendan Murphy; Maija and Simon Robinson; Alan Simpson; Kevan Nelson; Paul A. Golder; Sir Ian McCartney; Linda Bishop; and Paul Jeorrett.

Lightning Source UK Ltd.
Milton Keynes UK
UKOW01f0643070318
319037UK00001B/88/P

9 781781 326435